TIES THAT BIND US

TIES THAT BIND US

NICOLE KNIGHT

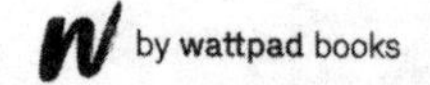

An imprint of Wattpad WEBTOON Book Group

Content Warning: This book deals with heavy themes of violence, drug use, pregnancy loss, organized crime, and murder. Please take care of yourself if any of these elements may be triggering for you.

Published in Canada by Wattpad WEBTOON Book Group, a division of Wattpad WEBTOON Studios, Inc.

36 Wellington Street E., Suite 200, Toronto, ON M5E 1C7 Canada

www.wattpad.com

First W by Wattpad Books edition: April 2025

ISBN 978-1-99834-122-1 (Trade Paper original)
ISBN 978-1-77729-003-0 (eBook edition)

Library and Archives Canada Cataloguing in Publication information is available upon request.

Printed and bound in Canada

1 3 5 7 9 10 8 6 4 2

Cover design by Emily Wittig
Images © jenmax via Depositphotos; © Hayri Er, © Kesu01, © emrahaltinok via iStock
Typesetting by Delaney Anderson

ONE

Ava

There's nothing graceful about a one-night stand.

The frantic scrubbing of last night's makeup from your face. The scavenger hunt for wrinkled clothes scattered across the hotel room floor. The way everything smells of regret and poor decisions . . . it's humbling, to say the least. And it's a spot I swore I'd never be in again.

Yet here we are.

Clutching my shoes in my hand, I glance over my shoulder one last time at the man I spent last night with.

He's twisted in the sheets, sound asleep, and blissfully unaware that I'm about to make a getaway. Nearly every inch of his tanned, broad shoulders is etched with a maze of intricate tattoos. His tight, bulging muscles are even more defined in the sunlight that trickles through expensive hotel blackout curtains, and the dark-brown hair I ran my fingers through last night is messy and tousled. Even as he sleeps his lips curve into the sweetest smile that pulls at my heart.

It's hard to imagine all the sinful things those lips were whispering to me last night. Not to mention what he actually *did* with them.

When he flinches and rolls over, I freeze, bracing for those deep, emerald eyes to blink open and find me, but they don't. He settles back into the bed, draping his arm over a lumpy hotel pillow that no doubt still smells like my perfume, and his breathing evens.

On the nightstand there's a fresh glass of water that I realize he must have put there for me after I fell asleep. Somehow, it makes it even worse knowing that I'm walking out on a guy who has some semblance of manners.

It would be easy for me to stay. I could set my shoes back down, take off my dress, and climb right back into that bed with him. If I did, I'm sure the sleepy stranger would indulge me and soon we'd pick up exactly where we'd left off—bodies passionately tangled together, whispering words only meant for the cover of darkness, ignoring every nagging responsibility that might come with the morning light.

But that wasn't the deal we made.

No strings. No obligations. *No names.*

A onetime thing. That's what we said.

It doesn't matter how intense the attraction between us was. Or that he kissed me in a way that already made me disappointed in all future kisses; that was so feverish and consuming that I was still seeing stars. Or that he had held my body like he owned it, his touch so electric that I'm still breathless thinking about it.

It doesn't matter that our connection was instant. Or that he made me laugh until my cheeks hurt. Or that we commiserated over our overbearing families and compared scars from previous relationships. Or that the last thing he asked of me before we drifted off to sleep was that I'd still be there in the morning and that I'd agreed.

It doesn't matter that somewhere between the conversation and the sex the lines got blurred and that, for a second, we both considered what it would be like if this turned into more than a one-night thing.

And that's exactly why I have to leave.

Last night was fun, but that's all, and it's time to go.

So, in my wrinkled cocktail dress, crumpled curls, and smudged mascara, I began my walk of shame down the hotel hallway—shoes in hand but dignity left behind.

Not one of my finer moments.

Thankfully, the elevator is empty on the ride down, but I can't say the same for the lobby. Even at six o'clock in the morning it's already bustling with people. For a hotel in downtown Manhattan, I expect nothing different, but I can't escape their judging eyes quickly enough.

With my car still at the bar, I'm stuck calling an Uber. I'm already pushing it timewise, and if I pick the car up, I'd for sure risk running into someone at my house, so I'll have to get it later. I've snuck in and out of that house so many times over the years that I could probably do it in my sleep, but explaining why I didn't come home last night isn't exactly something I'm up for this morning. Especially to my father, who might already be up and headed to work.

The ride home is long enough for me to stew over how I got into this mess. I could have done the responsible thing last night, finished my date, and gone home to bed at a decent hour. But responsibility isn't exactly my calling card—at least, not recently—so instead I chose to abandon the nice, dependable man my sister set me up with and spent the night in a hotel room with a mysterious stranger who was every bit as dangerous as he was hot.

Again, not one of my finer moments.

I can't blame it all on his charm, though. Maybe it was a bit of rebellion or maybe it was the alcohol clouding my judgment, but I decided to go with him all on my own. It's just one more bad choice in a long line of them, but you don't get the reputation of being the wildest Moretti child by making good choices, so I guess it tracks.

It wouldn't be quite so awful if my father wasn't Alessandro Moretti—notoriously vicious mob boss and equally threatening father. He lives and breathes the business, and people are only partly joking when they say he only had children to carry on the family legacy. As girls, my sisters and I are practically useless to him, and his attention is always focused on the boys. Unless, of course, I'm doing something to disparage his good name.

Like sneaking in after a salacious night out.

For the last several weeks he's been even less amused than usual with my antics, strongly suggesting it's time for me to find a nice man, settle down, and start a family. Well, he didn't even specify *nice*—just someone who would take me off his hands.

At twenty-three, getting married and starting a family sounds as good as a death sentence to me. Ironically, his threat was the reason I both accepted the date with my sister's friend and then ran from it.

LAST NIGHT

Damn it, I'm *really* late. I have forty-five minutes to get to the restaurant where I'm meeting Rob, and considering the NYC traffic, there's no way that's happening. Being late isn't the best first impression, but I'm not looking to impress anyone tonight.

In a moment of weakness I reluctantly agreed to go out with my sister Angie's friend, but I've been kicking myself ever since. Rob is so wildly far from my type that it isn't even funny. Angie used the word *wholesome* to describe him, and I must admit, that's one of the more creative ways I've ever heard someone labeled as boring. Maybe if I was looking for a babysitter or a tutor, but certainly not as a future boyfriend.

After a day of law-school classes, driving into the city is the last thing I want to do. But after a string of particularly wild incidents over the last few months, my dad has been on some sort of self-serving crusade to settle me down. I've turned down a long list of potential men, trying to buy myself some time, but I don't know how long he'll hold out before he just chooses someone himself. The only thing that sounds worse to me than getting married is getting married to a man my dad handpicks.

I sincerely doubt he and I have the same taste.

So when Angie mentioned this friend of hers, I jumped at the chance to show my dad I was making an effort. Maybe, just maybe, it would make him reconsider the whole thing entirely.

A girl can dream, right?

With one last coat of lipstick and a quick shake of my curls, I head down the stairs. As I pass through my parents' foyer, I hear voices come from the kitchen, and I peek my head in to say goodbye.

"Come on, Ma, let me try it." Vince chuckles, dancing around the stove as our mom tries to shoo him away.

"Vincent, we are eating in fifteen minutes. You can try it when everybody else does."

"Besides, you've had Mom's lasagna a million times." Bella fans her nails in front of her face without even glancing up. Bella's the middle child in our family. All in all, there are five of us Moretti children spread out over eight years: Vince, then Angie, then Isabella, and finally, me and my twin brother, Andrew. Well, I guess only me now. I swallow the emotion in my throat, shoving every thought of Andrew and his death away. Maybe someday the thought of him won't hurt so bad.

"It gets better every time!" Vince's smug smile makes me roll my eyes as he swings his arm over my shoulder when I walk into the kitchen.

"Kiss ass."

"Ay, Ava! Watch your mouth!" My mother whacks me with the towel she has draped over her shoulder, turning her glare toward me.

"You tell her, Ma!" Vince gets way too much satisfaction from my scolding.

"Here." My mom shoves a stack of plates toward him. "Make yourself useful."

"Auntie Ava, what's a kiss ass?" Vince's daughter asks as she comes around the corner.

"Ask your daddy, Gigi." I bend down and plant a kiss on her forehead. One of Vince's only redeeming qualities is that he married well and has the cutest little girl in the entire world. "I'm going to be late."

"Thanks a lot. Sophia's gonna blame this one on me," Vince calls over his shoulder, and disappears into the dining room to set the table. I swear, he may be next in line to take over our father's business, but he acts as immaturely as a middle-school boy.

"You're not staying for dinner, angel?" Deep frown lines crease my mom's brow and her face falls as if I've just delivered the most devastating news. For what my father lacks in affection and emotion, my mom certainly makes up for.

"No, Mama. I've got a date."

"With who? Dante?" Her mood pivots, eyes lighting up at the prospect.

"No, his name is Rob. He's a friend of Angie and Mike's." I grab a piece of garlic bread out of the basket and my mom reaches out to slap my hand away.

"What happened to Dante? Your father and I really liked him." She doesn't even try to hide her disappointment.

"Don't tell her that, Mom. That's the quickest way to get her to dump someone," Bella teases. As the youngest, I'm used to taking the brunt of their jokes, but I don't have the patience for it tonight.

"Very funny."

Bella smirks, popping a cherry tomato into her mouth. "Isn't that my dress?"

"I don't know what you're talking about."

Speaking of redeeming qualities, Bella's is that we're exactly the same size, and with both of us living at home, my wardrobe nearly doubles in size.

She rolls her eyes, attention back to her nails.

"How many dates did ol' Dante make it, anyway?" Vince makes his way back into the kitchen, not missing a beat of conversation.

"Five, thank you very much." Dating isn't exactly my forte. Well, that's not true. It's the dating I'm good at. Relationships . . . that's where I struggle. Can you be allergic to commitment? Because if you can, I definitely am.

"Wow! New record." Bella laughs. "Why isn't this new guy picking you up?"

"She needs her car in case she has to make a quick getaway, right, Avs?"

Vince isn't entirely wrong, but I don't give him the satisfaction of letting on.

"Wow, are you guys going on the road with this act?" I say. "You're hilarious."

"You two leave your sister alone!" my mom scolds them. "And you get out of here before your father sees you in that dress."

I don't need to be told twice. "See you guys later."

When I finally get to my car, I breathe a huge sigh of relief and I'm on my way. I love my family, but they can be a lot to handle.

Panchos is in Midtown Manhattan, and I agreed to meet Rob there at six o'clock. With traffic as bad as it is, I'm thrilled when I pull into the lot at six fifteen. Angie gave me a vague description of Rob, and I don't see anyone who fits, so I make my way to the bar and squeeze between people to find a seat.

A live band plays on stage beneath big colorful canvases in the restaurant's corner, and the room's stuffed to the brim with people. Everyone is talking and laughing and having a great time as a fun, upbeat energy pulses through. It's hard to imagine my conservative sister recommending it to us, because the atmosphere is kind of cool.

"What can I get for you?" the bartender asks as he pours another person's drink.

"A whiskey ginger, please." I lean against the bar on my elbows.

"You got it."

Across the bar I catch the attention of a handsome stranger. His piercing stare locks with mine and he holds my gaze for a few seconds longer than casual eye contact. Right away I notice he stands out, and it's not only because he's very obviously overdressed in his black suit pants and crisp gray button-down It's the air of confidence he carries. The arrogance. The command. He knows he's important and so does everyone else.

Tattooed forearms flex underneath the thin fabric of his cuffed shirt, and his sharp jawline is shadowed with thick stubble. Broad shoulders, dark tousled hair, and a pair of green eyes deep enough to drown in—now he's *exactly* my type. His hard stare takes the air right out of my lungs as the corner of his mouth turns up into a playful smirk, almost as if he's taunting me. Even from across the bar he looks at me with such intensity that I feel the heat as my heart races, the ferocious beat echoes in my ears.

The group of men around him are talking but he's got his full attention on me, not listening to a single word. It's like we're on our own little planet, the two of us completely alone. A ambiguous air hangs between us, and I can't tell if he wants to kill me or have sex with me, but somehow, that only excites me more.

"Here you go, ma'am. On the house." The bartender slides a glass across the woodgrain bar top.

"On the house?" I stumble over the words, still trying to get my wits about me. The guy had disarmed me with a simple look, and my imagination runs wild. What could he do with more?

"Compliments of the gentleman at the end of the bar."

An inviting grin meets my gaze, daring me to come over. I'm picking up my purse, ready to take him up on that offer, when I feel a hand on my shoulder.

"Ava?"

What awful timing.

I could just say no. I could say no and go meet the temptingly gorgeous man at the end of the bar. Angie would kill me, though, and Rob looks nice enough. That's the entire point of tonight, so I swallow my pride and turn around with a wide smile on my face.

"You must be Rob," I say, abandoning all thoughts of the tall, dark, and handsome stranger.

"I am. It's nice to finally meet you." He shoves his hands into his pockets, eyes sheepishly surveying me. "Angie wasn't lying. You are stunning."

This poor guy—we haven't even sat down yet and I already know I'm going to eat him alive.

"Thank you." I smile, leaning in close enough so that he can hear me over the pounding bass of the band. "Shall we go sit down?"

"I'd love to." He slips his arm in mine and leads me over to a table with a RESERVED sign on it. I steal one more glance over my shoulder at my mystery man, still conflicted about my decision. He raises his highball glass to me before turning back to the group he's with, and our moment passes as quickly as it came.

So long, stranger.

Rob and I sit down and chat for a few minutes as we scan the menu. A few times, I look up and catch bar guy staring at me, nursing his drink and politely laughing at something his friend said.

I look away, but it happens again.

And again.

Every time I look, his steely gaze is on me. We're stuck in this cat-and-mouse game as Rob and I wait for our appetizers, but eventually, bar guy disappears with the group and I can finally relax and try to enjoy myself with Rob.

"Your sister tells me you're studying to be a lawyer?" Rob begins with the first date small talk I hate so much.

"I am. A defense attorney, actually."

"Now that's a job that will give you a lot of great stories! How'd you get into that?" He's clearly intrigued.

"I guess I've always been interested in law. My family . . ." I clamp my mouth shut quickly. I can't exactly blab to this guy that my family needs their own defense attorney because they're part of the Mafia. That's at least fourth date material.

"Your family? Is that a family business, then?" Rob asks.

"Sort of, yes."

"A defense attorney, huh?" He leans back in his chair. "Does that mean you could help me get out of the assault charges I got a few months back? Silly little bar fight?"

"Oh . . . that's not exactly—"

"I'm totally kidding. I've never even gotten a speeding ticket."

I can't help but laugh. That certainly fits. Rob is really sweet, and pleasantly different from how I pictured him. He's safe and kind of comforting, so I start to relax. Maybe even have a little fun.

"What else do you like to do?" he asks.

"I love to travel. I get a little stir-crazy if I stay in one place for too long."

I don't even care where. Traveling is one of my favorite things in the whole world. There's nothing quite like experiencing a new country or culture for the first time. The sights and sounds and smells—it's all so exciting. I love that you can hop on a plane or train and be in a completely new place in a few hours where no one knows anything about you. It's always temporary, and you don't have to be tied to anything you don't want to be for very long. The freedom is almost intoxicating. "I spent some time studying abroad in Greece and Spain as part of my undergrad and I've been dying to get back ever since."

Rob nods in agreement with a distant look in his eye. "I know exactly what you mean. I used to travel a lot too. Now I'm so busy with work I hardly have the chance. Right now, most of my focus is on finding the right woman and starting a family."

His comment makes my stomach flip and I press my lips into a thin line, hoping I can ignore it and enjoy the rest of our evening.

We order more drinks and food to share, and Rob and I have a great time getting to know each other. He's charming and responsible—exactly like the type of guy my parents would prefer me to bring home. But that's entirely the problem.

I appreciate the security a guy like Rob provides, but what about the spontaneity and fun? What about the adventure and challenge and passion that a real relationship needs? Poor Rob is a nearly perfect guy, but he's about to be a casualty of my own personal battle. By the time dessert comes around, I'm anxious about the looming conversation. Luckily, Rob walks right into it and gives me my opportunity.

"Ava, I know this is fast, but I really feel like you and I click. I'd love to take you out again later this week. Do you like opera?"

I take a breath, setting my napkin on the table. "Rob, you're a great guy, and I've had a lot of fun tonight, but I'm not really looking for a relationship. I certainly don't want to waste your time. I'm not sure what Angie told you, but I'm not ready for that. I'm so sorry."

Rob gives me an understanding smile, but I don't wait around for an answer. I hate things like this, hate confrontation of any sort, and my instinct is always to bail as fast as possible.

Leaving some cash on the table for the check, I hurry away, trying not to cause even more of a scene. It isn't until I'm in a back hallway that I realize I've gone the wrong way.

Damn it. I can't go back out the way I came—Rob will surely see me and that will make things even more awkward for the both of us.

At the end of the hallway there's a doorway closed off with a black curtain. It's the only one not labeled as a bathroom or maintenance, and I have no idea where it leads, but I don't have many options. Hurrying toward it, I duck behind the curtain, and I'm almost immediately knocked off my feet by a server carrying a tray overflowing with food.

"Watch it!" the server yells.

Suddenly I feel like I'm standing in the middle of a ten-lane California highway. Somehow, I've found myself in the restaurant's kitchen, steps away from flaming grills and large wood-fired ovens. The heat is almost as overwhelming as the noise of the cooks hollering back and forth to each other. Through the smoke I can see another doorway a few yards away and make my move, trying to avoid another near collision.

When I slip through the doorway, what's on the other side isn't exactly an exit. It looks like an office. There's a large desk and tall filing cabinets, and it has the distinct woodsy smell of old books and cigars. What the hell is this place, a maze? Why can't I find my way out?

Because you didn't use the entrance like normal people, Ava. I grimace, covering my face with my hands.

"Looking for something?" A husky voice comes from behind me. Startled, I whirl around and come face-to-face with the dashingly handsome face of the stranger from earlier.

"I was . . . on my way out."

"I can't imagine why. Your date seemed riveting."

I bite my lip, the smug look in his eye disarming me. He's been watching me all night with Rob, which should turn me off, but it doesn't.

"You know, most people use the front entrance." He chuckles, holding his arm out and gesturing to a door I hadn't noticed before. "But by all means, don't let me stop you."

Don't do this, Ava. The door is right there. Don't . . .

"Maybe I'm not in such a hurry, after all." His eyes trace my lips as I speak.

Walking away from him once was hard enough, but twice? That's too big of an ask.

The guy is even more perfect up close. A masterpiece of high cheekbones, a sharp jawline, and a hypnotizing smile that has my stomach fluttering. I can tell I've amused him, but he's far too collected and poised to fully let it show. My knees feel weak as he strides forward, closing the distance between us until we're close. Intimately close.

He's blocking the only real exit, but I could step around him. I don't want to, though. Something keeps me here. When I don't move, his hand brushes my elbow with a touch so charged that I feel it in my bones. "I didn't catch your name."

I hesitate for a second, debating whether I should tell him the truth. I don't know where this is heading, but I shouldn't even be entertaining the thought of a guy like him. He basically screams trouble.

"How about 'Juliette'?"

He draws dangerously close. Close enough that I can feel the heat radiating off him and I blush. He catches onto the irony in my Shakespeare reference, as he puts his hand to my cheek, thumb brushing gently against my skin.

"Then I guess that makes me 'Romeo.' What do you say we get out of here and go somewhere a little quieter, 'Jules'?"

"Something to drink?" He drapes his dark suit coat over a chair in the suite. "You're a whiskey girl, if I remember correctly?"

When he glances up, he winks. A wink? Seriously? On anyone else the gesture would feel forced or cheesy, but when he does it I fall for it hook, line, and sinker. A slow burn ripples through me. I'm not used to being in situations where I don't have control, so my reaction surprises me a bit, and he picks up on that immediately.

"Perfect," I say quickly, trying to compose myself.

A smile spreads across his face, and then he disappears to make our drinks.

He moves around the suite as if he's at home, almost like he's done this before, and I hang back, an anxious excitement settling in my stomach. This was certainly not how I saw this night going, but so far I've got no complaints. It's certainly a step up in the hookup department, that's for sure.

The suite is incredible. Much nicer than any hotel room I've stayed in before. A small entryway opens into a spacious dining room and kitchen area. A long table with high-backed velvet chairs sits in the center of the room, set as if ready to host a dinner party with elaborate flatware and dishes and towering, fresh floral arrangements. The artwork on the walls rivals some pieces I've seen at the Met. The kitchen has granite countertops and nearly every appliance you could imagine, and I wonder who in the world would use those kinds of thing in a hotel room. Everything about this place is over-the-top and impractical, but somehow that adds to the fun of it.

The living room is every bit as impressive with its floor-to-ceiling windows and jaw-dropping views of the NYC skyline. I'm not afraid of heights, but as I stand and look out into the expansive city, I feel dizzy, like we're a hundred miles above everything below us. Four buttery leather couches frame a TV that's nearly as big as the wall it hangs on, and they're in such pristine condition it's hard to imagine they've ever been used.

Two bedrooms branch out from the main space, each with its own en suite bathroom and king-sized bed piled high with heavenly looking linens and pillows. For a second I consider flinging myself into the mass of white fabric just to see if it's as soft as it looks.

When a throat clears behind me I realize I'm not alone. "Romeo" is back, leaning against the door frame as he holds two glasses of amber liquid.

"I'm sure we'll make it there eventually." He nods toward the bed with a smug laugh. "But there's something I want to show you first."

"Lead the way." I take the drink he offers. It's a bigger pour than I was expecting, and I sip it slowly.

His hand falls, grazing the small of my back as he leads me toward the sliding glass door. When he presses a button, the entire wall of windows parts so that the living room is open to the patio.

"Wow." I'm speechless as I step outside, taking in the sights. It's absolutely breathtaking up here. A million tiny lights twinkle below us, the hum of the city completely silenced. "This place is really amazing."

"It is, isn't it?" he agrees, taking a big gulp of his whiskey.

"Maybe you could have gotten a better room," I tease. "It feels a little small."

"Sorry to disappoint." He chuckles, picking up on my sarcasm. "My usual room was taken. This was the best they could do on such short notice."

"Usual?" I arch my eyebrow. "Do you do this kind of thing often?"

"This kind of thing? You mean share a drink under the stars with a beautiful woman?" His smile is intoxicating, and now I'm not sure I'm dizzy because of the harrowing drop or because of him. My knees quake beneath me and a fire builds in my core. When did I become so easy to please? What is it about this guy that has me fawning like this? I'm almost embarsassed.

My teeth sink into my lip, and I force myself not to fall for his sweet words. "Con a stranger into leaving a bar with you for a one-night stand."

"It seemed pretty mutual to me." He leans his elbows on the railing. With every inch closer he gets, the more my heart thunders and I have to consciously slow my breathing. "But if it makes you feel any better, rarely. I'm not really into the dating scene."

Now he's speaking my language.

"It's hard to find someone who sparks my interest the way you did," he says.

"You know nothing about me," I remind him. We only met a few hours ago at most.

"That's kind of the point of these things, isn't it?" He chuckles, pressing the highball glass to his mouth and taking a slow drink. "But you're wrong. Part of my job is reading people. Picking up on their personality and habits from the way they talk. The way they act. I was watching you all night, so I know more than you might think."

"Oh yeah?"

"You must be adventurous, otherwise you wouldn't have agreed to come because I make you a little nervous. That's why you do that thing with your lip—biting back your hesitation. You don't want me to know, though, which is why you try so hard to hide it when you slip up." His thumb sweeps across my lip but I hold my ground, not wanting to admit he's right.

"And you know what you want," he continues. "I admired the way you cut to the chase with that guy back at the restaurant. You're beautiful and witty, and I'd love to know your real name." He gives me a hopeful smile.

"Don't you think it's better this way? Keeping things as impersonal as possible? Isn't that what you want? You don't strike me as someone looking for commitment."

"And now I know you're perceptive." He finishes the rest of his whiskey. "You're right, I'm not into commitment. Usually I leave things with as few strings as possible."

"Then that's what we'll do. Tomorrow we'll go our separate ways, and everybody is happy."

"Deal." He eyes me as if he doesn't believe a word I said, but he doesn't press.

His lips brush against mine. It's a small, gentle touch, but it opens the floodgates and ignites an inferno between us. Soon his hands travel all over me. Through my hair, down my back and ribs, around my waist as he presses his body against mine and eases me back inside off the patio, never once stopping our kiss. I backpedal until my ankles hit the couch and we both tumble back onto it.

With hands on either side of my shoulders, he towers above me in all his glory. For the first time I feel how much bigger he is, almost larger than life. It's not even fair how gorgeous he is, and all I can think about as I fumble with the buttons of his shirt is how outmatched I feel.

Sure, I'm not exactly lacking experience in the hookup department, but he's . . . this is . . . different. This guy is heads and shoulders above anyone I've ever been with before, the highest caliber of man. I can tell simply by the way he holds me. Dominant but gentle. Commanding but attentive. Every touch, every kiss, every nuance is intentional. It's pointed. It's direct. And it's already blowing me away.

Apparently, I'm moving too slow for him, because he rips his shirt off his shoulders and drops it to the floor, revealing his bare chest.

Oh my god. I expected him to be hot, but his body obliterates every misguided expectation I had. Chiseled broad shoulders. Sharp, washboard abs. A seriously impressive display of tattooed artwork. I can't tear my eyes away, but if he notices, he doesn't let on because within seconds his lips catch mine with a hungry, desperate kiss.

It's a kiss like I've never experienced before, and I'm pretty sure I never will again. Sensual, intrusive, possessive. It's so electric that I feel it to my toes, my core tingling as anticipation builds between us. He coaxes my lips open, and his tongue explores every inch of my mouth as his fingers tangle in my hair. With a gentle pull, he's taken full control over me. I'm at his mercy with a simple kiss.

There's a desperation in his touch that doesn't match his affect, and it's the only indication that he's as out of sorts as I am. Just as into this. Just as turned on.

"You are so fucking beautiful." His coarse whisper sends a wave of chills across my skin.

His lips trail to my neck, brushing along the sensitive spot along my collarbone. Between the cool wetness of his kiss and the warm blow of his breath, my senses are in overdrive. He works his way down across my chest, stopping along the neckline of my dress. I've never hated an outfit more, and the ache between my legs agrees. Even with his shirt off, there's way too much fabric between us.

Apparently he agrees, because his fingers trace the straps of my dress, gently tugging them down my shoulders. "You like this dress? Because I'm about to rip it off you."

"It's my sister's."

"I'll be careful then." He flips me onto my stomach and straddles me, his thick erection pressing into my butt. My pulse skyrockets as I try to remember to breathe. His lips graze my neck from behind, and then the dress loosens around me as he unzips it painfully slowly. He knows exactly what he's doing, deliberately making me wait.

He moans, running his fingers firmly down my ribs. The sensation makes me squirm, but it's nearly impossible under his hold. The resistance only turns me on more, my body literally raging for him.

He works the dress off and piles it on the floor with his shirt. He's got my bra off so fast it's magic, and I turn over, ripping at the buckle of his belt. When he steps out of his pants a flash of silver at his ankle catches my eye, and my heart skips. Is that a gun? I suck in a sharp, disoriented breath, wondering what I've gotten myself into. It doesn't scare me as much as it should. In fact, it almost turns me on more.

Yeah, something is definitely wrong with me.

Not missing a beat, he picks up on my apprehension and slides the gun and its holster off quickly, putting the set on the coffee table. "You're safe with me, baby. I promise."

And for better or worse, I believe him.

He wastes no time in taking control, pinning my wrists above my head and brushing a kiss across my lips before working his way down my body. He hasn't even made it past my chest yet and I'm about to come undone. As he drags his tongue along my breasts, his free hand plays with the elastic of my panties, softly snapping it against my skin. His fingers slip inside and barely graze my core.

"Ohhh . . ." An expectant breath slips out.

For a second I think I'm about to get what I want, but his touch is gone as quickly as it came. His hand is back on my chest, rolling my nipple between his finger and thumb with pressure that makes me wiggle again, jerking against his restraint of my wrists, but even with his one-hand hold, I'm no match for his strength and he keeps me firmly in place. There is nothing gentle about this man, but I love every second of his control.

"You are so hot." A smirk tips at the corner of his lips. "You liked that, didn't you?"

I can only nod, because words aren't coming to me.

"Tell me which part you like best. You like me being in control? Restrained?" His teeth drag across one of my breasts and I flinch. "Or was it the pain? That's what you're into?"

He waits for an answer, but when I don't give him one, he continues.

Taking my nipple in his mouth, he sucks and flutters his tongue against it. His teeth drag over it, eliciting just enough pain to drive me absolutely wild.

"Or was it this?" He inches my panties down for easier access. My breath hitches when his finger trace my entrance, but it's a tease. This man is the master of foreplay, and he's going to be sure I'm out of my mind with anticipation before he gives in.

A smirk plays on his lips as his fingers glide over my traitorous, already wet body. "You like being teased? Knowing I'm the one who decides what you get to feel? When you get to feel it?"

"Y-yes."

He nods, a flicker of playfulness flashing in his eyes as he pulls my panties all the way off.

"Close your eyes," he commands, finally letting go of my wrists. He edges my knees apart and moves his body between them.

I'm fully exposed to him now and a blush creeps into my cheeks. Still, I take a breath and do as he says, fluttering my eyes closed and dropping my head back. The flick of his tongue against my inner thigh makes me gasp. How is it possible he already knows my body so well? Exactly where to touch. How hard. How soft. It dawns on me that it's not only *me* he knows. It's sex, and that kind of knowledge only comes with practice. Lots of it.

The bitter thought is silenced by his lips on mine again in a possessive, confident kiss. His fingers press down my body until they reach my thighs. And by the devilish look on his face, he's enjoying every bit of what he's doing to me.

He holds my gaze as his fingers plunge inside of me, stroking slowly at first and then faster. His pace is ferocious as I arch my back, teetering on the edge of orgasm. He plays with me like I'm a puppet, dangling helplessly from his strings, and he's the domineering master watching me wiggle and squirm all for his pleasure. It should upset me. It should degrade me. But it doesn't. I'd do just about anything he asked of me, and we both know it.

Moaning, I rake my fingers along his back, holding on as if my life depends on it. Like if I let go, the moment might stop. No one's ever made me feel like this before, and I know I'll never get enough of him.

When he pulls his hands away, I worry he might be done, but he quickly replaces them with his tongue, delving it inside of me as I tug on his thick, dark hair. His hands are at my hips, angling me exactly how he wants me as he twists and sucks and dips inside of me. It's almost more than I can bear.

"This is incredible, but I can't wait anymore. I need you. Please." The first coherent sentence I'm able to form all night and I'm begging him? The me of a few hours ago would be absolutely appalled.

My neediness doesn't deter him. In fact, he matches it, frantically searching his pockets for a condom. When he finds one, I take it and rip into the foil, slipping it over his rock-hard length.

"I wanted to make this a little more special for you, but I can't wait either," he whispers.

"You need to feel good too." I lace my fingers together behind his neck, pulling him to me until our lips connect again.

"Give me your ankle," he orders. I lift my leg and he takes it, resting it on his shoulder as he strokes the sensitive skin of my thigh.

"You're sure?" he asks, checking to be sure I'm still okay with all of this. Even in the middle of rough, hot sex, he's a gentleman.

The only answer he needs is to see how wet and throbbing I already am for him, but I nod, assuring him that I'm more than sure.

I need this. Bad.

He doesn't need any further encouragement and slips inside of me. It takes my breath away at first, filling me up to the very brim as he eases himself in. He moves slowly, letting me get used to the feel as his hips pump against mine. My lips part in a moan, but he stifles it with his kiss. "Do you have any idea how fucking beautiful you are? This body. Those eyes. Every single bit of you. You're an absolute goddess."

Something about the way he says it makes me believe it.

His hips buck against mine a little faster, our bodies moving together in perfect rhythm. I arch my back, gasping sharply as each thrust goes deeper than the last. Stronger. Harder. Better.

I can't contain my moans and screams, but he doesn't seem to mind. Faster and faster he drives into me, edging me so close to explosion that my mind starts to blank. His body against mine takes me to a high I'm not sure I ever want to come down from.

"You feel so good," I purr, stroking his cheek.

I can tell by his thrusts that he's nearing the peak himself, and soon our bodies writhe against each other in pure ecstasy. We collapse back against the couch, both of us breathless.

"Wow." His voice is husky as he drapes his arm around my shoulder, and I settle into his chest.

"That was incredible," I say, trying desperately to catch my breath, but still sky-high in the clouds with pleasure.

"I'm not sure I'll be content with only once." He chuckles.

"Good thing we've got all night."

TWO

Nick

I don't like being surprised.

I don't like being unprepared. Caught off guard. I especially don't like being wrong. But when I wake up in an empty hotel room, that's exactly what I am.

For a minute I consider that I might have made the entire night up. That it had all been some sort of alcohol-induced fever dream. But there are remnants of her all over this room. Perfume on the pillowcase. Two half-finished glasses of champagne on the coffee table. Nail marks down my back. And is that lipstick on my neck?

Jesus Christ.

Clearly I didn't do all of this myself, so where the hell did she go?

I've had my fair share of one-night stands over the years, so I know that this is how they're supposed to end. They don't spill over into the daylight. They don't turn into first dates. They don't cross any lines.

Usually I'd meet a girl, charm her with my wit and good looks, and convince her to leave whatever establishment we were at for something quieter. I'd get a hotel room—never my own place—and take her back there, making my intention to sleep with her crystal clear. Over and over again I'd tell her this was a onetime thing, that we'd never see each other again after that night. But somehow that message would get lost in translation. Most of the time I'd try to sneak out before they woke up, but if I couldn't, it was always a fight. I'd wake up and they would be trying to get my phone number and planning when they could see me again, hearing wedding bells and wanting to meet my family.

After a lot of experience, I feel confident that the point of a one-night stand is completely lost on most girls. They like the idea in theory, but when it comes down to it, most girls can't leave the emotion out.

And that was exactly how I expected it to go when I sought this girl out. Maybe even more so because she was so damn hot. In the words of my brother, Leo, *No one looks that good and isn't batshit crazy*. Add that to the out-of-this-world sex, and this girl had to be certifiable.

So why the fuck am I the one waking up alone in a hotel room wondering where things went wrong?

Honestly, it went wrong the second she walked into my restaurant looking like a goddamn smokeshow. I'm supposed to be taking it easy in the hookup department. Getting serious about work and avoiding all distractions. I'd only dropped by Panchos to bring Leo some statements, which should have only taken a few minutes. A few minutes turned into a drink, which turned into two drinks and a sassy smile from a stranger, and the rest is now history.

Can you blame me, though? There isn't a hot-blooded man in the universe who could resist a woman like her—paralyzingly gorgeous doe eyes, pouty candy-colored lips, and thick, dark curls that fell over her slender shoulders like a damn waterfall. Dangerous curves, a set of tits that God must have sculpted himself, and a dress as tight as skin only completed the package. When I saw her across the bar, I was positive I'd found the most beautiful woman in the entire world. The type of girl every guy wanted but could never have. And the challenge only made it more enticing.

Leo thought I was insane when I said I was taking her home with me, especially considering at the time she'd taken the drink I'd bought her and gone to sit with another man. I waited patiently, though, watching from the safety of a private room all evening as she made small talk with that Boy Scout she called a date. For a while I almost thought she was interested in him, but when she excused herself, I made my move. And damn, was it fucking worth it.

Her company was great; the sex was even better. I had the most mind-blowing orgasm I've ever had in my life. Hell, I had the *five* most mind-blowing orgasms of my life. I had her on the couch, on the floor, against the window of our fiftieth-floor suite, in the shower, in the bed. The woman did something to me I'd never quite experienced before, and before the night was over, I was even rethinking my one-and-done policy.

I asked her to stay. Hell, I fucking begged. And yet here I am. No goodbye, no number to reach her at, not even a real name.

It isn't even just the sex I crave again. I want to talk to her. She proved to be as brilliant and witty as she was beautiful. In between rounds we compared scars from past relationships, bonded over the pressure we felt from our families to be something we weren't, laughed about our favorite TV shows, and told each other about our wildest fantasies. She challenged me and called me out, not letting me get away with the usual tricks I used to win women over. Her fiery attitude caught my attention immediately, and I've never been one to like a girl for her personality.

Why does her leaving bother me so much? Normally I'd be ecstatic to wake up to find myself alone, not having to deal with the morning-after mess. But at risk of sounding like a cliché, there's something different about her, and I don't think I'm ready to let it go.

What the fuck is happening to me?

We had a good time. A *really*, *really* good time. Or so I thought. Did I miss something? Did she not thoroughly enjoy every second right along with me? I almost laugh out loud at the thought. Of course she did. Her body's reaction left no question there. It had to be something else.

Maybe she's got a boyfriend. Would she have been so quick to leave with me, though, if she did? And he couldn't possibly be that joker she was at the restaurant with last night. That much was obvious.

Maybe she had somewhere to be this morning. She didn't mention it last night, but maybe she could have had an appointment or something. Or work. I forget that most people have normal business hours since my own are so sporadic.

Or maybe, just maybe, for the first time in my life, I've been beaten at my own game. Maybe I found someone who out-casuals the King of Casual. Maybe I've met my match.

I *must* find her. Tracking her down goes against about everything I stand for, but it's a pride thing at this point. But all I have left of the girl are a few memories and a fake name. My guys are good, but nobody is that good. How the hell am I going to manage this?

My phone buzzes on the nightstand, flashing Leo's face as the caller ID.

"Hello?" I answer, still groggy and rubbing the sleep out of my eyes.

"All right, shithead. Where are you?" Leo growls on the other end of the line.

"Good morning to you too."

"Did you forget what day it is? We were supposed to meet Dad at the warehouse an hour ago." Clearly, he's pissed off.

Damn it. In my confusion this morning, I forgot about the meeting. My father will blow a gasket. The day I take over for him as Don is fast approaching, and he's been on me constantly about being more responsible.

"You forgot." Leo chuckles nonchalantly. "You're lucky I covered for your ass. And that Frankie totaled his car last night so Dad had bigger fish to fry."

"What? Why didn't anyone call me? Is he okay?" I shoot up in bed, shoving a hand through my dark-brown hair. Frankie's our youngest brother and a total troublemaker. This accident is the latest in his long stream of recent screwups.

"He's fine," Leo assures me. "Might not be when Dad gets through with him, though. Anyway, the meeting got pushed back. You want to grab some breakfast?"

Most of what Leo says is lost when I stumble into the living room of the suite, finding her lacy panties still draped over the back of the couch. I bite my lip and groan, reliving the moment I slid them off her last night, tugging gently down each toned leg, inch by inch. The visceral memory is second only to the image I get in my mind of her walking out of here without them on. Damn, that does things to me that I am ashamed to admit, and I'm immediately transported back to the night before.

LAST NIGHT

A few minutes after the door shuts, "Jules" saunters back into the room holding two ice-cream sundaes. Mine with nuts, hers without. The hotel robe is held loosely around her by its belt, and one wrong move could make the whole thing fall open. Secretly I hope it will, so I can catch another glimpse of her body. She hands me my ice cream and then climbs back into the bed next to me.

"The room service guy called me Mrs. Sinatra when I answered the door." The playful look in her eye is adorable. "You even gave the hotel a fake name?"

I can't help but laugh. "What? I don't look like I have a good singing voice to you?"

"You look alive," she teases. "Frank Sinatra died years ago. Although you've got that whole Italian thing going for you. Dark hair, great bone structure, and I bet you wear the hell out of a fedora." She pauses, momentarily doubting herself. "You're not actually related to him, are you?"

I shake my head as she settles back into my chest while we enjoy our ice cream. Room service ice cream at three in the morning is a tall order, but people will do anything for the right price. And we certainly worked up an appetite.

"Flattered, but I'm no relation whatsoever. I'm a fan, and that was the first name I thought of when I made the reservation. You can never be too careful. No strings, remember?"

"For someone who says they've rarely done this, you certainly have a system," she quips. My cock twitches as her tongue glides across her upper lip, licking a bit of whipped cream off.

"That's what a few bad apples will do to you," I counter. "I've been on a little bit of a dating hiatus lately because so many girls have trouble understanding the no-strings thing."

"But you broke your streak tonight."

"I did." I nod. "Something about you told me you'd be worth it, and I certainly haven't been wrong so far."

"You're in luck. No strings is practically my love language." She takes another bite, lips bowing around the spoon. Jesus, I could watch her eat ice cream all night.

Easy, Nick. You guys are supposed to be taking a break. The self-coaching only goes so far, though, because anyone who's been through a sex-ed class knows exactly where my mind is.

I stiffen, composing myself. "Not looking for a relationship?"

"God, no!" Her face twists in horror as she continues, "Although I guess that depends on who you ask."

"Oh yeah?"

A woman like her probably has men eating out of the palm of her hand. She's the best kind of beautiful, not having any idea how incredible she really is. Her eyes grow cloudy, and I can't read her expression, but it weighs heavy on her.

"My family has a very different idea of what I should do with my life than I do."

"I can understand that. It seems like everyone always knows who you're supposed to be without even considering what you want." Family pressure—that's something I get.

"That's why I like this little world you've created up here. Even though all the stress will be there in the morning, tonight we're free to be whoever we want to be and do whatever we want."

"You're absolutely right." I kiss the top of her head. "And what is it you want to do next?"

"I want to finish my ice cream, and then I want to have sex with you in that shower." She points to the bathroom and flushes, almost like she's shocked herself by admitting it. "It's got four showerheads."

"Then we definitely have to try it." I'm not sure where the hell these thoughts are coming from, but all I can focus on is making her happy. We both admitted we don't do well in relationships, but this is something I could get used to. Her in my arms. In my bed. Maybe for longer than one night.

"Nick, did you hear me? Hello? Breakfast?" Leo barks on the other end of the phone.

Breakfast sounds great. If I get some food in my stomach maybe I'll be able to think clearer. "Yeah, pick me up in twenty minutes?" I glance at my watch, making sure that leaves enough time to get back to my penthouse.

"I'm already outside your building. Open up."

Damn.

Leo's going to want to know all the details of my night when he finds out I took the girl back to a hotel, and I don't want to get into it. I'm still licking my wounds from her untimely departure this morning. "I'm not at home."

"Where the hell are you?"

"At a hotel." I throw on my clothes so I can be on my way, but Leo's relentless and won't let me brush him off easily.

"You dirty dog." I can almost see him smirking on the other end of the line. "You took that girl back with you, didn't you? The chick from the bar?"

"Look, I'm fifteen minutes away. Can we talk about this at breakfast?"

"You did!" He ignores my ask. "Damn, I gotta admit I had my doubts. Was she as crazy as we thought?"

I chuckle to myself at the irony of the situation. She's crazy all right, just not in the respect we thought. "Even crazier."

"Beautiful. I can't wait to hear all about it. Meet me at Snooze in a half hour."

Thank god.

Clicking the phone off, I slide it into my pocket. Then I give the room a once-over, making sure that I'm not leaving anything behind—aside from my pride.

Because I can't let anything rest, I snatch my phone out of my pocket and quickly call my best friend, Zane. He's my right-hand man, but his legitimate job is private investigating. The guy's a whiz with computers and can track down nearly anyone. That certainly comes in handy in the crime world, and now, apparently, my personal life.

"Nick. How's it going, man?" Zane greets me when he picks up.

"Good, buddy." I wave at the receptionist on the way out of the lobby, signaling I'm checking out. This isn't the first time I've brought a girl back to this hotel, and despite my fake names, she recognizes me and gives me a condescending look before she charges my card. "Hey, I need a favor. I need everything you can find out about a girl from the restaurant last night."

"Business or pleasure?"

"I'm not sure yet." I laugh. "Thing is, I don't know much about her."

"No problem. All I need is a name," he says.

Yeah, me, too, buddy. My hesitation gives me away.

"Nick, tell me you at least know her damn name." Zane's voice is a mixture of amusement and irritation. He's been tied down for a while now, and while he enjoys hearing about my wild dating life, what I'm asking him to do is next to impossible.

"She said her name was Juliette, but that was a lie. I met her at the restaurant, so maybe try there. See if there are any credit card receipts or anything on surveillance," I offer, trying to give him a place to start.

"Description?"

"Brunet, dark-chocolate eyes. Five six, five seven, definitely Italian. Probably midtwenties."

"You realize you just described about thirty percent of women in New York. This could take weeks."

"I don't care how long it takes."

"Easy, killer. I didn't say I couldn't do it. I'll get on it and let you know as soon as I find anything."

"Thanks." I hang up without waiting for a reply.

It's about a fifteen-minute walk from the hotel to my building, and on the way I try to focus on anything and everything besides my mystery girl, but that's easier said than done.

When I get home I have only a few minutes to change clothes before catching up with Leo. If I'm going to see my dad, I at least have to look presentable. All he needs is another reason to tag me incapable of taking over for him. It's not like he'll hand it over to someone else, but he's put me through the gauntlet of prep lately and I can't stand to lose any ground that I've gained.

As the eldest of his three sons, I'm next in line to take over the Caponelli fortune and run one of the largest crime families in the United States. For most people it might sound intimidating, but I live for this shit. I grew up around it and there's never been any doubt one day I would take over for my dad as the boss and shape this organization into my own. It's only a question of when.

We're mostly in the weapons trade and counterfeiting. Thousands of guns, rounds of ammo, and fake bills come in for distribution every week through New York, and most of it passes through our hands. My dad dabbled in the drug trade at one point, but it was short-lived. That's Moretti territory, and, as a general rule of thumb, we stay away from all things Moretti.

The Morettis aren't exactly our rivals, but we aren't all that friendly either. My parents live in Harrison and the Morettis live in Oyster Bay, right on the other side of the Long Island Sound.

For as long as I can remember we've been battling for control of the ports. The Morettis' investment in illegal substances brings more police attention to the area than needed, and it's always a danger to shipments we bring in through that avenue. Years ago we tried pulling our forces together, but that ended in complete disaster, and the partnership was over before it even had a chance to begin. We're cordial with the Moretti family for business purposes now, but only when absolutely necessary.

When I get to Snooze, my brother is sitting in our regular booth in the back. We meet here at least once a week, sometimes more. Their breakfast burritos are out of this world, and a little grease and chorizo is exactly what this hangover needs. I make my way to him and sit down on the bench across from him.

"You look like hell," Leo asserts, sliding his coffee cup over to me. "You need this more than I do. Dad decided to meet us here instead of the warehouse."

I'm already so amped that caffeine is the last thing I need, but I take a drink anyway.

"Fantastic. That's exactly what I need after the morning that I've had." The booth squeaks as I shift my weight.

"Was she that bad?" Leo smirks, clearly on the edge of his seat for this story. Something tells me it's going to be less climatic than he's looking for.

"No, actually, she wasn't that bad. She was incredible. The best sex I ever had. Absolutely mind-blowing." He wants more details, but I'm not going to give them to him. At least not now.

The server slides two plates in front of us with our regular orders. They know us well around here. Leo shoots the new blond server a wink and she blushes. Poor girl has no clue she just gave him the in he was looking for. I have no doubt he'll be leaving here with her number. Part of me is jealous his escapades aren't scrutinized the way mine are, when he's way more of a fuckboy. He's also not the heir, so I get it.

"Really?" Leo looks confused. It isn't often I brag about my one-night stands, because it isn't often that I'm impressed the way I was last night.

I nod, taking another gulp of coffee. Maybe I needed this more than I thought, because it's starting to take the edge off. "And I woke up this morning, and she was gone. Slipped out without a fucking word."

"Then I'm not seeing what the problem is. You hate the morning after. Why aren't you jumping for joy about this? She was an awesome lay and completely detached. In fact, are you sure you didn't dream this? It seems too good to be true."

"I've never been ghosted before. No one has ever walked out on me like that," I grumble, shoving down some of my breakfast.

"You actually want to see this girl again?" Leo arches an eyebrow at me. Sometimes I hate how observant he can be.

"Can we drop it, please?" I hiss. So much for taking the edge off. Hopefully, Zane will have something for me soon.

"Drop what?" My father's voice comes from over my shoulder. He walks around my side of the booth and slides in next to Leo.

Gio Caponelli is an intimidating man. He stands tall at six foot six, is built like a linebacker and has a piercing glare that can make a person crumble on sight. He's fearsome, and evokes an uneasiness in people who don't know him well. Most people choose to stay out of his way entirely.

He's a good father, but he always demands the most out of us, and only now that I'm an adult can I understand why. This life isn't for everyone, and he's done his best to prepare the three of us to continue his legacy.

"Nothing," I snap.

The last thing I need is to relive the story for my dad. He'll have all kinds of unsolicited opinions I'm not sure I can stomach this morning. I've already heard them all—clean up my act, find a suitable woman to settle down with. Blah, blah, blah.

"Don't mind him, Dad." Leo laughs. "He's a little moody this morning."

"I'm not moody. I'm dealing with a minor crisis, and I would appreciate a little sympathy." I narrow my eyes at my brother, daring him to say anything else.

"What kind of crisis?" my dad asks, eyeing me suspiciously. His mind goes right to something being wrong with the business like usual.

"Please. You not being able to get in touch with your booty call is not a crisis." I kick Leo under the table. What the fuck? I thought I made it clear I didn't want to talk about this anymore. Especially in front of our father.

"Booty call?" My dad sighs heavily. "Don't you think it's time you grow up a little?"

And there it is.

I rub my chin harshly, careful with my response. I don't want to piss my father off, but I don't like what he's insinuating. My sex life isn't his business, and I certainly don't need to curtail it to run this business. I'm more than capable, and his assumptions are way off base.

"It's not a big deal. We have a lot going on at the warehouse this week that I'm stressed out about. That's all."

We run a legitimate shipping company that masks most of our illegal activity. By day we import and export all kinds of goods out of South America, and by night we bring in heavy ammo and artillery under the disguise of livestock shipments. Port authorities use scent dogs, and the animals always throw them off the scent of the illegal shit. It's the perfect setup. Until I take over for my father, I'm in charge of the day-to-day operations of the shipping business. My dad has his reasons for keeping me there, but all it really is is a headache for me.

"Right. That's what I wanted to speak to you both about anyway." My dad fills his coffee, thankfully not wanting to go down that road either.

"What's going on?" Leo asks.

"We might have a rat."

"What?" Leo and I both hiss at the same time. A traitor? There's no way. Our men are as loyal as they come, and we don't bring anyone new on without serious vetting.

My dad has always been sure to make an example out of anyone who crosses us, so no one would ever risk it. We have good relationships with all our men and treat them well. Did something slip through the cracks?

"Somewhere between the docks and inventory at the warehouse, we're coming up short. Just a little at a time. I have a feeling it might be a supplier, but I want to be sure before we do anything."

"How? I've been checking them in myself," Leo says. He's mostly in charge of shipments coming in at the dock and getting them to the warehouse and I handle redistribution after that.

"I don't know. We need to keep a close eye on things these next few weeks and find the problem. I don't want to draw any attention to it right now. See how everything shakes out and then we'll go from there." It takes a lot to rattle my dad, so when he's genuinely concerned, you know it's serious.

"And in the meantime?" I ask. "How will we make up the loose ends? We can't send our shipments out short."

"I've asked the Morettis for additional support." He sighs, not meeting my eyes. "They deal with a few mutual suppliers, and Alessandro said they're having some of the same issues."

"You're working with the Morettis?" I almost spit out my coffee. Signing a deal with them is like signing a deal with the devil himself. Alessandro isn't very far off.

"*We're* working with the Morettis," he corrects. "It's only temporary, and we're all on the same side here."

"I don't like this one fucking bit," my brother says.

"You don't have to like it, Leo. We need to figure out what's going on and go from there. We'll both be monitoring our own groups and then meet in a few weeks and see what we can figure out." Dad checks his watch. "I've got to run. You two behave yourselves."

He slugs back the rest of his coffee, then slams the cup back on the table.

"And you." He points at me. "No more booty calls. Find yourself a nice woman your mother will approve of."

I chuckle, shaking my head.

Dad waves and heads out the front door, as if he didn't just drop a bomb on us. Working with the Morettis is dangerous.

This is going to be a nightmare.

THREE

Ava

"How was your date last night?" Bella eyes me over the rim of her tortoiseshell sunglasses as she lounges on the pool chair next to me.

It's already blistering hot out here, the humidity making the pages of my trashy gossip magazine stick together when I try to turn them. If it was up to me, I'd still be snuggled in my bed, comfortable in the air conditioning, but Bella was in my room bright and early. She said she needed some company by the pool, but I know her better than that. She wants all the dirty details of my night.

This is something of a ritual between us—me recounting my dates and hookups while Bella eats it up, living vicariously through my bedroom adventures. Despite her other unruly tendencies, she's practically celibate. Unlike me, Bella's one goal in life is to get married, particularly in an arrangement to a rich and powerful man my dad chooses for her, and she's got it in her head that saving herself will make her more attractive to potential husbands.

I absolutely hate it. Not because I don't respect her virtuous choice, but because she's letting a man dictate her life. Not even a man; a *potential* man.

When I don't answer her immediately, she continues. "Must have been pretty good since you didn't make it home."

I guess it was stupid of me to think I made it undetected into a house filled with so many people. Bella and I both still live at home with our parents, and at least a few nights a week Vince is here after work, too, since he and his wife live farther north.

My parents have a sprawling estate in Oyster Bay Cove, about an hour east of the city and close to the warehouses and offices where my dad controls his empire. It was our childhood home, and while I've always loved the hustle and bustle of the city, there's something about the serenity here I appreciate. With its towering trees and expansive garden, it's like our own private nature sanctuary. When I was young it doubled as a fantasy land where my sisters and brothers and I would play pretend for hours, and also as a hideaway when I needed to escape the chaos of my family or my father during one of his fits of rage.

"Does Dad know?" If he does, it's not going to be pretty.

Bella shrugs. "I doubt it. So spill. How was it? Was he as boring as we thought he would be?"

Since Andrew died, Bella is the closest thing I have to a confidant in this family, but I'm still hesitant. Whether it's because I'm a bit ashamed or because I'm afraid of it traveling to the wrong ears, I want to keep the details of the night close to my chest.

"It was fine. He was nice."

Bella snorts. "Fine? Nice? And you stayed out with him all night? Something's not adding up there, Avs. Seriously, what happened? I can't imagine a single one of Angie and Mike's friends being interesting enough for you."

Maybe a few details won't hurt anything.

"Their friend wasn't. But the guy I left the bar with . . . he *definitely* was."

"Shut up! You left with another guy?" Bella jolts, twisting her body so that she's facing me in her chair. "You didn't meet up with Jimmy, did you?"

"Of course not!" I cringe.

Jimmy is the one guy my dad and I both agree was a bad influence on me. It wasn't always like that, though. When we first met, I thought Jimmy Bradford hung the moon and the stars, and by the time I saw him for what he really was, his claws were so deep into me that there was no way I could escape unscathed.

I don't want to tarnish the memory of last night by thinking of him, so I move on.

I give Bella a rundown of how I arrived at the restaurant early, only to catch the attention of a man across the bar who felt just as off-limits as he was hot. She's wide-eyed, completely engrossed in my story as I tell her about Rob wanting a second date and me not being into it. As I get to the part about running into the man from before in the kitchen of the restaurant, she's leaning so far forward in the chair she's almost in my lap.

"Wait. Why was he in the kitchen to begin with?" She scrunches her nose.

For the first time, I wonder about that too. "Actually, I have no idea. We didn't get that far."

Bella smirks, lips curling in a condescending way. "Okay, so then what?"

"He took me to a hotel a block or two away and we hooked up." I shrug, knowing she isn't going to let me get away with that simple of an explanation.

"And?"

And it was the best night of my life. So dreamy that I worry I made the whole thing up. I didn't, though. The deep ache in my legs and his marks on my body prove that. Even now, just thinking about his husky voice is enough to give me chills, and when visions of our night play through my mind, my breath shortens. The passion, the hunger, the dominance. I loved every single second of it, and for a moment I'm lost in flashbacks that nearly send me over the edge. It's almost unnerving how simple thoughts of him have this effect on me. I'd never let a man get to me quite like he did last night, and now I see that it's a double-edged sword. As good as last night was, the shame is setting in this morning, and I can't believe I did it.

Bad decisions seem to be part of my personality lately. Andrew's death rocked me, and being a little reckless is my twisted way of reckoning with it, but last night took it to an extreme that even I was shocked by.

I know better than to run off with a guy like that without telling a single soul, and yet I did it anyway. What if he was a serial killer? What if he kidnapped me and held me for ransom? I don't even know the guy's name. What if he has a girlfriend? Or a disease? God, what was I thinking? There were a million things that could have gone wrong, and it was a miracle that nothing did.

Not to mention, the second he gave me the time of day it was like I threw every moral I had right out the window. I left my date for another man and jumped into bed with him. Better yet, I let him use me like some glorified, high-priced hooker. He took me to a hotel, and if that wasn't enough of a red flag, maybe the gun he had strapped to his ankle should have been. He was dangerous to me in more ways than one, but never for one second did I feel threatened or afraid of him. He was attentive and gentle when I needed him to be, and underneath that tough, tattooed exterior, I felt an intimate connection with him. The guy is bad news—exactly the opposite of who I should be associating with—and yet, given the chance, I would relive last night a thousand times.

"Ava!" Bella rips me back to reality. "Hello? I want details. How was he?"

"Honestly, Bells, it was incredible," I confess. "He was perfect. And the sex was even better. It wasn't even just that, though. He was sweet and charming, and it felt like he was genuinely interested in me."

That's the part that surprised me the most. We were both clear from the beginning that this was all for fun, but somehow in the in-between it turned into something more. A level of understanding. A connection. A spark.

"Then why did you leave?"

I panicked and before there was any awkwardness, any possibilitiy of something more, any chance he could convince me not to, I left.

Maybe I walked out because it was the most intense connection that I'd ever had with someone, and I left before anything could happen to taint the memory. Maybe I wanted it preserved a certain way in my mind forever, untouched by the stickiness of the morning after, or, god forbid, a relationship. I'm not ready for that for a variety of reasons, and I never want to look back on last night with regret.

"It was a one-night thing." I shrug it off, trying to hide the defeat in my voice. The reminder is for my own benefit as much as it is for her. What happened last night certainly couldn't be repeated; we both agreed on that, and it was for the best.

"And you're okay with that? You seem really into this guy. And if he's as great as you say he is, maybe once isn't good enough."

"It doesn't matter what I want now, Bells. I agreed to a onetime thing. That's all it was. That's all he wanted."

"Did he actually come out and say that's all he wanted?" She looks at me like she knows he asked me to stay. Begged for me to be there in the morning.

Even I can recognize that I'm making excuses. "Not exactly, no. But guys like that . . ."

"Ava, I swear I'm going to murder you." Angie's voice announces her entrance long before she makes it out by the pool.

"Damn it. Hide me," I groan, ducking behind my magazine and sinking low into the chair. Bella I can handle, but Angie is another beast entirely.

"She's gotten scarier since she's become a mother." Bella snickers, her voice low.

"Do you want to explain why you ran out in the middle of your date with Rob last night?" She stands over me, hands perched on her hips as she glares down.

"I didn't run out in the middle of our date. He knew I was leaving, and I even left cash for the check. Now, do you think you could scoot over? You're blocking my sun."

She picks the magazine up off my face, rolls it, and swats me with it. I flinch but can't help laughing. Angie is only a year older than Bella, but it might as well be a decade. She acts more like a mother to the two of us than an older sister.

"Lighten up, Ang." Bella rubs some lotion onto her shoulders. "Just because Ava had fantastic sex last night and you haven't gotten laid in a while doesn't mean—"

"Bella!" I hiss, covering my face with my hands.

"Don't start with me, Bella. I only have time to kill one annoying little sister today, and Ava is at the top of my list." Angie arches her eyebrows at me, tapping her perfectly manicured fingernails against her side. "You ran out on Rob to go hook up with another man?"

Damn Bella and her big mouth.

"Angie, Rob's great, but there wasn't any connection between us. He's not the guy for me. Instead of dragging it out, I figured it was best to not waste his time."

"And you knew that from one conversation? Ava, Rob has a stable job. He comes from a good family. He's the type of guy who would take care of you. What more could you want?"

I bite back my laughter.

Adventure. True love. White-hot passionate sex with a man who touches me like he owns me.

Bella doesn't outright say it, but she agrees with Angie. My sisters are realists, the ideas of true love or soulmates completely lost on them. Angie married for practicality, and Bella will do the exact same thing. It's not like I consider myself much of a romantic, but I like the idea of at least enjoying the person I'm going to marry.

As twisted as it is, I don't blame them for their thought process. From the time we were tiny it's been ingrained in us that our only real responsibility as women within the family is to marry respectable men our father could profit from in some way. He and my mother have very old-school values, and even as children my sisters and I understood we were meant to be seen and not heard. We were expected to follow our mother's example, learning how to scrub kitchen cabinets and fold laundry, and have a hot dinner on the table when our father came home from a long day at work. It was something I resisted from the very beginning, which only got me into trouble.

As twins, the difference in treatment between Andrew and me was painfully obvious, and I wanted nothing more than to spend my days playing in the backyard and getting muddy with him. Instead I was holed up in the house learning how to polish the inside of the oven or put on the perfect dinner party. Vince and Andrew were immersed in every aspect of my father's business, whereas my sisters and I weren't even allowed to ask questions about it. It's a miracle in itself that my dad agreed to let me go to law school. Women don't need an education to be useful in his mind. In fact, sometimes an education makes them even more of a problem. Smart women have opinions, aren't as easy to control, and know there is more to life than being a homemaker.

I'm not against marriage entirely. I love the idea of finding my soulmate and raising a family with them one day, but I'm a long way from that right now. In some ways I'm still picking up the pieces of who

I was before I lost my brother, and that's hard for anyone in my family to grasp. I want to be a whole person again before I really start considering marriage or what comes next for me at all.

Of course, Angie doesn't understand this. She bought into the antiquated stereotype from the beginning. She found a good, wholesome guy my parents approved of in Mike, moved two streets away from our childhood home, and started popping out kids almost immediately. She never questioned it, wanted more, or strayed from the plan in the slightest, even when we were children. All she wanted to do was be a wife and mother, and while I respect her choice, it's the exact opposite of what I want.

"I don't need someone to take care of me, Angie. Look, I appreciate you setting up the date, but I'm not going to settle for someone just because everyone in this family thinks I need to get married. No offense, but that's not the life I want."

Angie scowls, obviously taking offense to my statement. "You say that now, Ava, but someday you're going to realize you're making a big mistake by passing these men up. You're going to wake up alone and wish you'd listened to us."

"I'm going inside," I say, standing up and grabbing my things. I'm not going to win this battle, and I have no interest in going around in circles with her.

Angie shrugs, then takes my spot on the chair. "Dad wants to see you in his office."

My stomach lurches. Fantastic. Does he somehow know about last night? That's the last thing I want to deal with right now.

I slip a cover-up on and pad down the hallway to my father's office.

I knock softly and hear him grunt on the other side. The door is heavy as I push it open and enter the office. It's dimly lit and smells like a mix of pine and cigar smoke. I don't know if that's what's making me nauseated or if it's the impending doom that is my father sitting behind his desk.

He's as intimidating as ever, glasses resting on the bridge of his nose as he looks down at the paper in front of him. He's barely acknowledged my existence, and he can wait all day, so I break the ice.

"You wanted to see me, Daddy?"

Despite the animosity between us, all I've ever wanted is for him to be proud of me. That's why I went to law school to begin with—to find something more useful to him than getting married. No matter what, nothing ever seems to be good enough, though, and even more so in the last few months. He's a hardened businessman, and his world doesn't have much room in it for children—especially wayward daughters.

"Ava." He sighs, finally looking up at me. "You didn't come home last night."

I bite my lip, holding in a sharp breath. I'm not sure why I thought I could get away with this to begin with. I'm an adult—it isn't like he can punish me in the ways he used to, but it still doesn't make this any easier. Standing in front of my angry father is every bit as terrifying as a twenty-three-year-old as it was as a nine-year-old.

"Ava!" my dad snaps, eyes narrowed on me as he waits for an answer even though he hasn't asked me anything specific.

"No, I didn't," I say quickly. "I stayed at a friend's house and—"

"You better think twice before you lie to me, Ava." He glares at me. "You're an adult and are capable of making your own decisions, but at least stand by them enough to tell me the truth."

I let out a slow sigh, contemplating my next move. I have two choices here: I can tell him the truth or I can continue to lie my way out of this. Neither seems like it's going to work, so I might as well quit while I'm ahead.

"Your mother and I are concerned. Things were better for a while, but I'm starting to see glimpses of who you were after we lost Andrew, and I'll be damned if we go down that road again."

It's a dark memory for all of us. Losing Andrew was like losing the other half of my heart, and for weeks I was so swallowed up with grief and blame that I couldn't even function. Eventually, I found the best way to deal with it—drowning whatever I felt in alcohol and drugs and partying until I couldn't remember why I was depressed to begin with. It was a slippery slope and even though it made me feel better temporarily, I quickly found myself in the throes of addiction. I've been drug free for a few months now, but it's been a long and grueling road to get here. I still have a lot of work to do, but I'm getting there, and his lack of faith in me stings.

"Dad, I'm not—"

"You're getting to the age where you need to become more responsible. You know, I have several nice men who would take care of you and be good for business." He scratches his chin, leather chair squeaking as he leans back.

My stomach drops at his degrading, misogynistic thought. "You can't seriously be suggesting an arranged marriage."

"What I'm suggesting is that you get a hold of your life, or I will be forced to do it for you," he threatens. "I won't have you running around recklessly giving our family a bad name. Is that clear?"

"Yes, sir."

"Ava, I only want what's best for you." His face doesn't soften in the slightest.

"I'm sorry, it won't happen again."

"See to it that it doesn't. I'm serious, Ava. I don't want to force you into anything, but I will if it means keeping you safe and our family name clean. Do you understand me?"

"Yes, sir." I want to crawl into a hole and die. What a horrible way to follow such an amazing night.

"Good." He stands up from behind the desk, walks around, then kisses my forehead. "I'm heading to the warehouse to meet with Gio. I'll see you at dinner tonight."

"Gio?" I ask curiously. As a rule of thumb, my father usually keeps my sisters and me as far away from the business as possible, but I know enough to know exactly who Gio Caponelli is. He and my father bring a whole new meaning to the term frenemies, and if my dad's meeting with him, nothing good is going on.

"Nothing for you to worry about, Ava. Shut the door on your way out." With that, he quickly ushers me out of his office.

Bella and Angie are still sitting outside, but I don't feel like facing them right now. My father's ultimatum leaves a bad taste in my mouth, and all I want to do is crawl back into bed.

I guess if I'm changing my ways, last night with "Romeo" is as good a night as any to go out on.

FOUR

Nick

It's been over a month.

Thirty-eight days.

Nine hundred and twelve hours since that woman walked out of my hotel room and simply vanished into thin air.

Zane and his team have been working around the clock for weeks, but we're no closer to finding her than we were the morning after she left. He brought me a few pictures to look through, but none of them even held a candle to the woman I'd spent the night with. I'm not easily deterred, but this feels like a fucking wash. And if I wasn't still haunted by her, I might be ready to throw in the towel entirely.

Since some of my business is run out of Panchos, it has a pretty substantial security system, but somehow she managed to elude the cameras most of the night. There isn't a single usable picture of her in the entire bunch. Every spare moment I had, I spent at the restaurant, hoping that by some stroke of luck she'd come waltzing back in. Of course, it couldn't be that easy, and my stakeout turned out to be a big fucking waste of time.

Leo was tolerant, but I could tell my obsession was wearing on him. More than once he'd suggested I let the whole thing go and take my frustrations out on another girl. *One who actually wanted to be with me.* It seemed like a good idea in theory, but it would never work. Every girl I've ever slept with pales in comparison to her, and it would only leave me disappointed and even more frustrated than I already am. Like drinking water after whiskey—dull, underwhelming, and pointless. The woman ruined me, and she doesn't even know it.

After they'd harassed me all week, I reluctantly agreed to join Leo and Zane at a yacht party out at Chelsea Pier. They thought it would be a welcome distraction and, honestly, I'm willing to try just about anything to get my mind off this girl. Not to mention I owe them after they've listened to all of my bitching and complaining the last four weeks.

Not being able to find "Jules" is only the tip of the disastrous iceberg my last month has been. There are all kinds of issues at the warehouse—the biggest being the bastard who's shorting our shipments. Turns out he was working with a Russian organization making its way into the city, and his focus was trying to discredit both us and the Morettis to our biggest customers. I'd spent the afternoon tracking him down and putting a bullet between his eyes.

Hits are my specialty. Quick, clean, and quiet. And I'm the strongest shot in the group by a long way. Rifle, pistol, revolver—the type doesn't matter. My aim and execution are without parallel. It helps that my dad had a gun in my hand early on and taught me both the caution and the craft, but I've got a certain natural talent for it that is hard to come by.

It's a highly coveted skill—one I would gladly give up, though. I have the blood of a lot of men on my hands, and even though every single one of them deserved death, there isn't a more harrowing feeling in the world than watching the life drain out of someone's eyes at your hands.

At least there will be enough alcohol and hot, desperate women at this party to clear my mind a bit. Kyle Archer is hosting, and every event he throws is like a fraternity party on steroids. The guy is a arrogant asshole who flaunts his wealth to anyone who gives him the time of day, and nothing irritates me more than that type of guy. He owns a tech company in the city that provides security at our main office, which is how I ended up on the guest list.

Owns is a loose term. His father started the company and then handed it over to his son a few years ago, and Kyle has narrowly avoided driving it into the ground in the short time he's had it. He's been bailed out by his father multiple times, but he's never a big enough man to admit it. The guy isn't exactly my first choice, but the security product his dad designed is unmatched, and cybersecurity is crucial to us. Unfortunately, that means playing nice with Kyle.

When our driver pulls into the marina parking lot, I'm already ready to leave.

"I can see this shitshow from here." Leo groans, slamming the door to the dark SUV shut behind us.

"Do you think Kyle's dad is paying for all of this too?" Zane scoffs, climbing out of his side and stretching his arms over his head.

"Is there anything in this guy's life his father isn't paying for? How long do we have to stay?" I ask.

"Would you relax and enjoy yourself a little?" Leo slaps my back, squeezing my shoulders as he gives me his version of a pep talk. "Let's go find you a pretty face in a tight dress to get you out of this funk."

"That's what I'm talking about," Zane agrees. He's even more motivated to get me off "Jules" than Leo, considering my search for her has more than monopolized his time the last few weeks.

Maybe it's a little arrogant of me, or maybe my tastes have always been more mature, but a party like this has never been my thing. Don't get me wrong, I like to have a good time with my friends and can drink any one of them under the table on any given night, but it's these big, out-of-control events that I don't like. Bodies slammed together, music so loud you can't even hear yourself think. Cheap, watered-down alcohol that tastes more like mouthwash than an actual drink. I can't believe people like this kind of thing.

"Let's see how the night goes, okay?" I say.

I'm not convinced, but not completely counting it out either. Hooking up with faceless, nameless girls wasn't out of the norm for me before her, so why can't I get back to that? There's a distinct chill in the air, signaling the coming of fall. It won't be long before the snow comes and parties like this are history. There's no harm in enjoying it while we still can.

The yacht is already overflowing with people when we board, and we squirm our way through to find the bar. Kyle intercepts us nearly at the door with that stupid, sly grin on his face.

"Gentlemen!" he greets us, shaking Leo's hand first. "Glad you could join us. There are some private tables in the back, a little quieter than this mess out here. I'll be sure they set one up for you." He winks like he's doing us some grand favor.

Play nice, Nick, I remind myself. "Good to see you, Kyle. The boat's amazing."

"Isn't it? The *yacht*'s perfect for landing bigger clients. You guys should invest in one. I could give you the number of my supplier." His voice hinges on the word *yacht*. Apparently, I've offended him by calling the damn thing a boat.

"We have a few," Leo boasts. "We normally don't have clients out on them."

Unless they're dead and we're taking them out to sea to ditch the body.

"Enjoy yourselves, and I'll catch up with you later." Kyle slithers into the crowd. That guy gives me the creeps. He's always up to something, and it's rarely ever good.

"Let's take him up on that private table offer. I don't feel like playing sardines all night with a bunch of drunk hipsters." Zane eyes the room, voicing my sentiments exactly. "I'll lead the way." He pushes a pathway through the crowd until we eventually reach the back of the boat. It's not necessarily quiet, but it's slightly more bearable than the front.

As promised, Kyle has a table set up with our name and a bottle of Grey Goose on top of it.

"Of course the motherfucker would give us the cheap shit." Leo laughs, picking the bottle up and turning it in his hands.

"I'm going to get a real drink," I say.

Zane and Leo settle themselves at the table and I start my trek to the bar on the upper level. It's usually a little less crowded, and I can scope the place out a bit and see what I'm dealing with. There has to be a girl here somewhere who can get my mind off "Jules," but so far, the prospects aren't promising. The place is crawling with girls, but most of them I wouldn't touch with a ten-foot pole. Bleach blonds with caked-on makeup who wear skimpy cocktail dresses even though they're very obviously freezing aren't exactly my type. Neither are girls too drunk to even stand up, and there's no shortage of those either.

I'm not into fake. I'm not into messy. Even for a casual hookup, I've got standards and I'm not about to drop them. Something tells me this is definitely not the kind of place to find a girl I could be into. *I don't need to be into them, though*, I remind myself. It's not like I'm picking a wife here. All I need is someone to get me off long enough to forget.

Fuck. It's every bit as crowded up here as it was downstairs, and I have to shove my way to the bar. I stay a few steps back, trying to find a place I can fit in and grab the bartender's attention, but I'm not about to wait around all night. Not when I have much higher quality shit back at my place.

As I'm about to turn back, a woman in front of me catches my eye. With her back to me, she leans over the bar, a tight black dress clinging to her dangerous curves. Her dark curls are loosely tied up at the nape of her neck, and she twists one strand between her fingers as she laughs with the bartender. When she shifts and her perfect, tight ass bounces, my cock twitches—a sensation I haven't felt in weeks. Maybe this would work out after all.

I make my way closer, positioning myself so I'll be the first thing she sees when she turns around.

"See you later, Ava," the bartender yells over the noise after he hands her a couple of drinks.

"Bye, Rick!" she responds, spinning back on her heels. She isn't watching where she's going and stumbles right into me, sending the drinks she's carrying sloshing over their rims as I dodge out of the wet zone.

"Oh my gosh, I am so—" she starts, glancing up at me. The second our eyes meet, she stops, swallowing her words as she presses her painted red lips together. Panic flashes in her eyes.

I let out a sharp laugh. "Well, I'll be damned."

Ava

"Come on." Bella slips her arm underneath mine and leads me to the side of the yacht that's parked in the marina.

Bella might be inexperienced in other areas, but she makes up for it in the social department. If there is an event happening in the city, chances are she knows about it and has already secured an invitation. Most of the time her drinking and partying make me look like an angel, but it always gets overlooked because she's already agreed to marry any man my dad chooses. Apparently, all is forgiven if you buy into outdated, suppressive Mafia tradition.

I bite back my bitterness, because none of that is Bella's fault.

I'm not even sure how she knows the host of the party tonight, but she insisted I tag along with her and her friends. I pulled out every excuse I could think of, but nothing worked, and so here I am.

"We'll have fun, I promise."

My sister and I have vastly different ideas of "fun." A hundred drunk, sweaty people crammed on a boat that could sink at any minute doesn't do it for me, but I indulge her, mostly because I haven't been easy to live with the last few weeks. Between my dad's looming ultimatum and stewing over my mystery man, I've been a wreck, and this is her last-ditch attempt at helping me get out of my funk.

This place is a nightmare. The air is heavy with the stench of sweaty bodies and alcohol, and the music's so loud I can feel my eardrums vibrating. "How long do we have to stay here again?"

"Give me a break. You had nothing better to do tonight than sit around and mope, so why don't you enjoy yourself for a change? Kyle set us up at a table in a great spot, and there's free alcohol all night."

"Right, because free alcohol is exactly what I need. Dad will shoot me if I come stumbling in drunk tonight." The thought of it makes me shudder. As a Don, shooting me isn't entirely out of the question. And honestly, it sounds better than the arranged marriage alternative he threw out last month. I haven't been able to get his threats out of my head since that day, and I've been on my very best behavior since. I'm not about to give him another reason to marry me off.

Bella doesn't quite comprehend what I'm trying to say. "Avs, you're being dramatic. Dad wouldn't marry you off just because you're enjoying yourself. You're young. This is the kind of thing you should be doing! I'm sure Dad's forgotten all about it."

I let out a sharp laugh. *Forgotten*. Yeah, I'm sure.

"Besides, you're out with me. He knows I'll watch over you, so it's fine." She waves me off. "Go get us some drinks."

"Fine. But if this night turns south, I'm blaming it on you." I forge through the swarms of people, opting for the upstairs bar in hopes I can get a little fresh air. It's going to take a very strong drink to get me through this disaster of a party, and if we're here a few hours, I'll have plenty of time to sober up before we go home.

Several months ago I would have thrived in this kind of environment. The booze and the partying and god only knows what is going on below deck—I would have been all over it. Now all it does is make me feel uncomfortable.

When I notice Rick behind the bar, I'm happy to see a familiar face. He bartends occasionally at my dad's parties and is a really nice guy. He fell in somewhere between boyfriends and lasted two dates. Luckily, the feeling was mutual, and we both agreed we were better as friends.

"Ava! Good to see you! What can I get for you?" Rick fills a few cups in front of him with alcohol. He works quickly, moving with such precision it's almost an art.

"Two whiskey gingers, please?" I smile as I slip a fifty-dollar bill toward him.

"You can tip me later if you want." He smirks, sliding it back to me and getting to work on our drinks.

"In your dreams, bar boy." He isn't serious, but the flirtation between us feels nice. Although after my month-long drought, any attention might.

Rick puts his hand over his heart, pretending to be hurt, and turns his back for a few minutes. When he returns, he hands me the drinks. "Have fun tonight. It's going to be quite the party. Bella here?"

"Yep, she's downstairs."

"Bring her around before you leave." He smiles, waving before he takes an order from someone else. "See you later, Ava!"

"Bye, Rick!" I gather the drinks in my hands and turn around. Not paying any attention to my surroundings, I take a step and fall right into something, or rather, someone.

"Oh, my gosh! I am so—" When I look up at the man, my heart leaps into my throat and I nearly drop the drinks. Instead, I grip them so tight that my knuckles turn white, the flimsy plastic bending in my hold.

"Well, I'll be damned."

It was him. *Him*, him.

He looks shocked to see me at first, but it doesn't take long for a huge grin to spread across his face.

"You know, you're a hard person to track down. Ava, is it?"

My knees weaken when he says my real name. How is it possible that he looks even better than I remember? I've drawn him like a Greek god in all of my fantasies, but seeing him in person again puts them all to shame. He's got on a pair of blue jeans and a tight black T-shirt that stretches over his biceps, with his hands shoved into his pockets. He's casual tonight, and informal looks good on him. Thick stubble lines his chin and his hair is tousled and even though he looks at me with confidence, there's a bit of boyish charm in his grin.

"Yes, my name *is* Ava," I say as blush tints my cheeks. Out of all the parties Bella could have dragged me to, we happen to be at the same one as the man who has been plaguing my thoughts for the last few weeks? Honestly, what are the odds?

"And here all this time I was looking for a woman named Juliette." His admission, though unintentional, catches my attention. He was looking for me?

"Right." I laugh, loosening up a bit. Mere seconds together and we're already slipping back into a comfortable flow, like we haven't missed a beat. "Like your name is Romeo."

"Nick, actually." He drags his thumb over his upper lip, eyeing me shamelessly. He doesn't seem to care in the slightest that I caught him staring. In fact, there's an amusement on his face that tells me he enjoys it. "I've been trying to find you since you snuck out of my hotel room a few weeks ago."

"Sorry about that."

"Why don't you make it up to me and go to dinner with me?" he says.

His hand brushes against my shoulder as he moves me out of the way for someone to get to the bar. Even the small gesture sends a shock wave through my body as I remember how he handled me that night. Attentive, but always in control. Dominant in a way that made me think it was my idea.

"Nick, I don't think that's such a good idea. Second dates aren't really my thing."

With any luck he'll take me at my word, because the more time I spend around him, the more likely I am to give in, and that could have hellacious consequences. I'm pretty sure an arrogant playboy who keeps a card on file at a local hotel specifically for his hookups is not the type of man my father has in mind for me.

"But fucking strangers in hotel rooms is?"

Fucking.

The term stings more than it should, because that's exactly what happened. Except it was more than that for me. And if his pleas for me to stay were any indication, it was more for him too.

"Didn't we agree on a one-and-done thing, anyway? Wouldn't dinner be breaking one of *your* rules?" He was the one who laid it all out, so plotted that it almost felt like a business plan.

A cool amusement fills his face as he leans in intimidatingly close.

"Ava, I don't care about the rules. You're worth breaking them. I haven't stopped thinking about you for a second since that night. The way your legs felt wrapped around my waist. The sound of your sweet voice begging for more." He's so close now that his lips graze my ear as he whispers, "The way your pouty lips bow when I make you come."

"Nick . . ." I put my hand to his chest, creating some distance between us because I know exactly where this will end up if I don't. Does he have some sort of hookup hotel on this side of town too?

"I'm used to getting what I want, Ava. And I'm not going to stop until I do."

His voice is like lightning through my veins, and desire ripples between my legs. I've never heard something so seductive and threatening all at once. Before I can say anything else, a drunk guy bumps into Nick from behind. He whirls around with an angry expression on his face, as if this guy had squashed whatever moment we had going on.

"Hey, man . . ."

This is my chance. I have to make my getaway. Otherwise I'll find myself right back in Nick's arms and, as tempting as that sounds, I can't afford the risk.

He's dangerous and consuming and above any responsibility—everything I don't need right now. Unless, of course, I want to wind up married to some old sleazebag as part of one of my father's business deals.

No, that can't happen.

Taking my opportunity, I duck away and find Bella as fast as I can.

"Bella, we've got to get out of here!" I practically throw our drinks down on the table and grab my jacket from the seat next to her.

"What? We barely got here. What's going on?"

"I'll explain everything later. We have to leave. Now." I tug at her arm, pulling her toward the dock.

She looks at me suspiciously but stands up. "Ava, I don't know what it—"

I don't even give her a chance to finish. He'll be looking for me soon and if he finds me, I'm not sure I would have the strength to look into those handsome green eyes and deny him again.

Bella resists at first, but when we are both off the yacht and on the dock, she takes her shoes off and runs alongside me.

"Would you slow down?" She's out of breath.

"Sorry. I just needed to get away from there," I say.

"What happened?"

"I ran into someone at the bar."

"And you couldn't talk to him like a normal human?"

"It *wasn't* a normal human, Bells. It was him. The guy I told you about from the hotel."

Bella's eyes widen as the weight of my words hits her. "Are you serious?"

I nod quickly, pulling out my phone to call an Uber as fast as I can.

"You mean to tell me you ripped me away from that party because the guy you haven't stopped thinking about the last month was there?" She's not confused anymore, just angry.

"It's not that . . ."

"Ava! We ran away from the one guy who has held your interest for more than a week in years?" She throws her hands up in exasperation. "Unbelievable."

She couldn't understand. She's not in the position I'm in, and that's painfully obvious. I'm the one who is always messing up, especially after Andrew died. I can't keep letting my parents down, and I need to get myself together this time.

And unfortunately, that means staying far away from any distractions. Specifically, distractions with big, strong hands and a killer smile.

FIVE

Ava

"You two are home early."

It's eleven o'clock at night, but for some ungodly reason, Vince is sitting at a bar stool in the kitchen with a bowl of cereal. He's close to the last person I want to see right now, second only to my father.

"Not by choice," Bella mumbles as she slides onto the stool next to him, unstrapping her heels and letting them clatter to the floor.

She's still mad at me, but started to come around on our ride home. If she had her way, we would have marched right back into that party, I would have found Nick, and all would have been right in the world.

That was *her* world, though. She doesn't have our father's threat hanging over her head the second she messes up. I barely escaped unscathed the first time Nick and I were together, and I might not be so lucky again. Although it is nice to finally have a name to put with the face.

"Anything interesting happen at the party? It was at Kyle's, right?" Vince's words are barely comprehensible through his crunching.

"It was on the boat, and only if you call Ava running away from an old date and making us leave early interesting." Bella rolls her eyes, grabbing the spoon from his hand and taking a bite for herself.

"Sounds like a typical Saturday night for you." He smirks.

"Don't you have your own family to go bother?" I snap, throwing the fridge open, not because I'm hungry, but because I need to hide the glaring flush in my cheeks. Between their teasing and the pent-up energy inside of me, I'm unraveling.

"Easy, Avs. I'm only teasing."

"Someone is a little sour that she actually has feelings for this guy, despite all of her best efforts not to." Bella seems eager to throw me under the bus as some sort of payback for ruining her night.

"Whoa, really?" Vince stops dead in his tracks and faces me.

"No." I slam the fridge closed. "I do not have feelings for him. I don't even know him." I try to sound convincing, but by the looks on their faces, neither is falling for it. That makes three of us.

"I'm confused. If you like this dude, why did you run?" Vince pauses. "Not that I'm opposed to my baby sister running from boys. In fact, forget I said anything."

"She ran because that's what she does. She runs from anything that even remotely resembles getting attached to anyone," Bella snipes. The little alcohol she had at the party has made her uncharacteristically hostile.

"Would you shut up?" I glare at her. Can't we be done with this conversation? For once it would be nice not to have to explain every decision I make when it comes to my love life.

"It's true, isn't it? You think you might be into this guy, and that scares the shit out of you. That's why you snuck out of his hotel room, why you ran from him tonight. You're scared of what that might mean."

My sister has no idea how right she is. The idea of being attached does scare me, because I know what it's like to lose someone you love. I don't want to go through that again; I'm not sure I could survive it.

"Back up," Vince barks, his face twisting in confusion. "Hotel? Why the fuck were you in his hotel room when you just said you didn't even know him?"

"Bella!" I hiss, covering my face with my hands.

"What in the world is going on down here?" My mother rushes into the kitchen, fury radiating from her as she wraps her velour robe around her shoulders. "I can hear your bickering all the way upstairs."

"Sorry, Mom. We didn't mean to wake you," Bella says. "We'll keep it down."

"What are you even doing here, Vincent?" Her eyes narrow on my brother.

"Decompressing, Ma." He gives her his most charming smile, immediately loosening up and dropping the protective big brother act, at least momentarily.

"Go home and *decompress* with your pregnant wife." She glares at him.

"But she's mean, Ma." Vince chuckles. "Pregnancy hormones are no joke."

"It's your own fault she's in that situation. You get your butt home and take care of her. And you two"—she points at Bella and me—"stop all of this commotion. I'll have you both scrubbing floors all day tomorrow if you wake your father up."

We all stand silent, like scolded children. She turns on her heel and is gone as quickly as she came.

"I'm going to bed," I announce, defeated and flustered. I've had enough of these two and this discussion for the night. In fact, I've had enough of it for a lifetime.

"Don't think this conversation is over, Ava." Vince raises his eyebrows. "I want to know why you were in some guy's hotel room."

"Go home, Vince." Bella slaps his shoulder, unexpectedly coming to my defense as she stands next to me. "Now isn't the time to get into any of this."

"Do you know how bad I begged for brothers?" Vince shakes his head. "So I wouldn't have to deal with all this shit. And what do Mom and Dad do? Go and give me three little sisters."

"Vincent!" my mother hisses in a hushed tone from the hallway.

"All right, all right." He puts his hands up in defeat. "Until tomorrow, ladies." He tosses a Cocoa Puff into the air, catching it in his mouth before disappearing out the French doors and jogging down the driveway to his truck.

"You'd think the moron could at least pick up his own dishes," Bella huffs, dumping them in the sink.

Gathering up my purse and jacket, I head toward the stairs, but my sister catches my wrist. "Hey, Avs, I'm sorry. What you do with that guy is your business. I want to see you happy. What if him showing up there was fate? What if he's a good guy and you could have a future together?"

"I am happy. I don't need to define my happiness by a man." I sigh. Why is that so hard for everyone to understand? "I don't want to get into all of this again, okay? It doesn't matter how I feel about the guy, Mom and Dad would never be okay with it."

"You don't know that. Maybe you should give it a chance. What if they surprise you and they love him?" She follows me up the stairs and to our rooms.

"And what if it seals the deal and Dad marries me off to some old guy he can make a deal with? Would you please let it go?"

"I will, but I want to say one thing first. You can't live your life always jumping to the worst scenario. Not everyone is going to hurt you like Jimmy did. But I'll let it go, only because I love you and I feel like I owe you one for outing you to Vince. Sorry about that."

"Thanks. 'Night."

"Good night, Avs."

When Bella brings up Jimmy, it's like salt in a wound I thought healed long ago.

We got serious right before my Andrew died, and it was the perfect storm in terms of timing. I clung to Jimmy like he was the one thing keeping me afloat, and instead of helping me work through my grief, he threw cocaine at the problem, catapulting me into addiction. It was like the deeper I got, the more I blamed myself for what happened to Andrew, and Jimmy was always there with another hit to take my mind off it.

Jimmy enjoyed the hold he had on me, and we were stuck in a vicious cycle. He was yet another person I trusted who ended up letting me down. Once I stopped using, I knew Jimmy was the first thing that had to go, but that was easier said than done. His father had been a friend of my father's for years, and I had to fight like hell to get myself to a place where I could break up with him for good. Even though my dad didn't approve of my relationship with Jimmy, the benefits of having his attorney father as a friend offset his opinions.

After the fact, I found out that he'd spent the last months of our relationship cheating on me too. Thankfully, the breakup had lasted, and Jimmy is a big reason why I don't want to get into any kind of relationship right now. I'm in a much better place mentally, but my stability is fragile, and who knows what could happen if someone I get attached to hurts me again?

Bella is the only one who knows the extent of what happened with Jimmy, and honestly, she's right. I've got it stuck in my head that everyone is going to hurt me the way he did, but even if it isn't true, I'm not really willing to risk it. It's easier to keep my distance and not even chance going down that road again. I know myself, and a tough breakup could be a lethal trigger.

For the most part, the rest of the weekend is uneventful. I successfully avoided Vince's judging eye for the majority of family dinner on Sunday, and spent the rest of the day working on homework.

Bright and early Monday morning, I have my Law and Ethics class. It's an awful way to start the week, especially since there won't be any ethics in the law I will practice. Like everything with my father, sending me to law school is a personal gain for him. It's always nice to have someone around who understands the law and can help find all the loopholes to make your business seem legitimate. In a desperate attempt to make him proud, I decided to be that person, and to my surprise, he went for it. Bella and Angie didn't even go to college, so this was a huge step.

The lecture drags on for about two hours before the professor finally lets us out. The hot August air hits me when I finally step outside of the building. I usually stick to my little corner of campus where the law school is and avoid this side entirely. For some reason, my Law and Ethics class is held in one of the main campus buildings with many of the undergrad sessions. It's always busy over here, but it's insufferable at the start of the school year like today. Trying to avoid the swarms of freshman trying to find their way around, I duck into the student union and the coffee shop catches my eye. I need another cup of coffee like I need a hole in my brain, but I scan the menu anyway.

The fresh-baked croissants catch my eye, but I'm meeting Bella for lunch in a little while, so I order my usual vanilla latte and work my way over to the pickup counter.

"We've got to stop meeting like this."

A deep, husky voice rumbles behind me, and I freeze. Why the hell does this keep happening?

I turn around to confirm my fears and, sure enough, standing in front of me in a fitted navy-blue suit is Nick. His smile catches me in a vise, and I can't bring myself to look away.

Something about him in that suit stirs unimaginable things inside of me. He's so put together. So professional. Between the deep woodsy scent of his cologne and the bit of chest hair that peeks out from the top of his unbuttoned collar, it's like I've got no control over my body. My legs lock intuitively, as if my body thinks he'd be bold enough to try something right here, in the middle of a packed student union. My heart almost wishes he would.

No, Ava! God, what is wrong with you?

Each time he catches me off guard like this, my resolve slips further and further. Soon I won't remember why I'm so adamant about avoiding him at all.

"I'm beginning to think you're stalking me." I grab my latte off the counter, wishing it was something stronger.

"Not stalking, just keeping my word." He follows me over to an empty table, already pulling another chair over so he can join me.

"Please, sit down," I say sarcastically. He's relentless. "What word exactly are you keeping?"

"That I'm not going to stop until you agree to go out with me," he clarifies, making himself right at home as he crosses an ankle over his knee.

He's cocky and arrogant, and it doesn't take more than a minute with him to pick up on that. Like he said, he's used to getting what he wants. Usually that would be a hard stop for me. This is a game for him. A conquest.

Nick will be gone the second he gets what he wants. Letting myself think otherwise is a recipe for disaster.

"And, for the record, I'm not stalking you. I had business near here this morning. Running into you was a pleasant coincidence." Man, that smile is intoxicating.

"Business?" I ask. "Are you a student?"

Nick laughs, choking a little on his coffee. "A student? No. I was here as a guest speaker. A friend of mine teaches in the business school and asked me to come talk about working with customs to run my shipping company."

Realization sets in and a panicked look sweeps across his face. "Wait. Are you a student here?" He pauses. "How old are you?"

"How old do you think I am?" For once I have the upper hand with him, and I enjoy watching him squirm.

"Don't play with me, Ava." He gets serious. "Are you legal?"

"I'm twenty-three." I smirk, finally letting him off the hook.

Relief washes over him. "Thank god."

"Isn't it a little late to be asking that question?" I take a gulp of my coffee and set it on the table between us as if I'm creating some sort of barrier.

"What are you studying?"

"Law. I want to be a defense attorney." His eyes trail my every move as I tuck a rogue piece of hair behind my ear.

"Wow." He brushed his thumb over his lip. "Beauty and brains . . . are you excited?"

He called me beautiful the night we were together, but there's something different about hearing it in the sober sunlight.

"You mean am I excited to spend the next two years of my life studying for some stupid test only to work eighty hours a week in a stuffy corner office with a nice view of a park I never get to actually go to and spend my days defending drug dealers and thieves?" I arch my eyebrow at him, feeling somewhat cynical this morning. "Thrilled."

My answer catches him completely off guard. "As hot as the thought of you in that corner office is, why are you doing it if you're already dreading it so much?"

"Daddy issues." I shrug, unable to stifle the small laugh on my lips. Pitiful.

"Now that might be something I can help you with." His domineering grin is almost enough to make me ask him to describe what he has in mind—almost. He might be joking, but it's a glaring reminder of where his head is at.

"Nick, it was nice to see you again, but I need to be going." Bella's words echo in my ear like she's the devil sitting on my shoulder.

"Ouch!" He puts his hand over his heart, feigning injury. "I've been called a lot of things in my life, but nice isn't one of them."

"Do you prefer pleasant? That's what you referred to me as a few minutes ago, right?" I tease. Despite my worries, I can't stop egging him on either.

"I'll call you whatever you want if it means you won't run away from me again."

"I didn't run away." I can't even bring myself to say it, because I literally did run away from the boat that night.

"You're a textbook runner." Nick gives me a knowing half smile. "When things get too hard or too real, you bolt."

"Well, for my entire life, I've been conditioned to believe that the only person I can ever actually count on is myself." I shift, crossing one leg over the other underneath the table, his words hitting me like a raw nerve. "Maybe I do run, but I also know how to protect myself. So don't think you're going to come in here with your smooth talk and arrogant charm that works with all the other girls."

Nick chuckles, rubbing his stubbled chin, and I can't quite tell what he's thinking. "What happened to you?"

"What do you mean?"

"You don't become this distrustful overnight. Someone does it to you, so what happened?" His face is soft, and he waits.

Nick already knows way more about me than I want him to, so I don't give him an answer. I stand up and grab my bag. "Goodbye, Nick. Have a nice day."

As I turn to leave, he catches my wrist, his firm grip holding me in place so dangerously close that his breath is hot against my ear as he speaks. Images of him manhandling me in that hotel room flash through my mind, and a wave of heat hits me. "Have dinner with me, Ava. Please."

The student center suddenly feels very small. Nick's eyes lock with mine and everything around us disappears. The shuffle of students moving from class to class, the static radio playing over the loudspeakers, the thirsty looks Nick draws from nearly every woman in here. All his attention is focused on me.

"I don't think that's a good idea."

"And why is that?"

"Because I'm not your type," I say flatly, his daring expression enough to make me forget my reasons entirely.

"Ava, what makes you think you even know enough about me to say that?"

"Because." I stiffen. "You can't get through a single conversation with me without making some kind of sexual pass, you have every woman in this entire student center fawning over you, and if you remember right, you were the one who explicitly said one night and we'd never see each other again. That's what we agreed to."

If it's possible, Nick leans in even closer to me, keeping his voice low. "Circumstances have changed, and you can't tell me you're not the slightest bit curious what—"

"Goodbye, Nick." I pull away, cutting him off abruptly.

"You're wrong, you know."

I pause, stealing a glance over my shoulder as I make my way out of the café. "Oh?"

"This isn't a game to me, Ava. That's not the person I am. Give me a chance to prove that."

"I'm sure you'll find somebody willing to take you up on that offer. And if you don't . . ." I shrug. "I have a feeling you'll figure out some way to find me."

SIX

Nick

Zero for three.

I haven't won a single round with this girl. She has a stubborn streak that rivals my own, and if I was any other person, I might have given up already. I'm no quitter, though, and Ava's rebukes only solidify how much different she is than any other woman that I've been with.

Despite leaving me hanging three separate times, she still hasn't flat-out denied me. It's always *I don't think this is a good idea* or *We shouldn't do this*. Never a straight no, and I'll take what I can get.

When I pull into the warehouse, it's already busy. My father was meeting with Alessandro Moretti this morning, and that would mark the end of whatever alliance we have with them. The supplier issue is taken care of and now we can all be back in our own lanes—the way it should be.

Our relationship with the Morettis hasn't always been so volatile. About four years ago things were peaceful, and we worked alongside each other and helped each other out, functioning as a cohesive team instead of bitter rivals. To say we were friends might have been a stretch, but we were, at the very least, civil.

Nothing stays civil for very long in the Mafia world, though.

Andrew Moretti's death was a turning point for both of our families, and nothing would ever be the same. It was almost four years ago that he died. That I watched my friend bleed to death on a dirty apartment floor. The deafening ring of the gun, the vacant look in his eyes as his body slumped over, the crimson spattered on the wall behind him—those are the things that haunt my nightmares to this very day.

Alessandro has five children, but I've never met his daughters or even his wife, as is typical for a lot of the families we work with. He has a strong philosophy of keeping them out of anything to do with the business, and to be honest, I hardly know they exist.

Andrew was his youngest son, and when we met, we instantly clicked. Both of us carried chips on our shoulders, eager to prove our worth to our families. I was a little more reserved, but Andrew wanted to be involved in everything. He was loyal and sincere, and had a heart for others, but he was also cocky and impulsive. He'd seek out any confrontation he could, and dragged us into some really shitty situations.

Eventually, I had to pull back and watch his crazy antics from afar. It was as if he was a junkie and danger was his drug. He craved it, almost thrived on it. My father always used to say that his rash decisions would wind up getting someone killed, but no one imagined it would be Andrew himself. Or that the shot that killed him would come from me.

It ended any chance our families ever had of working together unless it was absolutely necessary. There's so much animosity between us now, and battle lines have been drawn. We can come together when there is a common enemy or threat, but aside from that, it just doesn't happen.

Jesus, I haven't thought about Andrew in a while, and I certainly don't have time to go down that rabbit hole today. After my run-in with Ava this morning, I'm distracted enough. Somehow, I've got to find a way to end my infatuation.

When I walk into the office, I'm surprised to see Leo sitting at the desk. Normally he'd be at Panchos on a Monday, regrouping after the weekend rush. The place is technically mine, given to me years ago in a business deal by a guy who couldn't pay off his debt. At the time I had no use for a floundering restaurant, but Leo took a special interest in it and I passed the management of it off to him. Now it's one of our most lucrative side businesses, and one of the most popular spots in the city.

I throw myself into the chair in front of him, sighing dramatically as I loosen my tie.

"Long morning?" He keeps his eyes fixed on the stack of papers in front of him.

"I saw her again," I mumble, wallowing in my own self-pity. How pathetic can I get? I'm not used to being on this side of things, and so far, it fucking sucks.

"You what? The girl from the hotel?" Now I've got his attention. "What the fuck happened?"

"I was speaking to a business class this morning. Turns out she's studying to be a lawyer. We ran into each other and then she left. Again." I shove my hand through my hair in frustration. Rejection certainly doesn't suit me, and admitting it out loud to my little brother only adds insult to injury.

A smirk grows on Leo's face and soon, he's all-out laughing.

"Something funny to you?" I glare, gritting my teeth. I'm already in a foul mood even without his unneeded amusement at my expense.

"She's denied you, what, three times now?" *Thanks for the reminder, Leo.* "When are you going to give it a rest?"

"Never." His suggestion isn't even worth my time.

Clearly, he doesn't understand, and I don't expect him to. A few weeks ago I wouldn't have either, but a few weeks ago, I hadn't tasted Ava. Hadn't held her in my arms. Hadn't connected with her so far past something just physical. The night I spent with her in that hotel room ruined me in the best and worst of ways, and that isn't something a person can understand until they feel it for themselves.

He shakes his head in disapproval. "I'm all for you chasing after love, bro, but that's not what this is. This is a game to you—you like her because she doesn't like you and you can't accept that. You better stop this shit before you get yourself in over your head."

Maybe he's right. I've never been rejected like this by a woman and it's really eating at me. Deep in my heart, though, I know that isn't all this is. It might add to the attraction, but it's much more than that. For the first time in my life I have a genuine, purposeful connection with a woman, and the thought terrifies me.

I understand Ava. And I'm sure if she gives me half the chance, she'll understand me too.

"When are you gonna get your head on straight, man?" Leo asks.

"He better have his head on straight right now," my father chastises us from behind me, coming into the office and slamming the door behind him. He's not necessarily angry; he just always likes to put an emphasis on things. I got good at distinguishing real anger from what was for show early on in my life.

"Don't listen to Leo. Everything is fine." I glare at my brother. "How was the meeting?"

My father shifts his weight, setting his jaw. I can tell immediately there's something on his mind, and I have a feeling I'm not going to like it.

"Meeting was fabulous. Alessandro was thrilled with the way things went down, appreciated you taking care of the hit, and everything is back to business as usual." There is an eeriness in his calm demeanor.

"But?"

"But . . . as always, it's a little more complicated than we expected. The Russians are getting more brazen. To put a guy into our supply chain and try to discredit us is passive, but it also proves their real motives. They want to take us down. Both us and the Morettis. Alessandro and I think it might be good to work together on a more permanent basis."

What the hell does that mean? An alliance?

"What do you mean 'more permanent'? Don't you remember when we did that before? It didn't work," Leo says. As usual, my brother and I are on the same page. "I thought we were done with them."

After his meeting, my dad's patience is already thin, and he rubs at his temples. "Leo, can you keep your mouth shut long enough for me to get this out? I understand you're skeptical, but it's not your place to question my choices."

Leo lowers his head like a scolded puppy.

"I thought the idea of an alliance was out of the question," I press, treading carefully. Unlike a lot of Mafia organizations, we're governed by a council. My great-grandfather put it into place with some of his top advisors so no one man could ever run our organization into the ground. My father is Don, as I will be one day, but the majority of his big decisions have to go through the council first. Years ago, alliances were deemed out of the question for a variety of reasons, and I can't imagine anything has changed.

"It is." My dad nods. "We cannot form an alliance with them in the traditional way, but we have something else in mind. A union would allow us to work alongside each other without actually being one body."

"A union?" Leo finds his voice again.

His word choice is intriguing, especially because a union only has one meaning in the Mafia.

"Yes. It's the only condition that was set by your grandfather and the rest of the council. The only way for us to work long-term with the Morettis is if a member of our family and a member from theirs . . ." He trails off.

"Marriage." As soon as the word is off my lips, my stomach flips. I know the council decree backward and forward, so the idea isn't new, but I never in a million years thought it would be enacted.

My father sits in silence as Leo and I absorb exactly what this means. It can't be just anyone in the organization; it has to be the acting Don. Considering our parents were going on thirty years of the most nauseating pure love in the world, there isn't a shot it would be him. So that means this falls on me, and my father will be forced to step aside.

"Is this really necessary?" There's a bit of panic in Leo's voice that I'm not used to. "We've been functioning fine without Moretti support for years. Why the change now?"

"It's getting to be complicated. There are a few soldiers from the Asnikov group who moved into a neighborhood in Newark. It's a small sliver of land that's right between our territory and the Morettis'. Like I said, they're getting more brazen, and now they're not only trying to discredit us, but they're moving in on our turf. Neither of us is strong enough to take down the Russians on our own, and if we aren't proactive, we'll all be at risk. By joining with them, we double our strength and there will be no way Asnikov and his men can compete with that."

I know my dad well enough to know that he wouldn't be suggesting this unless absolutely necessary, but I honestly can't believe what I'm hearing.

This has to be some kind of joke. There's no way he's suggesting I marry some girl I've never even met. Some fragile little wallflower I'll no doubt hate if she's related to Alessandro.

The timing couldn't be worse. After a long history of serial dating, I've finally found a girl who holds my interest for longer than it takes to get her clothes off. Ava is special, perfect in every way, and the more time I spend with her, the more I'm convinced of that. Convinced that there might be something there. Something deeper. Something long-term.

And now I'm about to get engaged.

There are a thousand things I wish I could say, but they all get stuck in my throat. There's no fucking way.

We don't even operate in the same field as the Morettis, but maybe that's the point. With an alliance, our territory doubles and we have much more influence than either group could obtain on their own. Still, Alessandro is a loose cannon. He's power hungry and greedy, and he often draws unwanted attention—from other groups and law enforcement alike.

Combining forces is risky, but my dad is as thorough as they come. I'm sure he's thought about this from every angle and doesn't need me to remind him. He knows what he's asking of me.

"What exactly do we need to do?" My question feels somewhat rhetorical, but I ask anyway.

My dad scratches his head, glancing at me and then looking away quickly. That tells me everything I need to know. I'm going to fucking hate what's about to come out of his mouth.

"Nick is going to marry one of Alessandro's daughters."

The last place in the world I expect to see Ava is at one of Alessandro Moretti's parties. She's the first person I notice when I walk into the foyer, looking like an absolute smokeshow as she makes small talk with an older man I don't recognize.

She's all legs in a lacy cocktail dress—lean and toned and accentuated by the sky-high heels strapped around her feet. An absolute vision in red. Painted lips and soft, bouncing curls. I don't know how she manages to look even better every time I see her, but she does.

What the hell is she doing here? Of all the times. Of all the places. For the first time, I wish I hadn't run into her.

I'm walking into this party, about to meet my fiancé and form an alliance with a man I want nothing to do with, and the woman who has had me by the balls for the last several weeks is here to bear witness to it all.

Fucking perfect.

Over the last several hours I've resigned myself to the fact that my dad is right. I hate how much sense it makes for me to marry one of the Moretti girls and take over for him as Don, a position I've been vying for for years. A merger is the perfect tactic for holding off the Russians. Anything more direct or violent could send us into an all-out war, and we're liable to lose some of our men. This is cleaner, less risky, and it just might work.

The only problem is there is no way I'm going to go through with this. There must be other ways, and I'm confident if I can stall long enough, I'll come up with something. No way in hell am I going to be a part of an arranged marriage, even if it means becoming Don.

I have a plan—pretend like I'm going along with the arrangement but make the girl absolutely hate me so that she's the one to call the whole thing off. It's a win-win. I look like the dutiful, dedicated son ready to step in for my father, and the marriage is over long before it can even begin. I give it a few days tops before I'm in the clear.

And in the meantime, it buys me a little more time to sell Ava on that second date.

When I look up again, she's alone, with her back to me. Seizing the opportunity, I take her wrist, pulling her into a closed-off room by the foyer. She lets out a gasp, whirling around as I shut the door into Alessandro's office behind us.

"What the—" She stops suddenly when she realizes who's grabbed her. As much as she tries, she can't hide the tiniest bit of satisfaction in her smile. She's somewhat happy to see me.

"You've got to be fucking kidding me."

"Such a dirty mouth for such a pretty girl." I chuckle, closing the distance between us.

She narrows those beautiful eyes at me, and my heart thunders in my chest. If I'm about to sign my life away, why can't I have a little fun first?

"I was kidding about the stalking thing earlier, but now I'm not so sure," Ava quips, teeth sinking into her lower lip.

"I was here first, which would mean you're stalking me. If you wanted to see me again, all you had to do was ask."

"Oh please." When she rolls her eyes, my cock hardens and all I can think about is fucking that attitude right out of her.

I reach out, softly stroking her cheek as I lean in dangerously close. "Please what, baby?"

She flinches under my touch, but not because she doesn't want it. The complete opposite, actually. There's no denying the way her body melts into me or the way her breath shallows. She's flustered, so hot and bothered that she might let me have her right here in this office.

When she steps to the side, she inadvertently backs herself against the wall and flattens herself against the door. She looks up at me through thick, dark lashes and a smile pulls at her lips. "Please," she repeats. "Kiss me again, Nick."

She says my name like a dare, and without much time to waste, I take her up on it.

"Whatever you want, baby," I whisper through my grin.

Finally, I have the permission I've been waiting for. My fingers fumble with the hem of her dress, my hand grasping her bare thigh as my lips crash into hers. My hands tangle in her hair as I push her against the door, a hold firm enough to excite her, exactly like it did before. Every bit of pent-up anticipation and passion explodes through the kiss. It's everything I thought it would be. Everything I built it up to be. Everything and so much more.

My hand inches closer to the feather tattoo on her upper thigh—I remember that well. I'd traced it with my tongue ten times over during our night together. Her knees part slightly, as if she's egging me on. Tempting me to go further. And I want to. Jesus Christ, do I want to.

But, in what could go down as the cockblock of the century, I remember what I'm doing here. I'm about to meet my future wife, and as badly as I want to bend Ava over this desk, it's not fair to her.

What the hell am I thinking? I can't do this to her. Am I really that selfish? Leading her on like this when I'm currently promised to another woman? It won't always be like this, but right now it is. And one thing's for sure, I'm not a cheater.

"We should stop." Each word feels like a blade to my groin as they come out. "Someone might catch us."

Ava shies away, both disappointed and confused by my sudden change of heart.

"You're right." She composes herself. "This definitely isn't the place. It's a little brazen to show up at my house, don't you think? Even for you."

Wait a second. Did she just say . . .

"Your house? You live here?"

Ava's face twists, clearly confused, and for the first time I notice a photograph hanging above her head on the wall. It's a picture of the Moretti family—Alessandro and his wife at the center, flanked by both Andrew and Vince, and right there, clear as day, is Ava.

I glance back at her and then at the photo again. "You're . . . your dad is . . ."

"What is the matter with you?" She grimaces, fixing her hair to be sure she's presentable to go back out to the party.

"You're Alessandro Moretti's daughter?" I almost choke on the words.

"Yeah, and if he catches us in his office like this, he'll kill us both." She glares at me, throwing the door open and disappearing into the sea of people arriving.

Oh, this is definitely going to be more fun than I originally thought.

SEVEN

Ava

I hate everything about these parties.

I hate the small talk. The socializing with sleazy old men who work with my dad. The role I have to play in his happy little family fantasy.

Tonight is as unbearable as ever, but that may have more to do with the sudden and unexpected appearance of Nick. I have to say, the man has some nerve showing up here like this. I knew he was stubborn, but this is a whole new level of determination. I don't even want to think about how he got my address or found out about my dad's party, but thankfully no one has questioned his attendance. He moves around the room, mingling a bit and fitting right in with the crowd.

Thank god.

Every time I look up his eyes are on me, and it's starting to irritate me. If his intention was to prove that he wasn't playing games, he's done the exact opposite. The second I gave in, the second I let my guard down, he backed off. He got the satisfaction he wanted, so why is he still here tormenting me? What exactly is he trying to accomplish?

"Ava!" Bella's voice brims with excitement as she slips into the chair next to me. "I just got the best news ever! Dad is announcing the man that I am going to marry. Here. Tonight. Can you believe it?"

Every fleeting thought I have about Nick evaporates and my mouth falls open. That's what this entire party is about? Bella is getting engaged?

Her brow furrows. "I know it's not really your thing, but you could at least pretend to be happy for me."

"I am happy for you, Bells," I assure her, wrapping her into a tight hug. "That's amazing. I'm sure he's going to be a great guy."

It's not a lie. I really am happy for her because it's exactly what she wants. I, on the other hand, would rather walk across boiling glass than marry a man for the sake of helping my father out. Ugh, gag me.

"I think so too." She's content with my response, even though I practically choke on the words as they come out of my mouth. "I'm going to go find Mom. I can't believe it's finally happening."

There's a bar set up out on the balcony with contracted bartenders like usual, and when Bella leaves, I make my way there. A little air and some alcohol might do me some good, but just one drink.

"What can I get you, ma'am?"

"A glass of Chardonnay, please." I give him a tight smile as he fills a wineglass and hands it to me. "Thank you."

"No whiskey tonight?" When I turn, Nick is standing out on the balcony with me, leaning back against the railing. I have a fleeting thought of pushing him right over it and into the pool. I made the jump more than a few times as a teenager, so the fall wouldn't kill him, only seriously bruise that monstrous ego.

I shake my head, joining him. "Nope. Taking it easy."

"Too bad." He chuckles. For a minute it's quiet except for the hum of the party behind us. "So you're a Moretti?"

My stomach flips. He obviously knows the name, but I wonder what else he knows. I'm used to the reputation of my family preceding me, and that's one reason I gave Nick a fake name to begin with. The less association I can have, the better.

"Guilty." I swallow, pressing the wineglass to my lips.

"Why didn't you tell me that sooner?"

"Because it's not really something I go around bragging about, Nick." I roll my eyes. "Besides, it didn't seem to matter to you what my last name was when I was naked in your bed, did it? Or the other day when you offered to help me with my daddy issues? Or even just now when you felt me up in my dad's office?"

Nick clenches his jaw. "I deserve that. But you're right. It didn't matter then, and it doesn't matter now. In fact, it's even better."

"In what way?" I fold my arms over my chest.

"Ava." He runs his fingers through his hair anxiously. "It's time for us to formally meet. My name is Nick Caponelli. My dad is—"

"Gio." My blood runs cold, and I almost feel like I might faint on the spot. Nick is Gio Caponelli's son—rival crime boss and my father's sworn enemy. Suddenly, it all makes sense. The gun on his leg. The secrecy. Him showing up here tonight. I couldn't have picked a worse person to fall into bed with.

"What . . . How . . ."

Did he know all along? Was this some sort of scheme to get to my dad?

"Do you want to take a walk? We can talk some more, and I can answer all your questions."

Right then the patio door opens and a man I recognize as Gio Caponelli walks out. "Nick, it's time."

Nick swallows, nodding again, and then turns to me. "Later?"

"Later," I agree.

Before he disappears with his father, he glances over his shoulder one more time and flashes me a reserved grin. It conjures up a barrage of feelings that I'm not sure what to make of.

Anticipation. Anger. Desire. Lust.

For better or worse, the guy has my number, and I want to hear him out.

Nick

"Ready?" my dad asks, handing me a sweating glass of whiskey. He's almost more anxious than I am.

In fact, most of my objections about this entire thing went right out the window when I realized Ava was Alessandro Moretti's daughter, the woman I'm about to be engaged to marry.

What an incredible stroke of luck.

It's quite a jump from where we are, but in the world of arranged marriages, I've struck gold.

I haven't put much thought into the Moretti girls over the years, but I guess I always expected them to be meek and wholesome. Alessandro is harsh and set in his old-school ways, and I picture him raising daughters who don't speak out of turn or stray away at all. Quiet, obedient, submissive.

And that's certainly not Ava. I doubt the girl has a submissive bone in her entire body. Every interaction we've had has been charged and full of a contagious energy that I can't even describe. With all the fire and spice inside of her, it's a wonder she and Moretti can even exist in the same room, let alone as parent and child.

Those daddy issues are making a hell of a lot more sense.

"Nick?" My dad clears his throat, drawing me back. "I asked if you were ready?"

"As ready as I'll ever be." Even if I'm coming around to all of this, I can't let my dad in on it yet. When he and Alessandro introduce us, I'll have to pretend that it's the first time I'm meeting Ava, and hopefully she'll follow suit.

We can sort everything between us out later, but right now, we have to play our parts.

"Okay, then." My dad nods. "Let's go meet Alessandro."

I follow my dad into the center of the great room, where Alessandro is standing among a group of people. Mostly his partners and heavy-hitting clients. An official engagement party will come where both sides are invited, but tonight is about the show for him, and he's clearly in his element.

"Ah, Gio, Nick, please join us." He waves us over.

I follow my dad's lead, and we make our way through the crowd, on edge, as most of the men in this room hate our guts. It's a weird feeling being the guest of honor, but also so obviously disliked. These guys better get used to it, though, because as soon as my and Ava's marriage goes through, I'll be at the helm of both organizations.

"Ladies and gentlemen, tonight is special. It marks the start of a brand-new chapter both for us and for the Caponelli family. After years in competition, Gio and I have finally decided that we're much stronger together, and that's how we plan to move forward."

The room erupts in superficial applause, and I want to throw up. Even the way he speaks to his own guys is patronizing as fuck.

Alessandro continues. "To commemorate the merger, we are thrilled to announce the engagement of our children—Nick and Isabella."

I take a step forward, but pause. Did he say Isabella? Who the hell . . .

A girl steps forward, gushing as she clings to my arm, and my entire body stiffens. Everyone around us cheers, showering us with congratulations and good wishes, but I feel like I've been hit by a freight train.

Isabella must be Ava's sister—another Moretti daughter. They have similar enough features, but Isabella's are highlighted with an incessant amount of makeup. Her floral perfume already gives me a headache and she digs her powder-pink fingernails into my bicep.

Not in the hot way. Not in the way I like. Not in the way her sister did.

I realize I severely misjudged the situation, and I anxiously scan the room for Ava, desperate to explain this to her. She already thinks I'm an arrogant fuckboy and this, well, this might be the final nail in my coffin with her.

"It's nice to meet you." Isabella smiles up at me, wide-eyed and expectant. "I've dreamed about this day for so long."

Dreamed about the day your father uses you as a bargaining chip and marries you off to a man you've never even laid eyes on before? Yeah, this is exactly the type of girl I expected Moretti to raise.

"It's nice to meet you too," I say through gritted teeth.

Isabella's got one of those high-pitched voices that sounds like nails on a chalkboard. Maybe I'm being dramatic, but Jesus, can this mess get any worse?

"Should we kiss?"

Come on, Nick. Get a hold of yourself. Play the part. "Uh, yeah. Sure."

I lean down toward her tiny frame, giving her a quick peck because I can't stomach much else, knowing Ava is somewhere in the room watching this play out.

This mess goes from bad to worse when I pull back and see Ava standing across the room by the double doors leading out to the patio. The look on her face would silence the most lethal of criminals, and it's like a blade straight to my chest.

I want to explain, but what's the point? I have to marry her sister. I have to sit at Sunday dinners next to Isabella while Ava's across the table. I have to bite back every urge and craving I have for her, and pretend like it doesn't make my skin crawl. I have to pretend like the night we spent together wasn't the best of my life.

Yeah, there's no way in hell that's happening. I've got to find some way to fix this.

Ava

I hear the words come out of my dad's mouth, but for some reason it takes a second for them to set in.

Nick and Bella.

He's marrying my *sister*.

The man who took my world and completely spun it upside down. The man who's been tracking me down for weeks. The man I've been hopelessly vying for ever since the moment we met . . . is marrying my sister.

It's almost funny at this point, but only because if I don't laugh, I'll probably cry.

When he catches my stare across the room, my heart slams against my chest. He has no right to look at me that way. Not anymore. Not after this. Any chance we had is squashed, and I can't get away from it fast enough.

I burst through the double doors onto the patio, bracing myself against the railing. It's cold, so cold that no one else is brave enough to be out, which is perfect, because facing anyone and having a conversation about how happy I am for my sister feels next to impossible right now.

When the cool air doesn't give enough shock to my system, I realize I need a drink. Something strong. Preferably strong enough to knock me right out.

When I get to the bar, the bartender glances up. "What can I get you?"

"Whiskey, please."

He fills my glass, and I don't even leave the pop-up bar before slugging it back.

"Another?" he asks, and I nod.

"Make it two."

Nick's voice elicits chills across my spine that have nothing to do with the temperature out here. Ferocious anger boils inside of me, and I take a deep breath before slowly turning around.

"Please let me explain," he says quickly, ushering me away from the bar with his hand on my elbow.

I let out a sharp laugh, jerking out of his grasp. "You know, being engaged is bad enough, but engaged to my *sister*? Do you get off on that kind of thing? There's another one of us, if that's what you're into."

"Ava, stop," he demands. "I'm sorry. Believe me, I know how this looks, but when you and I—" He glances around to be sure no one else is in earshot. "When we met, I knew nothing about this. In fact, I only found out earlier this afternoon."

"You knew when you had your hand up my dress a few hours ago?"

"No. Well, yes, sort of." It's almost endearing how flustered he is. Almost.

"Which is it, Nick?"

"I knew I was coming here to meet my future wife, and when you said you were Moretti's daughter, I assumed I'd be marrying you. I literally met your sister two seconds after your father made the announcement. I fully expected to see you up there."

"And yet you didn't mention a word of that to me when we were out here earlier."

"I should have, but I didn't. I fucked up, and I'm sorry. I never, ever wanted to hurt you. You're all I've thought about the last few weeks, and I swear to god, this was never a game to me. I felt a connection with you. More than a connection, Ava. It was . . . I can't stop thinking about you."

"Well, you should. We should probably both forget that night ever happened and pray that Bella doesn't put any of this together."

"Ava." Nick sighs.

"There you are!" Bella croons, joining us on the patio. "Wow, it's freezing out here!" She shivers. It's cold, but not that bad. She's fishing for Nick to give her his jacket in a romantic gesture, and like the gentleman he is, he obliges.

"Here, take this." He shrugs it off, and for a second, I remember the way he did it in our hotel room that night, my traitorous body betraying me as a rush of heat spreads through my core. As he slips it over her shoulders, I make every effort to bury the memory as far down as I can.

"What are you two doing out here?" Bella asks innocently. She hasn't picked up on any of the energy between Nick and me—the friction or the attraction.

"I was introducing myself to your new fiancé." I smile, refusing to look at Nick anymore. "I'm so happy for you, Bells. But I'm not feeling very well, so I think I'm going to sneak out a bit early and head to bed."

"Oh." Bella pouts. "We can celebrate tomorrow. Hope you feel better."

I'm already reaching for the door when Nick calls after me. "Good night, Ava. It was lovely to meet you."

"You too." I press my lips together, biting back emotion. "Goodbye Nick."

EIGHT

Nick

"Damn it!" I slam my hand against the wall so hard that the pictures rattle, nearly shattering to the floor.

I just spent the better part of an hour explaining the mess that is this marriage to Leo and Zane, thinking that it might help to talk it out, but all it's done is enrage me—even more so than it did last night. The adrenaline and alcohol have worn off and now I'm faced with a harsh reality.

An arranged marriage. A dream girl who wants to forget she ever met me. A brother and a best friend who have no better advice than to make a deal with Bella so that I can still see Ava. As if either of them would ever go for that.

I could always try to drive her away like I had in mind to begin with. Bella seems so eager for this to work that it might not be so easy, which, I guess, puts me back to square one.

"Maybe it won't be as bad as you think. Maybe Bella is really similar to Ava."

She's not. I already know that.

"On the bright side, you're about to become Don," Zane offers.

He's right. If even the tiniest of silver linings can be found here, it's that. Not only am I about to take over as head of our organization,

I get control of the Moretti group as well. That part is a dream come true, and maybe I need to shift my attention to work, the one thing I can count on.

"You're right," I say. "Let's focus on that."

I spend the rest of the morning going over some shipment details with Leo and Zane. With the merger happening soon, we have several loose ends to tie up, and I can't trust them to just anyone. Leo and Zane are eager to help, and before long we've got it all ironed out with plans to finalize everything within the week.

It's refreshing to have something swinging in my favor.

There's a knock at the door and one of my guys appears. "Nick, there's a woman here to see you."

"Yeah?"

He nods. "Tall brunet. Smoking hot."

For a split second, I consider it might be Ava, but one look out the window of my office to the front of the warehouse confirms it isn't. It's Bella.

"She's visiting the warehouse?" Leo arches an eyebrow.

It's no secret that we don't bring many people around the warehouse, and it's out of the ordinary for someone to show up unannounced like this, but she doesn't know that.

"I'll take care of it."

I can't help but feel bad about all of this. By all accounts, Bella is great. She's cute and sweet and I'm sure she would make 99 percent of men very, very happy. It's a shame I fall into that other 1 percent, though. Ava ruined me in more ways than one. It's not even just Bella I'm not interested in right now—it's the entire female population, because I know no one will ever measure up.

"Hi, Bella." I greet her, coming down the stairs. "How are you?"

"Hi!" She beams. "I'm good! I was in the area and thought I would come by and bring you some lunch. We didn't have much time to talk last night." My reaction must fall short of what she was hoping for because she quickly adds, "I hope that's okay."

"That's great. I'm glad you came by." I force a smile. "Why don't we go upstairs to my office?"

I guide her up the stairs and through the door to my office, shutting it firmly behind us. Bella starts pulling out a huge spread of food, setting it up on top of my desk.

"Wow. This looks great. Where is it from?" I sit down across from her, making myself comfortable.

"Um, I made it, actually." She blushes. "I didn't know what you liked, so I brought a bunch of options."

She isn't kidding. She's got everything from pasta salad to a huge selection of meats and cheeses, and she's only halfway done emptying her bag. Somehow, this makes me feel even worse. Bella deserves more than what I can give to her, and I have a feeling that neither one of us is going to be all that content with this marriage.

"You didn't have to do all of this for me."

Bella shrugs. "I enjoy it. Besides, I wanted an excuse to come talk to you, and this seemed like a good one."

"What did you want to talk about?" I grab a sandwich, realizing this is my first meal of the day. I was too distraught to eat breakfast this morning, so I survived on coffee until now.

"Logistics," she says. "Like, how soon can we get married? And when should I move in? And I know this is kind of your thing, but do you want to see pictures of rings that I like?"

Bella talks about a hundred miles an hour, but my mind goes blank the second she mentions getting married. What's the rush? Don't these things usually take time to solidify? I'm still barely wrapping my head around the idea, and she's wanting to move in. Things are moving way too fast, and now I'm sure there will be no driving her away. She's in it for the long haul, unless I can figure something else out.

"A lot of those details will be laid out in the contract. That's usually how these things work."

"Oh, right." She nods. "And the ring?"

"The ring." I swallow, having lost my appetite. "I have something in mind. But you know what, I totally forgot I have a meeting this afternoon, so I'm going to have to cut lunch short."

"No problem." She smiles. "How about dinner? Are you free?"

"I might be late." That's a lie, but I don't want to commit to anything right now. "How about I call you when I'm leaving?" I help her collect the rest of her things and show her to the door.

"Sounds great. It was really nice to see you."

"Bye, Bella. Have a nice rest of your day."

She opens her mouth like she wants to say something, but I shut the door before she can. Finally, some peace and quiet.

Bella is intense, and despite her best efforts, there's just nothing there between us. I don't feel the slightest bit of attraction toward her, and she seems about as disinterested. The girl wants to get married, and anyone could stand in my place. There is absolutely no way I can go through with this, but if I don't figure something else out fast, I won't have a choice.

One of the worst parts of this deal is the increased contact with Alessandro. I can barely stomach the guy on a bi-yearly basis, and now I'm headed to my second dinner in five days with the man. I suspect once Bella and I get married, it will only get worse.

As if this dinner wasn't going to be unbearable enough, my dad had something come up at the last second, and now Alessandro and I are having dinner on our own. Kill me now.

The restaurant he chose is on the lower end of the city, and it's nice enough, but I'm already ready to leave. After my lunch with Bella, I'd been in a nasty mood all afternoon and the only thing that will take the edge off is a session in the gym. There's a punching bag waiting at home with my name on it. No, Alessandro's name. When they say visualization is good for your mental state, I'm sure this is exactly the scenario they have in mind.

"I'm glad we could do this tonight, Nick. Especially since you and I will be working so closely together in the next few months."

"I am too," I lie.

"How have things been going with Bella?"

I wipe my mouth off with the napkin, setting it back down on the table. "We're just getting to know each other, but good so far," I say. "She's very sweet."

"She is," Alessandro agrees. "And she'll make a model Mafia wife. Agreeable. Quiet. Knows how to keep house and her opinions to herself." He chuckles. "Now if only I could get her younger sister to do that."

I cringe at his mention of Ava. For most of the afternoon I'd been able to focus on other things, but when Alessandro brings her up, I can feel myself getting riled up again. "What is your plan for her?"

I have no right to press, and knowing is probably only going to make things worse for me, but I can't help myself.

Alessandro sighs, leaning back in the booth and stretching out. "Ava, she's a different story. She's . . . spirited. It's going to take a firmer hand. I've been in talks with Drake Tatum for a while. I won't get much out of that deal, but he'll be able to break her down, and I might be able to negotiate some more port access."

The way he talks about Ava makes me sick, and I have to hold myself back from lurching across the table and knocking him out. As if I need any more reason to hate him.

Drake Tatum is a notoriously awful guy. Deceitful and gruff and downright abusive. Alessandro knows full well the kinds of things a man like Drake Tatum is capable of, and I can't imagine any father who loves his daughter would willingly hand her over to him. Ava won't last a week with him.

There's no way I can let that deal go through, but if it happens before I'm married to Bella, I'll have absolutely zero say. Unless . . . The words spill out quickly.

"What if I take Ava off your hands?"

Alessandro chuckles to himself, rubbing his chin. "You want both Bella and Ava?"

"No, I'm only talking about Ava," I say quickly. "When this deal goes through, I'll have most of the control over both groups, and that's a bit of a sacrifice for you. I might be willing to sweeten the deal in a way that helps us both out."

"What exactly are you saying, Caponelli?" He narrows his eyes on me.

What the fuck *am* I saying? I haven't even mentioned any of this to my dad. Hell, I hadn't even thought of it until just now. In a moment of panic I flipped the script entirely, and I have to tread lightly here or risk blowing the entire deal up.

"Better port access benefits all of us," I say, hoping this will work. "Like you said, Bella is already perfect wife material. What if you arranged another deal for her with Savino? We could get access to the southern ports that way, and we all come out ahead."

Alessandro scratches his chin as he thinks over what I've said. Even I'm surprised at how much sense it makes, considering I had to come up with it all on the spot.

"And you'd be okay marrying Ava to secure the treaty?"

"For the sake of the deal, I would," I say. "Maybe if you throw in one of your stockyards down in the valley. We need another storage facility and that could work. I'd be more inclined to take her off your hands if there was something in it for us."

Talking about her like she's a piece of property rubs me the wrong way, but for this to work, I have to speak his language.

Even with the stockyard, the offer is too good for him to refuse, and we both know it. I've really outdone myself with this one. If he agrees, I'll have single-handedly negotiated myself out of a marriage I can't stand the thought of, saved Ava from her impending doom and bought myself another shot with her, *and* I'll have a stockyard to give my dad to smooth over not running this by him first.

Alessandro is quiet for a minute, but ultimately, he agrees.

"You're sure you're up for that? Ava's . . . She's tough. Comes with a lot of baggage and a lot of attitude."

I can hardly contain myself. "I'm up to the challenge."

"Let me be sure I've got this straight." My father rubs his chin. The stiff leather of his armchair creaks as he leans back. He's had that ragged old thing in his office for as long as I can remember. He could have replaced it a thousand times over, but he insists they don't make them that comfortable anymore. I came straight here after my dinner with Alessandro to explain what happened.

"You took it upon yourself to renegotiate a deal that took Alessandro and me weeks to fine-tune without evening mentioning it or clearing it with me first? Let alone the council? Do I have that right?"

"In so many words, yes." When he puts it like that, it sounds a hell of a lot worse than it was. "I'm sorry. I should have talked to you first, but when he said that he was going to marry Ava off to Drake Tatum, I couldn't control myself. I couldn't let that happen, and so I did the first thing that popped into my mind."

My dad sighs. "I can appreciate you wanting to help her, Nick. I really can. But that was a massively unnecessary risk. You could have handled the situation with Ava after you and Bella were married. Even mentioning a change like that could have derailed the entire deal."

"There was no other way. And Alessandro was more than happy to switch things up. He even threw in one of their stockyards for us to use as a storage facility."

My dad perks up at that bit of information and chuckles slowly.

"What? What's so funny?"

"You took a big risk with Alessandro, but somehow came out ahead. You might be more ready for this position than I give you credit for."

His approval makes my heart soar. Succeeding him is all I've ever dreamed about and it's nice to know he thinks I'll be good at it.

"You're okay with it?"

My dad nods. "But don't make a habit of changing things on your own like that. The council is in place for a reason, and if you make too many rogue decisions, they'll come down hard."

"Got it. Won't happen again."

"This Ava, you really like her, don't you?"

"Yeah, we met a few weeks ago, and I had no idea who she was, but—"

"The girl from the hotel incident?" My dad arches an accusatory eyebrow at me.

I wince. I thought I'd done a good job of keeping that on the down-low, but I guess not. "How do you know about that?"

"There isn't a single thing I don't know about this family. Someday you boys will realize that."

I laugh. We'd never been able to pull anything over my dad's eyes when we were little, and apparently nothing has changed in adulthood.

"She must be special if she's got you so worked up, and I'll be happy to see her again."

My dad is a romantic at heart. He and my mother are the very definition of soulmates, and deep down, that's what he wants for all three of us boys as well. I know he agonized over asking me to do this to begin with, so maybe this lets us both off the hook.

NINE

Ava

Maybe things are turning around.

Maybe my sister getting engaged to the man I spent a salacious night with is the jolt I needed, and my universe has finally decided that I've been put through enough.

Maybe my dad is finally seeing me as more than a bargaining chip.

I'm an optimist, but I'm also not delusional enough to think that all three of those things are true.

In all of my life I can't think of a time when my father has involved my mom in any of his business, let alone one of his daughters, so when he called me this afternoon to ask that I meet him for dinner, I was immediately thrown off. He said he was meeting with Gio to finalize details of the treaty and needed my help drafting the contractual details for the aboveboard business elements and the prenups.

Part of me feels like he's up to something, but I eagerly agreed. Despite everything I'm still desperate for my father's approval and validation, and even the smallest possibility that his offer is genuine is enough.

It could be true, right? I mean, he's shelling out a small fortune for me to go to law school. Why waste all that money if he doesn't intend to reap the benefits?

I spend the better part of the afternoon scrambling through all my old textbooks on contracts, studying up so that I'm sharp when they have questions. It's my one chance to prove myself to my dad, and I'm going to do everything I can to make it happen.

Between the adrenaline and the library espresso I snagged this afternoon, I'm practically vibrating by the time I get to the restaurant. It's crowded, and I step to the side while I wait. A few minutes go by, and a deep humidity fills the air as the front door opens. I glance up, expecting to see my father, but it's Nick, and my stomach drops.

Why is he here? My dad didn't say anything about him joining us. If he had, I might have reconsidered coming. Well, probably not, but I could have at least prepared myself, because right now I feel completely blindsided.

"Ava. Hey," he stammers. He seems somewhat surprised to see me, too, which makes me even more suspicious about all of this.

"Hi." I press my lips together, trying not to throw up. I feel heat rumbling deep in my core, and bite the inside of my cheek hard enough to draw blood in order to recoil it. Apparently, my body doesn't know that the man in front of us is engaged to my sister and entirely off-limits, no matter how good he looks in that button-down. "What are you doing here?"

He steps out of the way of other patrons and inadvertently closes the distance between us. The closer he gets, the more intensely my heart pounds. "I'm meeting our dads for dinner."

"Oh." I swallow the lump growing in my throat. I have to sit across from him all night? I take back everything I said about the universe being back on my side. What kind of cruel and unusual punishment is this?

Wait a second. Maybe that's exactly what this is. Maybe my dad found out about the night we hooked up and that's why we're both here. Suffocating fear ripples through me at the thought. If he knows that I slept with Bella's fiancé—even if they weren't together at the time—he might honestly kill me.

"What are you doing here?" I barely hear his question over the whooshing in my ears as panic sets in.

"I, um, I'm meeting them too," I manage to get out. "My dad asked for my help drafting the contracts."

"The contracts?" He looks confused by what I said. "What contracts?"

Now I'm positive something fishy is going on here. I can feel it in my bones. "The ones for your and Bella's marriage."

"Fuck," he mutters under his breath, looking stunned.

He shoves his fingers through his hair. "You mean he didn't tell you?"

"Tell me what?"

"Ava . . ." Nick opens his mouth, but he's cut off by the sharp ringing of bells on the door.

Gio and my father walk in at the same time.

"Ava, Nick." My father grins, greeting us warmly. His chipper mood might as well be a giant, flying red flag. "Sorry we're running late."

Nick shoots him a hideous glare, and I wonder what it's about. "No problem. We had a minute to talk. Ava tells me she's here to help draft the prenup for my marriage to Isabella."

My dad tenses. "That's right. She's studying to be a lawyer, and I thought it would be good to have another set of eyes since there have been some changes."

Nick scoffs, turning his back in fury without even acknowledging what my dad said.

"Why don't we take this to the table?" Gio suggests.

He checks us in with the hostess and she leads us to a secluded booth in the back of the dining room. We all slide in on our respective sides, and I quickly realize that sitting next to Nick might have been the better choice. He wouldn't dare touch me with my dad here, and it's agonizing to have to stare across the table at him all evening.

Whatever tension there was between my dad and Nick is brushed aside as dinner starts. It's every bit as unbearable as I imagined it would be. Gio and my father, and occasionally Nick, discuss a few work things vaguely, but it's mostly pleasantries. I'm on edge the entire time trying to figure out why I was included, especially since no one's really even spoken to me after the introductions.

"So." Gio turns to me, a gentle grin spreading across his face. "Ava, I'm so glad the four of us could get together tonight and discuss some changes we want to make to the treaty. I trust your father has explained to you while we're all here?"

"Actually, I haven't had the chance," my dad says before I can get a word in edgewise. He's unusually antsy. "Ava has been busy with school, and I haven't seen much of her since we met a few days ago."

Gio sighs with disdain as he eyes my dad. "Right. Well, as you know, your father and I have come to an agreement to combine our forces, and the way we did that is through a marriage treaty."

I know all of this already. Wasn't that the point of their announcement the other night? Why is Gio treating me like I'm fragile? Like I need to be coddled?

"Right, which is why Bella and Nick are getting married." I smile but it quickly fades the moment I feel Nick's knee brush against mine underneath the table. Whether or not he did it on purpose, he yanks away so we're no longer touching.

"Actually, we've had a change in plans, Ava." My dad shifts his weight, uneasy. "I need Bella to marry a man who is going to give us access to some southern ports we've been missing. She is already aware of the change and knows she won't be marrying Nick anymore."

Well, that was about the shortest engagement in all of history.

"Bella is of much more use to both of our families by marrying

Savino, and Nick has offered to still go through with the marriage, but with you in Bella's place. It was his idea, actually."

I must have misheard him, because I think I heard my father say that I'm the one who will marry Nick.

"His idea," I repeat, glaring at Nick. He graciously meets my eyes, but offers no explanation.

Unfortunately, I don't need one to recognize what's happening. I am about to be written into an arranged marriage, and it was all Nick's idea.

"We haven't talked about this, sweetheart, but it is really for the greater good. It is safer for all of us, and I wouldn't be asking you to do this if it wasn't necessary. I don't like involving you girls in any of this."

Every part of my body tingles as painful realization washes over me, and suddenly, even breathing feels like a feat. Married? Me? To Nick?

"Your father is right, Ava. This would normally be the last thing we would do, but with the Russians moving in—"

"She doesn't need to know the details." My father cuts Gio off before he can explain any more, glancing around the room to make sure the conversation hasn't been heard by anyone else.

"I thought you needed my help with the contracts." My voice is shaky, and I'm surprised I can even form a coherent sentence.

"Technically, we do. We need your signature." A wave of nausea crashes into me. *What?*

"You want me to get married?" I stutter, looking back and forth between all three men. "To him?"

Nick

If I had any doubts that Ava knew about any of this before, the look on her face is glaring proof she didn't.

After promising me he'd talk to her about this before we met, that motherfucker didn't even warn her. He's marrying her off and didn't even give her the courtesy of letting her know it was happening. Got her here under some stupid guise that he needed her help with contracts. He really has no shame.

And then he skirted the blame and said it was entirely my idea, leaving out some very key details. Now I look like the bad guy, when all I really wanted was to protect Ava. Save her from the man Alessandro was planning to ship her off to and give her somewhat of a normal chance at life. His antics shouldn't surprise me anymore, but somehow, they do.

The anger on her face hurt me at first. I guess I had some half-baked idea of what this would be like in my mind. In my fantasy, Ava would be thrilled. She'd be excited at the prospect of marrying me and we'd ride off into the sunset together. But that was before Alessandro royally screwed everything up in a way that only he could.

I have some serious work ahead of me. Because of the treaty, I'll have her either way, but I'd prefer her to marry me willingly. I'm all for domination in the bedroom, but forcing a girl to do anything against her will isn't my thing.

"Yes." Alessandro doesn't even bother giving her more. "You're marrying Nick."

"You can't just make a treaty and be done with it?" Ava's breath hitches, but she's the picture of composure otherwise, fighting to keep herself together. It's impressive, really. If I was in her shoes, being delivered this news without any kind of consideration or even warning, I would have lost my mind. And knowing Ava, she's about to. I can't imagine she'll take this lying down. Not from what I know of her.

"No," Alessandro answers adamantly. "Your marriage is the only way. It's not open for discussion."

I wait, expecting her to yell, to cause a scene, to have a loud, pointed reaction, but she doesn't. When she lets her head fall without a word,

I'm shocked. This is not the Ava I'm used to. Her fiery, opinionated spirit is one thing that draws me to her, but tonight there is a meekness about her that doesn't sit right with me. Somehow, I know Alessandro is to blame.

"Okay." Her voice is soft, and she refuses to even look up at me. I can't say that I blame her, though. After the last few weeks, and then being told by her father that it was my idea to force her to marry me, she probably thinks I'm a psychopath.

That's the last that is spoken of our marriage over dinner. Dad and Alessandro carry on, and I interject a few things here and there, but I spend most of my time studying Ava. She picks at her dinner, moving pasta around the plate and pretending not to notice when I look at her. She's blindsided and hurt, and this is not the way I want to start things off with her.

"Who wants dessert?" my dad asks, scanning the menu once we've finished. Neither Ava nor I have eaten much of the meal at all.

I can't even think about more food when the night has unfolded like it has. I hate seeing her so deflated, a shell of the girl that has had me so captivated the last several weeks, and I can only assume its because she's scared of speaking up in front of her father. As angry as she is, I've never been more sure that I made the right choice. She'll never have to be fearful of her father again, as long as I'm around.

"I'm going to head home," Ava says suddenly. "I have to be up early tomorrow, and I'm exhausted." She stands, grabbing her purse and not giving anyone an opportunity to object. "It was a pleasure to see you again, Mr. Caponelli." She smiles and extends her hand to my father.

A smug smile sweeps Alessandro's face, sickeningly proud of how well mannered she acts, exactly as he groomed her to be. Personally, I want to shake the politeness right out of her. I want her to yell. To scream. To throw something across the room. Anything that resembles the girl I first met.

"It was wonderful to meet you, too, Ava. I am looking forward to getting to know you," my dad says as I stand up next to him.

"Nick." She presses her lips into a tight smile, offering a stiff hand to me, as if she hadn't held my erection in it a few weeks ago.

"Let me walk you out," I offer, reaching for my coat.

"That's not necessary," she snaps defensively. The last thing she wants right now is to be alone with me, but I can't let her walk away without knowing my true intentions.

"It's late, Ava. Let him walk you to your car. I'll see you at home," Alessandro says, ending any protest she has.

She lets out a discreet huff that only I see and turns to the door. It takes me a few paces to catch up to her. Damn, she's quick, even in those heels.

"Ava, please, wait," I call after her, as she rushes through the door.

"This was your grand plan?" she asks, big, angry tears threatening to fall from her eyes. "I won't go to dinner with you, so you force me to *marry* you instead?"

"That's not what happened, Ava. I never wanted to marry Bella and—"

"You traded for me like a new pair of shoes, then? Did you ever, for one second, stop to think about how I would feel about this?"

"Ava, I thought about you through *every* second of this. In fact, I only suggested this for your sake."

"My sake?" She bursts out laughing. "I've told you for weeks how I don't want to even be in a relationship, let alone get married, and somehow you've convinced yourself this is for me?"

Several people in the parking lot glance over at us now. I grit my teeth, trying to ignore the venom in her voice. After all the revelations tonight, she needs someone to take her frustration out on, and I can be that for her.

I grab her wrist and pull her toward her car. "Would you keep your voice down, please? I'm not the one you should be yelling at. If you would let me explain, you might understand that."

"Fine. Explain it to me. How did this happen when less than a week ago we were celebrating your engagement to my sister?"

"It would have been someone else if it wasn't me, Ava. No matter what he's told you, that's been your dad's plan all along. And the man he had picked out for you, he's awful."

I don't know if she shivers from the cool air or the realization. "Why should I believe you? It's not like you've been very forthcoming with me since we met."

"You can believe whatever you want, but the truth is that that marriage would have been a death trap for you. I couldn't let it happen, so I intervened the only way I could think of, and I offered to marry you instead of Bella."

"So what? Am I supposed to fall down at your feet in gratitude now?" Her bitter anger slowly fades, and now she's mostly overwhelmed and hurt.

I shake my head, resting my palm on her cheek as my thumb brushes along her rosy skin. "No, absolutely not. All I want is for you to understand that I wasn't trying to set you up. Or hide anything from you. Or to hurt you."

She scoffs and looks away, but she doesn't pull from my touch.

"The situation's a lot for both of us, so why don't we just take this day by day and see where it goes?"

"There is no seeing where it goes, Nick. Once the treaty is signed there won't be any going back." A few tears trickle down her face, the pain in her voice stinging us both.

She's right, of course. As soon as the ink is dry on our signatures, we'll be married—for better or worse. She's got even less choice in it than I do.

"There is still time, you know. You can go back in there and tell him you want to marry Bella. The only thing she wants in life is to be the perfect wife to someone like you."

The way she talks about herself like some sort of consolation prize breaks me.

"And what about you? Send you off so Tatum can beat the shit out of you and keep you chained up in a tower somewhere?"

"You said it yourself. I'm a runner. It wouldn't be that far-fetched for everyone to think I took off."

"You dad would find you before you were even out of the city, and then what?"

She sighs, not wanting to admit that I'm still her best option.

My hand settles on her chin, lifting gently so she has no choice but to look at me. "Ava, this is ridiculous. You're the one I want, and I think I've made that pretty clear over the last few weeks."

"You like the chase."

"Let me prove you wrong."

She hesitates, her resolve breaking just long enough to give me my opportunity.

"I want to take you out tomorrow," I say.

"Nick, I—" She starts to protest, but I don't give her the opportunity.

I kiss her, rough enough to remind her of the spark we had but gentle enough not to push my luck. My tongue glides across her lip, and she moans at the slight bite of my teeth. She's tense, but she lets me go a little further. My fingers tangle in her hair, holding her body close to mine as heat builds between us, but I stop short of anything else.

"Let me make this up to you. We completely started out on the wrong foot and at the very least, I owe you a proper date."

"Fine." She's reluctant, but she agrees. "One date. That's it, and I want you to keep your hands *and* your lips to yourself."

"Why is that?"

"Because I can't think straight when you touch me, and I need to sort this out."

"Deal." I chuckle. "I'll pick you up tomorrow."

"See you tomorrow."

"Good night, Ava." I open the door for her, and she climbs into her SUV. The engine revs, and she pulls out of the lot. I watch until her taillights disappear into the darkness.

It might not have gone like I'd envisioned, but it's a start.

TEN

Ava

When I wake up the next morning, I have a raging headache. I was hoping to find this was all some sort of twisted nightmare, but I get a sinking feeling in my stomach when I realize that's not the case.

I'm engaged.

Engaged to a man my father picked out for me.

Engaged to a man I'm very obviously attracted to, but whom I'm still not sure how much I can trust.

A dull ache radiates throughout my body, and my stomach is in so many knots that I'm scared that if I move too quickly, I might throw up. Kind of like having a hangover without any of the fun that leads to one.

An engagement and a wedding should be exciting. At least that's how I always pictured it. The start of a new chapter in my life—one I'd spend with a man I was head over heels for. We'd start a life together, build a family, and be nauseatingly happy and in love.

My idea of marriage has always been distorted, but I never imagined it would come under these circumstances. That I'd be twenty-three, not even out of school, and promised to marry as part of a business deal. My mind spins like I'm standing at the edge of a cliff, teetering on the edge as I balance on one foot. My entire world, and every possibility of what my future could be, is crumbling underneath me.

I've been raised around Cosa Nostra soldiers, so men like Nick aren't new to me. They're controlling and demanding, and they get what they're after by any means necessary—Nick even admitted that to me himself. So far, he's been nothing like the soldiers I'm used to, but who's to say that shine won't wear off? That the real Nick is every bit as fearsome and tyrannic as my father? The thought gives me chills.

It was only weeks ago that my dad promised me that if I got my act together, it wouldn't come to this. I'd been busting my ass for weeks, trying to show him I was making an effort, for none of it to matter.

It's nearly nine in the morning, and if I'm going to make my class, I'll have to rush. Columbia is over an hour away from my house, and I still have to shower and make myself presentable. On second thought, what's the point anymore? In the last twelve hours, any hope I had of proving myself as more than a bargaining chip to my father has been obliterated. Why get my degree at all if I'm just going to be some kind of glorified housewife?

A whole lot of time and effort for nothing.

After a quick shower, I head downstairs. I slept through breakfast, but didn't eat much of my dinner last night and I'm hungry. Bella and Vince are in the kitchen, and I consider picking something up on the way instead. I don't want to deal with them yet, but I'm running late already.

"Come on, just for a few hours," Vince whines as I come around the corner.

Bella completely ignores him.

"Good morning to you, sleeping beauty," my sister says.

"We thought you were dead." Vince puts his hand over his heart, feigning shock.

"I might as well be," I grumble under my breath, slouching onto the bar stool next to Bella.

"Hey, I have a great idea. Why don't you ask Ava to do it? I'm sure she'd love to."

"Do what?" I haven't even been awake for fifteen minutes and they're already trying to rope me into something.

"Avs, can you take Sophia to the mall this afternoon?" my brother begs. "She's losing her mind because none of her clothes fit and shopping really isn't my thing."

I should have known it had something to do with his wife, Sophia. As excited as he is to have another baby, the idea of pregnancy absolutely terrifies Vince, and he's here at least once a week trying to get one of us to step in and hang out with Sophia. She's at the end of her pregnancy, hormones flaring, and so he's been spending more time here to stay out of firing range.

"As thrilling as that sounds, I can't. I have class." I grab a banana from the fruit bowl and peel it. "Why don't you call Angie? She loves that kind of thing."

"Because Angie is already on my back about this. She thinks I need to man up and take care of Soph."

"I kind of agree with Angie on this one. She's your wife. Remember all that in sickness and in health stuff you promised?" Bella chimes in.

Vince throws his arms up in exasperation. "You guys don't get it. She threw a curling iron at me this morning. A fucking curling iron, and it was hot. She's going to murder me in my sleep one of these days."

"Speaking of crime . . ." Something outside the kitchen window catches Bella's attention. "Nick Caponelli just pulled up."

My stomach lurches. Talk about terrible timing. What the hell is he doing here? I agreed to go to dinner, but it's not even lunchtime. Not to mention, Bella and I haven't had a chance to talk about what happened. Even if she's content with the change, like my dad claims, it doesn't feel great to throw it in her face this way.

"What the fuck does he want?" Vince grimaces, eyes trained on Nick as he makes his way up the path toward the front door.

"Oh, I don't know, Vince. Maybe he's here to see his fiancé?" Bella gestures to me.

Vince scoffs. "Which one of you is it today?"

"You'll have to ask Dad, I guess," Bella says.

When the doorbell rings Vince charges forward, and Bella trails close behind. Before she can leave the kitchen, I catch her wrist.

"Hey, Bells, we're good, right? The whole treaty switch—"

"You think I'm upset about this thing with Nick? God, no, Ava! I should be thanking you. Nick's hot and all, but honestly, he's a little boring."

I have to laugh out loud. If only she knew. After my experience with Nick, boring is about the last thing I'd call him.

"Paul Savino is much more my type. I'm sorry you got roped into all of this."

"Thanks, Bella."

She smiles back at me over her shoulder before joining Vince in the foyer. He's peering out the window but hasn't actually opened the door yet.

I have a fleeting thought of running up to my room and locking myself in, but that won't do me much good. Sooner or later I'm going to have to face my future.

"I'll get it." I suck in a sharp breath, pushing past them both.

Nick has his back to me when I open the front door. He turns at the creak of it, and I nearly melt. Hating him would be *so, so* much easier if he didn't look so good all the time. He's got on a pair of blue jeans and a charcoal waffle-knit long-sleeve that's shoved up his muscular forearms. He lights up when he sees me, a big grin splashed across his face.

"Hey!"

"Hi." I give him a reserved smile, closing the door behind me and forcing a bit of privacy. Bella and Vince will watch, but at least this way they won't be able to hear our conversation.

My body is pulled to his like a magnet, but I resist. At least my brain is still weary enough to keep him at a distance. "How did you get past security?"

"Your dad put me on the list."

"Are you here to see him?"

"Nope." Nick smirks, shoving his hands in his pockets. "I'm here to pick you up. Our date, remember?"

"Aren't you a little early?"

"I didn't specify dinner when I said I'd be picking you up. Come on, I've got something I want to show you." He nods at the sleek black truck parked at the end of our driveway.

Bold of him to assume I don't have any plans this afternoon.

"I have class."

"So? You don't want to be a lawyer, anyway. What would one afternoon hurt?"

The worst part about him being right is that he knows it, and a subtle, barely detectable smirk raises at the corner of his mouth.

Despite my brain's screaming protests, I'm truly considering Nick's offer. It sounds mildly better than sitting in a lecture hall while the professor practically taunts me with law strategies I'll never use.

Nick reaches for my hand, and I let him take it. His touch is warm. Familiar. A little comforting. "I'm only asking for an afternoon. I want to get to know you better. Don't you think we should do that if we're going to be married?"

Married.

Hopefully at some point that word stops giving me an immediate headache.

Honestly, the only thing I want to do is lie around here moping and feeling sorry for myself all day, but that won't do me any good. I can't change what's happening regardless.

"No touching, no kissing." Nick grins, holding his hand up in a fake salute as he swears to adhere to the terms I'd set out last night. "Just two people hanging out, talking and enjoying each other's company. I promise."

"Nice start," I tease, nodding at my hand gently resting in his.

When he pulls his hand back, he smirks. "From this point forward."

That's a promise he probably won't be able to keep, but I'm not sure I mind.

He can't ever seem to keep his hands to himself when we're together. Not on the yacht. Not in my father's office. Certainly not that night in the hotel. Every touch is so pointed, so personal, so intimately confident. Like I'd given him a blueprint to my body, a map to every sweet spot I've got. The one behind my ear, inside my elbow, on my inner thigh. He knows exactly how to play them all.

Nick clears his throat, drawing me back to reality.

"Sorry." I straighten up. "Sure, I'll go with you. But I can't be back late. My father won't be happy with you if I'm out all day and night."

"Not much of his business anymore, is it?" Nick shrugs.

His words catch me off guard a bit. If it's not his business anymore, then whose? Nick's?

"One thing's for sure, Ava. You'll never have to answer to me the way you answer to him. Or be worried about how I'm going to react to something. As long as you're straight with me, I'll be straight with you."

There's a grit in Nick's voice that piques my interest. It's not like I know the finer details of his relationship with my dad, but his words make me think there is a bit of animosity there. And that makes me think that maybe my assessment of him is off.

Maybe he's different.

ELEVEN

Nick

"I'll just be a minute."

Ava starts up a long, winding staircase in the foyer of the Morettis' house.

Damn, I could watch her walk away a million times over. The ripped-at-the-knee blue jeans that hug every curve of her lower half, messy curls tied into a ponytail trailing down her back, white ribbed crop top that's anything but innocent. She clearly wasn't expecting me, but I don't mind catching her off guard, because this laid-back side of her is one I haven't seen before. Usually, she looks like she just walked off the current-trends page of a magazine. Even when I saw her that day at Columbia, she was the pinnacle of current fashion.

This, though, her casual, relaxed look, might be my favorite yet. So goddamn gorgeous.

"Don't change. You look absolutely perfect," I call after her.

"What?" She laughs nervously, tucking a loose strand of hair behind her ear.

Fuck. So much for keeping it cool.

"What you're wearing is perfect for what we're going to do."

Ava gives me a funny look, and she's not buying it. "Whatever you say."

I'd be embarrassed, but if she doesn't realize that I am into her by this point, then she's purposely ignoring it. She disappears down the hallway at the top of the stairs, and I turn around. When I come face-to-face with Vince, my heart nearly stops.

"You've got a lot of nerve showing up here, Caponelli." Vince clenches his jaw, fists balled at his sides as he stands in front of me.

"I don't want to start anything, Vince. I'm only here to pick Ava up. I wouldn't have come if I'd known you were going to be here."

We have a tumultuous history. Things got especially icy between us when everything went down with Andrew, and they've only barely begun to thaw. That was pre–marriage treaty, though, and judging by his reaction, we're on rocky terms again. Marrying Ava means that I'll take control of both of our families, effectively knocking Vince off the top of the list to inherit the Moretti organization.

"My bad, I thought you were here for Bella. Oh wait, it was *last* week you were engaged to her. Hard to keep up."

"Vince, that's not—"

"Is my family some kind of game to you, Caponelli?" he sneers. "Gotta fuck one, marry one, kill one?"

That statement is truer than he knows. At least, I hope he doesn't know about the night Ava and I spent together.

Vince steps toward me, readying himself for a fight, but I want nothing to do with that. I'm not one to back down from a challenge, but somehow, I don't think knocking Ava's brother out cold would help my case with her.

Luckily, she comes down at exactly the right moment.

"Vince, don't you have anything better to do than harass my boyfriend?"

She slings a bag over shoulder, nearly skipping as she comes down the stairs. Despite her skepticism, she's kept the same outfit on, but let her hair down and thrown on a pair of white sneakers. White isn't the best choice for what I've got planned this afternoon, but I'm not about to spend any more time here cockfighting with Vince.

"Trust me, I have much better things to do than sit here and talk to Caponelli any longer than absolutely necessary." His attempt at intimidation falls short, but I don't make a show of it.

"All set?" I turn to Ava, who gives me a soft smile and a nod. "Great. Let's head out then."

I want to reach for her hand, but my promise rings in my ears and I think better of it. Might be better to ease her into this at whatever speed she wants to take. I've waited weeks for this girl; it can't hurt to wait much longer.

"Bye, Vince," she calls, waving over her shoulder. "Good luck with Soph today!"

Vince mutters something under his breath, slamming the door behind us.

Ava is a few steps in front of me as we walk to my truck, and I open the door for her as she climbs inside. "Boyfriend, huh? That's what we're calling it?"

"Would you have preferred I introduce you as 'Romeo'?"

"I would have preferred you introduce me as your fiancé." I arch a hopeful eyebrow at her, only halfway teasing.

Ava purses her lips, a small smirk pulling through. "Don't push your luck, Nick. Let's see how the day goes."

"You got it." I grin, shutting the door before going around to my side. Ava is unlike any girl I've ever been with, and I can already tell I'm going to have to jump through some serious hoops to make this work. For a guy who usually only puts minimal effort into relationships, that should sound like a nightmare, but I'm oddly looking forward to it.

"Sorry about Vince," she says as I back out. "I wish I could say you got him on a bad day, but he's kind of always like that. If I'd known you were coming, I could have made sure he was gone."

"He's not so bad, just being protective," I say. "And how would I have let you know I was coming? You haven't even given me your phone number yet."

"You're kidding, right? You have the entire Mafia at your disposal. You can't do a little research and find it for yourself?"

She's spicy this morning, and I love every second. Such a difference from last night. "Well, of course I *can*, but I'd rather you give it to me on your own terms."

"How chivalrous of you."

We make small talk on the drive, arguing about my taste in music and who has the best pizza in New York. It's a start, but it only scratches the surface of what I want to know about her. Hopefully, that will change after today. About an hour and a half into our drive to Montauk, I turn into a long, tree-lined driveway. It's a good thing I know this drive so well, because I can't stop watching the light in Ava's eyes as she stares out the window, taking in the sprawling meadows all around us.

"Where are we?"

A prideful smile hits me as I realize she's already enjoying herself. "You'll see."

Up the road a little ways, the barn comes into view. As we get closer, the property opens up. Endless white fences line the pastures where horses graze. Others are being ridden in the outdoor arena. Off in the distance, you can barely see the training track. I get a sense of nostalgia every time I come to this place. We used to come a lot as kids, and I have nothing but happy memories of the place.

When we step out of the car, an earthy scent hits us, and the air just feels light and clean.

"What is this place?" Ava asks as I park the truck.

"My family's stables. One of my father's big moneymakers is horse racing. He's got some of the best athletes in the sport here." I lead her into the barn. It's busy today, both horses and riders coming and going.

"Nick, this is incredible." Her eyes are wide as we walk farther down the line of stalls. "I love horses."

"Good, because we're going for a little ride."

"Seriously? We get to ride them?" Ava looks at me like I've offered her the keys to the kingdom. This is a risky first-date option, but I had a hunch she'd be into it, and it's paying off.

"Once Dad's horses retire from racing, they become leisure horses. There are ten of them here for days like today, when one of us can get out and ride. Come on, I'll show you." Her pinkie brushes mine as we walk deeper into the barn, and I fight every natural urge to grab her hand. A few of the horses peek their heads out of their stalls, curious about us. This side houses my dad's racehorses, and they're not used to many visitors.

"This is Onyx." I stop in front of a stall where a huge white horse peers out. "He's one of the top horses right now. He's young, but give it a year and he'll be nearly impossible to beat."

"He's beautiful." Ava approaches slowly, offering her hand for him to sniff before scratching his nose. Onyx snorts, eating up her attention.

I lead Ava around the backside of the barn where the horses we'll be riding today stay.

"This is Pain, and this is Panic. The two we'll take out today." I ruffle the mane of Panic, who's been my horse for several years now.

"Interesting names." Ava laughs curiously.

"Have you ever seen *Hercules*? My brother and I named them when we were young."

"I didn't take you for a Disney fan," she teases, her guard dropping lower and lower by the second.

"I was seven. Give me a break," I defend my choice, inching toward her a bit. "Have you ever ridden before?"

She nods. "My mom's sister has a ranch in Colorado."

"Great." I smile. "I'm going to go get our saddles and I'll be right back. There are carrots in the bucket over there if you want to give them some."

I leave Ava to feed the horses while I go round up all the tack we'll need. By the time I get back, she's got both horses nuzzling into her as she giggles. Apparently, I'm not the only one under her spell.

As I lay everything down, she works her way down the row of stalls, stopping in front of Cassio.

"Careful with that one," I warn her. "He's not very friendly. Fast as lightning, but next to impossible to get a saddle on. His trainer is about the only one in the world who can touch him."

"Maybe he's just misunderstood." There's a knowing look on her face as she watches him, slowly stepping forward and grasping the bars of the stall door. "Why does he have bars while all the rest are open?"

"Try to pet him." I know exactly how this is going to end. It's cute she thinks she'll have some kind of magic touch with him, but Cassio is a different kind of horse. He doesn't like interaction in the slightest. His poor jockey has to fight tooth and nail to get him ready for a race.

Ava timidly sticks her hand through the bars, trying to give him time to warm up. Instead, he rears back, shrieking and neighing like someone's trying to kill him. Startled, Ava jumps back and bumps right into me. I wrap my arm around her waist, catching her just before she falls to the ground.

I don't even have to say I told you so, because her expression tells me she knows I was right. She lingers in my arms for a few seconds longer than I expect before she pulls away and dusts herself off.

"Have you ever tacked a horse up before?"

Ava shakes her head, and I sling the saddle over Pain. "I'm surprised you have. Don't you have stable hands to do this kind of thing?"

"We do, but my dad always insisted that if you're going to ride the animal you should know how to take care of it. And that includes getting them ready."

"I better pay close attention, then." She steps closer. If she knows how much she's tempting me, she doesn't let on, listening to every word I say as I do my best to focus on the task at hand.

I ignore the way her body grazes against mine when I show her how to tighten the straps of the saddle. I ignore the fresh, beachy scent of her hair when she stands in front of me as we slip the bridle on. I ignore the perfect view I've got of her tits when she leans forward to check the girth. I ignore the way that denim fabric stretches, my hand on her delicious ass as she swings her leg over Pain and I help her up.

"Good boy," she coos, patting his neck once she's settled.

Yeah, Pain is most definitely what I'm going to be in after riding all afternoon with the throbbing erection I've got.

I get Panic set up, and then we're off. One of the best parts about this place is the scenery. One minute you're riding on sandy beaches and the next you could be in a thick, dense forest. We ride for about a half an hour before I lead her into a clearing.

"Wow." Ava is almost at a loss for words, which I haven't seen very often. "This is so gorgeous."

"Almost as gorgeous as you." I grin, securing the horses to a tree where they can rest.

"Does that line work on all the girls you bring here?" She laughs, playfully glancing up at me as we walk through the wildflowers.

"You're the first girl I've ever brought here, so you'll have to tell me."

Ava blushes, and my words seem to surprise her. She's got it in her mind that I'm a huge playboy, and while she isn't entirely off base, she severely underestimates how I feel about her compared to anyone else. "This place is special to me, almost sacred, and I wouldn't share it with just anyone, Ava."

"How did you find it?" The color in her cheeks intensifies, and she changes the subject.

"Well, my brother Leo and I came across it one day while we were out riding. Honestly, we only stopped because we knew when we got back my dad would make us muck all the stalls out before we could go home, so we were buying time. After that we came here when we wanted to escape. From chores, from our tag-along little brother, from work.

"You tend to see a lot of tough stuff when you grow up in the Mafia. I guess you know how that goes, though." I lay out the picnic blanket that I brought and sit down.

"Actually, I don't." Ava sits next to me, knees slightly bent as she looks up. "My dad always kept my sisters and me as far away from it as he could from anything to do with his work."

I could understand if Moretti wanted to shelter and protect his girls by keeping them away, but nothing with him is ever that deep. It's always about power, and keeping them out of the business meant keeping them in their place. A lot about the Mafia is rooted in tradition and misogyny, and Moretti really takes that to heart. In his world women aren't important enough to understand the inner workings of the business. Not important enough to make their own decisions or even be involved in them. Not important, period, beyond building and raising a home and family.

Things are much different in our family.

There are definitely things I'll keep private for her sake, but if Ava doesn't know what she's up against, how can she ever protect herself? With as many enemies as Moretti has made, it's a wonder nothing happened to her or his sisters growing up. That's a chance I'll never take.

"Hey, I got something for you," I say, reaching into my pocket and pulling out a small black box.

Her breath hitches when she sees what it is, teeth sinking into her lower lip. "Is that—"

"It's an engagement ring," I say, unfastening the ring and holding it out to her. "Ava Moretti, will you marry me?"

She lets out a sharp laugh. “Pretty sure my dad already gave you an answer.”

“He did.” I nod. “But I want it to come from you. I know that this is a lot to handle, and it’s probably not what you had in mind when you pictured your engagement. As fucked up as the situation is, I want it to be as authentic as possible for you.”

Ava is stunned into silence, staring down at the diamond sparkler in my hand. She lets me take her hand and slip it onto her finger, and it’s a perfect fit. Almost like it was made for her. I thought it would take a while to find the right thing, but when I saw the three-carat oval-cut solitaire sitting in the jewelry store’s display case on my way home last night, I knew it was the one. Simple, dainty, and elegant. I chose to take it as some kind of fateful sign.

The sunlight hits the perfect angle, and it sparkles on her hand.

“You might not have had a choice in the matter, but I hope that you won’t ever regret us. When I have earned your love and trust, I’ll ask you for real, and I hope your answer will be yes. But until then, this”—I hold her hand to my lips and kiss the ring—“is my promise to you that I will spend every day working on our relationship with you, making the most out of it and giving you everything you deserve. That I’ll never force you to do anything you don’t want to do, and that I won’t ever take you for granted.”

“Nick, I . . .” Tears well in her eyes as she bites her lip, and I can’t tell if they’re happy or sad ones.

“You don’t have to answer me now. Let’s see how things go.”

“Thank you.” Her lips curve into a small smile. “It’s absolutely beautiful.”

“I’m glad you like it.” I squeeze her hand. “Now, how about some champagne?”

I pull a bottle from the small basket I brought and pour us each a glass.

"You've thought of everything, haven't you?" She presses her lips to the glass, ring on full display. The sight makes my heart skip—and my cock twitch. I've never been so jealous of a glass before.

"I like to be prepared for anything that arises." The condom in my pocket is further proof of that, however optimistic it may be. Today is a ruthless exercise in restraint that I could have done without.

Ava looks up, and her eyes meet mine. "Who exactly are you, Nick? The sweet, charming romantic or the rough, domineering enforcer?"

"Maybe a bit of both," I say. "I like my job, and I'm willing to sacrifice a lot for it, but I also don't hate the idea of finding someone I'd love to spend the rest of my life with."

"And you honestly think that could be me?"

"I want to find out. We both know we've had a connection from the moment we met. Even before that, when I saw you across the bar, I wanted to know more about you. Everything about you, actually."

"Like what?"

"Like why you ran away from me that first night."

Ava winces at the memory, pressing her lips together as she contemplates. "I guess I felt it too. That connection you've been talking about. My dad had already been after me to find someone I could marry and settle down with, and it was why I was on that date in the first place. Ironically, I thought you were the last guy he would approve of, and I was trying to prove myself to him."

She pauses. "It's the same reason I went to law school. I had some misguided idea that if I got my law degree, I could be useful to him. Not in the arranged marriage sort of way but, like, with the big stuff. I thought there was no way he'd dump all that money into me and my education only to marry me off, like he might be proud of me, but I was wrong."

"You guys have always had a tough relationship?"

She laughs sharply. "Tough is kind of an understatement. It wasn't always so bad, but things changed after my twin brother died."

Twin brother? My heart jumps into my throat when she mentions Andrew. I knew they had to be close in age, but *twins*? Right then I understand she doesn't have any idea what really happened. She wouldn't speak so nonchalantly if she did.

"I didn't take it well when he was killed. Got into some shit I shouldn't have and my dad wasn't thrilled."

"What did you get into?" I ask.

Ava's eyes glass over and she's quiet for a second. "Andrew was my best friend, and losing him was . . . I had to find a way to forget. To numb everything I was feeling. I was dating a guy that ran drugs for my dad and I—"

"Cocaine?"

She nods. "Mostly, but I wasn't picky."

Oof. My heart shatters for her. Losing a brother is incomprehensible to me, and now that I know she doesn't know the truth, I'm even more concerned. What's going to happen when she finds out she's been lied to? That it didn't happen as cleanly as Alessandro's led her to believe? That I did it?

I can't broach this with her until I know what exactly he told her, and that kills me. Seconds ago, I promised to be straight with her, and I'm holding a catastrophic secret. Even though I can't give her the full truth just yet, maybe I can offer her something.

"I knew him, you know."

Her eyes widen. "You did?"

"Yeah." I nod. "We worked together a bit. He was a great guy."

Ava swallows. "He was."

"I'm sorry you didn't have anyone you could turn to." I want to take her hand, but she's emotional and I don't want to take advantage of that, so I don't. "Tell me more about the cocaine."

"It's over now," she says quickly. "I spent some time in treatment, and I haven't used in a long time. It was just a phase, I promise."

I want to believe that, but drug use is a slippery slope. "Good, and I hope that if it ever gets bad again, you'll come to me about it. As my wife, if you don't handle it, I will."

It comes out harsh, but it's the truth. Drugs are a serious thing for me, regardless of circumstances.

My threat strikes a nerve. "And how do you intend to do that? Beat me into submission?"

"Is that how your father would handle it?"

She doesn't answer, but that silence speaks volumes. I've always known that Alessandro is a hardass, and it's not out of the ordinary in the Mafia, but for some reason, it's only now dawns on me that he's physically abusive. Rage nearly blinds me as I think about all the shit that man has put her through.

"Ava, I want you to know that things are going to be much different with me. I'll never, ever hit you or raise my hand to you like your father did. Ever. No matter what. What I meant by that was that I'd get you back into treatment, or whatever else I needed to do to help. Not hurt you even more than you already are. Partying isn't a good way to cope, and it has to stop."

I lift her chin so she'll meet my eyes, wanting to be sure she hears every word of this. "I love that you're independent and can handle yourself. It's one of the first things that drew me to you, and I can promise you, I'll never do anything to discourage that, but my highest priority will always be your safety. You might not always like it, but you should know that everything I do will be with you and your best interests in mind."

She presses her lips into a reserved smile. "You certainly have a way with words, Mr. Caponelli."

We sit there for a while in silence, the cool breeze whipping through the trees. I'm not sure how long we've been gone, but the sun will probably be going down soon. The quiet between us is comfortable, and when I stretch back against the blanket, so does she.

Her body is so close to mine, our hands nearly brushing as they rest between our hips. A single heartbeat could be enough to propel them into each other.

"It's a shame you've got that no touching policy . . . all this privacy and seclusion, and we can't even put it to good use."

Ava glances down to where our hands sit so close on the blanket and slips her hand underneath mine, a smile tipping her glossy lips. "Hand holding is okay."

"Why exactly are you so set on this, anyway? I mean, after the places on your body that my hands have been . . ." I click my tongue, raw memories rushing through me.

"*That* is exactly why. We jumped right into bed and I barely know anything about you. What if you're a serial killer?"

I put my hand on my forehead, unable to swallow my laughter.

"What?" She bites her lip playfully but there's a hint of truth to what she's saying. "You've shown up randomly all over the place the last few weeks and you've openly admitted to searching the entire city for me, which is serious stalker behavior. Serial killer isn't all that far off."

"More like a contract killer, actually."

Her face drops. "What?"

"That's my job." I clench my jaw, debating how much of this I should share with her. I made a promise to be straight with her, so ultimately, I continue. "I'm the best shot in our group, so when someone needs to be taken care of, that's what I do."

She pales a little, and I can feel her body tense all the way through her fingertips. "How often?"

I shrug. "Whenever it's needed."

"What does *needed* mean?" The wheels turn in her mind as she questions me. There is a hesitance in her voice that tells me she's not sure if she even wants to know the answers.

"Look, I promised I'd tell you the truth whenever I could, but if this is too much—"

Ava shakes her head, cutting me off. "I want to know."

"If someone's betrayed us. Or is an imminent threat." I turn toward her, propping myself on my elbow. "But I've never killed a single person outside of absolute necessity." My thumb sweeps across the back of her hand. "Does that worry you?"

"Probably not as much as it should." She presses her lips together, and her eyes darken. She disappears into her mind for a second and I want to press, but this has already gotten much heavier than I intended, and I want to salvage all the progress we've made, so I cut it off before we can go any further.

"It's getting late. How about we check out that pizza place you were talking about on the way home and I can see if it's as good as you think it is?"

Ava smiles. "That sounds perfect."

TWELVE

Ava

Nick looks at me expectantly. "What do you think?"

He's so cute that I hate to break his spirit, but I have to. "It's very average." I frown, scrunching my nose as I brace for his reaction.

His face twists in disgust, acting like I'd insulted his mother and not a piece of overpriced, way-too-doughy pepperoni pizza. "You've got to be kidding. It's the best slice in the entire state. Maybe even the entire East Coast."

"Sorry." I shrug with a wince. "Not my favorite."

One thing that Nick and I have in common is our love for pizza, so we've spent the better part of the week trying out new places all across the city. It's been fun and low pressure, and I'm almost embarrassed to admit that I'm coming around to all of this. Coming around to Nick, specifically, because he's been amazing.

Attentive and sweet and, so far, he's kept his hands to himself. Out of pure respect for me, he hadn't pushed it further than a simple kiss good night every night when he dropped me off, and it's almost making me want him more. My hands-off rule is backfiring and now I'm the one feeling unsatisfied.

It's not like we haven't crossed that line before. Haven't touched, haven't kissed. We've done way more than that several times over, but somehow it feels too personal right now. That first night was casual, but now that I'm engaged to the man, it feels uncomfortably intimate.

"Okay, this weekend, we're going to my parents' house. My mom ran a pizza shop when they first met, and she's got some tricks up her sleeve that you've got to be impressed by." Nick smirks, shaking his head.

"Deal." My stomach flips as I agree. Getting to know Nick's family feels like a bigger step than it is, especially considering they'll soon be mine.

"Man, I had no idea you were such a pizza connoisseur." He leans back in the booth, stretching an arm out over the fading leather. It's late, and we're the only ones left in the entire place.

"You should hear my opinions on ice cream." I arch an eyebrow at him.

"Don't tempt me with a good time." He grins. "There's ice cream just down the block. Interested?"

It's already eleven o'clock, and I have class in the morning, but I'm not ready to go home. Nick has my hand in his as we walk down the block, and his fingers play with the ring on my finger. Sometimes I forget it's even there. I don't know how, considering how big and heavy it is.

"You've been wearing my ring for a week. Made any decisions yet?"

Of course, decisions have been made. They were made by our fathers, but even so, I appreciate what Nick is trying to do.

"Before all of this, I never thought I'd even get married," I admit, avoiding his question. I'm not ready to answer, but I'm also afraid Nick will start to lose his patience with me. So far he's been patient and considerate, but everyone has their limits. My dad already agreed to this, so Nick could whisk me away and marry me whenever he wants. That he's waiting at all is an accommodation he doesn't have to give.

"Really?" Nick looks at me curiously. "You mean you haven't had your wedding day planned out since you were a little girl like most women?"

"I've thought about it, but I figured it would happen in a few years. Or like twenty."

Nick lets out a sharp laugh. "Twenty? I told you I'd wait, but I'm not sure I can wait that long." Our hands fit together perfectly, and he gives mine a tight squeeze. "Not interested in the black tux, white gown thing, or what?"

"More like the relationship kind of thing." I pause. "I've never been very good at that."

"Nobody is good at relationships," Nick says. "We live in a country where half of marriages end in divorce. And that's not even counting failed relationships that don't even make it down the aisle."

"Is that supposed to make me feel better about our marriage?"

"You're right. Horrible choice of words." Nick runs his fingers through his thick hair anxiously. With a step forward, he spins in front of me, taking both of my hands in his. "Ava, I can't tell you I'll be any better at this than you. I'm gonna mess this up. I'll be hard to love, I'll drive you insane most of the time, and I don't like admitting when I'm wrong, but I can tell you we'll figure it out together as it comes. Like I told you, we're a team."

"And what if we don't figure it out?" Nick is so casual about all of this in his attempt to reassure me, but it doesn't change the fact that we're stuck together forever.

"We will." He is adamant. "Divorce won't be an option for us. It would send both of our families into complete turmoil."

Meaning we'll have to suffer through whatever might come.

"Don't you ever get tired of all the pressure?" I bite my lip, letting the weight of his words fall on my shoulders.

"Pressure makes diamonds." Nick flashes me his Hollywood smile and I can't help but return it. "Speaking of diamonds . . ." He lifts my hand to his lips and kisses the back of it.

"I'll marry you."

Nick is surprised that I actually said it, and I'm surprised by how good I feel about it.

"You will?" His face lights up like a little kid's on Christmas. His excitement eases my apprehensions.

I nod, sinking my teeth into my lower lip. Before I know what's happening, his lips crash into mine in a desperate, hungry kiss. He coaxes my lips apart with his tongue, dashing inside of my mouth and sweeping it around. Bricks dig into my back as he pushes me into the wall of the building we were passing, but the little bit of pain is a nice complement to the elation that spreads through the rest of my body. My stomach tingling. My heart racing. My core throbbing with an ache that only he can remedy.

When he pulls away to take a breath, he's still smiling and tugs my hand, nearly jerking me forward. "Come on."

"Nick, where are we going?" I giggle, putting up a bit of a protest.

"Back to my place. Where we can celebrate properly."

"What about the ice cream?" Dessert is the last thing on my mind, but I kind of like playing with him.

"We can order some rocky road takeout if you have your heart set on that, but I can't stand to be out here another second when all I can think about is how good this dress will look on my bedroom floor."

"Rocky road? Ugh, just when things were going so well."

An evil smirk wipes across Nick's face. "Your choice, Ava. You can come with me now or I can rip your dress off you right here and fuck you in that alley."

Is he serious? Why do I feel a little excited about the possibility?

"Is this a bad time to tell you that I'm saving myself for marriage?"

There's a little bit of sinister in his laugh. "Go on, have your fun. You're only digging yourself a bigger hole, my *smoking-hot fiancé.*"

"Nick Caponelli," a gritty voice sneers from only a few feet away. Nick cranes his neck toward the voice, his mood immediately souring.

"What the hell are you doing here, Alek?" Nick snarls in a voice I've never heard before. His tone is paralyzing, as he instinctively moves in front of me and shields me from whoever this man is.

The man smirks, chuckling at Nick with a threatening posture. His chilling eyes rake over me, and I duck back farther behind Nick.

"Aren't you going to introduce me to your smoking-hot fiancé?" Alek steps forward, closing the distance between us, and my eyes fix on the gun-shaped outline of his hip. "I have to say I agree with your assessment of her."

He shoots me a harrowing look.

"Back up, Alek. Before I do it for you." Nick stiffens, his grip on my arm tightening.

"No need to get defensive, Caponelli. I had to come and see it with my own eyes. I heard about the infamous Caponelli-Moretti union, but I didn't think it was true."

"Well, believe it." Nick's stance is wide, like he could launch himself at the guy and beat him senseless at the drop of a hat. I haven't seen this side of him yet, and even though his anger isn't directed at me, it's intimidating.

Alek ignores Nick and turns his attention to me. "Ava, is it?"

"Yes," I say, pressing my lips tightly together and appraising the situation.

"Nice to finally put a face with a name. You know, you're the one they are counting on to bring down the Asnikovs. My family. With this bullshit marriage."

"I don't know what you're talking about."

"Well, of course you don't, darling. Why would a woman know anything about what's going on behind the scenes?" Alek chuckles, taking another step forward.

Nick snakes his arm around my waist again, pulling me painfully close. "I don't know what your endgame here is, Alek, but I suggest you get out of here before you start something you can't finish." Words spew like venom from Nick's mouth.

"Oh, this is far from over, Caponelli." Alek turns his back to us and walks away, but before he disappears, he glances over his shoulder. "I look forward to seeing you again soon, Ava."

When he turns the corner, I find my voice and whisper, "Who was that?"

"No one for you to be concerned about," Nick says, turning me and leading us in the opposite direction.

So much for that team thing, huh?

"Nick?"

He ignores me and continues to walk.

"Nick!" My voice is sharp as I pull my hand away from his.

"What?" he says sharply, the interaction having put him completely on edge.

"Who was that? Why does he know who I am? Why does he know what we're doing?" I cross my arms over my chest defiantly, determined to get my answer.

Nick drags his hand through his hair in frustration. "Damn it, Ava. Do we have to do this tonight? We should be celebrating! We should—"

"You told me you would be straight with me."

He knows I'm right, and he drops his head with a shake. "That's Alek Asnikov. He's the son of a Russian Mafia leader and his family is encroaching on the city, which is a big reason our families are joining."

His honesty takes me by surprise, because it's the first time I've ever been told any information about what was truly going on. It's both strange and refreshing.

"If he's after us, why didn't he do something right now?" I ask, trying to wrap my mind around this new information.

"Because he's a coward, and that's not how this kind of thing works. If he attacked us unprovoked it would start an all-out war, which he certainly doesn't want. He'd have both of our families breathing down his neck, trying to get justice. He's taunting us, so don't let him get to you."

"But why do the Asnikovs even care if we get married? It has nothing to do with them." The whole interaction has me rattled, and I'm not ready to let it go as easily as he is.

"It has everything to do with them, Ava. If our families join, it could be the end for them. And there's no way in hell they go down without a fight."

I've been so focused on what this marriage means for myself that I didn't even consider the ramifications elsewhere. Including how it affects Nick.

Other organizations are bound to be upset, to attack, to converge, to do anything to stop it from happening, and my dad knowingly put me in the cross fire of the brooding Mafia war.

"Ava." Nick sighs and slips his arm around my waist, immediately sensing the heaviness on my mind. "Can we not do this tonight? All of this bullshit will still be here in the morning, so can we just put it out of our minds and enjoy our engagement for one night?"

That seems easier said than done, but I'll give it my best shot. "Sure."

"That's my girl." Nick smiles, swiping his lips across my neck in a rejuvenated kiss. "How about we renegotiate that saving yourself for marriage thing?"

He relaxes a bit, but I can tell that Alek and his family are weighing on his mind too. It's like a cloud looming over us, and even though we both do our best to ignore it, I can't help but feel like a train is barreling down the tracks toward us, and we have no way of stopping it.

THIRTEEN

Ava

The more time Nick and I spend together, the more it feels like we're in a genuine relationship. We've spent nearly every night together since our engagement, but he's been gone since Tuesday on a work trip, and the hours are dragging by. It's amazing how quickly I went from avoiding Nick entirely to missing him when he's not around.

Luckily, I have some distraction today in the form of my sisters, who are all too eager to hear how things are going.

"I don't get it." Bella dangles her toes into the crystal-blue water of the pool. She's on the wall across from me and Angie sits next to her, with my nephew Jax on her lap. "Three weeks ago you never would have even considered something like this."

"It's not like I have much choice, Bells. I'm trying to make the most of it," I defend myself for what feels like the millionth time. She knows exactly how this works, because she's involved in an arranged marriage herself. What does she want from me?

Despite her initial denial, I can tell there's some animosity any time I bring Nick up. Bella is more than content with Savino, who's already showered her with expensive gifts and lavish luxuries, but it's still weird.

"Well, I'm really proud of you." Angie bounces Jax on her lap, and he coos each time Bella flicks a tiny drop of water up at him. "From what it sounds like, you hit the jackpot with Nick. I've never heard of a man from the Mafia letting the woman have any kind of choice once a deal like this was done."

"Right, because you know so much about the Mafia," Bella scoffs. "Although, I will say he's got good taste in jewelry."

She holds up my hand out next to hers, comparing our rings. They're about as different as our personalities—mine, simple and timeless, while Bella's is intricate and busy. "When is the wedding going to be? I hope not before November, because that's when Paul and I are thinking."

"It won't be before then." It's September, and that means November is only a few short months away. I'm in no rush to get to the altar, and Nick and I haven't even talked about setting a date. Even the idea of planning a wedding has me overwhelmed, and I can't imagine how I'll feel when it comes down to making decisions. "Nick wants to plan an engagement party in a few weeks, though, so we can officially celebrate."

"It's cute how excited he is," Angie continues. "Mike wanted nothing to do with any of it after he gave me the ring. I was basically on my own until I met him at the altar."

Bella shoots her a condescending glare. "Ang, you had three wedding planners. I would hardly say you were on your own."

"What is your problem today?" Angie glares back at her. Bella *is* more short-tempered than usual today. As sisters, it should be fun that we're planning weddings at the same time, but it's feeling more and more like a competition.

"It's a little fishy." She shrugs. "Ava screws a guy in a hotel, and two months later, they're engaged to be married, the golden couple that's supposed to save Dad's organization from ruin." She flashes us both a dirty look. "No one finds that odd?"

"We're *both* getting married to help Dad, Bella," I remind her. "And

Nick and I running into each other before was a complete coincidence."

"You're sure quick to trust the guy. What happened to the girl who thought *marriage* was a dirty word?"

My phone rings before I can even respond. Nick's face flashes across the screen, and I'm thankful for the distraction.

"Hey, beautiful, are you at home?"

"I am." I stand up, walking over to one of the patio chairs. "I'm hanging out by the pool with Bella and Angie. What are you up to?"

He doesn't answer for a minute.

"Nick?"

"Sorry," he says with a laugh. "I was distracted by the visual of you in a skimpy bikini. Anyway, I got home sooner than expected and my parents asked us to come over for dinner. What do you think? Are you up for that?"

Spending more time with Nick's family is the next obvious step for us, but the thought is still a little daunting. I'm excited, but weary because this isn't just any family we're talking about. Growing up, the Caponellis were our competition. The enemy. Walking into their house for a friendly meet and greet feels odd.

"Sure," I say, hoping he can't detect the hesitation in my voice.

"Great. I'll pick you up in five."

"Minutes?" I wince. After sitting at the pool all afternoon I'm a sweaty mess, and that's not the way I want to make an impression. A little warning would've been nice.

"Yeah. Will that work?"

Panic surges through me. No, of course, that's not going to work. I need two business days to prepare for something like this. It's my own fault, though, because we've been talking about doing it for a couple of weeks. I guess I thought it was more of a figure of speech. "Sure. You can just wait while I get ready."

"Sounds good. See you soon, babe."

Nick hangs up without another word, and I scramble to gather my things on the patio.

"Who was that?" Bella eyes me suspiciously.

"Nick," I say. "He's coming to pick me up for dinner, so we'll have to continue this discussion another time."

"You better not leave without bringing him out here to meet me," Angie warns. Jax shrieks, as if echoing her demand.

"Yeah, yeah," I call over my shoulder.

Miraculously, in the six minutes that it takes Nick to get here, I change into a blue sundress, brush out my hair, and put on a bit of makeup before grabbing a jacket out of my closest. I'm not thrilled, but it will have to do, because right as I fasten the buckle of my shoe, I hear the doorbell ring.

I hurry down the stairs, because I don't want to take the chance of someone else answering the door. I've had my fill of Bella and Angie for the day, and even though I promised to take him outside, after four days apart, all I want to do is see him.

The moment I open the door, Nick steps forward and closes the distance between us. His kiss crashes into me like a tidal wave, relief and solace washing over me. He snakes his arm around my waist and pulls me deeper into his as his tongue slips between my lips and sweeps through my mouth.

When he pulls away there's a grin on his face. "God, I've missed that."

"I missed you too. How was your trip?"

"Successful, but I've never been happier to be home. Ready to get going?"

I nod, shutting the front door behind me as he leads me down the path into his truck. He opens the door and I hop inside.

Nick

Fuck, Ava is a sight for sore eyes after the week I've had. I wasn't lying when I told her that the trip was successful. It just didn't come easy.

News of our marriage is traveling fast, and organizations are panicking. I had to visit Boston to calm some fears from one of our allies, and it went as well as it could. Understandably, they're uneasy about someone my age taking over for my father. Hell, I'm uneasy about it. I thought I had years left before this happened.

The stress melts away the second she's in my arms, though. Her petite body presses against mine as the sweet smell of her hair consumes me.

"Is this okay?" she asks, twirling around a few steps in front of me.

"You look incredible," I say.

"You're sure? We could go upstairs and you could help me pick something else out if you want," she purrs seductively against my ear, batting those long lashes at me. It makes me so fucking weak when she looks at me that way and I almost take her up on it.

"Ava." I groan. "You and I both know that if we go upstairs we won't make it to dinner." I graze her thigh with my fingers, fiddling with the hem of the dress and lifting it slightly. "I promised my parents that we'd be there, but as soon as we're done there, I'm going to take you back to my place and make up for all the time that we've missed this week. I'm going to peel this dress off you, lay you back in my bed, and make you come so many times that you can't even keep your eyes open."

A furious blush covers her cheeks, and she tilts forward, hips brushing against mine. "Promise?"

"Promise." The only problem with getting Ava riled up is that it has the same effect on me, and I have to adjust myself before I get in the truck.

The drive from the Morettis' to my parents' house is a little over an hour, so she fills me in on everything she's been doing since I've been gone as we drive.

"What should I expect tonight?" She's adorably nervous, fidgeting in her purse to take her mind off it.

"Don't be worried," I tell her, reaching across the console to take her hand. "This is really casual. My family is excited to spend some time with you."

"Will your brothers be there too?" Ava stares out the window.

"Yeah, Leo is making the trip, and Frankie still lives there."

I spend the rest of the drive telling her random little details about my family, and soon I pull off the road toward their house. They are on the opposite side of the water as the Morettis, and there's a stiff ocean breeze in the air tonight.

Ava takes my hand as we walk up to the door, nervously tucking her hair behind her ear.

"Relax," I whisper, brushing a kiss across her cheek. "They're going to love you."

Opening the front door, we step inside. Right away, a heavenly smell wafts from the kitchen.

"Hello?" I say.

"In here!" my mom calls from the kitchen.

I take Ava's jacket and hang it with mine in the hall closet. The kitchen sits at the back of the house and we wind our way toward it. Her eyes wander to the hallway walls cluttered with pictures and photographs that depict my childhood. She smiles, nodding at one of me in a baseball uniform, oversized hat covering my eyes and a bat sitting on my shoulder.

"Okay, that's adorable."

I laugh, clutching her hand in mine. "Give me a break. I had to grow into the jersey."

"And that?" She points to another picture of Leo, Frankie, and me all huddled around the Christmas tree in matching pajamas. "That doesn't exactly scream threatening crime boss."

"Mmm. You're right. Not the best look." I narrow my eyes at her, keeping my voice low. "But if you need something that *screams crime boss* I'd be happy to give you a better idea later tonight."

Ava shivers, darting her eyes away and continuing down the hallway.

When we get to the kitchen, my mom is at the stove, stirring something that smells incredible, while Leo and Frankie are parked on two of the bar stools. Leo's coming from work, still in his jeans and button-down, while Frankie is less presentable. My dad isn't anywhere to be found, but I assume he's in his office, finishing things up. My mom glances back at me, and does a double take when she sees Ava. Grabbing a towel, she wipes her hands and hurries over to us.

"Ava," my mom gushes. "I can't tell you how wonderful it is to meet you properly." She pulls Ava in for a hug and eventually turns to me. "Oh, hi, honey. Nice to see you too."

"Hi, Mom." I chuckle, bending over to give her a hug. She's not all that small, but when you have a husband and three sons who stand more than six foot four tall, you appear that way.

"Ava, these are my brothers, you remember Leo from the party, and this is Frankie."

"It's so nice to meet you guys. Nick has told me so much about you." If Ava is still anxious, she doesn't show it, smiling confidently as she turns to them.

"Everything he said was a lie. Unless, of course, it was good." Leo smirks.

"Definitely good," she says.

"You know Nick has been completely infatuated with you ever since he met you. He's hardly talked about anything else," Leo teases.

"Oh, Leo, give your brother a break," my mom scolds. "I hope you guys are hungry. Ava, Nick mentioned you like pizza, so I pulled out a few of my old recipes. I hope that's okay."

"That sounds perfect. Thank you so much. Is there anything I can do to help?"

My mom glances over her shoulder at me and winks with her approval. "You can cut these up if you want."

She hands Ava some cucumbers, and Ava gets to work while I grab us both a glass of wine and take a seat next to my brothers. After a few minutes, my dad joins us.

"Ava." He grins. "So glad you could join us."

"Hi, Mr. Caponelli."

"How'd everything end up in Boston?" He slaps my back.

"No work talk tonight." My mom glares at us. "Gio, make yourself useful and set the table."

Dinner goes so smoothly that it's almost boring, and I sit back in awe as Ava and my family get to know each other. The way she fits is remarkable, like she's a missing piece we didn't know we had. She picks my mom's brain about different ways to cook the pizza dough, and she and my dad bond over their love for horses. She and my brothers share a few laughs at my expense, but I don't even care, because this is going better than I ever could have anticipated.

Family is big to me, and finding a girl who fits just right has always been a top priority. Ava checks absolutely every box that I've got, and then some, and I can't believe my luck.

Of all the bars she could have gone to that night. Of all the nights I could have been there. It's almost enough to make a man believe in fate.

When we've finished our dessert, Ava and I say our goodbyes so that we can make our drive back into the city.

"It was nice to meet you, Ava. I can't get over how much you look like your brother," Frankie marvels. The blood in my veins turns to ice. The kid has pretty much been mute all evening, and he chooses now to bring up something so contentious?

"Oh." Ava flinches, unsure how to respond. "Nick told me you guys worked with him a bit. We were twins, so I get that a lot."

"He was always a good guy when we were working together. We were so sorry for your loss." Leo quickly jumps in, smoothing things over.

"Thank you." She gives him a tight smile and then turns to my parents. "Thank you for everything tonight. I had a great time, and dinner was delicious."

"Oh, sweetheart," my mom says, "we loved having you. Please come over anytime! With or without Nick."

"Very funny." I smirk, leaning down to kiss her. "I'll call you tomorrow, Mom."

"Drive carefully, okay?"

Ava and I load into the truck, and I can't help but notice her spirit has fallen a little, no doubt thanks to Frankie and his big mouth.

"You okay?" I ask her.

"Mhmm." She nods. "Just tired."

I take my jacket off, wadding it up and offering it to her as a pillow. She leans against it, and soon everything is still and quiet and she's asleep. I rest my hand on her thigh as I drive, happy to be in the moment with her.

I need to have a conversation about Andrew with her soon, but before I do that, I have to talk to Alessandro. Despite his attempts to dodge my calls the last few weeks, it can't wait any longer.

FOURTEEN

Nick

The only thing worse than a last-minute work trip is a last-minute work trip where my dad and future father-in-law accompany me.

Especially now that I've got Ava, these trips are becoming more and more draining. I'd much rather be home with her, but instead, I'm at some dingy Irish pub east of New Jersey.

"To a job well done!" Alessandro holds a glass of scotch up across the table from me, celebrating the success of our first official deal together.

"And to a future of many more," my dad agrees, nodding and clinking his glass against Alessandro's.

I join them in the toast, but I'm ready to get home. It's been a long few days. Ava occupies my every spare thought, and I ache to get my hands on her. With any luck, the last few days apart will be the final catalyst she needs to fully commit. We've hooked up plenty, but she is still holding out on having sex with me.

I don't pretend to understand the hesitation. It's not like it's the first time. But it's important to her, so I've held back, no matter how badly I want to lay her down and pound inside of her until she's dizzy with pleasure. That sinful body tangled up in the sheets—my own this time. Her gentle whimpers and moans in my ear. Those dark curls wrapped around my fist. I've thought about it so many times, but I can't think too hard or I'll get myself in serious trouble.

One more dinner with Alessandro and my father to get through, and then I can see her.

We are on our way home from St. Louis, where we've been meeting with the weapons dealer for the last few days. Finally, we agreed on terms, and hopefully this arrangement will bolster our arsenal enough to be ready for anything the Russians throw at us.

"Eager to get home, Alessandro?" my dad asks, making small talk.

Alessandro chuckles, leaning back in his seat. "Actually, I'm enjoying the quiet. Traveling is like pure bliss for me. I'm telling you, you lucked out having all sons. I love my girls, but they are so much harder than the boys ever were. Guess you'll get a taste of that soon enough, Nick. By the way, how are things going with Ava? She seems to be coming around."

I grimace, feeling oddly defensive of her, even against her own father.

"Things are great with Ava. We've been getting to know each other, and she's incredible."

"Give her time." He chuckles. "She is the most trouble out of all my three. You'll need to keep a close eye on her. Feisty, that one."

The traits that annoy him most about her are the ones that I love so much. Her passion, her sense of adventure, her independence and fight. The one good thing about this trip is that Alessandro can't keep dodging my calls and attempts to meet. It's time we have an overdue conversation.

"I've been meaning to ask you . . . it doesn't seem like she knows the whole story about Andrew. She was surprised that I knew him at all." I finish what's left of my glass. I don't actually like the taste of scotch, but one of the lessons my dad taught me early on is that when you want something from someone, you drink whatever they're having, so you've immediately got common ground.

Alessandro stiffens at the mention of his younger son. It seems like anything to do with Andrew is off-limits in that family, because Ava reacts similarly when he's brought up. Like if you ignore the problem, it will go away.

"She doesn't know the full story. Sonya and I decided it was best to tell the girls as little as possible, so they believe he was killed by a rival gang—end of story."

End of story. I fight the urge to laugh. In typical Alessandro fashion, he left out any other details that pointed blame to him, where it actually lies. "And Vince?"

"Vince?" Alessandro lets out a heavy breath. "He read into the situation and thought Andrew was left unprotected during an ambush. He blames you guys."

Does anyone in that family besides Alessandro know what actually happened? I'm beginning to think they don't.

"After Andrew died, Ava pretty much lost her mind. They've always been so connected, she—" He shakes his head slightly. "It was bad. We went through a period when she was constantly out partying, almost threw her entire education away, and nearly killed herself while she was at it. Vince found her at a party one night on the verge of an overdose, almost comatose in a hot tub with this prick she was dating, and we forced her into a treatment program after that. We decided it was best to let things lie where they were, and I didn't expand with any of my kids."

I suck in a short breath. Ava glossed over her partying and drug use, and I didn't realize how extensive it really was. My heart shattered for her. She was working through the loss of her brother, and Alessandro didn't even have the decency to tell her the truth about how he died. He severely underestimates Ava. The girl I know is strong and courageous, and knowing what happened might've helped her cope instead of sending her into a self-destructive spiral.

None of that matters to Alessandro, though. All he cares about is saving face.

"It's your choice, Nick, but I don't think it's in either of your best interests for her to know that you shot her brother," Alessandro cautions me, effectively ending the conversation. There's obviously nothing else to say, because Alessandro won't ever admit that his son chose to die rather than disappoint him.

He put me in an impossible position. Soon a day will come when she'll know everything. I can only hope we'll be able to work through it.

Ava

Nick promised that we could take things slow, but everything seemed to go into hyperdrive over the last few weeks. A big family dinner where everyone could meet got scheduled, and an engagement party after that. A wedding date set in February, only five short months from now.

In the grand scheme of things, this marriage means more to Nick than it does to me in terms of how much daily life will change. Three months after our marriage he'll take over as Don and have control of both of our families. They will still be separate entities, but he and my father, and even Vince, will have to work together and Nick will have the final say. That's a lot of pressure to be under, and I wonder what that means for me as his wife.

So far, everything has been great. Nick's been nothing but a complete gentleman, and I'm already falling for him. It's the last thing I ever expected from an arranged marriage, but he treats me well, he respects me, and he's actually open and honest with me.

For the last few days he's been away on another job, and I haven't been able to talk to him much. I've been a little stir-crazy, so, despite my better judgment, I let Bella convince me to go out with her tonight to the Jaguar, a club across town. Things between us have been off lately, and I'm desperate to patch them up. Not to mention with Nick gone, I need something to keep my mind busy.

The Jag is one of the few clubs where we can avoid being seen by anyone who knows our dad. It's in Newark and draws more of a local crowd than most clubs in New York City. It's a small, dark place, and probably has about a hundred health violations, but the music is good, the drinks are strong, and their scanner doesn't pick up on fake IDs.

We've been doing this since we were teenagers, and even though we're old enough to be out drinking now, we still choose it most of the time. Maybe it's for nostalgia, because it definitely isn't for convenience. It's a hefty drive, both there and back. Although that means we are less likely to run into anyone who could let our father know what we are up to. Old habits die hard.

The club is packed when we arrive, but we've been here enough over the years to be friendly with the bouncers, and they usher us in right away.

"God, I've missed this," Bella squeals, squeezing my arm as we go in. She's almost giddy, thriving on this type of thing. "You find us a table, and I'll go get some drinks."

She scurries off before I can protest.

Winding through the crowd, I spot a high-top table toward the back. It takes a few minutes, but I finally maneuver my way there. Just as I'm getting situated, a familiar voice comes from behind me.

"Look who decided to grace us with her presence." Jimmy grins, leaning in to give me a peck on the cheek. "It's great to see you, Ava."

A pit forms in my stomach. I'm trying to be on my best behavior tonight, and I certainly haven't had enough alcohol to equip myself for seeing my cheating ex-boyfriend.

"Hi, Jimmy." I smile uncomfortably. It's been a long time since

Jimmy and I have had a normal conversation, and it's going to take some getting used to.

"You look well." He takes my hand in his, studying the diamond on my finger and arching an eyebrow. "The rumors are true?"

"They are. I'm getting married."

"Good for you, Avs. And to a Caponelli no less. Which one? Frankie? Leo?" He slides into a chair at the table, inviting himself to join me as I glance desperately over my shoulder, looking for my sister. What is taking so long?

"Nick, actually." I shift, putting as much space between us as possible.

Jimmy is shocked. "The heir himself, huh? You're practically Caponelli royalty now."

"I don't know about that." I laugh nervously, holding my hands together. "I didn't have much say in the matter, anyway."

"Oh, don't let her fool you." Bella smirks, setting four sloshing drinks down on the table. "She's hopelessly in love with the guy."

"Hey, Bella. It's good to see the two of you out again. It's been a while," Jimmy says.

Bella seems to fall right away for his charming smile, the one that only repulses me now.

"Tell me about it." Bella rolls her eyes. "Ava gets engaged and it's like she turns into some kind of saint or something. No more drinking, no more partying."

"That must make Cap happy." Jimmy eyes me carefully.

I feel the need to defend myself, but I don't, opting for a large sip of my drink instead. I'm going to need this, and probably many more, to get through the night.

Bella and I dance for a while, and then I am finally able to drag her back to the table. I've managed to only have two drinks, keeping myself in check, but I can't say the same for Bella. She's on number four and starting to blur the line between tipsy and drunk. Tipsy Bella is a good time. Drunk Bella is an instigator, and I can already tell things are about to go south.

"Hey, Jimmy." She waves him back over to our table. "You got anything to lighten my sister up?"

"I've got the perfect thing." Jimmy's eager to oblige, pulling out a small, clear bag from his pocket and setting it on the table.

Just looking at the white powder burns my veins. It's been months since I've done cocaine. I hate what it does to me, the downward spiral it brings me to. I'm not going to risk that now.

"No, thanks." I slide it back to him.

"Of course not." Jimmy smirks. "Caponelli wouldn't approve of that, now, would he? You already think you're too good for us now that you're joining them."

"It's not about that. I just—" I shift in my seat.

"Come on, Avs!" Bella begs. "A little won't hurt anything! You know how good it makes you feel."

I swallow, trying to find my strength. I hate that she's right. When I was high I felt like I was flying. All my problems disappeared and I was light, drifting in a sort of alternate universe. I used to crave it worse than just about anything, and as much as I hate to admit it, it sounds good right now.

If I only have a little, what harm can come from that? I've stopped before on my own. I can do it again. One taste won't really hurt anything, will it?

Yes, it will, Ava. It'll ruin everything. You're stronger than this.

"You know you want to, Ava. Don't be so pretentious. One more time, for old time's sake." Jimmy's voice is enticing as he slides the packet toward me again.

I could do this. I could have one taste and be content. I deserve to let loose and have a good time with Bella and our friends tonight. I'm about to give my life away to the Mafia. Why not celebrate a little?

Because it's more than that, and you know it.

The nagging voice in my head is usually quiet, but it's loud and merciless tonight. I slowly open the baggie, slipping my finger into the silky white powder. If I press it into my gums it'll absorb quickly and the high won't even be that strong. No one will guess.

"That's it," Jimmy coaxes.

There's a commotion on the dance floor, which makes me pause long enough to get a hold of myself. What the hell am I doing? "No, I don't want it. Thank you."

Cool relief floods through me.

"If you're going to be such a wimp then give it to me." Bella lays out a line in front of her and then snorts the white powder.

The drug gives Bella a shock of energy that she doesn't need, and we continue to dance and party with Jimmy. The more I drink, the more I loosen up, but I still feel uncomfortable here, and to combat that feeling, I have quite a bit more. I finally start to enjoy myself, and before I know it, it's two in the morning.

I leave Bella and her group of friends briefly to go get a few more shots, and head for the bar.

There's a man leaning against the high-top, nursing a crystal glass of whiskey. He's tall and intimidating, and his eyes are trained on me. It's dark in here, but the closer I get, the more I recognize the man as Nick.

"Hi!" Surprised to see him here of all places, I throw my arms around his rigid neck and plant a sloppy, alcohol-induced kiss on his cheek. "I missed you. What are you doing here?"

He doesn't answer immediately, so I take his hand, ready to lead him back to the group. "Let's go get a drink, and you can tell me about your trip."

Nick's grip on my hand tightens, and he yanks me back rougher than I expect.

"What are you—"

He cuts me off with a ferocious glare, and for the first time I realize that he's angry. "I think you've had plenty." His jaw is set, nostrils flaring as anger pulsates off him.

My pulse quickens, and in my state, I can't tell if he looks more terrifying or sexy when he's angry. I don't say that out loud, though, because I doubt he'll find it amusing.

"Come on." Nick plows through the crowd and to the front door at a punishing pace. I look over my shoulder but don't even have time to say goodbye to Bella, who is still totally oblivious on the dance floor.

"Would you slow down? You're hurting me." Technically, it's the shoes that are hurting me, but his near sprint isn't helping the matter.

Once we're outside, several people around us stare at the scene we're making.

"Have you completely lost your mind? Has this been going on the entire time I've been gone?" Nick growls.

"No!" I defend myself, hot tears welling up in my eyes. "Bella begged me to come with her, and I thought one night wouldn't hurt anything. I haven't had that much to drink, really."

"I watched you take seven shots in the last thirty minutes."

My stomach turns, wondering just how much he'd seen.

"I'm sorry." Tears stream down my face, the reality of what I've done catching up to me. I've backed myself into a corner, and there doesn't seem to be a way out. "I just wanted to have a little fun."

"Ava." He sighs exasperatedly. "I didn't tell you to stop partying because I didn't want you to have fun. I did it because I'm concerned about your safety, especially when I'm not with you. What if you stumbled into another guy tonight? Or Alek? God knows what would've happened."

"It was stupid," I continue, the weight of my guilt feeling like a ton of bricks on my shoulders. It was all stupid, and I never should've been here.

"This is a terrible part of town. Now that we're getting married, it's even more dangerous for you. This place is a shithole, and this is exactly the neighborhood that Alek Asnikov moved into. Not to mention the fact that you completely disregarded what I said. I thought we had an understanding of what would happen if you used again." His tone holds an ominous threat.

I've never been scared of Nick, and, despite his vow to never hurt me, that's exactly how I feel right now. I know what I'd have coming if my dad was the one to find me, but I have no idea what to expect with Nick.

"I didn't. It was only a few drinks." He's not interested in more excuses and doesn't respond. "Nick, I'm sorry."

Knowing that he's upset is a terrible feeling. It's the complete opposite of how I used to feel with my dad. I liked to see how far I could push him, but with Nick, the idea of him being even slightly upset with me is heart-wrenching. I wipe the remaining tears off my cheeks.

"Apologizing doesn't change what happened tonight." He takes my hand, leading me to his truck. The disappointment and anger in his voice sober me up at record speed.

"Where are you taking me?"

"I can't exactly take you home to your father like this." He scratches his stubbled chin. "I have a guest room at my place. You can sleep in my bed, and I'll stay in there."

I grimace. We've been apart for days. "You don't want to—"

"No," he snaps quickly, opening the truck door for me. "This is not exactly how I want to remember the first night I wake up to you in my bed."

As if I could hate myself even more than I already do.

"What about Bella? We came here together."

"I called Paul when I saw the two of you. He'll take care of her." Nick slams the door and goes around to the other side. I jump at the noise.

Forget everything I said earlier—angry Nick is terrifying.

FIFTEEN

Ava

I've been to Nick's penthouse a few times before, but it still feels foreign to me, almost like a museum. Everything has its place and the floors are so clean you could probably eat off them. Someday it will be my home, but right now, I feel like a guest.

Nick grunts when we get inside, grabbing my hand and leading me down the hallway. He's still pissed off and hardly said two words to me on the way home. As the alcohol wears off, all my emotions seem to converge at once.

He's got every right to be upset. We'd talked about this before, and I still let myself get out of control. I know my limits better than most people, and if I'm not careful with them, I could wind up exactly where I was a few months ago, or worse. Alcohol is a gateway for me, and sure, I've been strong enough to deny the drugs tonight, but I don't know if that will always be the case.

Tonight I disregarded all of Nick's concerns, and I deserve his anger. I'm upset enough with myself, and coupling that with the fact this is the first time Nick's been upset with me, the guilt is suffocating.

"You can sleep in here." He opens the door to his bedroom, letting go of my hand. He rummages through his drawers, a harsh glare still painted on his face as he tosses a T-shirt to me.

"Nick, please," I beg. The silence between us is torture. Seeing how disappointed and angry he is breaks my heart.

"Ava, you're too drunk and emotional right now, and I'm way too fucking pissed off. We'll talk about it in the morning."

In a moment of reprieve, Nick walks over to me, setting his hands on my shoulders as he presses a kiss to my forehead. "I'm glad you're safe. Sleep well."

I muster a weak smile, irritated with both myself and the situation. Nick shuts the door quietly behind him, and I can hear him moving around in the living room for a little while before another door closes and it's silent.

Slipping off the stupid skintight dress, I don't even bother to fold it, and toss it in a heap on the side. It reeks of cigars, smoke, and alcohol, and all the bad decisions I've made tonight. Nick's bed feels like a cloud as I climb into it, but it's also cold and lonely. I hate that he's sleeping in the guest room in his own home, and that I put us in this position. I lie awake for hours, rehashing the evening in my mind.

There's a part of me that is angry with him for being so upset and controlling. He's spent so much time telling me how different he is from my father, but tonight it didn't feel that way.

The worst part of everything, though, is that I know he's right. I put myself in a bad situation with Jimmy, and even with Bella, because of my history. When I lost my brother it sent me into a complete tailspin, and I found myself in more than a few rehab centers. Nothing worked until my dad pretty much scared me straight.

When a Mafia father is angry, it triggers a whole different level of fear. He figured out his normal tactics of screaming and beating me weren't working, so he resorted to something even worse. He threatened to throw me in a cell for a month until everything was out of my system and I could appreciate the life he and my mother had given me. The way he paraded me around down there, making sure I was clear how serious he was, still gives me nightmares.

All it made me do was resent him, and I pushed back. It wasn't until I overdosed that I realized how serious it was. I fought endlessly to get clean for myself, and I'm so proud of what I've accomplished. Tonight I came dangerously close to jeopardizing that.

I groan. Yeah, there's no chance I'm getting any sleep tonight.

It isn't just me I have to worry about now, and even though Nick may have overreacted, he's trying to protect me. For most of my life Andrew was the one who protected me, and when he died I got used to doing it myself, and not relying on anyone. Letting Nick take care of me the way he wants is going to take some getting used to.

When I can't take it anymore, I throw the covers off. I don't care if he doesn't want to talk about it—I do.

I pad down the hallway to what I presume is the guest room, and see a soft light peeking out from under the door even though he went to bed hours ago.

I open the door softly and I'm surprised to see Nick sitting up in the bed, completely awake, with his laptop on his lap. When he looks up, there's still a frown on his face, but he's got a softness in his eyes that he didn't before.

"You're awake." I stutter over the words.

"So are you," Nick says flatly, staring at me as if he expects me to make the first move.

"I couldn't sleep."

Nick shifts a bit on the bed and sets his laptop to the side. "Neither could I."

His expression is unreadable, but he pats a spot next to him on the bed for me to join him. Before he can change his mind, I hurry to sit down next to him and we're quiet for a few minutes.

"I'm sorry," we both finally say at the same time.

Nick smiles, reaching for my hand. "I overreacted. I've known Jimmy as a dealer for a long time, and when I saw you together tonight, it all came together for me. He was the boyfriend, wasn't he?"

I nod.

"I figured as much." Nick frowns. "Seeing you with him threw me into a jealous rage, even before I saw how much you were drinking, and it made me break the promise I made to you about never hurting you or treating you the way your father does. I didn't like what you were doing, but I should've handled it better, and in the future, I will. You have my word."

It's hard to believe a guy like Nick really even exists. He's amazing, and it makes me even more upset to have hurt him.

"Thank you for saying that, but I'm the one who needs to apologize. Nights like tonight are exactly what got me in so much trouble, and I don't want to go down that road again. I'm used to doing this on my own, you know? I don't trust people easily, and have a really terrible habit of pushing even harder when someone tries to control me. I know you're not like my dad. You're nothing like him. But that's all I'm used to, so it's going to take a little time for me to adjust."

Nick puts his arm around me, pulling me closer to him. I nestle in beside him and lay my head on his chest. God, this feels good. "I'll give you all the time you need. As long as you promise to give me some time to adjust too. I'm used to giving orders and people bending over backward to follow them. I don't want that to be a relationship."

"Neither do I," I agree.

"Good." Nick kisses the top of my head.

"Does this mean you're not mad at me anymore?"

Nick chuckles. "I wasn't as mad as I was disappointed. You have to understand that as my fiancé, and eventually my wife, your safety and well-being are my top concern, and tonight you took both for granted. I need to know that you're going to take care of yourself and not put yourself in dangerous situations when I'm not around. I mean Jesus Christ, Ava, Jimmy Bradford? The guy is a walking danger zone. Especially when he was your supplier and you're recovering from drug addiction."

"I get it." The seriousness in Nick's tone sends a fiery burn to my cheeks, as if he's reprimanding me. It isn't condescending, but much sharper than his usual banter.

"Do you?" He turns to me suddenly. "Ava, I know you're an adult and you're going to make your own choices, but you have to consider there are bigger things at play. I'm not just talking about you partying. When you put yourself in a situation like that, you're vulnerable to all kinds of attacks. We have enemies on both sides, and I would rather die than see you hurt."

"I'm sorry."

"You don't need to say you're sorry anymore. You need to see it from my perspective. I'm not trying to control you, but I'll do whatever I have to do to keep you safe."

Nick's arm around my shoulders comforts me in a way I didn't know I needed. No one's ever shown their concern or worry for me the way he does, and it blows me away. "How did I end up with a guy like you?"

A wicked grin spreads across his mouth. "Let me refresh your memory a bit."

Nick slips his T-shirt over my head and a hand around my neck, pulling me into him with a rough, insistent kiss. My lips part, and his tongue forges though, a cool minty taste on his breath. As he scours my mouth, a rush runs through me that lights up every inch of my body, from the tips of my toes to the top of my head. It's dominating and possessive, and as his teeth pull at my bottom lip, it conjures memories from our first night together that leave me so desperate for him I can hardly stand it.

"Mmm." A groan rumbles in the back of his throat when he comes up for air. "It's been too long since I've tasted you."

In one smooth motion, he lays me back on the bed, arms on either side of my shoulders as he hovers above me. Without the cover of his shirt, the only thing I have on is the skimpy thong I'd worn under my dress, and Nick makes quick work of inching it down my legs until I'm completely naked underneath him. He looks at me like he's about to devour me, ravage my body and soul, and I want nothing else. The feral glint in his eye makes my heart skip. He's unstable in the very best of ways.

Somehow, even though I am lying beneath him, completely vulnerable and exposed, I've never felt safer.

His eyes trace every inch of me, thirsty and eager.

"So perfect, Ava," he whispers.

As I let my head fall to the side, he strings a row of frenzied, hungry kisses along my neckline. He moves mercilessly, not leaving an inch of my skin untouched as he works his way down my body. Down my neck, along my chest, over the swell of my breasts. My nipple hardens as his tongue flicks across, followed by his teeth a second later.

I gasp. The mix of pleasure and pain is enough to unravel me right there, and he knows it.

"Nick . . ." I moan, arching my back as his kisses reach my inner thigh. My need for him is insatiable, and as good as this feels, I need his skin against mine. We've been playing around for weeks, and I'm not interested in that tonight.

Grabbing the hem of his shirt, I slide it up over his head and expose his chest. My breath hitches as I run my fingers down his strong, rippled skin, tracing the sharp lines of his muscles. I stop short at the band of his boxer briefs.

"Ava." Nick grabs my fingers, stopping me from pulling them down as a husky smile plays on his lips. "If we keep going, I'm not gonna be able to stop myself."

I run my tongue along my upper lip, unable to turn my eyes from his piercing stare. "That's what I'm counting on."

Without another word, Nick lifts my body effortlessly and repositions me underneath him. "I wanted this to be more romantic." He breathes against my ear, fumbling with his underwear. "But I've got to fucking have you."

His words only amp me up even more. He wants this as much as I do, and it can't happen fast enough. Usually, I like the foreplay, but tonight is a completely different story.

He works meticulously, kissing every part of me, and slowing only to pay special attention to my inner thighs, because he knows how much I love it. As his teeth drag across the sensitive skin, a soft whimper escapes my lips, and Nick leans back with a telling smirk.

He swipes a finger through my slick folds, and I gasp. The feel of his fingers between my legs is intoxicating, even better than I remember.

"You're already so wet, baby." A look of satisfaction spreads across his face as he slides a finger inside. Then another. Then another.

Wet is an understatement. I'm soaking. Dripping. Flooding. And the man has barely touched me. It's almost unfair how well he knows my body and how he can get the response he wants.

He pumps his fingers faster and faster, alternating between rough and tender strokes, and each one drives me wild in a completely different way. His touch is like fire, burning with a feverish heat and leaving cool devastation in its wake. It's like I'm starved for it. Desperate. Desolate.

"Nick, please." His name rolls off my lips in a needy beg. I won't be able to take much more without exploding.

"Not yet." He pulls his fingers away abruptly, leaving me empty and breathless. "Let me see you."

He edges my knees apart, hands traveling over every inch of my bare skin, and never once taking his eyes off me. The look in them is almost animalistic. It's raw. Untamed.

Like making love to me is the most natural thing in the world.

With my knees spread, he brushes a teasing finger across my clit, eyes locked on me as desire winds up through my core and radiates across my entire body. There isn't an atom of my being that doesn't want him.

"Do you have any idea how long I've been waiting for this? How long I've dreamed about seeing this perfect body again? That dark hair splayed out against my pillow, those perky tits bouncing in front of me, my fingers buried deep inside of you?"

His words make my mouth water, and he looks at me like he worships me.

"Every time I saw you. Every time you tempted me, teased me, left me hanging, I thought about what it would be like to be inside of you again. I thought about your legs wrapping around my waist, your nails digging into my back, the sound of your voice screaming my name so loud that the entire fucking city knows who you belong to."

"Mmm." Do I even know how to speak? I can't remember.

"I thought about touching you here." He plants a rough kiss on my neck. "And here." Another one between my breasts. "And here." One at my panty line. He glances up with a grin. "And here."

He dives, and I gasp when I feel his tongue against my throbbing flesh. *Oh my god.*

I cry out, my fingers pulling at his hair. It's so damn good. Almost too good, and I squirm, but he holds me firmly in place and continues to lick and suck.

Nick's magic touch robs me of my most basic faculties. I can't think. Can't speak. I can't even breathe without forcing myself. Why the hell did I deprive myself of this for so long?

Thankfully, when Nick comes back up, he's ready for release. His erection is at full attention as he rips into a condom and slides it on.

"What did you think about, Ava? All those nights that you lay in bed by yourself, did you think about me touching you? Did you picture me throwing you back against the bed, pinning your arms above your head and ramming my thick cock into that tight little pussy?"

I whimper again, so ready for him that I might combust if he doesn't give in soon.

"Be a good girl and beg me for it, Ava. Show me how much you want me." That gravelly tone makes my core pulse, and when he calls me "good girl," I'm all but a puddle.

"Please, Nick . . ." My voice comes out like a violent whine.

With his hands on either side of me, I'm pinned to the bed, and he leans down, pressing himself into me—slow and gentle at first, and then steadily, until he's fully inside.

I close my eyes, letting pleasure wash through me, as I feel the fullness of him inside of me. My body tightens around him as he strokes my cheek, moving his hips back and forth against mine. "Keep your eyes on me, baby. I want to see you."

I flutter of them open, locking on his gaze.

"There's my girl." He moves quicker, the friction building between us. Over and over again, he thrusts into me. Each plunge is harder and deeper than the last as I hook my legs around his waist and draw him in farther. Nick tilts, bracing me with his strong hands, pounding into me with a delirious fury. There's nothing soft or gentle about him tonight, and it's exactly what I need.

"Jesus, this is good, Ava. So damn good," he says. "Ah, I've fucking missed you."

It's better than good. It's explosive. It's relentless. It's straight up domination. At the very edge of climax, I claw his back. My mind clouds, and all I can think about is his body wrapped around mine.

Weeks of pent-up frustration. Weeks of denying him. Weeks of trying to convince myself I didn't want this. It all comes to a head as his body rocks into mine in a merciless, punishing rhythm.

"Nick," I call out, reaching the point of not being able to stand it anymore.

"Mmm . . . fuck!"

Nick latches on to me as his orgasm hits, our bodies simultaneously riding that sweet release. A few breathless seconds pass before we fall away from each other against the bed. When he reaches for my hand, I am still so high that I can't even make sense of which way is up, and we lie tangled together.

"You okay?" he asks, brushing his thumb across my chin. "Was that too much?"

I shake my head. "It was incredible, Nick."

He grins, settling into me. "I hope you don't take this the wrong way, but I've had a lot of sex."

I let out a sharp laugh.

"But nothing, no one, has ever compared to you. You're perfect, Ava."

I'm not sure how long we lie there before we both drift off to sleep, but being in his arms, it's the best sleep I've gotten in years.

SIXTEEN

Nick

As it turns out, planning a wedding and getting ready to take over two different criminal organizations is a little time-consuming. Ava and I only go without seeing each other a few days at most, but I miss her like it's been weeks. Not to mention, dropping her off at the Moretti house after each date feels excruciating. Why she isn't living with me yet is beyond me, but as soon as she's ready, I want her with me full-time.

Over the last several weeks my father has trained me for when I take over once the marriage is official. Until now, I never fully comprehended all that he handles, even just within our family. After the wedding, the pressure and responsibility will both double.

First on my list of jobs is figuring out a way to deal with the Asnikovs that will send the right message to our enemies. Since word of our merger has gotten out, this will be my first opportunity to show the Mafia world the type of leader I'm going to be, and it can't be taken lightly. With all that we have going on, I'm certainly feeling the pressure.

When I pull into the warehouse and see my dad's car parked outside, I'm a little concerned. He rarely ventures out here unless it's a special circumstance, and my mind immediately goes to the worst. Hurrying inside, I make my way to the upstairs office. He's already in there with Leo, Zane, and another one of the council members, Russell. At least they're all smiling and laughing. That's a good sign, but I'm still a little uneasy.

"Hey," I say, shutting the door tightly behind me. "Everything okay?"

"For now, yes." Zane rubs his forehead. "But we've got a little problem."

"What kind of problem?" I raise an eyebrow, tossing my bag into the corner. This is about the last way I want to start my day.

"The kind that smokes cheap cigars and has a shitty accent." Leo smirks confidently.

My dad rolls his eyes. "As your brother so eloquently put it, Asnikov is making moves. One of our clients out of Miami called me this morning to cancel a shipment. Apparently, he's getting the same caliber of guns, but cheaper, from Alek."

"You're serious? How?"

"We aren't sure," my dad spews. He's not used to having a problem you can't solve, and this one keeps popping up. "But they need to be dealt with before we lose any more customers."

"The timing of this is too coincidental. It's got to be about the announcement of the engagement."

"That's what I'm thinking too," my dad agrees. "But we can't expect it to end here. They're only toying with us now, but who knows when it could escalate."

"Does Ava need protection?" The thought of her in any kind of danger debilitates me.

"She's not in any danger right now. No sense in worrying her over nothing," my dad assures me.

"What do we need to do, then?" I fold my arms over my chest. I have a hunch where this is headed, and I don't like it.

"They had a guy named Vic seal the deal. He needs to be eliminated." Leo doesn't mince words, and he's right. I hate that he's right, mostly because it's my job to make sure it happens. While executioner is only my role in the organization for the time being, it wears on me.

Andrew was the first person I ever shot, and maybe that's why each kill is hard for me. I always think about him whenever I carry out a hit. I think about our friendship, and how badly his family was hurt, and because of that, it gets harder and harder for me to separate.

My father used to say I had too much of a heart to be in the Mafia, and for a long time I tried to prove him wrong. I hid how I feel about killing so that no one knew how much it bothered me. I dealt with it at night on my own, where only God could see.

Something feels different this time, though. Maybe it's the responsibility I feel about taking over the group, or maybe it's that I finally have someone else I care about that I need to protect. Suddenly, I'm hyperaware of the cool metal pressing into my back, where my gun is tucked into my pants, and I've got an itch to use it. Where Ava is concerned, I'll stop at nothing to make sure she's safe.

"Nick, I know that you don't particularly like—" my father begins to reason with me.

"I'll do it." I cut him off sharply. "But it's the last time."

Everyone else looks at me in surprise, but my father gives me a knowing nod. My compliance comes from a place of concern for my future family.

For my fiancé.

"Quick and quiet," Russell instructs. "They have a safe house that he's holed up in, but he goes outside every day at five for a smoke. If you go now, you should be able to catch him."

"I'm supposed to meet Ava at the restaurant at six."

Leo nods. "I'll be there. I'll let her know you're running a little late."

"And it might be time to consider moving the wedding up, Nick. With the added pressure, the Russians might move along quicker than we expected," my father cautions me.

I want to laugh. Yeah, Ava's going to be a hard sell on that. We barely got a date set, and things are progressing well. I promised her we would take it slow, and I have every intention of keeping that promise, so I won't let a mosquito like Alek get in the way of that. "Let's take care of this first and see where we are."

"Let me know when it's done." My dad nods and he and Russell head out the door. Leo and Zane soon follow, leaving me to prepare for the hit alone.

I need to get in the right headspace, and normally I can't do that in the company of others. I have to separate myself from the man behind the gun, almost as if it's a character I'm playing.

Ava

I've been sitting at the bar waiting for Nick for almost thirty minutes now, and I'm getting frustrated. Leo let me know Nick was going to be late, and even kept me company for a while, but eventually he had to get back to work. Turns out he and Nick own this restaurant—the same one I came to with Rob the night that we met for the first time.

Not wanting to make the drive home first, I came here right after class this afternoon, so I was already exceptionally early, and I've been doing my best to occupy myself.

I know Nick is busy, but he was supposed to take tonight off. That was the point of meeting here for a date. We haven't seen each other for a few days and tonight was supposed to be only about us. Instead, I'm sitting here nursing my second drink a half an hour after we were supposed to meet. Just as I'm about to leave, I see him weaving through the crowd.

"Is this seat taken?" He flashes me a reserved smile as he appears next to me. As much as he tries to hide it, I can tell something is off.

"By all means." I smile, gesturing to the chair. "I'm waiting for my fiancé."

Nick sits and waves down the bartender, who places a glass in front of him without even taking an order. "Lucky guy, your fiancé." He shoots me a devilish wink.

"He is." I trace the top of my wineglass with my finger, keeping my eyes low. "But he's late."

Nick cringes, downing the whiskey in his glass and pushing the glass toward the edge of the bar for a refill. There's a bite to his voice, but I don't think it's directed at me. "I bet he's sorry."

"He better be," I say.

He's flustered in a way I've never seen before, and it catches me off guard.

"He is," Nick agrees, leaning forward to give me a harsh kiss. It's been too long since I felt his lips against mine. "How was your day?"

"It was good. I had lunch with Bella. She and Paul officially set a date. November tenth. Which will be interesting since Sophia is due the week before that." I sip my Chardonnay. "How was your day?"

"Nothing unusual." He can't hide the distance in his voice. I get the feeling that something happened at work today, but he doesn't seem like he wants to talk about it, and so I don't push him.

Nick turns to me, putting his arm around the back of my chair, leaning in so his lips are only a few inches from my ear. "I was planning on having a nice dinner here with you, but seeing you in that dress, all I can think about is getting you back to my place. What do you say?"

I try to mask the fire inside of me that his voice ignites. Honestly, that's what's on my mind, too, but I want to make him work for it a bit after leaving me waiting so long. "I'm hungry." I twist a piece of hair between my fingers.

"Oh, I'll give you something to eat." He smirks, settling his hand on my thigh.

"You are awful."

Nick slaps a fifty-dollar bill down on the bar to cover our drinks. I follow him out of the restaurant, and he waves at Leo on our way out. Leo seems confused as to why we're leaving, but Nick doesn't notice.

He drives quickly and whips his truck into the garage of his building even quicker. The entire elevator ride to the penthouse he can't keep his hands to himself, like a rabid animal. It's not his usual gentle touch, but aggressive. Urgent.

When we get into the apartment, he doesn't waste a single second before hoisting me up on the kitchen island and ripping my dress over my head. He stands between my legs, burying his face in my chest with harsh, desperate kisses.

"Nick." I pull away slightly. "Take a breath."

"I need you, Ava," he growls, his voice cracking with emotion.

He strokes his hands up and down my inner thighs, not taking his eyes off my chest. It looks like he's holding back tears. I've never seen him like this before, so detached and unhinged, almost like he's out of control, and it's scaring me a little.

"Hey." I put my hands on both of his cheeks, forcing him to meet my eyes. "Are you okay?"

"I'm fine." He shakes his head, snapping himself out of his daze. "It was . . . Fuck, I had a bad day at work, and the only thing that got me through it was the thought of seeing you tonight."

Part of me is screaming to ask him what had been so bad, but the other part knows it's probably difficult for him to talk about. He seems in such disarray, a stark contrast to his usual calm and collected personality.

"I'm sorry I ruined dinner." He shakes his head in frustration.

"Nick, you didn't ruin anything. I'm just worried about you. You seem—" I'm not even sure how to finish that sentence. Stressed? Lost? Scary?

"I killed someone today," he says flatly, staring back at me, his face a picture of confliction.

The directness catches me off guard. I press my lips together tightly, not trusting what might come out of them. It's not the first time, but it's different to hear the words out loud. Nick killed someone. *My* Nick. My future husband.

My brain wants me to hightail it right out of here, but my heart sees the amount of pain he's in. I can't bring myself to leave him, no matter how logical it is. I can't run from this, run from him. He needs me to tell him it's okay, that he did what he had to do, that I understand. He needs me to make some kind of sense of it, to talk him off the ledge and make the world seem right again.

This is ripping him apart, and in a sense, that's comforting to me.

He doesn't like to kill. It pains him. It hurts him. It makes him crazy.

That's so different from what I'm used to. All the men I grew up around had no problem killing. Sometimes they even did it for sport. If anything, this is only further proof that Nick is different. He stares back at me expectantly, but the right words won't come. Instead, I reach forward and pull him closer to me. He's hesitant at first, but then he gives in and comes willingly. Wrapping my arms around his neck, I pepper it with kisses, running my tongue along his tender skin slowly.

"What are you doing?"

"Let me help you," I whisper, running my fingertips across his forearm.

"Ava, you don't need to do this. You should be repulsed by me."

"You're a good man, Nick. What happened today doesn't define you, and it doesn't change how I feel about you. It's your job," I continue. "You're frustrated. Why don't you take some of that out on me?"

Our body language will help when words fail me. I can't make this okay or any better for him, but I can show him that I'm not going anywhere and that I understand. Oh, how I understand. I've never had to kill anyone, but I've been forced to do so many things in this life that I didn't want to do because that was the nature of the Mafia.

A genuine smile spreads across Nick's lips, and he leans forward until our foreheads touch. "You're way too good for this world, you know that?"

SEVENTEEN

Ava

Wind rips through campus as I hurry from my class to meet Nick across the street at the burger place for lunch. My morning had been nearly unbearable as I sat through Law and Ethics, almost falling asleep to the sound of my professor's voice, so when Nick asked if I wanted to meet for lunch, I welcomed the distraction.

"You know, I'm starting to think you're avoiding me." The voice behind me turns my blood to ice.

Jimmy.

"Hi, Jimmy." I put on my bravest face and turn around. "Not avoiding you. I've just been busy."

That's a lie. I've been avoiding him like the plague since Bella and I ran into him at the club, but seeing him on the street corner is about the last thing I expect. I know Jimmy enough to know that he's bad news, and I know myself well enough to know that he can find a way to break me down eventually. But even talking to him is dangerous—Nick's no fool and he won't tolerate me having anything to do with Jimmy.

The burning in my veins is a painful reminder. I want nothing to do with him anymore, but he knows my weaknesses, and he knows exactly how to play them against me to keep me drawn in, exactly where he wants me. That was his intention the other night. He knew one taste would pull me back in and have me craving the high for days. But I'm stronger now than I was before, and I won't fall back into my old habits. Jimmy is like an angry wasp, though. The more you slap it away, the more intent it becomes on attacking you.

"I've heard getting married will do that to you." Jimmy smirks. "Caponelli was pretty pissed when he found you in the club the other night. Not exactly his style?"

When I don't answer, he continues. "I never expected you to let him make all your decisions for you." Jimmy scowls, reaching into his pocket and flashing a little white bag of white powder.

My throat dries at the sight. "Jimmy, I can't. I told you the other night, I don't want it. Take your blow and stay away from me. I'm staying clean."

"Clean? You and I both know you won't be able to stay that way long. It makes you feel too good. Makes all that stress disappear." Jimmy's ruthless. "Wonder what your new fiancé will think about that habit of yours."

I never want Nick to find out how bad everything got. It seems like a lifetime ago, like I'm not even that person anymore. I've worked too hard to get myself to a good place to let Jimmy jeopardize that.

"Anyway, you can relax. Getting you high isn't the reason I'm here." I know better than to ever relax around him. At even the slightest sight of my guard coming down, he'll pounce. "I have a business proposition for you."

"What sort of business proposition?"

"My father is looking for an intern at his law firm. He heard you were looking for a position for next semester, and he's got space."

Cautiously, I take the card that he offers. I *do* need an internship, and an offer is exciting, but Jimmy never does anything without some kind of ulterior motive.

"Look, you're in a rush. Call him and find out the details. It could be good for you." Jimmy sounds somewhat sincere. He reaches into a pocket again and pulls out the little baggie and presses it into my palm. "Just in case."

"Jimmy, wait! I don't want this!"

He ignores me, picking up his pace and disappearing around the corner. I consider dropping the bag, but I'm in public and could get in all kinds of trouble for even having it. Slipping into my pocket, I vow to flush it down the toilet the second I can.

Now I'm running late, so I jog across the street. My interaction with Jimmy has me completely flustered, and I can only hope that Nick doesn't pick up on it.

When I walk into the restaurant, Nick is already sitting at the table with Zane and Leo. I bite back my disappointment that they're joining us. I love them both, but between my school schedule and Nick working so much, we barely have any time for the two of us.

Nick's face lights up when he sees me, immediately washing away the irritation that built inside of me from my interaction with Jimmy. Just being in his presence is calming. Making my way to the table, I slip into the open seat. Nick leans across it and kisses me.

"Hey, baby."

"Sorry I'm running so late. I got stuck with a professor." The lie is off my lips before I can stop it, and it makes my stomach twist.

"No problem. We haven't been here long." Nick's hand finds a resting spot on my leg underneath the table.

Zane scoffs. "You're the first person in the world that I've ever seen Nick tolerate being late."

He and Leo share a laugh.

"Would you two shut up?" Nick says.

"He left me waiting the other night. Guess we're even now," I tease.

"Holding him accountable—I like that."

"Why don't you two fuck off and go actually do your jobs?" Nick grumbles, shooting both of them an icy glare. He's in a sour mood, and I hope it has more to do with what they were talking about than me.

"Gladly."

They both stand up and we say our goodbyes. Nick loosens up the moment they're gone, confirming his frustration is with work.

"You seem a little tense today."

"And you're a little feisty. What's got you all riled up? How was your morning?"

"It was fine. Class was boring, but I might have gotten a job offer." Why can't I just keep my mouth shut? Nick will probably lose his mind if he finds out that I was late because I ran into Jimmy. How am I going to explain that his father is trying to offer me a job?

"Really?" His mood has completely shifted. "That's fantastic. Doing what?"

"I don't know too much about it yet, but it would be with Bradford and Chambers. I need an internship to graduate. It might be worth checking out." I wait on eggshells for Nick's wrath, but it never comes. He processes my words carefully before speaking.

"Bradford wouldn't be related to Jimmy, now, would it?"

"His dad's firm."

"Are you sure that's a good idea?"

Honestly, I'm not. Nothing with Jimmy comes without strings, and I want to stay free and clear of him.

"Probably not. There are a lot of internships I can find with other firms."

"And any of those firms would be lucky to have you. Although you know you don't have to work if you don't want to, right?"

"Thank you, but I need a job. I can't stay home all day or I'll go crazy." Marriage is already pushing me enough out of my comfort zone, and I need some type of outlet.

"Not even with our children?" Nick suggestively tilts his head.

My eyes widen. We haven't talked about it more than simply saying we both wanted them eventually, but it sounds like Nick might have a different timeline in mind. "I'm talking about right now. We've got several years to think about kids."

Nick bites his lip, obviously holding back something that he wants to say. He's not satisfied with my response, but neither one of us pushes it.

"You're right." Nick's tone is shallow, jumping on the same page as me. "Let's not ruin the day. Are you excited about tonight?"

"What's tonight?"

"You forgot?" Nick teases, a smug grin plastered on his face as he waits a second for me to process. "The dinner at your parents' house? Our families getting together for the first time?"

"Damn it." I completely forgot about that. Nick's entire family is coming over and having dinner with mine.

Nick chuckles. "Come on, it won't be that bad!"

Personally, I think he's way too optimistic.

Nick

Six hours later, Ava and I sit at a large, beautifully decorated dining room table amidst both of our families. Sonya spared no expense on this dinner, serving course after course of elaborate dishes and sides. By the time dessert was brought out, I didn't have enough room in my stomach to even *look* at it.

I'm surprised at how civil the entire night has been. It's borderline friendly. My father and Alessandro sit at the end of the table, lost in their own conversation for most of the evening, and, somehow, I manage to keep myself from bashing Alessandro's head in when I see him. That feels like a major feat, considering the things that Ava has shared with me about him over the last few weeks.

I can't stand the thought of anyone disrespecting or hurting her, and it makes me sick to think that it happened at the hands of her own father. On every single level the man disgusts me, and I can't get her out of this place fast enough. The rest of her family is terrific, though, and I love watching Ava interact with her sisters. Their playful joking and banter remind me so much of my brothers and me. And it's nice to know that there are no hard feelings between me and Bella after everything went down.

As a pleasant surprise, even Vince is starting to come around. He keeps his distance for most of the night, but he hasn't tried to start anything with me, which I consider a victory. He's fiercely protective of Ava, and I can never fault him for that. Leo speaks with him for a while, running interference for me, but most of the night, Vince is occupied with his wife and his daughter.

Seeing him with his family is like seeing an entirely different person. I'm used to his ruthless, hotheaded side, but he is anything but with his beautiful little girl. She clearly has him wrapped around her finger, and as I watch them interact, I wonder what my and Ava's daughter might be like.

I rest my hand on Ava's thigh underneath the table. She's angled away from me as she talks with Bella about Bella's upcoming wedding plans. I can tell she's already tired of listening to Bella, but she doesn't let on. Ava's got an uncanny ability to make everyone she talks to feel like the most important person in the room, and she lets Bella run through all the tiny, insignificant details like they're gold.

When she finally turns back to me, her cheeks have a rosy hue from the wine.

"It sounds like Bella has this wedding thing figured out. Maybe we should hire her to plan ours." I'm only partly joking. It would certainly move things along if someone else was involved. Aside from the date, Ava won't touch wedding plans with a ten-foot pole.

She scoffs. "Only if you want to get married in front of five hundred guests at St. Patrick's Cathedral with a full-blown marching processional and horse-drawn carriage.

"That elaborate?" I chuckle, once again thanking my lucky stars I ended up with Ava.

"Maybe worse. I don't even want to think about how extravagant their wedding is going to be."

"Yikes. Maybe we should consider moving ours up. That way we don't have to worry about following an event like that up." I shrug, pressing the long neck of my beer bottle to my lips.

"Wow, smooth." Ava smirks, narrowing those gorgeous eyes at me. "What do you say we get out of here?"

Leaning forward, I brush my lips across her cheek. "You took the words right out of my mouth."

I've been on my best behavior with her dad and brother around, but now all I can think about is getting her back to my place. Ava gives me a look that tells me she agrees and now I can't get out of here fast enough.

We begin to say our goodbyes, and we're all standing in the foyer when my dad speaks with my mom at his side. I wrap my arms around Ava protectively, pulling her in until her back is flush with my chest.

"Alessandro, Sonya, we want to thank you both for opening your home to us tonight. We are thrilled to be welcoming Ava into the family and are so glad that we can all put our differences aside to—"

Vince snorts loudly, and everyone turns their attention to him. "Differences? That's what you call your son killing my brother?"

Oh god, no. Not here, Vince. Not now.

"Vincent." Alessandro's voice holds a strong warning but Vince doesn't seem to care. He walks slowly toward us, and Ava tenses in my arms.

"What?" She turns to me in hurt and confusion. "What is he talking about?"

All the opportunities that I had to tell her over the last few weeks flash through my mind. Why didn't I just explain it? It was an accident; surely, she'll see it that way. Why did I feel like I had to keep it from her? Right now, there's nothing I regret more.

Vince's eyes fix on Ava. "You don't know, do you?"

"That's enough, Vince!" Alessandro bellows, and charges toward him. Vince throws his grip off as if it's nothing, determination flashing through his dark eyes.

"You are all content to let this go on, and she doesn't even know the truth?" Vince yells to no one in particular, wobbling slightly from the alcohol in his system.

"Vince, what are you talking about?" Ava steps away from me as she looks at him.

"Did you ever think to ask your fiancé how he knew Andrew, Ava?" Vince hisses, poison spewing from his tongue.

"We should go." I take Ava's hand, trying to move her forward to the door, but she's frozen in place.

Vince pushes me away from her, positioning himself between us.

Alessandro lunges toward him, slamming his son against the wall with a thud. "Vince, I'm warning you. Shut the fuck up."

The room seems to freeze as everything unfolds.

"Ava, let's go." I pull her hand, desperate to get her out of here, but she lets go and her vision tunnels on Vince.

"What is it, Vince?" Her voice breaks.

"Ava, leave with Nick," Alessandro demands. "Now!"

As if she doesn't hear him, she stands exactly where she is, looking desperately at Vince for some kind of explanation. The confusion in her eyes chokes me, and all I can do is watch this nightmare unfold.

"It's his fault Andrew is dead. And before you go through with this wedding, you need to ask him why." His words are like bullets spraying into all of us. I stand still, paralyzed as I watch her process what he said.

I can't blame Vince; this is all my fault. Thanks to Alessandro, Vince doesn't even know the whole story himself.

Ava should've heard the truth from me long ago, the second I realized who she was. I should've told her before we even got to this point, before it could be twisted or taken in the wrong context.

"Enough!" Alessandro shrieks, carting Vince out of the room. It's too late, though. The damage is done.

Ava turns around, her eyes immediately seeking me. The pain that pools in them is excruciating and nearly knocks the wind right out of me. "Ava, let me explain."

Before I can say another word, she flies out the front door as if she can't get away from me fast enough.

I chase her onto the porch, reaching for her arm just before she goes down the stairs. "Ava, please."

She jerks away from me so roughly that I'm afraid she might lose her balance. "Is that true?"

Hot tears streak down her face. Her body trembles with betrayal and she can't seem to catch her breath.

I hesitate and then nod. I can't lie anymore. "Yes. I was involved with Andrew's death."

"What exactly does *involved* mean?" she spits, narrowing her eyes at me.

I suck in a sharp breath, knowing this could have the potential to ruin everything.

"It's my fault he's dead. I shot him."

EIGHTEEN

Ava

When I leave my parents' house, I have no idea where I'm going. I need to get away from the house. Nick lied to me, my parents lied to me—there's no one I can trust. I can hardly see the road through my tears, but I can't get away fast enough, so I start driving.

It's my fault he's dead. I shot him.

Nick's words echo in my mind, and my chest. I trusted him. I believed him when he told me how different he was, how much he cared about me, how he would never keep things from me the way my father did. The potential was so exciting that I foolishly fell for it all. And all this time, I wasn't worth the truth.

Nick shot him. My fiancé murdered my twin brother. My father knew it all along, and he still shipped me off to the Caponellis like some sort of olive branch. It's a cruel irony that my life was handed over to mend fences, when it was Nick killing Andrew that broke them in the first place.

Right now, I don't know who I'm angrier at—my dad or Nick.

What kind of person could look me in the eye, knowing the truth about what happened? How could Nick lie so effortlessly to me, making me think he was falling in love with me, that he only had the best of intentions for me? This is all probably some sort of sick fantasy for him and I played right into it all. I've never felt so mortified in all of my life. God, the things I let that man do to me.

Twenty minutes ago I was joking about my wedding with Nick, ready to let him whisk me back to his place without the slightest bit of hesitation. Like he was some kind of hero riding in to save the day. Now I feel like an absolute fool with no one I can truly trust. Vince obviously knew. What about my sisters? My mom? Did they all lie to me?

The more I think about it, the more the pressure builds inside of my mind and if I don't find an outlet soon, I think it might explode.

I need Jimmy, not because I can trust him, but because I want to get high. To slow my mind down. To forget any of this ever happened. Erase all of it. Nick, the dinner, losing Andrew. Tomorrow all this bullshit will still be here, but for tonight, I want to forget.

If I didn't leave my stupid jacket back at my parents, I would be doing that right now. The bag Jimmy gave me earlier is sitting conveniently in the pocket, and now I'm going to have to beg him for more.

I must've blacked out, because I don't know how I end up in the parking lot of the Jag. I throw my SUV into Park and cut the engine, checking myself over in the mirror. I'm an absolute mess, but this is the kind of place where people don't ask questions.

It's more crowded than I expect, and I fight my way through to the bar. I glance anxiously around, searching for Jimmy. I need a fix—that's the only thing that can make this hurt a little less—and I don't care about the consequences.

Making my way from one end of the bar to the other, I finally set my eyes on Jimmy at a secluded table in the back. The entire place gives me the creeps, and I want to get out of here as soon as possible, so I make my way to him.

Jimmy is flanked by two rail-thin girls, so strung out that they can barely keep themselves vertical as he sleazily drapes his arms over their shoulders. I shudder, remembering that not long ago, one of them was me. It's enough to make me reconsider what I'm about to do, but only briefly. I would never let myself fall that deep again.

I gather up every ounce of gumption in my body and walk toward him. He does a double take when he sees me, and then a sinister smile spreads across his face.

"What do we have here?" He's much too excited to see me in this dump.

"I need something, Jimmy." My voice is hoarse from all the crying I've done; I almost don't recognize it when it comes out.

Jimmy chuckles. "Girls, can you give us a second?"

The two women on his arms glare at me, and then stumble away in their doped-up state.

I bite my lip, knowing this is my last chance to reconsider. I could call Nick to pick me up and go home. *Yeah, call the guy who lied about murdering my brother. That's a great idea.* Instead, I slump into the chair across from Jimmy, propping myself against the table on my elbows.

"What happened to what I gave you earlier? Out so soon?" Jimmy arches an eyebrow at me.

"It's at home. I can't go get it and I need something now."

Jimmy considers my words for a second, and then laughs. "Oh, how the mighty fall. What was it you said to me earlier? You're clean?"

"Never mind. I'll find someone else." I stand up, ready to go. I didn't come here to be ridiculed; I'm well aware of how pathetic this is.

He grabs my arm roughly. "I'll give you what you want, but on one condition."

I should have known he wasn't going to make this easy for me.

"What?" I ask, afraid of what the answer might be. I can't pay him; I ran out without my purse. By some stroke of luck Nick left the keys in the car, and that was the only reason I could drive.

"Do it now. In front of me."

"What?" My voice shakes. He can't be serious.

"I want to watch you. I'm not going to let you run out of here again and let my good shit go to waste. I want to see your face the second it hits your system." He leans in. "I used to love to watch you get high." His harsh whisper bristles across me skin, and I squeeze my eyes shut.

Get up, Ava, get out of here and run. Go back to Nick.

I should, but my brain and my body are on two completely different pages and I can't make myself do it.

"Fine."

Jimmy reaches into his pocket and pulls out a bag of cocaine. He lays a line out and gestures to it expectantly. I stare at the line in front of me for a few seconds. There won't be any going back after this, but what exactly do I have to go back to? The second I get home my father will hand me off to marry a murderer and that will be it.

None of this makes any difference. I'll still have to marry Nick despite the fact that he killed my brother. And my father will make sure of it. But this right now, this is my choice. It's something I can control, so I let out a deep breath, committing to my misery.

Without another thought I lean down and sniff the powder into my nose. It hits me almost instantly, washing over every inch of my body like a tidal wave. A wretched smile twists on Jimmy's face as he watches the sensation take hold of me.

Within seconds my world is spinning. I leave him to be with the girls from before, and go to the bar to order myself a drink. I can feel the drugs pulsing through my veins, everything in hyperdrive as I sit down.

Time passes both fast and slow as I sit at the bar. I'm so wrapped up that I don't register anything that happens around me.

"What's a pretty thing like you doing here all alone?" a deep voice says from the chair next to me.

I'm not in the mood for company, and I turn to the man, intending to tell him so. He's handsome, but nothing like Nick. Lighter and longer hair, a few more freckles, and patchy facial hair. He certainly looks like better company than Jimmy, though.

"What makes you think I'm here by myself?"

"I've been watching you for a while. And trust me, no man in his right mind would leave you alone in a bar for this long looking like that." His eyes travel up and down my body, and I'm as uncomfortable as I am annoyed under his gaze.

"Are you trying to hit on me?"

"Is it working?" His smile is genuine, and I'm desperate for anything to occupy my mind, so I don't completely shut him down.

"Why don't you ask me that again after a few drinks?"

"What's your name?" he asks, scooting a little closer.

I consider lying for a minute, but it doesn't make much of a difference at this point. "Ava."

"I'm Nick." Am I hearing things? It's like I can't escape the constant reminder of him.

I wince at his words, and then twist my lips into a smile. "You look more like a Shaun. Can I call you Shaun?"

"You can call me whatever you want, babe."

We spend the next few hours talking and drinking. I'm not exactly enjoying myself, but he's a warm body who doesn't know who I am or what's going on in my life, and he takes my mind off it all.

"It's closing time. You guys want to settle up?" the bartender asks, clearing our empty glasses.

Shaun reaches for his wallet, but I push his hand away. "No, let me get this. You've helped me more than you know."

"Are you sure?"

"Absolutely," I insist, reaching for my purse. Damn it, I don't have it. I forgot it back at the house.

The sparkling ring on my finger catches my attention and a vengeful, hideous thought crosses me mind. This could be the perfect *fuck you* to Nick.

Despite every shred of reason I've got left screaming at me to stop, I slide it off my finger and onto the bar top. Both the bartender and Shaun stare at me in shock. "I don't have any cash on me, but will this do?"

"We'll call it even," the bartender says, reaching for the ring. My heart skips when it disappears, but I ignore the twinge of regret I feel and fully commit to my misery.

"Why don't you let me take you back to my place?" Shaun says, helping me off the bar stool.

For a moment, I consider it. Eventually I'll come out of this state of mind and I'll need something else to distract me from the shambles my life has turned into. And the longer I can put off having to see Nick, the better.

"She's already with someone." A dark, menacing voice comes from behind me. This time I know exactly who it is, and my heart jumps into my throat. I'd recognize that voice anywhere.

Shaun, or Nick, or whatever the hell his name is, chuckles. "Maybe she's tired of her boyfriend."

"Fiancé, actually," Nick growls, picking up my left hand, expecting to see his ring. When he doesn't, he clenches his jaw, and a sinking feeling grows in the pit of my stomach. "I think it's time to go home, Ava."

There's nothing in the world as sobering as a pissed-off Nick.

"You don't have to go anywhere with him if you don't want to," Shaun says, angling his head toward me. Nick's hands clench into fists and the reality of the situation hits me. The drugs, the alcohol, giving my ring away. Nick is only getting angrier by the second, and it won't bode well for me, or for this guy who's egging him on.

"Let's go, Ava," Nick demands, grabbing my arm.

Shaun steps forward. "Hey, man, don't be so rough with—"

Before he can finish the sentence, Nick's fist lands squarely on his jaw and knocks him backward. "Stay the fuck away from her."

"Nick!" I shriek, latching on to his arm as I try to pull him away.

"Get your ass outside."

"Nick, please stop," I beg.

He leans close to my ear, voice so low it sends a threatening rumble through my body. "Get your ass outside before I drag you out of this place. Do you understand?"

I manage a meek nod and hurry to the door. Nick is close at my heels, and it might be a hallucination, but I swear I can feel the anger radiating off him.

"You can be as angry as you need to be, but you can't pull this shit," he growls from behind me.

"You have no right to do this," I say angrily through my tears. The words are jumbled in my head, and I can only hope they make sense as I say them. "I'm not a child."

I fumble with the keys but Nick quickly snatches them from me. "Are you high right now?"

I can't bring myself to face him. I hate him for lying to me, but I also hate the idea of disappointing him, and it's an unfair paradox. He grabs my chin, forcing me to look up at him, and on instinct, I reach out to slap him. He catches my wrist firmly before I can make contact, and I cry out in pain.

"You're not going to do this, Ava. I messed up, but that doesn't mean you get to throw all your progress away. You owe it to yourself to let me explain."

I open my mouth to speak but nothing comes out. There's a raging battle inside of me like I've felt before. Part of me doesn't want to give him the time of day after all the chances he's had the last several weeks, but another part is desperate to hear what he has to say. The push and pull is relentless, and my mind spins out of control.

"Ava, please get in the truck, and I will tell you everything. I swear." His voice cracks with emotion.

"Now you want to talk? You've had weeks to tell me the truth and now that you've been caught, it's a priority?"

He glances around. "It's always been a priority, Ava, but the situation is a little more complicated than you know."

"Obviously." I let out a sharp laugh.

"I wanted to tell you, but your dad—"

"Don't do that." I glare at him, tears streaming down my face. "Don't pass this off on my dad. I know exactly the kind of man he is. I don't expect any kind of honesty from him, but you? That's all you've been preaching to me for weeks. How I can trust you. How different you are."

Nick is silent because we both know I'm right.

"You're a grown man, Nick, and you could have easily chosen to tell me before we got to this point."

"You're right." He looks up at me with a brokenness in his eyes. "I'll tell you everything you want to know. Please, just get in the truck and let me get you home."

I hesitate, but nod. He opens the door for me and I climb inside.

"What happened?" I ask once he starts to pull out of the parking lot.

"Not now. You need to be sober to hear the whole story."

I wait for him to reach out and put his hand on my leg like he normally would, but he doesn't. His eyes are locked on the road, jaw flaring every once in a while.

And all I can do is cry.

NINETEEN

Ava

When I wake up the next morning, I feel like I've fallen off a cliff. My entire body aches, my throat burns, and my eyes are so heavy that I can barely keep them open. It's been so long since I've felt like this, and I never thought I'd feel like it again.

I blink several times, trying to adjust to my surroundings. Why am I in Nick's room? Why am I wearing his T-shirt? Did I stay over at his house? The reality of what happened last night hits me out of nowhere.

Nick confessed to killing my brother.

All of my initial feelings hit me like a tidal wave. The hurt, the betrayal, the realization that everyone lied to me about it for years. I must've . . . god, what did I do? My mind is completely blank.

A cup of water sits on the nightstand, still full of ice. Nick probably put it there recently. I sit up carefully and reach for the cup. The cold water hurts my burning throat at first, but then it soothes it. It does nothing to help the splitting headache I have, though. I haven't felt like this since . . .

The night comes back to me in small pieces, and every bit of it is gutting. Everything was great at my parents', and right as we were about to leave, it all blew up. The confrontation with Vince, Nick's admission, me going to the Jag and finding Jimmy. I can almost see the line of coke he laid out for me and almost feel the way my body tingled at the sight of it. I would give anything to erase what happened next, but it's so vivid in my mind.

The other guy at the bar. The way his head snapped back when Nick punched him. Our fight in the parking lot. I cradle my head in my hands in frustration. How did I let things spiral so out of control? I've worked so hard over the last several months, and now all of it is gone in one moment of stupidity and selfishness.

Right now, I'm not sure who I'm more upset with—myself for breaking my recovery or Nick for making me feel so safe all while keeping this monumental secret from me. It's not like this is a little white lie.

Nick played a part in Andrew's death, and whatever that means, it should've been one of the very first things he told me. We were supposed to be building a life together, and he was hiding some pretty serious shit from me.

I have every right to be upset, but what I shouldn't have done is go crawling back to my old habits. I set myself back in a giant way, and who knows how long it will take me to reach that point in my recovery again. It's a daily battle and while I'd like to say it was a onetime thing, it's a slippery slope. What comes next is unknown, and that's the scariest part.

Hearing Nick say he shot my brother still haunts my mind. It makes me sick to even think about it. After all his preaching about honesty and treating me like an equal, it's out of character for him to keep me in the dark like he did. If I'd been thinking clearly, I might've realized that and given him an opportunity to explain.

After giving myself some time to think about what happened, I have to talk to Nick before making any kind of judgment. We both have some explaining to do. I jump out of bed much too quickly and a raging pain pulses through my head. In the bathroom I splash some water on my face to make myself look like I'm not quite as strung out as I am.

My eyes are dark and sunken in, and I pinch my cheeks to try to get a little bit of color on my pale skin. The sight of my bare left hand makes my heart drop. *Oh my god.* I gave my ring to the bartender! If I thought Nick would be upset before, this will surely be the icing on the cake.

The hallway is filled with the smell of breakfast. He can't be all that mad if he's cooking for me, can he? That's a good sign—at least, I'm choosing to take it that way.

Nick stands with his back to me, wearing just a pair of sweatpants. I don't have to see his face to know that something is different this morning, because his body language says it all. His shoulders are slumped forward, and he moves slowly and timidly. The confident air that he usually carries is gone, and it's replaced by brokenness and remorse. He hears me come in and turns to face me after a few seconds, clearing his throat.

"Good morning," I say sheepishly.

There was never any doubt in my mind that Nick would be livid. What I didn't prepare for, though, is the look of torment and hurt on his face. It's like a dark cloud hangs over the both of us. It's not anger, but pure anguish. Neither one of us wants to move first, for fear of igniting the other, so we stand facing each other with our eyes locked for several seconds.

"Good morning," he finally says. "You look—"

"Hopefully better than I feel."

"I'm making breakfast. There are painkillers in the cabinet if you need them," Nick offers, turning back to the eggs sizzling on the stove.

I don't have the heart to tell him, but the thought of eating right now is enough to make me want to throw up on the spot. I sit in silence as he cooks, and after a few minutes, he joins me at the bar, sliding a plate of food in front of me.

"You didn't need to do this." I force back tears. I didn't expect to get emotional, but the second I feel his hand on my knee, all of that goes out the window.

"I've been trying to think of what I want to say to you for the last several hours, but nothing really seems appropriate." His voice is even and calm as he stares forward.

"I guess we've got a lot to talk about."

"We do," he agrees, turning to me.

I take a deep breath, debating where to start. The ring feels like as good a place as any. "I did something really stupid last night."

"One thing?" He teases a smirk, trying to lighten the mood.

"Valid point. But this one is probably the worst."

"Go on."

"I lost your engagement ring." Tears bubble in my eyes again as I blurt it out.

Nick studies my face for a second, scratching his chin before he responds. He reaches into his pocket to fish something out.

"You mean this?" He holds the oval-shaped sparkler in front of me and my heart slams into my chest.

"How did you . . . ? Where . . . ?"

He clenches his jaw, turning the ring over and over in his hand. "The bartender's a friend. He's the one who called me when you showed up. And he kept hold of this after you used it to pay for another guy's drinks."

"God, Nick, that's mortifying. I can't apologize enough." I burst into tears.

"The thing is, Ava, I couldn't care less about this thing." He holds the ring up to me. "I care about you. And your safety. That's what I'm pissed off about. What you did last night—you could've gotten yourself killed. And I get you were upset. You have every right to be, but you should've come to me and talked about it, not gone to fucking Jimmy."

His voice breaks. This is painful for him. Having someone so concerned for my safety is a whole new experience for me. With my parents it was always about how my behavior reflected on them.

"I owe you an explanation. I'm going to tell you everything that happened with Andrew, and I'm going to set this here." He puts the ring on the countertop. "And after we talk about all of this, you can decide whether or not you're going to put it back on."

I nod.

"But if you do, some things are going to have to change. I'm sorry I didn't tell you this from the beginning. I assumed your dad did. I didn't find out that you didn't know the truth until a few weeks ago, and I've been trying to figure out the best way to bring it up ever since," he starts. "I knew Andrew for a long time. I should've recognized you the moment that I saw you that night because your faces are so similar. I don't know why I didn't." Nick hesitates. "He was one of my best friends."

"Mine too," I say.

Nick squeezes his eyes shut, as if he's getting himself up for what he's about to say.

FOUR YEARS AGO

Nick

"What the hell?" The sound of someone banging on the door wakes me up abruptly. Usually, it's Leo, having forgotten his keys. I throw some shorts on and stomp out of my room and down the hall.

I'm annoyed as hell when I open the door. "Bro, seriously, you've got to start . . ."

It isn't Leo who stares back at me, though; it's Andrew. He paces on the porch, frantic and looking like he hasn't slept in days.

"What's going on?" I ask, confused to see him standing at my door at three o'clock in the morning.

"I need help." His voice is hoarse.

"Come inside." I usher him in, looking around to be sure that no one is watching us. "What the hell is going on?"

"I screwed up, Nick. I took the deal from the MS-13 dude." He runs his fingers through his hair, continuing to pace back and forth in my living room.

"Are you out of your damn mind?" I bark. "Do you have any idea how dangerous it is?"

A few weeks ago he came to me about this whole thing. He'd royally screwed up a weapons shipment for his dad and was trying to get it replaced before anyone caught wind of it.

MS-13 is a gang—they don't run things like we do in the Mafia. It's fast and loose and you can't take much of what they say as truth, so when he told me about the deal they offered him, I knew it was bullshit.

They said they would replace his guns for him. All he had to do was go to their supplier and get the replacements, plus their next shipment. Getting involved with them in any capacity is a death trap, but Andrew wouldn't listen.

"I know, I know!" he says. "I should've listened. But, shit, Nick. It's bad." His panic pulses, and he's bitten off more than he can chew. What he tells me next, though, I never could've been prepared for.

"What happened?"

"You should've seen this place, Nick. Guns fucking everywhere! Most I've ever seen in my life. No way they can keep tight inventory on that shit. I figured . . ."

My heart nearly stops. "Andrew, tell me you didn't steal from them."

"I only took a few! I didn't think they would even notice they were gone. And my dad would've been ecstatic if I brought more home than we paid for. He's always talking about what a screwup I am. For once, I wanted him to trust me like he trusts Vince." His voice is pained, and he's almost in tears. He's under a lot of pressure, but I don't understand how he could've been so damn reckless. "But they did. And now their suppliers after me, and so are they."

"I told you I'd get you the guns, man!" Now I'm pacing too. We have to figure this out fast. You don't mess with these kinds of people, and I'm furious at Andrew for dragging me into it.

"There's no way you could have without my dad finding out."

"And this is better? They're going to kill you!"

Of course they were going to find out. These are weapons we're talking about—thousands of dollars' worth of weapons.

"They're not going to kill me, Nick." He pulls a gun out of his waistband. "I'm going to kill myself."

"You really are out of your damn mind. Put that thing away," I hiss, growing angrier by the minute. He isn't thinking straight. We need to get our dads and figure out what to do.

"Nick, please. I'm here to say goodbye," Andrew pleads. "They'll come after my family. They don't care that this shit is my fault."

"We need to tell your dad." I rake my hand through my hair as I try to form a plan.

"No." He shakes his head wildly. "This is my fault. If I get him involved, more people than necessary will get hurt."

"This is insane. You can't do this. How does this solve anything?"

"Their war is with me, and if I die, it'll die with me." Andrew continues to drone on, but I'm not hearing much of what he has to say. It's all nonsense. Him dying is no way to handle this. We can figure something else out.

"Drew, this is ridiculous," I plead. It's concerning how much he has planned this out.

"Nick, I'm dying. One way or another. I screwed this up so bad, and there's no way out. My dad can't protect me, you can't protect me, no one can. I'm okay with that. I've come to terms with it, but I can't come to terms with anything happening to my family because of the shit I got myself involved in."

"Andrew—"

"This is the only option, Nick. They'll hurt my family. They may even come after you if they've got eyes on me already."

I stare back at him, standing in silence. This seems so drastic, but he's right. The second he agreed to that deal and then stole those fucking guns, he signed his own death certificate. God, I'm so fucking pissed at him for being the stupid.

"Goodbye, Nick."

He raises the gun and I lunge at him, refusing to let it happen. I get a hand on the barrel and Andrew and I struggle over it.

"Nick, let go!" he growls, pulling as hard as he can against me. There's no way I'm going to let him go through with this.

"Come on, man." I grunt, trying my best to get good footing so I can wrench the gun away from him.

We struggle against each other for what feels like forever, each of us trying to get the upper hand.

Suddenly, Andrew's elbow hits my chin and sends a searing pain through my jaw. I lose my hold on the gun, and then a deafening shot rings out.

Everything else happens in slow motion. Andrew's face freezes, and he stumbles backward, clutching his stomach. His shirt seeps crimson with blood as he drops to his knees, letting the gun fall to the ground.

"Fuck!" I kneel in front of him, putting as much pressure as I can on the wound. It's no use, though. I can see Andrew fading quickly in my arms, and after a few seconds, he's completely gone. Tears pool in my eyes as I stare at his lifeless body in front of me. How the fuck did this happen?

Honestly, I don't even know if I pulled the trigger or if Andrew did, but it doesn't really matter. He's dead, and I couldn't stop it.

I sit next to him, trying to steady my breath, and figure out what to do next. Finally, I do the only thing I can think of.

I call my father.

TWENTY

Nick

"Ava, I swear to god, I did everything I could to stop it. He was determined, and there was nothing anyone could've done. You or me, or probably even your dad," I explain. "At first your dad didn't believe me, but Andrew had left him a video to explain. After that, we stopped working together completely. There was just too much animosity, and obviously, Vince still blames me."

Ava hasn't said a word since I started telling my story. She stares back at me, so emotionless that she's almost despondent. I can't tell how, or even if, she's processing it, so I keep talking.

"When I found out you were his sister, I never in a million years thought you wouldn't know the truth. I always figured your dad would've told you, but after a little while, I realized you had no idea about any of it."

The words sting in my throat, but my hurt is dismal compared to what she must be feeling. "I'm sorry this is the way you found out, and I'm sorry I didn't tell you sooner. It's something that I'll regret for the rest of my life."

She has no idea how true that statement is. I think of Andrew constantly. Every time I have to kill someone, I relive that entire night.

"Nick—" Ava searches for the right words, but there really aren't any. A heaviness sets in between us and I'm desperate to know what's going on in her head. "I don't even know what to say."

"I can't imagine what you're feeling right now."

Until now I've been trying to give her some space, but I can't take it anymore and reach for her hand. It surprises me when she doesn't shy away, and a sliver of relief hits me.

"Thank you for telling me." Ava purses her lips. "I'm sorry that I didn't give you a chance to explain. Losing Andrew is like a pressure point for me, and when something triggers it, it's like I black out."

Ava buries her face in her hands, heavy sobs racking her entire body. The sound of her whimper guts me, a blade straight to my insides.

"Hey." I scoot closer, wrapping my arms around her as she cries. She turns into me, burying her face in my chest and I stroke her hair gently. "It's okay, Avs. You can cry all you want to, and I'll be right here when you're ready to talk."

For a few minutes, we stay that way—her resting in my arms as I soothe her. Eventually she sits up, pulling back and taking a deep breath to compose herself. She wipes her tears off her cheeks and then turns to me. "I'm sorry," she says.

"You have nothing to be sorry about." I almost cringe when she says it, because she's been conditioned to believe her emotions are an inconvenience. Maybe if Alessandro had taken the time to help her work through them back then, we wouldn't even be here right now.

"I'm the one who's sorry, Ava. For what happened. For not telling you. For all of it," I say. "I wanted to find the right time, but you told me what an awful time you had after he died, and I didn't want—" About halfway through, I realize how this is going to come off.

I don't need to finish for her to recognize where I'm going with it. "You thought I would start using again," she says quietly. It's harsh, but it's exactly what happened.

"I need to know how bad this is, Ava." I let out a heavy breath. "I was honest with you about Andrew, and now I need you to be honest with me about this. You're about to be my wife."

"You still want to marry me?" The shock on Ava's face catches me completely off guard.

"Of course I do. What would make you think I didn't?"

"I don't know. I thought you might want to give me back after what happened last night. How I acted."

Her face falls in defeat. Every time this side of her comes out, I'm reminded of how much she's been beaten down by Alessandro for the last twenty-three years. I hate seeing her so shaken and insecure, and I hate that she expects that kind of reaction from me. Reaching over, I scoot her chair closer to me, resting my palms on her thighs.

"First of all, you're not some kind of object that I'm going to return the second it stops working how I want it to. The last thing I want is for you to go back to that house. I care about you, Ava. I'm not going to throw you to the side when you screw up. That's not what love is."

My admission softens her, and she presses her lips together gently.

"And second of all, I'm the one who should be worried about you calling off the wedding. I kept a huge secret from you. And you know what? I can't guarantee that this will be the only thing that I screw up in our life together, but I don't expect you to dump me to the side when that happens either."

She nods, on the verge of tears again.

"We're going to get through this together—if you want to." I gesture to her ring on the counter.

That's all it takes, and the floodgates open. Thick, heavy tears trickle down her cheeks, her emotions getting the best of her. "Nick, of course I do. I'm so sorry."

"Don't be sorry. I messed up, and we need to hold each other accountable. Although in the future, I hope you choose another method besides giving your ring to a bartender and getting high."

There is a smile at the corner of her lips, but she isn't giving it up yet, still consumed by her guilt.

"I need you to explain it to me. I can't help you if I don't know what you're going through." I'm not going to let her off the hook here. Regardless of what I did, her reaction worries me, and it's something we have to talk about, no matter how difficult it is.

"Nick, I'm not using again. Last night, I was . . . I got pissed off, and I didn't know what to do, and I just snapped." The words seem physically painful for her to say.

"That's the only time you've used in our entire relationship?"

"Yes," she says. "It's the first time I've used in many, many months. The night I went out with Bella we ran into Jimmy, and he tried to get me to do it then, too, but I refused. I was so proud of myself for being strong enough to tell him no, but I threw it all away last night."

Running to drugs used to be a trauma response for her, and it makes sense she'd slip back into her old patterns after a night like last night. There's a difference between a full-fledged relapse and a slipup, and I hope that we're dealing with the latter.

"You didn't throw it all away, Ava. It was a mistake. A terrible mistake, but there are going to be bumps in the road. What matters is how you come back from it. No one expects you to be perfect, and you shouldn't expect that from yourself either."

What I have to ask next makes me anxious, about both her reaction and answer. "How bad did it get?"

A darkness washes over her, and I can tell she doesn't want to tell me.

"Ava." I cup her chin, slanting it up so that I can see her. "Nothing you say is going to make me think less of you. I just want the truth."

"It was bad," she finally says. "For several months after Andrew died, I was rarely sober. I was using constantly because it was the one thing that brought me any kind of relief. I didn't care about the pain or the embarrassment or what I was doing to anyone else." Painful memories swarm in her eyes.

"How did it start?" I press.

"Losing Andrew was like losing a huge part of myself. He was the only one who ever protected me, and I felt lost without him. Right before that, things had gotten serious with Jimmy, and in the beginning, I really thought he was trying to help me. But all he really wanted was somebody to get high with. At first, I didn't mind because I could forget. My dad lost his mind, and he tried everything he could think of to get me to stop. He tried to beat it out of me, and when that didn't work, he threatened to throw me into his prisoner cells for a month so that I knew how good I had it."

She swallows, biting back her tears, and rage wrecks my body. Fucking Alessandro.

"It became a power struggle between us, and I pushed even harder. But one day I overdosed. I was at a party with Jimmy, and somehow Vince found me. I guess at that point, I realized how bad it was, and I agreed to do whatever my parents wanted me to do. First, it was a rehab program, and then I started seeing a counselor. I stopped that day, and I didn't have anything again until last night."

Ava talks fast, like she's worried if she slows down, she might not get it all out. Finally, she takes a breath. Hearing it from her is harder than I imagined, mostly when I hear about the way that Alessandro handled it. His daughter was crying out for help, and he treated her like one of his captives. He's a fucking monster.

"I wasn't completely honest when we talked about this before. It wasn't just casual, I got hooked. Addicted." Her face falls. "But I swear, it's not like that this time. It was a slipup, but it won't happen again." She assures me with a desperation in her eyes that makes me a little nervous.

I want to believe her, but I also know how things like this work. I won't let her fail, though. The difference between this time and last is that she has me to support her, and I'm going to keep her as far away from her bastard father as I can.

"I don't want you to see Jimmy anymore." I grit my teeth; even saying his name infuriates me. I hated the guy long before I even knew what he'd done to Ava.

"Done," she agrees.

I reach for her left hand, taking the ring off the granite countertop.

"Can I put this back on now?" I wait for her permission. Ava's never been given much authority over her own life, and that makes it even more important that I follow through when I say I'm going to do something.

"I'd like that." Her voice cracks with emotion.

My heart practically leaps when I slide it back into place. A few minutes ago, I wasn't sure it would happen. "Promise me that if you ever feel like you want to use again you'll come to me. That you'll let me help you."

"I promise, Nick." She blinks back tears. "You don't have to worry about it. I don't ever want to get back to that point, and I'll do whatever it takes."

Bringing her hand to my lips, I kiss the back of it softly. "Good. But if it happens again, you'll get professional help. I care about you too much to watch you self-destruct like you did last night. I'll be here every step of the way, but understand that if you start using again, even at all, I'll get you professional help and it won't be a choice."

"It won't come to that."

"That's my girl." My mouth covers hers in an intense kiss. A kiss that holds greater meaning than any that we've had before. A kiss that reaches new levels of intimacy because of everything we've shared. A kiss that binds us. "I do have one more condition."

"What's that?" There's a hint of apprehension in her tone.

I grab her hips, pulling her onto my lap. My boxers look good on her, but it's time she gets clothes of her own here.

"Move in with me." It's not much of a request. Most of my reasons for wanting her here are selfish, but as of late, the idea of sending her home to her father makes my skin crawl.

"You want me to move in here?"

I nod. "We talked about it a few weeks ago, but I'm ready to make it happen. I don't want to play around anymore. I want you here with me all the time."

"Wow." She lets out a sharp laugh. "This is not at all how I expected this morning to go."

"It's not the kind of conversation you're used to, but it's how things are going to go with me. Like I said, I want us both to be accountable, but it's not my job to make you feel bad about what happened. If I had to guess, you've already been doing that."

I can't read her expression as she weighs my offer. She's not really going to fight me on this, is she?

"Nick, my dad won't go for that. At least not until we're married."

"I don't give a shit about your dad, Ava. Do *you* want to move in with me?"

Ava reaches out, resting her hand on my cheek as her thumb sweeps across it. "I want to be here with you, Nick. One hundred percent. Every day for the rest of my life."

"Then let's do it." I grin. "And I'll handle your dad."

TWENTY-ONE

Nick

Leaving Ava back at my place, I head straight for Moretti's warehouse. It would probably be better for me to take a couple of days to cool off and get my head straight, but time isn't a luxury I have. Ava's right—he's not going to be thrilled about her moving in with me before we're officially married, but there's no way in hell I'm having her go back there. Not after the things she told me about him this morning.

When I pull into the parking lot, I cut the engine, readying myself for an argument with Alessandro. His door is open, so I don't bother knocking to let him know I'm here.

When I clear my throat, he looks up from his desk

"Nick! Good to see you. I didn't know you were coming by." He stands up to greet me and shake my hand.

"We need to clear the air after last night." I sit down in an armchair across the desk from him. "I told Ava the truth about Andrew. That he came to my house that night because he wanted to kill himself rather than disappoint you."

Alessandro's face hardens, the vein in his neck pulsing. "We agreed to keep her out of it."

I can't help but scoff. Sometimes he and I have two completely different conversations when we talk. "*You* agreed, Alessandro. I'm not lying to my soon-to-be wife about what happened, especially when our marriage is on the line. And Vince's outburst didn't give me much choice."

"Your marriage was never on the line," he spits. "Ava will do what I tell her to do, despite what she knows or doesn't know."

"That's where you and I differ. She should know things that pertain to her. From now on, she will."

Alessandro stiffens in his desk chair. "You're forgetting that she still belongs to me. You're not married yet."

I do my best to curb my temper, gripping the arm of my chair with such force that my knuckles turn white. "She doesn't *belong* to anyone, Alessandro."

His deep chuckle only irritates me more. "You're naïve, Nick. She's got you fooled."

"No, I understand things pretty well." I stand, stalking toward him and bracing myself against his desk. "I need to be sure that you do. I know everything, Alessandro. The things you've done to her. What you've put her through. And if you so much as look at her the wrong way and I find out about it, I will slash you into so many pieces that they'll never find them all. And I'll enjoy every second of it, so give me a fucking reason."

Alessandro sets his jaw, the threat looming between us. The shift in our dynamic is glaring. He doesn't have the upper hand anymore, and he's starting to unravel at the revelation.

"Get the hell out of my office."

"By the way, Ava's going to be moving in with me. Starting today. And unless you want an even bigger problem on your hands, I don't want to hear a thing about it." I smirk. "Have a nice day, Alessandro."

My adrenaline is high when I walk out of the warehouse. I'm sure my dad will have a lot to say about how I handled that, but honestly,

I'm thrilled I showed the restraint that I did. Today wasn't only about being a good Don; it was about being a good husband, and sometimes that has to take precedent.

Ava

Now that I've been living with Nick for a few weeks, his place is finally starting to feel like home. We've settled into an easy routine. Breakfast on the patio together. Our own sides of the bed. My leaving my coffee cup in random places throughout the house and Nick giving me a hard time about it. It's even better than I could have imagined.

My parents' house is out in the middle of the suburbs, with all the space and fresh air a person could want, whereas Nick's penthouse is right at the center of Manhattan. We have all kinds of space, but the city never shuts off and most of the time I feel like I'm staying in a luxury hotel. He doesn't pay much attention to decoration or personal touches, but I've already got some ideas to make this place a little cozier. Honestly, I'd stay in a cardboard box if it meant I got to come home to Nick every night. I don't know why we didn't make this decision sooner.

Nick is headed to Miami this afternoon, and although I'm going to miss him, a little quiet doesn't sound all that bad. I woke up this morning with a little headache, but after a day full of classes and a meeting with a wedding planner that my mother insisted on, it's turned into a raging migraine by the time I get home.

All I want to do is take some painkillers, have a nice hot bubble bath, and then curl up on the couch for the night. When I get inside, though, all I can manage is to find a sappy Hallmark movie and collapse on the couch. I type out a message to Nick letting him know that I'm not feeling well and I'm going to lie down, and barely get it sent before my eyelids become unbearably heavy. Maybe I'll feel better after a nap.

When I wake up an hour later, I'm a little disoriented. The TV is off, and I remember falling asleep to a movie about a billionaire who falls in love with a small-town bakery owner. Not to mention that I have the distinct feeling that I'm not alone.

I want to sit up but the throbbing in my head and my achy body say otherwise. It takes me a second to realize that Nick is sitting at the end of the couch. He's hacking away at his laptop and my feet are draped over his lap. I've never seen him wear glasses before, but it's definitely a good look on him. If the thought of moving didn't make me want to vomit, I might make a move on him.

"You really should lock the front door when you're here by yourself." The corners of his mouth lift into a barely detectable smile, but he doesn't look up.

"So creepy men don't sneak in and watch me sleep?"

"Precisely." He smirks, shutting his laptop and turning to face me. "How are you feeling?"

"I'm fine," I insist, propping myself up. The sudden move makes my head feel like it's going to explode, and it hurts to talk.

"You don't look fine." Nick presses the back of his hand across my forehead. "And you're burning up. How does your head feel?"

"It hurts. A lot," I admit. Although it feels a bit better as I reposition myself on the couch so that I can snuggle into his chest.

Nick frowns, wrapping me into a tight embrace. "Why didn't you tell me you were so sick? I thought it was just a headache."

"Why aren't you in Miami?" I ignore the question.

"Because I came home to check on you before I left and you were burning up, so I canceled my trip. There's no way I'm going to Miami when you're sick like this." His fingers stroke my arm gently, almost lulling me right back to sleep.

"You didn't need to do that." Secretly, my heart is bursting at the gesture. I'm already starting to feel better now that he's here.

"I wanted to. You need someone to nurse you back to health. Speaking of which"—he leans forward, careful not to jostle me too much and grabs a glass from the coffee table—"drink this."

"Yes, sir," I tease, but I take it from him eagerly, hoping that whatever is inside will calm my burning throat. It doesn't, though. A horrible taste fills my mouth and I nearly spit it back out all over the living room. "Ugh! What is this? It's awful."

"It's a vitamin superpack. My mom used to give them to my brothers and me when we were younger. It's supposed to build your immune system back up."

"Well, it's disgusting." I cringe, handing the glass back to him without taking another sip.

"You're going to be a difficult patient, aren't you?"

"Did you expect anything less?" A small smile escapes my lips, and I shut my eyes, ready to fall back asleep on Nick's chest.

"Not at all." He shimmies out from underneath me, propping a pillow underneath my head. It feels nice, but it doesn't have the same effect. "Does anything sound good to eat? Maybe some chicken soup?"

"Sure, soup sounds good," I say, expecting that he'll order takeout. Honestly, the thought of eating sounds tortuous right now, but it will make him feel better.

"Sure." Nick's smile is unsure. "I can do that."

He disappears into the kitchen as I fight to get comfortable on the couch. First I'm too hot, then it's too cold. Even the thought of moving makes me entire body ache. It's been a while since I've been this sick, and it couldn't have come at a worse time.

Between searching for a new internship, classes being in full swing, and all the wedding planning, I have too much on my plate to slow down. Next week our families are hosting an engagement party for us, and while I'm looking forward to it, a part of me wishes we could sneak away and do things on our own terms. On top of that, Nick had to cancel his entire trip to take care of me. He'll never admit it, but he's under a lot of stress as he's preparing for his new role.

He's gone for nearly an hour without a word. I drift in and out of sleep during that time, wondering what could possibly be taking so long. The café in the lobby of our building even has chicken soup. Did the delivery driver have to kill the chicken himself? After what seems like an eternity, Nick emerges from the kitchen with a tray filled with food and a bouquet of flowers.

"Okay." He sighs, setting the tray down on the coffee table and arranging a few things. "This is my first attempt at making chicken soup, so cut me a little slack."

A wave of emotion strikes me as I stare back at him, realizing that he's made the soup himself. This man canceled his entire work trip to take care of me, has waited on me hand and foot, and now tried to make me chicken noodle soup, even though he hardly knows how to turn the oven on. And that's just in the last few hours. Nick is incredible. He's everything I could've ever asked for and then some. No one has ever cared for me quite like he does, not even my family.

"Why are you looking at me like that?" He laughs anxiously, running his fingers through his hair.

"Nick, I love you," I blurt, admitting my feelings to him for the first time.

Nick bites his lip, letting out a sharp laugh as he sits down on the couch next to me. "Is your fever making you delirious? You just told me you loved me."

I shake my head. "It's not. I meant it. I love you."

"I love you, too, Ava." He leans forward, resting his forehead on mine. And we stay like that for a few minutes, taking it all in.

"Now, will you please eat this so you can get some rest?" Nick tilts his head at me, offering me a spoonful of chicken soup that smells like heaven.

"Of course."

The moment isn't glamorous. We're not at a fancy restaurant or on some grand adventure. We're sitting in sweats on the couch in our living room, but it's perfect all the same.

TWENTY-TWO

Ava

By the time Friday rolls around I'm feeling much better. I even get up early so I can make some breakfast before Nick heads to work. He's been home with me all week, nursing me back to health and taking care of anything that came up. Yesterday he couldn't avoid going into the office for a little while, but it was the first time he left me all week.

I'm just starting to mix up some waffle batter when my phone rings. I rush to get it so it won't wake Nick up and pick up without looking at the number.

"Hello?"

"Hi, sweetheart." I nearly have a heart attack hearing my father's voice on the other end of the line. It's been weeks since we've even spoken, and it isn't like him to call me out of the blue.

"Hi, Dad. How are you? Is everything okay?"

"Oh, everything is fine, sweetheart. I've been meaning to call for the last few days."

"Oh, really?" I'm weary of his sudden interest in me. This is new, and it's suspicious.

"Yes. Terry Bradford called me a few days ago. He said he has an internship open at his office next semester and that he's been waiting for your call."

I swallow a lump in my throat. "Oh yeah. Jimmy mentioned something about that. Sounds like a good opportunity, but I'm not sure that's something I should be doing right now."

"Nick wants you to quit school?"

The way he twists my words has me jumping on the defense. "No, nothing like that. I'm going to finish. I just . . . I don't know if it's a good idea, with my history with Jimmy. There are a lot of internships out there and—"

"Oh, nonsense, Ava. It's a great opportunity. Jimmy has nothing to do with it. You should be flattered that Terry would consider you for something like this."

"Maybe."

"I set up an interview for you. He will be expecting you at eleven o'clock."

My eyes widen. "Dad, today is really not a good day with the engagement party tonight. And I don't really—"

"Ava, it's rude not to respond. Terry is a friend of mine and I was completely mortified when he said you didn't even bother to call. The least you can do is go and see what it's all about."

"Sure. There's no harm in that," I say reluctantly.

"Good. Let me know how it goes." He hangs up without waiting for a response.

I throw my head back, swallowing a groan. Why do I let him do this to me?

I look at my watch, realizing that it's close to ten o'clock now. I don't have any time to spare if I'm going to make it to Bradford and Chambers by eleven. There's no way I'm going to show up late and run the risk of pissing my dad off even more.

I put the waffle ingredients away and grab a banana on my way to the bathroom. I don't have time to shower, so I slip on a professional-looking black dress and run my fingers through my knotted curls. I lean against the counter, applying a healthy coat of red lipstick and smacking my lips so that it's even.

"Wow! You certainly look better today." Nick comes into the bathroom shirtless and sweaty, having just finished his workout in the home gym. He sneaks his arm around my waist, sweeping me into him as he peppers me with salty kisses. "Where are you off to dressed like that?"

His eyes rake over me as he holds me out in front of him, hands on each of my shoulders. I blush under his gaze.

"Thank you." I laugh anxiously. He isn't going to be thrilled when he finds out where I'm headed. "I'm going to Bradford and Chambers. I have an interview at eleven."

Nick's face falls and his entire demeanor stiffens, as if he's preparing for a fight. "You're what? I thought we talked about this."

"We did." I nod, turning back to the mirror to finish my makeup so I can be on my way. "But my dad thinks it's a good idea if I go. It's a really prestigious firm and—"

"It might be prestigious, but it's also a direct line between you and your drug-dealing ex-boyfriend." He reaches for my wrist, spinning me back around so I can't avoid his stare. "Ava, you know how I feel about Jimmy. I don't want that scumbag anywhere near you, and if you're working for his father, it's easy access."

"I'm sorry. I obviously wasn't planning to follow up on Jimmy's job offer, or I would've told you about it sooner. My dad set this up without even talking to me first. How am I supposed to say no?"

I don't think he means to look at me as condescendingly as he does. "Pretty easy, actually. You don't have to listen to him anymore. I don't care who he's friends with. Jimmy didn't tell you about the offer to help you, Ava. He wants to see you fail, and he wants you to owe him. He's made that very clear the last few weeks, don't you think?"

I rub my temples, immediately feeling my migraine coming back. "There's no harm in me going down there and going through the motions. Even if it's just for practice. I'm trying to make everyone happy."

"You don't have to make anyone happy with you, baby. Fuck your dad. He hasn't called in weeks and now suddenly you hear from him because he wants more from you? It's bullshit."

Somehow, the tension between Nick and my dad has gotten even more pointed over the last few weeks, and I'm stuck in the middle.

"He's still my dad, Nick." I fold my arms across my chest in frustration. This is the last thing my nerves need this morning. I'm anxious enough as it is. "Please, let this go. It's not like I'm going to take the job."

"You say that now, but what happens when your dad tells you to take the position? You'll miraculously stand up to him then? It's fucking sick that he's even okay with you being around Jimmy in the first place."

"Nick, it's his dad!" I throw my hands up in exasperation. "Jimmy won't even be there."

"If you believe that, Avs, you're being naïve. Terry Bradford knows full well that his son is in love with you. That's why he wants to hire you," he says harshly. "That, and it'll put him in your father's good graces."

Nick's words hit me like a bullet from a gun. He doesn't mean it in the way it sounds, but all I hear is that he doesn't think I can get a prestigious internship like the one Bradford and Chambers is offering on my own merit.

He immediately regrets it. "Babe, I didn't mean that how it came out. You could work anywhere you want, and you deserve to be somewhere that hires you for more than your connections. And you're in such a good spot right now. Are you sure it's healthy to put yourself in a situation where you'll be around Jimmy and that kind of temptation?"

"You don't think I can resist getting drugs from Jimmy if I see him again," I say flatly. That stings worst of all. I've been fighting this as hard as I possibly can, and to hear that he doesn't have faith in me is a tough pill to swallow.

"No, no, no. That's not what I said." Nick holds his hands up as he backtracks, remorse in his eyes.

"I need to get going." I take a quick breath and grab my phone from the counter. I need to put some space between us before things get worse. "I'll see you later."

"Ava, please." Nick follows me. "I'm sorry. That's not what I meant. I trust you. I'm only—"

I hold my hand up to quiet him. "That's bullshit, and you know it. I'm working as hard as I can to turn it around and you can't throw my addiction in my face every time we're arguing. You don't get to bring it up when it's convenient for you. I told you I have no intention of taking the internship, but I'm going to go down there and meet with him because my father asked me to. I'll talk to you later."

I hurry out of the room before he can stop me again.

Nick

When I arrive alone at Ava's parents' house for the engagement party, the place is already packed. Having to mingle and make small talk without her sounds miserable, so I duck into Alessandro's office to hide out until she gets here.

I wasn't thrilled about this party to begin with, and after my argument with Ava this morning, I'm absolutely dreading it. She dodged my call and texts all day, and I wanted to hash this out—not pretend that everything was completely fine between us in a room full of our fathers' closest friends and soldiers. There is all of this production around our wedding, and it's wearing on me. Especially when the performance gets in the way of our actual relationship.

Things quickly got out of hand this morning, and I was mostly to blame for that. Ava's need for her father's approval is something I will never understand, but that's because I've never had to beg or fight for it the way she has. My dad can be difficult but I've never once questioned that he loves me and is proud of me. And the more I hear about the way Ava grew up, the more I realize that's a luxury.

Hopefully, someday, she won't feel the need to appease him, but until then I can be a little more understanding. And as soon as she gets here I plan to tell her as much so we can make it through this evening together.

Tonight is the first formal event that Ava and I will attend as a couple, and first impressions are everything in the crime world. It's our chance to show both of our organizations that we're committed and united as one. My father had been talking about that for weeks, as if I needed the reminder.

When I hear her voice in the foyer, I peek out and watch as she greets a couple who came in a few seconds in front of her. I don't recognize them, but she seems friendly, so I figure they must be friends of her parents.

Damn, she looks good tonight. Her curls are loosely pulled back in a half-up half-down style, and her candy-colored lips curve into a grin as she hangs her coat. My heart races as I trace her curves, thinly veiled under the tight fabric of that floor-length black dress. There's no doubt in my mind that she chose the dress with the thigh-high slit as a bit of added punishment for this morning, and it's working.

My slacks tighten across my crotch as my erection grows, craving her so badly it hurts. Yeah, there's no chance in hell I'm making it through the night without taking care of the urge.

I watch impatiently as she chats with the older couple, smiling politely and nodding at something they say to her. All the while I imagine all the ways I want to have her in this very office. Stretched out on the couch, bent over the desk, pressed against the window. There's an endless array of opportunities. Once they walk away and she's finally alone, I reach for her hand and pull her into the darkness with me.

"Wh—" I quench her protests with a thirsty kiss, pressing her back into the wall. When she realizes it's me, she relaxes into the kiss, a gentle moan escaping her lips.

"Are you still mad at me?" I whisper, grazing my lips against her ear. She smells so fucking good. Delicious enough to eat, and I just might.

"Of course I am."

"That's fine. Makeup sex is my favorite, anyway." Edging her knees apart, I position myself between her legs and slant my body into hers so our hips rub against each other. If I can't convince her, I'm going to have a serious problem on my hands.

"Generally, someone has to apologize for it to be makeup sex." The bite in her tone isn't angry as much as it is playful.

"I'm sorry." I chuckle. "Better?"

Ava's mouth parts like she has something she wants to say, but as my fingers trail up her thigh and underneath the material of this taunting dress, she swallows any argument she's got.

"Nick . . ." Something about the way she whispers my name makes me weak. It takes my breath away and lights a raging inferno inside of me that's insatiable.

"Everyone is waiting for us," she reminds me, as if that has ever stopped me before. When she tries to wiggle out from underneath me, I take her hips, bracing them against the wall.

"It's our party. Let 'em."

She puts her hand on my chest, painted pink fingernails drumming against the buttons of my shirt as she bats those thick lashes at me. "Don't you want to hear how my day was?"

The girl knows exactly what she's doing to me, and I let her have her fun.

"Eventually, yes. But right now, all I want to do is get this dress off you."

"Nick, seriously." She slides away, this time successfully. "This is my father's office. He could walk in at any second."

"Then lock the door, if that's what you're worried about." I'm not going to be talked down easily. Ava might have started this game with her outfit choice, but I'm going to finish it.

"You're impossible." Ava steps to the door and reaches for the knob. At first I think she's about to walk out on me, but instead she trips the lock. "You've got ten minutes."

I let out a sharp laugh, stalking toward her. My arm slips underneath her ass and I set her on the edge of the desk. Loosening my tie, I drop to my knees in front of her and nudge them apart. "I only need five."

TWENTY-THREE

Nick

“Thank you,” I say, taking my drinks and sliding a few bills across the counter to the hired bartenders.

Our parents went all out for this party, catering the event and bringing in a whole slew of vendors. With the Moretti estate as big as any venue, this party is like a mini wedding itself. I'm having a good time, but all I want to do is get Ava home. A few stolen minutes in Alessandro's office were nothing but a tease, and I'm even more frustrated than I was to begin with.

I spot Ava across the room. But as I start to make my way over to see how much longer we have to stay, I'm intercepted by Vince.

“Hey,” he says gruffly.

“Hey.”

The last time Vince and I spoke he accused me of murdering Andrew, and I definitely don't want another scene like we had that night.

“I wanted to say . . .” Vince mumbles, scrambling for words. I know where he's heading with this, but I want to hear him say it. “I reacted badly the other night. I didn't understand the truth about what happened with Andrew, and if I had—”

"Hey, man." I hold up my hand to stop him. "I get it. I probably would've reacted the same way."

"I'm sorry if I caused problems with my sister," he says genuinely.

"You didn't. It was a conversation I should've had with Ava a long time ago, and that's on me."

"Yeah, I heard you paid my dad a visit last week too," he says.

I don't respond. I expected news of our little exchange to get out and that reactions would be mixed.

"I respect the way you handled the situation. The way you stood up for her," he says. "My dad always has some sort of ulterior motive where Ava is concerned."

"What do you mean?"

Vince shakes his head. "Look, all I can really say is that you need to be careful who you trust around here." He glances around the room as if he's worried he'll be caught saying too much to me.

"Your dad?" The marriage treaty was his plan from the very beginning. Why is he not happy with it now?

"He likes to use Ava as a distraction," Vince says quietly, his voice barely audible over the hum of the party behind us. "I don't know what he's planning, but you need to keep a close eye on things. She'll wind up getting hurt if we don't take care of this soon."

"We?" I raise a curious eyebrow at him, his insinuation surprising me.

"Don't let it go to your head, Caponelli. I still can't stand you, but I'm willing to compromise where my sister is concerned."

"Noted." I laugh, taking a drink of my whiskey. This is progress for me and Vince. At least we can agree on one thing—Alessandro isn't going to hurt Ava anymore.

"I'll let you get back to your party, but I'll be in touch soon." Vince slaps me on the back and disappears.

This isn't the time or place, but I need to talk to my dad and Leo as soon as possible so we're not caught off guard. Alessandro is a loose cannon and needs to be dealt with.

The only advantage I have is that he doesn't know I'm suspicious of him.

Ava

"Well, there's the blushing bride herself." Jimmy grins.

He saunters toward me as if he owns the place, his father next to him. Somehow, I've managed to avoid both Jimmy and Terry for most of the night, but he must've been lying in wait. The second Nick leaves me to get a drink, he pounces.

"Hi, Jimmy," I say politely. I can't get away from this conversation fast enough. Especially considering Nick will be back at any second. "Mr. Bradford."

"Please, call me Terry," he says. "I was sorry to hear things didn't work out at our office. We were really looking forward to having you."

"I really appreciate your offer." I give him an awkward smile. "The timing is a little off for me."

Exactly as I told Nick, I had no intention of taking the job with Mr. Bradford. I was able to appease my dad and still follow through with what Nick and I decided, and honestly, that feels like a major win. After Nick ambushed me in the office, I didn't have a chance to tell him.

"I hope you find a good placement." Mr. Bradford smiles. "Now, if you'll excuse me, I need to go find your father."

He excuses himself, slipping through the crowd, and Jimmy and I are left standing alone. There are about a million other places I would rather be. Jimmy makes me uneasy. It isn't that I don't trust myself around him, it's that I don't trust *him*. For whatever reason, he seems hell-bent on driving a wedge between Nick and me. I look around anxiously to see if I can find Nick, but he is still on the opposite side of the room.

"I haven't seen you around the last few weeks," Jimmy observes, standing uncomfortably close. "I'm surprised that your gatekeeper even let you out of the house tonight. Is he the reason you turned down my dad's offer?"

"I turned it down because I don't think it's the right place for me. And honestly, I don't see how this is any of your business."

"Relax, I'm teasing. That's what friends do, right? They tease each other. Although you and I have never really been good at the *friends* thing. We were much better as a couple."

"We were a pretty shitty couple, from what I remember." I scowl. "And I was a completely different person back then."

"Yeah, keep telling yourself that." He smirks, but then his expression softens. "You can do much better than that guy, Ava. Why don't you tell your dad you don't want to do this?"

"Because I do, Jimmy. I love Nick—"

Jimmy nearly spits out his drink. "I'm sorry, did you just honestly say you love Nick? You're practically strangers."

My lack of response doesn't seem to bother Jimmy, and he continues.

"This is a business deal for Nick. He stands to inherit two very powerful organizations the second you say I do. I'd be doing everything in my fucking power to make sure the wedding happened, too, if I were in his shoes. Don't kid yourself into thinking he actually cares about you." Jimmy's words are like venom, burning as they hit my ears. He's trying to get to me, but it still stings.

"Don't listen to him, babe." Nick's arm snakes around my waist territorially, and I've never been happier to feel him next to me. "If I had wasted my opportunity with you and was staring at your fiancé right now, I'd be jealous too."

Jimmy chuckles, finishing the rest of his drink and setting it on a nearby table. "Trust me, Caponelli, I am far from jealous of you. The two of you have only known each other a few months, and now, all of a sudden, you're rushing to the altar. Seems a little convenient to me."

"When you know, you know," Nick says confidently, tightening his grip on me.

"What's Ava's favorite movie?" Jimmy presses, not showing any sign of backing down. Unfortunately, Nick doesn't, either, and I have a bad feeling about how all this is going to end.

"Our relationship is none of your business," Nick growls through gritted teeth.

"Nick, let's go . . ."

"It's a simple question, Caponelli. What is your fiancé's favorite movie? What's her favorite food? Hell, I'll even be satisfied if you know her favorite color."

Nick clenches his jaw. I'm impressed with his restraint, but if Jimmy pushes much further, this won't end well.

"I get that she's good in bed, but you should know a little more about a girl than her favorite position before you pop the question." Jimmy's wry smile sends a rush of chill across my body and a pit forms in my stomach.

Before I know what's happening, Nick jerks away from me and rears his fist back, landing it squarely on Jimmy's jaw. Jimmy returns the hit and a fight breaks out. The two morph into a tangled mess of flailing bodies and punches, and all I can do is stand back and watch.

I'm no match for either of their strengths, and the idea of me trying to break them up feels completely hopeless.

"Hey!" Vince bellows, rushing in to pull them off each other as the rest of the partygoers whisper and look on.

Once he's got them apart, Vince grabs Jimmy's arm and leads him away. Nick swipes some blood dripping from his lip and turns back to me. His face is bruised and bloody, but not nearly as bad as Jimmy's. If

I wasn't so angry at Nick for sinking to Jimmy's level, I might find some amusement in this. Jimmy deserves everything he gets, but not like this. Feeling the scrutinizing eyes of all the partygoers on us, I hurry out of the room, desperate for some air.

They sure know how to break up a party.

TWENTY-FOUR

Ava

"Ouch!" Nick winces, squeezing his eyes shut. He sits on the edge of the bathtub in my childhood bathroom as I wipe at the blood on his face. "I know that you're pissed, Avs, but it hurts when you jab at my face like that."

He can't help but laugh.

Personally, I can't find the humor in any of this. We still have a hundred guests downstairs and here I am, dressing his injuries because he punched out my ex-boyfriend in front of everyone. I'm torn—I loved seeing him come to my defense like he did, but impulsive and hotheaded is probably not the impression Nick wants to give to my father or his future soldiers. Not to mention it was embarrassing to watch the two of them fight like overly testosteroned high-school kids while everyone looked on.

Ignoring him, I press the warm washcloth to his cut.

"Hey." He reaches out and takes my hand, running his thumb along the back of it. "I'm sorry. I shouldn't have hit him. I just can't fucking stand that guy, Ava."

"I know." I sit down beside him on the edge of the tub. "Which is why I didn't take the job."

Nick's eyes widen. "You what?"

"Nick, that's what I was planning to do all along. I explained that I was only going to the interview to make my father happy. They offered me the spot, I turned it down, and then spent the rest of the afternoon looking for other options."

"Baby, more than anything, I was upset that your father would ask you to work with someone who might take advantage of you. I'm sorry I didn't explain that better. Jimmy is a snake, and he's hell-bent on destroying us for some reason."

"But he's some valid points." I let out a shaky breath. "There's so much we don't know about each other."

He chuckles, a broad hand gripping my thigh, and then he's quiet for a second. "Purple."

"Huh?"

"Your favorite color is purple. Favorite food is pizza, and your favorite movie is *The Parent Trap*."

I press my lips together. "Okay, but—"

Nick puts a rough finger to my lips to silence me. "You like to sleep on the side of the bed opposite the door whether we're at home or in a hotel. Your right leg twitches right before you fall asleep every night, and you're a shameless cover stealer. When you're concentrating on something, you bite your lip. You sing in the shower when you think I can't hear you, and you leave a trail of hair ties wherever you go. There's always an empty cup or water bottle in your car, and even though you're not very confident about it, you're a great cook. Your biggest fear is disappointing others, and there isn't anything in the world you wouldn't do for the people you love. Your dream would be to sell everything we own and go travel the world. If you don't eat, you get feisty, and you hate to admit that. You don't like to be wrong and you're stubborn as hell, and no matter how many times we talk about it, you don't use a coaster on the coffee table."

With tears in my eyes, I let out a sharp laugh.

"You're driven and ambitious and adventurous, and when I think about my life without you, I can't breathe. And you know what? Even if I didn't know all those things about you, that would be okay, because I want to spend the rest of my life learning every single detail about you. The ones that stay the same, and the ones that change as we get older."

A tear falls down my cheek. I played right into Jimmy's game. Nick already knows me on a deeper level than Jimmy ever did in the entire time we were together.

Nick leans forward, pressing a soft kiss to my lips. "This is a big change for both of us, but no matter what Jimmy tries to make you believe, I love you. And I'm so excited about our future together."

"Why are you so good to me?" I rest my head on his thick shoulder, our hands intertwining.

"Because you deserve it. And I plan to spend the rest of my life convincing you of that."

"For the record, I wasn't upset that you had a fight with Jimmy. He deserves that and worse. But maybe having it in front of our guests in the middle of our engagement party wasn't the best idea."

Nick stands up, glancing at himself in the mirror and running his fingers over the cut above his eye. "Girls are still into scars, right?"

"Oh yeah." I laugh. "Especially when you get those scars trying to defend their honor."

"Perfect." He winks. "You ready to get out of here?"

"Absolutely."

By the time Nick and I get back downstairs, the crowd has dispersed. The fight broke up the celebration, and only a few guests and our families are left. We say our goodbyes quickly and head home.

We spend the rest of the evening tangled up together in the sheets. Every time we make love, it amazes me how balanced he is. Powerful and commanding. Collected and intentional. Gentle and attentive. He moves my body into any position he wants with ease, knowing exactly how to get to me with each touch. I'll never get tired of the feel of his lips on mine, as if he's starved for me and can never get enough. He makes me feel so thoroughly loved that by the end of it, I can't even keep my eyes open.

When I wake up the next day, I'm lying on his chest in the same position I fell asleep in. Careful not to wake him, I wriggle out from underneath his arm to get ready. An hour later, I'm sitting in a bridal shop with my mother, Mrs. Caponelli, and my sisters, searching for a wedding dress.

Bella chose this boutique, and it must have nearly a thousand options. The dress consultant showed me all kinds of different styles, and at least thirty of them sit in the dressing room right now, waiting for me to try them on.

This is one of the first big things I've done for the wedding, and the closer we get, the more real it becomes, especially since moving the date up. February was hard enough to digest, but now Nick will be my husband before Christmas, and I actually feel excited. Putting on a white dress, regardless of whether or not it will be the one I choose, gives me butterflies. If I close my eyes, I can already imagine Nick waiting for me at the end of the aisle, and the image doesn't immediately send me into a panic attack.

"What do you think?" I smile nervously, turning around to face the group in a dress that's clearly not my style. It's enormous, with pillowy sleeves and a train so long that I'm already positive I'll trip on it.

I came in with an idea of what type of dress I wanted, but unfortunately, so did everyone else.

This was my mother's pick, and although it's beautiful, it's a bit more dramatic than I'm going for.

"Oh, Ava!" My mom gasps, covering her mouth with her hands. Tears pool in her eyes like it's my actual wedding day.

"She looks like a cupcake." Bella cackles, sipping her champagne.

"That dress weighs as much as you do." Angie smiles from her perch on the side of the velvet couch.

"Oh, stop, you two." My mom glares at my sisters. "It's perfect. She looks like an angel. What do you think, Diana?"

Nick's mom and I share a smile. "You'll be absolutely stunning in anything, Ava."

"Thank you." I spin back around, holding some of the fabric up as I look in the mirror. "You guys don't think it's a little . . . big?"

Bella and Angie dissolve into giggles.

"Mom, it's enormous, and Ava is trying to be nice, but she thinks it looks hideous." Bella stands up and goes to browse through a row of dresses. She stops at one, pulling it out and holding it up against her body. "How about this one?"

The dress is incredibly sheer, skintight, and a little too skimpy for my liking. Bella's trying to get a rise out of my mother, and it works immediately.

"Isabella!" she scolds, shaking her head.

"How about something in between the Queen of England and a stripper?" Angie quips. "Try the one I picked out."

"Let's get you out of this and try something a little simpler." The consultant smiles, turning back to the dressing room.

The sound of glass shattering rings through the store. I'm not well-versed in my dad's business, but I know enough to recognize gunshots and screeching tires. Bullets riddle the front windows of the shop, pouring in from somewhere outside. Screams fill the air and people drop to the ground, searching for cover and protection as glass fragments rain down. A few seconds later, everything is still and quiet again, gun smoke and dust settling in the air.

Frantically, I sit up, searching for everyone else, and the movement causes a searing pain in my ribs. I look down, noticing the crimson-red stain soaking through the dress. As I clutch the wound, blood seeps through my fingers and I start to tremble.

"Ava!" I hear someone say my name, but I can't tell the direction it comes from. Suddenly, my arm starts to tingle and my vision gets spotty. I try to take a deep breath but the air gets stuck in my throat and I slump to the side.

Everything around me goes black.

TWENTY-FIVE

Nick

I take a swig from the coffee cup sitting in front of me. We've been sitting here long enough that it's cold, and our server is nowhere to be found. My dad, Leo, and I are having breakfast. For as long as I can remember, we've had a standing Saturday-morning meeting as a point of catch-up, but in light of recent developments, we had some serious business to attend to.

"Vince didn't have any idea what Alessandro was planning, but he said we should be on the lookout." I rub my forehead, trying to force a headache away. Even before my conversation with Vince, I've been overwhelmed with all that's on my plate.

Leo shifts into the booth with a frown. "One of our spies says Alessandro met with Asnikov last week and didn't mention it."

"Why the fuck is he meeting with the Russians and not telling us?" I growl. Alessandro is turning out to be quite a problem. Loyalty is law in the organized crime world, and Vince coming to me behind his own father's back has me uneasy. He wouldn't take the risk unless there was some major shit going down.

My dad clears his throat. Until now, he's been silent. "Is it possible Ava is involved?"

"What?" I spit. "Of course she's not involved."

The idea is as funny as it is ridiculous. There's no way in hell Ava has anything to do with what her father has going on. That's not me being jaded or biased; it's reality.

"Easy, Nick." My dad holds his hand up. "I had to ask. You know her better than anyone, so I trust your judgment."

No, he didn't have to ask, and the fact that he did only irritates me more.

"Maybe he's trying to use the Russians against us," Leo says, scratching his chin. "Alessandro has always wanted more control, and maybe he thinks if he blinds us with this arrangement he came up with, we'll start a war with the Russians. Then we'd have no choice but to merge under any terms he wants."

"If he wants full control, why would he hand Ava over to be in the cross fire?" my dad asks.

"He couldn't care less about Ava. We should've realized that the second he was so quick to change the deal," I snarl, still sore about the memory. Alessandro is a fucking coward, and if I wasn't marrying his daughter, who, for whatever reason, still feels attached to him, I would've offed him already.

"Look, I think we all need to take a breath here. I don't want to make any rash decisions," my dad says. If it were up to Leo and I, we'd act big, and we'd act fast. My dad is much more controlled, though, and it's probably good that we have him to keep us level.

My phone buzzes on the table next to me, and my mom's number pops up. She'd gone with Ava to try on wedding dresses this morning, and I love that the two of them are getting close. When I pick up the phone, there's an urgency in her voice that makes my heart stop.

"Nick, honey, there was a shooting at the dress shop while we were there this morning. I need you to meet me at the hospital."

My throat goes dry, every bit of air sucked out of my lungs. "What happened? Are you okay?"

"I'm fine, Nick, but they just took Ava in the ambulance to Mount Sinai. You need to go to her." My mom's voice breaks as sirens wail in the background. I feel like I'm going to throw up right here.

"I'm on my way."

Lunging out of the booth, I head for the door without any explanation. All I can focus on is getting there and making sure Ava is okay.

"What's going on? What happened?" my dad and Leo ask, trailing behind me.

"There was a shooting at the dress shop. Ava was there. Mom too." I have to focus on every word I say in order for it to make sense. My chest is heavy with panic and terror, but other than that, I'm completely numb. "Mom's okay, but they took Ava to the hospital."

Leo turns white. "Just as a precaution, right? She's okay?"

"I don't fucking know, Leo. I wasn't there," I bark, raking my fingers through my hair. My fury is very obviously misplaced, but I can't help it. Not having all the information makes me insane.

What if she isn't okay? What if she was hit and she's really hurt? What if our life together is over before it even begins?

"We'll go with you." My dad is stone-faced, used to being the source of composure amid the panic.

Thankfully, I have the two of them, because I don't know how I'd get to the hospital otherwise. I'm used to things like this, but with Ava involved, it changes everything. All I care about is getting to her, and I won't be able to function until I can see for myself that she's all right.

I don't even wait for the car to stop before jumping out and sprinting inside. The emergency room is an utter chaos, crawling with reporters and police.

I catch sight of Bella out of the corner of my eye, standing outside a room with Paul, and I rush toward her.

"Nick!" She sobs when she sees me.

"Where is she?"

"She's inside. Vince is with her," she says, pointing to the door behind her.

I don't knock, forcing my way in. Ava sits on the edge of the bed, wearing a white wedding gown drenched in blood, and the sight guts me. Her body heaves with sobs as Vince sits next to her, a doctor and a nurse crouched in front of them.

"Ava." I breathe a sigh of relief, thankful to see her up and talking. That's a good sign.

"Nick!" Her voice breaks with anguish when she sees me.

"It's okay, baby, I'm here now." I wrap my arms around her gently, careful of where she may be injured. "Are you okay? Where are you hurt?" I hold her out in front of me, scanning her body for any signs of injury. She's a bloody mess, but I don't see anything right away.

"She'll be fine," the doctor assures me. "I'm Dr. Fraser. Ava wasn't hit directly by a bullet, but she's got some pretty nasty cuts from the glass and shrapnel. My nurse, Ashley, is going to help Ava get changed so I can have a better look. Do you think you two can give them a minute?"

Vince and I share a look, neither of us wanting to leave her alone.

"No!" Ava is hysterical, burying her face in my chest. She shakes violently, completely inconsolable. "Please don't go."

"It'll only be a minute, baby." I stroke her back, her pleas breaking me. I don't want to leave her any more than she wants me to, but it's important that the doctor sees what's going on.

"And if you're okay with it, he can come back and stay for the exam as soon as we get you changed and cleaned up," Dr. Fraser says.

"Are you okay with that, baby?" I cradle her chin in my hands, fear swirling in her eyes.

Ava hesitates, but nods. "That's fine."

"I'll let you know as soon as we're ready," the nurse says.

I give Ava a quick kiss and follow Vince into the hallway. The door is barely shut behind us before his entire demeanor shifts.

"Is Leo here?" he asks through gritted teeth.

"He's in the waiting room with my dad. What the fuck happened?"

Vince stiffens. "You focus on her, and I'll fill you in later. I'm going to go find Leo."

I want to press him for more, but the most important thing right now is Ava. I wait for a few more minutes, and then the nurse invites me back in while we wait for Dr. Fraser to come back.

Ava sits up in the hospital bed now. She sniffles, some of the color returning to her face. I take a seat next to her, reaching for her hand. "I'm so glad you're okay."

"They killed her, Nick." She chews on her lip, refusing to meet my eyes.

"They killed who, Avs?"

"The saleswoman. She was standing right in front of me," Ava whimpers, a heavy sob rattling through her again.

"Oh, baby," I whisper, dropping my head.

"She was right in front of me, Nick."

"I can't imagine how awful that was for you, Avs, but we're going to get through it, okay?" There's nothing like seeing another person die, and although Ava might be physically okay, this is going to take some time.

Ava is quiet and doesn't say much more. The tattered dress she had on is still draped over the chair, and the sight of it makes me so sick I almost throw up. I've dreamed about the day I'd get to see her in a big white wedding gown, but I never imagined it to be this way. I'm not sure I'll ever get the image of her sitting in front of me in bloody, torn lace out of my mind.

After a few seconds, the doctor is back.

"You look a little better." He smiles. "Mind if I take a look?"

Ava nods, moving over so the doctor has room to work.

Dr. Fraser comes around the side of the bed and gently pulls Ava's hospital gown back. When I see the wounds on her side, my whole body tenses. It may only be from debris, but Ava's wounds are deep and jagged all along her side.

The doctor is gentle as he cleans the wounds, but Ava is in a lot of pain, squirming and wincing as he dabs at them. "Everything looks okay. No major damage, but there's some glass embedded in here and you'll need stitches. How are you feeling otherwise? No other places that hurt?"

"I'm feeling okay." Ava's voice is shaky.

"No headache or anything like that?"

She shakes her head.

"Good." He nods. "I'm confident that you lost consciousness from the shock and not because of any of your injuries, so as soon as we get your cuts sutured, you'll be able to go home. You'll need to take it easy for a few days, and you can expect to be pretty sore for a while. It's all very normal, but if you notice any signs of infection or major bleeding later tonight, then come straight back in."

"Okay," Ava says, clinging onto my hand.

"Thank you so much, Dr. Fraser." I stand to shake his hand, letting out a huge sigh of relief.

Ava is calm enough that I leave while the doctor stitches her up, and I speak with the detective on the case. He doesn't have much information except that it was a drive-by, and he assures me that they're pulling security footage.

Hopefully my guys will get to it first. I want the police as far away from this as possible so I can handle it myself. There's no lawful punishment strong enough for what happened today.

Once Ava is ready to go, we collect her things and head out. She's calm now, but completely drained. Over by the front doors, Alessandro is talking to my dad, Leo, and Vince. He's about the last person I want to deal with, but it seems unavoidable.

"How are you feeling, sweetie?" he asks when he sees us. The insincerity in his voice nearly kills me.

"I'm okay," she answers, tightly gripping my hand.

"Why don't you come home with me? Nick has a lot to deal with, and your mother and I can keep an eye on you while you're recovering," he offers.

"I want to go home," she says. "With Nick."

"Are you sure?" he asks, and turns his attention to me. "Aren't you going to Las Vegas tomorrow?"

"I'm not going anywhere. I'll take care of her," I say through gritted teeth. *She needs to be with someone who sees her as more than a pawn.*

"Nick's right, Dad. No sense in changing things for her now," Vince cuts in. "I'm sure he'll take good care of her. Is that what you want, Ava?"

Ava nods as Alessandro clenches his jaw.

"Why don't you wait for me right over there, baby? I'll just be a second," I suggest, pointing to some chairs in the waiting area. When she doesn't put up a fight, I'm a little surprised, because usually she'd want to be included in the conversation.

"What have you got so far?" I ask, without taking my eyes off Ava.

Leo hands me a playing card that has the Asnikov family symbol on the bottom of it. "This was left on their car out front."

"This is your fault," Alessandro hisses. "This is about the hit you guys made a few weeks ago."

"Are you sure it doesn't have something to do with you? They didn't mention anything when you met last week?" I hiss back.

His jaw twitches as he realizes he's been caught. "I don't like what you're insinuating." *Give me a reason, Alessandro. Give me a fucking reason.*

“Nick, you need to take Ava home. Everyone is stressed, and this is no time to discuss this. We’ll meet first thing in the morning,” my dad intervenes, and it’s a good thing he does because Alessandro and I are damn close to coming to blows.

“Call me if anything changes,” Alessandro spits.

He takes off without another word or even glance at Ava, the daughter he’s supposedly so concerned about.

TWENTY-SIX

Ava

After the trauma of the day, all I want to do is crawl into bed, preferably with Nick's arms wrapped around me as I sleep.

The hospital gave me some Valium to help me relax, but so far it isn't working. It might have calmed my body a bit, but it's done nothing to quiet my mind. I can't get that vision out of my head, and I'm not sure I ever will. The sounds of splintering glass and my sisters screaming. The look on that poor woman's face when she fell against me. The smell of gun smoke and blood, a combination that still makes me nauseated.

The memory is so vivid that it strangles me. Desperate for a little air, I go out onto the balcony off of our bedroom, bracing myself against its wrought-iron railing. Below me, cars pass and the streets are full of tourists. It almost feels surreal how easily life continues. A woman died, and life continues as if nothing happened. She was someone's daughter, someone's friend, and now she's gone.

Nick wants me to believe that this isn't about us, but I know better. I watched as he scoped out the parking garage when we drove in, opting for a space closer to the entrance than our usual assigned spot. I watched as he held me back, refusing to ride up the elevator with another group and insisting we wait until we could go ourselves. I watched as he double-checked the locks on all the doors behind us, even tripping the dead bolts that we rarely ever use. He's worried about something, and that scares me more than anything.

After a few minutes I hear the bedroom door open, but I don't turn around. I can tell by the footsteps it's Nick. When he comes out, he approaches slowly, leaning against the railing next to me and giving me a bit of space.

After a few minutes of quiet, he reaches over and sets his hand on top of mine. "Leo brought over your prescriptions. I'll keep them with me, but let me know if you need anything, okay?"

I nod. I can tell by the flat tone in his voice that he's concerned about me taking the medication, and so am I.

"Are you doing okay?" he asks, thumb sweeping across the back of my hand as he holds it.

The question sounds disingenuous, but he doesn't mean it that way. He wants to help, but I don't know if I'll ever actually be okay again.

"I just can't get it out of my head," I admit.

He swallows, an unreadable expression on his face. "I wish that I could tell you it's going to get easier, but you went through something really traumatic and sometimes that takes time to work through."

"How many people have you seen die?"

Nick hesitates for a second. "More than I would like to admit." He tucks a piece of hair behind my ear, his touch so delicate it's like he thinks he might break me. "What you're feeling is totally normal, Ava. It's never easy, but the first time is the worst."

"The first time," I repeat, realizing that this probably wouldn't be the last time.

Nick doesn't respond, because there isn't much to say. This is my reality now. Or maybe it always has been.

"Do you know who did it?"

"I don't want you to worry about that. Your focus needs to be on getting better."

"I am going to worry about it," I argue. "A woman died in my arms today, all because you and I are getting married. That doesn't bother you at all?"

"Of course it bothers me, Ava. I would rather die than have you in danger like you were today." He cups my chin in his hand, gently angling it toward him. "Look at me—what happened today has nothing to do with you and me getting married. It has nothing to do with you, period. You have to trust me. In the scheme of things, our marriage doesn't mean all that much. Certainly not enough for someone to want to kill either of us. Something bigger is going on, and I need you to trust that I am going to take care of it."

"If it has nothing to do with us, then who does it have to do with? My father?"

"I don't know who it is yet. But I swear to you, I won't stop until I do. And I will make sure whoever killed that woman today pays for it." Nick sets his jaw, a distance in his eyes that I don't quite know how to take. He's defended me before. He's made promises and even threats regarding my safety, but the weight of this one feels different. It feels personal and intimate on a completely different level.

I want to believe him, but I'm not convinced. The way I see it, the shooting is directly related to us, and the thought that someone might be trying to kill me is paralyzing.

"Why don't I get a bath ready for you? It might help you relax," he suggests, effectively ending the discussion. I won't get more information out of him right now, and I don't have the energy to argue.

I nod and follow him into the bathroom. A bubble bath does sound relaxing, and hopefully it will help quiet my mind so I can get some rest.

Nick runs the water and leaves me for a few minutes to undress and get settled. I have to be careful not to get my bandages very wet, but they are high enough on my ribs that I can keep them out of the scalding hot water. I stare at my skin where the nurse cleaned off the blood, but I still feel like I can see it. Like I'll never be able to get it all off. Like I'll never feel completely clean again. I scrub at my skin, but it isn't working. My mind knows that the blood is gone, but my body still feels it there. I scrub and scrub until my skin is almost raw.

"All set?" Nick's face falls when he sees me frantically washing my skin. "Ava, what's wrong?"

There is no way I can explain this to him. He comes over and kneels beside the tub, taking the loofah from me and holding both of my hands in his.

"You're okay," Nick soothes me, kissing the backs of my hands. "I'm going to get in there with you and help you clean it off, okay?"

I nod. At least if he's with me, I won't be left alone with my own thoughts. Nick slips his clothes off quickly and steps into the tub, positioning himself behind me. He rubs my skin gently with a washcloth, up and down my body, grounding me until I slowly come to my senses.

Nick drains the tub and fills it with clean water so I don't have to look at the blood anymore. I lean back against him and he drapes his arms over me. Bubbles cover both of our bodies as we sit, melting into each other.

My mind clears with his touch, and suddenly I'm overcome with need for him. It hits me like a brick wall, and a loud ache builds inside of me. I need Nick to make me forget this day ever even happened.

As I drape my head back against Nick's shoulder, I press my hips against him. He sweeps a kiss across the exposed skin on my neck, hands traveling all over my body as the realization of what I want dawns on him. I moan into his touch, dissolving all other thoughts in my mind besides the feel of his skin on mine.

"Ava, are you sure—"

I lift my chin, crashing my lips into his and silencing his protest.

That's the only invitation he needs. Nick leans forward, nipping my earlobe softly. One hand trails down my chest, over the swell of my breasts and along my stomach. His touch is gentle, but it's almost too much for me as a deep, sweltering heat winds through my body.

I'm impatient, but Nick is calm and intentional as he rubs and massages my body. He holds me like I'm breakable, each stroke of his finger more dainty and delicate than the one before. I've come to expect his domination, his control, his authority. This is different, and it hits me right in the feels.

My knees fall open, because even though there's a fragility in his touch, I need it. His fingers creep up my thigh until they reach my core, and he tenderly traces my entrance. Without much wait, he slips a finger inside of me, swirling and twisting as I buck against him. He moves at a gentle, indulgent speed that satisfies me as much as it surprises me.

"Please, Nick." The intensity of my request feels more intimate than usual, because I don't just need Nick in the physical sense. I need him to make this okay. I need him to make me forget. I need him to hold me like he believes we can make it through this.

Nick grunts, shifting himself in the tub as he grabs my hips. He lifts me up, positioning me on top of him and guiding me down. I love feeling him against me. Our bodies pressed together, morphing into one.

His lips trace designs on my stomach and breasts as his fingers still slide along my curves. He's careful to avoid my cuts, softly kissing each bandage. Draping my leg over the edge of the tub, I press farther into him, begging him for more. He's steady, but in a way that puts me in control, and he follows my lead.

When I moan, he quiets me with a kiss and slips his tongue into my mouth.

"There we go," he coaxes, easing me down on top of him and slipping into me with a slow, deep plunge. It takes my breath away at first, and his body tenses against mine. No matter how sweet and gentle he wants to be, he can't deny his own desire, and his pace intensifies. Still, he's careful. Our bodies rock against each other, moving in a perfect, uninterrupted rhythm.

With each thrust, he gets deeper and deeper, filling me up and erasing every dark and depressing thought in my head. His fingers dig into my back, holding me in place as he pushes against me and I slip further and further into a euphoric bliss.

I had no idea how badly I needed this. How badly I needed him. Nick is my refuge—saving my life time and time again.

Finally, we collapse against each other, panting and breathless. Even if for a brief moment, the pain of today is gone, and I'm safe in his arms.

TWENTY-SEVEN

Nick

It takes me hours to get Ava finally settled enough to rest. Once we get home, the shock and adrenaline wear off and reality sets in. She's horrified and scared, and there's a part of her that feels guilty that she even survived. I know from experience that those emotions are hard to sit with, and it shatters me to watch her go through it.

Unfortunately, there isn't much I can do to help besides be with her as she processes it. Not being able to fix this for her guts me. There's no simple answer, no magic wand I can wave, no right words to make her feel better. I've never been good at the emotional stuff, and so I turn to what's familiar.

The violence. The vendetta. The vengeance.

With Ava sleeping soundly in the bedroom for the time being, I head into the kitchen. I call Vince, and he picks up on the first ring.

"Everything okay?"

"Fine here. Are you somewhere you can talk?" I ask, reaching into the liquor cabinet for a bottle. I think better of it, though. My mind needs to be as sharp as possible right now, and bourbon certainly won't help with that.

"Leo and I are at the coffee shop a block from your place."

With everything that's been going on, it isn't far off to think that the Russians, or even Alessandro, are monitoring us, but I don't want to leave Ava. She'll be hysterical if she wakes up and I'm gone. "I don't have much time. I don't want Ava to wake up alone."

"We'll come to you then. Meet us outside your building?"

"Sounds good."

I slip my shoes on and grab my keys quickly before peeking in on Ava one more time. She's relatively peaceful, but I don't know how long that will last. I double check the alarm, and by the time I get downstairs, Leo and Vince are waiting.

"Ava doing okay?" Leo's voice is full of concern. Everyone has grown to love her in the last few months, and she's already a part of this family, so this hits deep for us all.

"She's all right. I finally got her to sleep. She's having trouble processing everything."

"I don't blame her. I'm having trouble processing it myself," Vince says.

So am I. The escalation doesn't make sense, and that's what has bothered me from the beginning.

"Have you guys found out anything?"

Vince reaches into his jacket and pulls out a manila envelope. "This is the guy. So far, all we can tell is that he showed up at the dress shop a few minutes after they got there. Seems like a spur-of-the-moment attack. No one was casing the place or following Ava or any of the girls beforehand."

My hands shake with rage as I hold the black-and-white surveillance pictures in my hand. I don't know what I was expecting, but this guy isn't it. He looks anxious, almost like he's strung out on something, glancing around and fidgeting. He doesn't even make any effort to hide his face or the giant Russian tattoo on his neck because they want us to know who is responsible. "Where can I find him?"

"Look, man." Leo shoves his hands into his sweatshirt pocket nervously. "I don't think you should handle the hit on this."

I almost burst out laughing. Not handle the hit? He's fucking delusional if he thinks I'm going to go for that. I want this bastard all for myself. Plotting exactly how I'm going to make him pay is the only thing that's kept my sanity for the last several hours, and I have some very innovative ideas.

"You're too close to this, Nick." Vince backs him up. "It's already got a lot of eyes from the cops and the media, and we need to be careful. Especially if this is really about my father."

"Of course it's about your dad. If this was about us, they would've come after me, not Ava. You don't think I can keep my head on straight because she's involved?"

"No one is saying that." Leo shakes me off. "This is Alessandro's fight. If you get involved in this shit, they'll come after you and they'll come after Ava."

"They already did come after Ava." This is bullshit. I want the guy. I want his blood on my hands like a goddamn trophy.

"We don't know that," Vince insists.

Seems pretty clear to me.

"Look, whatever my dad is mixed up with, it's unraveling, and anyone close to it is going to be in danger. My mom took his car to the dress shop, and they were inside before the guy showed up. It's highly possible that the hit was coming for my dad and they thought he was inside when they saw the car."

"What the hell does your dad have going on with the Russians?" I'm tired of being two steps behind. Alessandro is jerking us around like puppets, and we've let him in the name of keeping the peace. Well, fuck that.

He's dragging us into a war that we want nothing to do with. This arrangement is supposed to keep the Russians at bay, not incite them even further.

"I don't know. I'm working on it." Vince grits his teeth. "In the meantime, you and my sister stay as far away from this as possible. Get her out of the city, do whatever you need to do. But let me handle this. This is my father's fault, until proven otherwise, and it needs to stay that way."

I don't like the idea of being pushed away from this fight, but Vince has a point. Until Ava and I are married, she isn't officially part of the Caponelli family, which means I can't allocate resources to protect her without council approval.

"Nick, Dad wants you to think about moving the wedding up again. Alessandro doesn't want it to happen, and if he backtracks on the deal there won't be much we can do. It's the best thing for us, and it's the best thing for Ava too. We can protect her better."

This time, I can't stifle my laughter.

"You think I'm going to convince her to move the wedding up after what happened today?"

"You can't protect her like she needs to be until she's your wife," Leo continues. "And if you're married, Alessandro won't have a leg to stand on."

"She's never going to go for that." I shake my head, already imagining how telling Ava would go.

"Then convince her," Vince snaps. "If my dad gets his way, there will be no wedding at all, and then what? You'll be content handing her back to him?"

"Absolutely not. I'm never letting your father anywhere near her again." Deal or no deal, I would die before letting Ava be hurt by him again. She's been suffering the consequences of his horrible decisions for too long as it is.

"Yeah, well, you won't have much choice if you don't seal the deal," Vince reminds me.

He's right. Nothing feels safe, but at least if we're married, I have control.

"We're all in this to make sure Ava is safe. Let Vince do what he's good at, and you focus on getting her better. Alessandro won't get away with this, I promise you that." Leo puts his hand on my shoulder.

I'm quiet as I decide whether or not I'm going to go against my better judgment and hand the reins to Leo and Vince.

"Nick, I had just as much at stake in that shooting as you did," Vince stutters, his voice breaking slightly. "And Soph is due to have the baby any day now. The last thing I want is for this bullshit to last any longer."

I hope I won't regret this. "I want to be kept up-to-date on everything."

"Of course." Leo nods.

"And the second you find out what Alessandro—"

"You'll be the first to know."

"Fine," I say reluctantly. I'm not usually one to let go of things easily, but if it means keeping Ava safe, I'm willing to try anything. As weird as it is to be on the same side as Vince, it's a nice change of pace.

Leo and Vince leave and I head back upstairs. Now the only thing I've got to focus on is how to coax Ava down the aisle . . . like, tomorrow.

TWENTY-EIGHT

Ava

"Ava?" Nick calls, shutting the door to the penthouse quietly. Every move he's made around me lately has been quiet. Restrained. As if he expects anything too harsh or too loud to send me into hysterics. For all I know, it might.

I've relived that day a thousand times over, barely able to think about anything else. It's on my mind when I wake up in the morning, the last thing I think about before I go to sleep, and it occupies most moments in between.

The bullet-riddled bridal shop. The shredded, bloody wedding gown on my body. The look of horror on the consultant's face when she realized she'd been hit. The images have plagued my nightmares for days.

Nick refuses to leave my side no matter how restless I am, and neither one of us has gotten much sleep. Each time I have a nightmare, I wake up cradled in his arms. I don't think I've slept a solid hour in the week since the shooting.

He'd finally made it into the office today, but only at my insistence. He's only trying to help, but the way he treats me like I'm made of glass is driving me crazy.

"Ava?" he calls again.

"In here."

"Hey!" He comes into the living room, sitting down next to me on the couch. "How are you?"

"I'm doing okay." I muster a smile, hoping it looks more convincing than it feels. I can't take another night of him placating me.

"Good," he says. "You look better. Did you get outside today?"

"Mhm."

He doesn't respond, just bends down and kisses my cheek. "I've got a surprise for you."

"Oh yeah?"

Nick smiles, offering me his hand to help me up. "Go change, we're going out."

Suddenly, his surprise doesn't sound all that appealing if it requires me to put on real clothes and leave the penthouse.

"Don't look at me like that. We're going." Nick angles his head, chucking. "You need to get out of this house, and don't tell me you went outside today. You're lying. I watched you lie here all day."

"What do you mean, *you watched me*?"

Nick points to a frame on the mantel with a barely detectable smirk on his face, so small that it's clear he doesn't want me to see he's finding humor in this. "There's a camera in there."

"A camera?" I shoot up, throwing the blanket off and bolting upright. "You installed cameras to spy on me?"

"No, I have cameras installed all over the apartment for security purposes. And they were here long before you were, so relax." Nick takes my hips possessively, pulling me closer to him. It's the first time he's manhandled me since the shooting, and god, it feels nice. We had sex in the bathtub that night, but other than that, he's been treating me like a porcelain doll. Feeling his firm hold on my body again is enough to make me consider whatever it is that he has in mind.

"Besides, I'm worried about you. I understand you're still processing what happened, but it isn't healthy for you to stay cooped up here all day thinking about it. You need to get back into the swing of things. Keep yourself active. Busy."

"And that will help?"

"I promise it will." His lips find mine in a deep kiss. A cool ache consumes me the second he pulls away, but there's a charge and energy through my body that I haven't felt in days. His kiss is like magic. "There is a box on your bed—I want you to go change into what's inside and meet me here in fifteen minutes. No more questions, no more protests. Am I clear?"

I nod, excitement creeping through my body. Maybe this isn't such a bad idea after all.

Scurrying into the bedroom, I'm eager to see what he brought me. I have no idea where we're going or what we're doing, but I'm already feeling slightly better. Having something else to concentrate on is nice.

Just as he said, there's a white box tied with a beautiful gold ribbon sitting on our bed. Careful not to crease the ribbon and paper, I open it carefully. There's a black jogger set inside that's exactly my size. Nick's got good taste, that's for sure. The material is so buttery soft and luxurious that I moan as I slip into it. It feels like heaven on my skin, and it's so warm and cozy it almost defeats the purpose of getting me out of the house entirely. It's so comfortable I could fall asleep right now.

Fighting the temptation to crawl into our bed, I find my sneakers and lace them up. I even put on a little makeup and fix my hair so I don't look like an absolute train wreck for whatever he has planned.

When I get out to the living room again, Nick has his back to me as he stares out the window into the darkness, his phone tightly pressed against his ear. He's tense and his voice is so low that I can barely make out what he says.

"I want to be kept up-to-date on everything. He leaves the house for a second, you call me. I don't care if he's walking the fucking dog, I want to know about it."

Silence. His harsh voice sends chills up and down my body. It always catches me off guard when he slips into crime boss mode—fierce, lethal, and terrifying.

"Yeah, everything is taken care of on my end." Nick shoves his fingers through his thick hair in frustration. "Don't fuck this up, Vince. This may be our only shot."

Vince? My brother Vince?

"Got it. Talk to you soon." Nick ends the call and whirls around.

Startled by his sudden move, a small gasp escapes my lips.

"Hey, baby," Nick says, his demeanor taking a hard turn. "You look incredible. Ready to go?"

My head tells me to let it go, but my mouth has other plans. "Why are you talking to my brother?"

Nick's brow furrows into a frown. He starts toward me slowly, each step making me more anxious. I have no idea why—Nick's never made me feel scared in the entire time we've known each other, but I can't push the feeling down.

"You were listening to me on the phone?"

"Stop avoiding my question." I hold my ground. "Why are you talking to my brother?"

He sighs heavily. "Ava, Vince and I are working together to figure out who was behind the shooting at the dress shop. There is no reason to get worked up. I figured you'd be happy we're getting along."

In reality, I am, but I can't help but feel like I'm being kept out of the loop about something.

"I didn't tell you because it's still such a sore subject for you. Seriously, Ava, I wasn't trying to hide it from you. Call Vince, and he'll tell you the same thing."

Of course there is a simple explanation. Why wouldn't there be?

Why do my mind and body jump to the worst-case scenario so fast? It's like ever since the shooting, I'm on the defensive.

"Okay." I nod. "Sorry, I guess my nerves are still a little on edge."

Nick wraps his hand around the back of my neck, drawing me into him as his lips find mine. "I'm sure they are, which is exactly why we're doing this. I want you to be able to relax and forget about everything for a while. Does that sound okay?"

"That sounds incredible." I smile. "Where are we—"

He silences me with another kiss. "No questions, remember?"

We drive for a while, and the entire time I try to figure out where we're headed. It's nearly midnight, and most places won't be open. Nick offers no hints, and I can't even tell what part of town we're in through the darkness, so I'm totally baffled. Which seems to be exactly what he wants.

When Nick finally stops the car, we're in the middle of nowhere.

I climb out of the truck, shivering in the stiff breeze. Even in the sweats, it's a cool fall evening and the wind is relentless out in an open field like we are.

"Wait for it." A smug grin stretches across his face, thrilled with himself for whatever he's pulled off.

I wait patiently, but nothing happens. Nick scowls, and I have to stifle my laughter. It doesn't seem like things are going according to his plan.

"One more second . . ." he coaxes, a tight grip on my hand.

All of a sudden a giant roar comes from the sky above us. As I look up, an airplane flies by, so close that the wind it generates makes me feel like I'm inside of a tornado. Heart racing, hair all over the place. No clue what's going on.

"Jesus, Nick, this is your idea of relaxing? Are you trying to give me a heart attack?"

Nick grabs my shoulders and spins me around. There's a personal jet behind me.

"No, baby. That plane is going to take us to my idea of relaxing."

A trip? "Nick . . . what are you . . . I don't . . ."

"Shhhh," he says, pulling me toward the plane by my hand. "No protests, remember?"

"I agreed to that before I knew you were trying to take me out of the state," I quip.

"Country."

"What?"

"I'm taking you out of the *country*. To Saint Lucia." Nick grabs a bag from the back seat of the car and then locks it behind him.

"Nick, we can't pick up and leave. I don't have any clothes, I have class, I have to find a job . . ."

Nick rests his hands on his hips, letting me rattle off my list of reasons why this won't work. "Are you out of excuses yet?"

"I am, yes, but that doesn't mean this is a good idea."

"Ava, the beach is always a good idea." Nick smirks. "You don't have to find a job yet, there will be plenty of time for that. And you already got approval to take a few weeks off class because of the shooting. As for clothes, I packed a bag for you and it's waiting on the plane, but I assure you, clothes won't be necessary for the things I have in mind."

"Nick, we can't. What am I supposed to tell my parents?" My protests are shallow. I want to get onto that plane and fly away from everything with him more than anything in the world.

"You don't have to tell them anything, Ava." Nick throws his hands in the air. "We need a break. Both of us. Things have been stressful lately, and it's only going to get more chaotic with the wedding coming. When we first met, you told me how much you like to travel. And there's no better way to start feeling like yourself again then getting back into the things you enjoy."

He reaches into his back pocket and produces both of our passports.

"Humor me, okay? I rented us a villa right on the beach for five days. Nothing to worry about but all the places we're going to make love."

"You're insane, you know that?'

"Come on, baby. You're really going to turn me down after all the effort I put into putting this together?"

Now he's playing the guilt card. "Are you sure this is a good idea?"

"Oh, I'm positive it's a good idea. I've already decided we're going, but I'm trying to give you the illusion of control before I haul you over my shoulder and throw you onto that plane." Nick narrows his eyes.

"You wouldn't."

He shrugs, closing the distance between us in one smooth stride. His arms wrap around my waist and he effortlessly tosses me over his shoulder, exactly as he promised.

"Nick!" I giggle. "I'll go! Just let me walk!" I can hardly get the words out because I'm laughing so hard.

"Nope, you had your chance." Nick slaps my butt lightly. "Now we're doing things my way."

TWENTY-NINE

Nick

The second we touch down in Saint Lucia, it's like a huge weight lifts off Ava's shoulders. I can almost see the stress melting away before my eyes. At first I was hesitant about traveling so far away, but after seeing her reaction, I'm positive it was the right thing to do. Getting her out of New York is the only way I can protect her until she's my wife, and if all goes according to plan, the next time we touch down in the city, she will be.

We get to Saint Lucia at six thirty in the morning, and it's a quick trip from the airport to the resort. Our villa is about a hundred yards into the ocean, right in the middle of the beautiful turquoise water. There's a boardwalk out to it, and fish race along the side of us as we walk.

There are a few other villas out here, but we're far enough away to have privacy with our own hot tub and pool on the deck. Back on shore, there's a beach club where more resort guests stay. A world-class spa, large, sparkling pools, and a restaurant with about every global cuisine you could imagine. Ava is like a little kid at Disney, the ocean air breathing life into her that I haven't seen before. She's over the moon to be here, and so am I.

Neither one of us slept much on the plane, so after a walk on the beach and some breakfast, we decide to take a nap. She's asleep within seconds of lying down on the giant feather bed, and I take advantage of the moment alone to call Vince.

He picks up on the third ring.

"Can you just fucking leave this alone and enjoy your time away?" He chuckles, knowing full well that it's not in my nature. I don't have it in me to be so hands-off.

"Trust me, I am definitely going to enjoy my time away, but I want to make sure things are in order there first." Even thousands of miles away, I have to have my hands on this somehow.

"They're in order, Nick. Joey took your credit card and booked a room in Chicago. He's got the burner phone attached to your number. He's going to stay there the entire weekend and be sure he's not seen by anyone. I already planted the seed with my dad that Ava is in Cape Cod visiting some friends and that you are out of town on business, but he doesn't know where. He thinks I'm house-sitting." Vince chuckles. "Anyway, if he shows up in Chicago, then it proves he's tracking you."

With all the groundwork we laid, hopefully Alessandro will take the bait.

Since Alessandro has close tabs on most of us, we decided to use Joey as a decoy. He's been with us for years, and he's as trustworthy and loyal as they come. Usually he comes in to do the cleanup work, so when we suggested that he spend the weekend in a fancy hotel downtown pretending to be me, he jumped at the chance.

After a bit of digging, Vince, Leo, and I concluded that Alessandro might be trying to take me out. If he is, and he needs an opportunity, we gave him one: a solo business trip to Chicago where "I'll" be alone all weekend. To be on the safe side, I booked the Saint Lucia hotel under a false name—"Sinatra," for the memories—and we took a private plane so that Alessandro can't find out where Ava and I really are.

"I'll call you if anything develops, but if I don't, don't call me. We can't take any chances of my dad seeing us in contact."

"Got it. I'll have my hands full here," I chide, letting his mind wander where it may.

"Watch it, moron. That's my sister you're talking about."

"You're the one who told me to find something to keep me busy."

Vince growls. "I'm hanging up before you say something that's going to make me slit your throat."

"Fine. Keep me updated."

I make my way back to our room to find Ava still fast asleep. Her sweats are draped over a nearby chair, meaning she's completely naked beneath the sheets—exactly how I want her. I bite my fist, trying to contain myself from ambushing her. We both need some sleep, and the rest can come later. Stepping out of my own clothes, I climb into the bed next to her and wrap my entire body around her protectively. She stirs but then melts into me.

"Good morning." A sleepy smile plays at her lips.

"Shush. It's not morning yet. Go back to sleep," I try to coax, pulling her into me tighter and burying my face in the bare skin between her shoulder blades.

Ava pulls out of my embrace, not having any of it. "No, come on," she whines. "We're at the beach. We can sleep later."

"For someone who was so vehemently against this trip a few hours ago, you've certainly had a change of heart."

She giggles, pressing a kiss to my cheek. "Please?"

Ava jumps out of bed and rummages around in her suitcase until she finds one of the swimsuits I brought. She slips it on and ties her long hair into a bun on the top of her head.

"All right, all right, all right." I fake frustration, swinging my body out of the bed. So much for a little rest. "We can go swimming on one condition."

I walk toward her slowly, snaking my arm around her waist as her body presses into mine.

"What's that?"

My fingertips trace up her spine until I reach the back of her swimsuit, and then I gently tug at the strings. She gasps as it falls to the floor, and I lean in, grazing my lips against her ear. "This stays here."

"Nick, no . . ." She's appalled at my suggestion, but her protest falls on deaf ears. I booked this place with this very moment in mind. I put my finger to her lips to quiet her.

"No one can see you but me. It's completely private out here." I smile, trailing my lips down to her collarbone and slipping my fingers into the waistband of her bottoms. I slide them down painfully slowly until they're wrapped around her ankles, and she steps out of them. "Now we can go swim."

I sink my teeth into her tender inner thigh, and she yelps, playfully twisting out of my grasp and diving into the pool.

She's a perfect masterpiece.

Ava

Everything about my vacation with Nick is perfect. We spent the morning lounging by the pool of our villa, taking full advantage of the privacy, and munching on fresh fruit and juices that room service delivered. Now we're sitting on the beach watching the waves roll in while we eat our lunch. This place is pure paradise, and Nick was exactly right: I'm feeling more like myself than I have in a long time.

I want to forget about everything at home, but I can't shake the feeling that Nick is hiding something from me. He's been on his phone most of the morning, looking at texts and emails, and even when he isn't, his mind is elsewhere.

He's going to go after the person who attacked the dress shop. It's his job—something that he does often and is good at—but I'm not sure I'll ever get past the anxious feeling in my chest when I know he has to kill someone.

It's dangerous, and I'm worried for him. I'm worried for us. I don't want it to ruin our time here together, but it's hard not to think about what might happen when we get home. We can't ignore our responsibilities forever.

"What do you want to do this afternoon?" Nick asks, stroking my leg as we lie by the water, finally giving me his full attention.

"I don't know. Do we have anything we have to do tonight?" He took a brief dip in the ocean, and his hair is still salty and damp as I run my fingers through it. It's a little longer than I'm used to, and I love it.

"We have reservations at one of the restaurants, but not until eight. The afternoon is all yours." He winks, stretching his arms high above his head. I pretend not to notice how the motion pulls his swim trunks down a bit, his abs glistening in the sunlight.

When his phone rings, the noise startles us both.

"Hold that thought." He grimaces. So much for the afternoon being mine.

"Hello?"

I can faintly hear the voice on the other end, but I don't recognize it.

Whoever it is sets off alarm bells for Nick, though, because he stands up abruptly and walks farther down the beach so that I can't hear. I hate that he isn't telling me what's going on. He's promised over and over that he won't hide things from me, but over the last few days, it feels like that's all he's doing.

Nick is on the phone for a while, and his call doesn't show any sign of ending soon, so I take it upon myself to enjoy our vacation. The water is beautiful and the sand feels so soft between my toes that it's like walking on clouds. There's a little shack down the beach where you can rent water equipment, and I decide to snorkel. The resort is set along an absolutely stunning reef with thousands of colorful fish, stingrays, and even a few sea turtles. I've never seen anything like it in all of my life and I swim until my skin gets pruny.

When I finally make it back to shore, Nick is still on the phone pacing next to our chairs.

He's determined to make me relax, but maybe he needs a little encouragement in that area himself. I get an idea, and come out of the water right as he's hanging up the call.

"You seem like you're having a good time." He grins, eyes locked on my chest. The swimsuit he packed for me leaves very little to the imagination. In fact, I'm not even sure it qualifies as a swimsuit. Dental floss would be more accurate.

"I am. It's beautiful out here." I smile, reaching out and snatching his phone out of his hand.

"What are you—"

Without another word, I throw the phone as far as I can out into the ocean.

Nick looks at me like I'm absolutely insane, his eyes widening in horror as he watches it sink beneath the waves. He lets out a sharp laugh. "Have you completely lost your mind?"

I turn back to him, taking his hand in mine and dragging him into the water. "Do I have your attention now?"

"Oh yeah, you've got every bit of my undivided attention now, baby. But I think you just bit off way more than you can chew."

Nick sprints through the water after me with a taunting smirk on his face. His arms sweep around me and he tackles me into a wave. I'm no match for his strength, but I also don't put up much of a fight.

"Nick!"

"You know what happens to naughty girls?" he purrs, effortlessly lifting me and throwing me over his shoulder.

"Nick, stop!" I pound my fist against his strong back, but it's no use. I'm completely at his mercy, and we both like it that way.

"They get punished, Ava." He laughs to himself, sticking his fingers in the waistband of my bikini bottoms and yanking them down.

"Nick, oh my god—"

He works my bottoms off and tosses them into the water. I come up in time to see him catapulting them into the ocean, never to be seen again.

"What's that saying about karma?" He runs a rough finger along my chin, tilting my head up to give me a salty kiss.

THIRTY

Nick

Saint Lucia brings out an entirely new side of Ava, and damn, could I get used to it.

Without the heaviness and pressure of home, she's happy and completely carefree. I don't think I've seen her quite like this in our entire relationship. Easygoing is a good look on her, and as each minute passes, she's more and more at peace. The look in her eye makes me want to buy her a whole damn island so that we can do this more often. Or at the very least, a jet, so that it's accessible on a whim.

After our romp in the ocean, Ava and I spend the day kayaking, snorkeling, and enjoying the resort. This place is heaven on earth, and I'm pretty sure we could be here for a month and never run out of things to do.

When we finally drag ourselves back to the room, it's time to get ready for dinner. Ava hops in the shower, and as badly as I want to join her, I'll have to scrounge up some kind of phone, since mine is now sitting at the bottom of the Caribbean. Her tactic was dramatic, but effective. Without a phone, I have no way of staying in touch with what's happening back home, and it was nice to forget for a while, but now it's time to face the music.

Alessandro is a manipulative bastard. I guess I already knew that, but Joey's phone call solidified it beyond my wildest dreams. Last night was the first night in our stakeout to catch Alessandro tracking me, and he'd fallen right into our trap. Apparently, I severely underestimated his hatred for me, though.

I expected him to send some soldiers to prove a point by roughing me up a bit, but what I didn't expect was for him to send two prostitutes to the door in a blatant attempt to set me up. The motherfucker is brazen, I have to give him that.

From the very beginning he was planning to use Ava to control and manipulate our family, and now he's counting on her to be the one to break the deal off. And he's willing to do it by any means necessary.

I'm sure his plan was to photograph me at the door with those women and use the pictures to convince Ava that I'm cheating on her. That this really is just about business, and I'm lying about my feelings for her. Then she'd walk away, and it would be her fault the treaty fell apart.

The man is spineless, and the longer this goes on, the more he can see her pulling away from him. If I had any doubts about coming home with her as my wife, now I'm fucking positive it's a good idea.

Ava doesn't know that her dad is double-crossing us, and I've had conflicted thoughts about telling her. Knowing what he's up to might only hurt her more. I promised not to keep things from her, but Ava is fragile, especially right now. Regardless, lying isn't a path I want to go down again.

I knock on the door, unsure if she's still in the shower. When she doesn't answer, I push it open and go in anyway.

"Avs?" I call, glancing around the room. A few of her dresses are strewn out across the bed and, from the bathroom, I can hear her singing. She's so happy and relaxed here that I almost can't bring myself to ruin it.

I nudge the bathroom door open, and she's leaning against the counter in only her towel. Dark, damp hair cascades down her back as she does her makeup. Each time she leans forward, the towel rides up and I get a glimpse of her perfect bare ass. She's got no idea what a tease she is. *Jesus Christ.* This woman is everything.

"What are you doing?" Ava raises an eyebrow at me. I was so distracted checking her out that I didn't even realize she knew I was here.

"I, uh . . ." I stammer, running my fingers through my hair. "I was going to apologize for earlier."

"Apologize? For what? We had a great day."

"We had an incredible day." I grin, sweeping my arm underneath her. The towel doesn't provide much coverage, so when I do, my hand finds her bare skin, and it's all I can do not to strip the entire thing right off her.

Patience, Nick.

It's physically painful to ignore the ache in my groin, but I'm in here for a reason.

I set her up on the bathroom counter, edging her knees apart and positioning myself between them. "But this is supposed to be about us getting away from everything back home, and I wasn't abiding by that earlier. I promise you that from now on, you are the only thing on my mind."

"Somehow I find that hard to believe," she says. Ava isn't stupid, and a simple apology isn't going to cut it. She's been taking shit like this from men for her entire life, and I have to prove to her that I'm different.

There are so many details about her father that I've tried to spare her from because I knew they would hurt her, but now I don't have a choice. "Ava, you are the most important thing in my life. Do you understand that?"

She bites her lip in anticipation, an uneasy look in her eyes.

"I made you a promise that I'll be honest with you, even if what I have to say is going to hurt." I pause. "Your dad—he's into a lot of shit, Ava, and we don't even know the half of it yet."

The subject already strikes a nerve, and she tries to pull away, but I don't let her.

"Ava, the truth is this vacation isn't just about you and me getting away from everything. That's part of it, but it's also because of what's going on back at home. Your dad was responsible for the shooting at the dress shop. He didn't pull the trigger, but it was in retaliation for a bad deal he made with the Russians. I needed to get you out of town for a while so we could evaluate the threat we're under."

"No, there has to be some mistake. My dad wouldn't . . ." She shakes her head, but realization hits her as little pieces fall into place.

"He did, baby." My arms are loose around her waist as I stroke her back. "He planned to use you to control our organization once we were married. That's what he promised the Russians." When she closes her eyes, a few tears trickle out and I wipe them away. "Ava, he can feel you pulling away from him, so he is doing anything he can to protect himself. He knows he can't control you anymore, so he's desperate for another plan."

"How do you know all of this?"

"Before we left, one of my men booked a hotel in Chicago under my name because we thought your dad was tracking me. Vince was monitoring—"

"Vince?"

"Yes. Vince knows about this. He has been working with Leo and me since we found out." She's quiet. "Your father put a track on my credit card, which is how he knew about the room in Chicago. Then he booked two prostitutes under my card to convince you I was cheating on you so you'd call off the wedding. That way he wouldn't have to come clean about what he had really been planning and could use you as a scapegoat."

"Nick, this doesn't seem right. He's a bad person, but he couldn't . . . Why would he do something he knew would hurt me?"

"I need you to trust me, Ava."

"He's my dad, Nick." Her voice breaks.

"I know, baby. This isn't what you want to hear, but I wouldn't lie to you. He's too deep with the Russians. If he doesn't deliver, they'll be out for blood. They've already shown that with the shooting, and believe me, if they come back, they won't miss this time."

Covering her face with her hands, she continues to cry as I wrap her in my arms and pull her into my chest. She buries her face into me, clinging to my shirt.

"Ava, I won't let anything happen to you, okay? Do you understand that? I am going to do everything in my power to make sure no one ever hurts you again. Not your father, not the Russians, no one."

I plead with her, her tears ripping me apart.

"We're going to figure this out, but I need you to trust me. Can you do that?"

"Yes," she whispers.

"I love you, Ava. I have since the second I met you, even before I knew who you were. And I'm going to make this right, okay? All of it."

She nods, but I can tell she isn't sure. Honestly, I'm not, either, but I sure as hell am going to do everything in my power to try.

THIRTY-ONE

Ava

When I was eight, I heard a noise out in our backyard.

I've always been a little anxious, so I don't know what possessed me to go and investigate on my own, but I left whatever I was doing on my bedroom floor and followed the sound. I opened the sliding glass door, letting myself out onto the patio as I looked around. Everything seemed to be normal, except I could hear water running in the shower behind the pool. Peeking my head around the stone wall, I saw my dad.

At first I was relieved that it was just him, but the relief quickly turned to confusion and then to fear. He was standing underneath the showerhead fully clothed as the water rained down, washing blood off his skin and clothes.

A lot of blood.

I must have been in some kind of trance because I don't know how long I stood there, trying to figure out what was happening.

"Are you okay, Daddy?" I asked softly. He craned his neck in my direction, anger flooding his face. He shut the water off quickly and stomped toward me. If I had been thinking straight, I probably would have run, but instead, I stood with my feet cemented to the ground. The sharp sting of his hand hit my cheek and then he grabbed my shoulders with a bruising hold.

"You're not supposed to be out here," he hissed, shaking me violently. "Get in the house," he said, shoving me toward the still-open door. "And don't tell your mother about this."

When I finally got my bearings, I raced inside and shut the door behind me, squeezing my eyes shut to stop my tears, and hurried to my room. I didn't dare look outside again for fear of getting caught.

That was my first real clue that something was off about my dad, that what he did wasn't normal, not like what my friends' fathers did. They were doctors and lawyers and stockbrokers—they didn't come home with blood all over them and take a shower outside so their families didn't see.

So when Nick tells me that my dad is the reason I almost died, I'm not all that surprised. I want to be, but I'm not.

All night, I lay awake trying to remember little bits and pieces of my childhood.

Until I met Nick, I hadn't realized how oppressive it really was. My dad never let my sisters or me anywhere near the business; he didn't even talk about it in our presence. We weren't allowed to ask about it or be involved at all. I always thought he was trying to keep us out of it to keep us safe, but maybe that wasn't the case.

I did have happy memories with my dad—birthday parties and movie nights and him teaching me how to ride a bicycle. When I was young he used to let me get all dressed up once a month and would take me to do whatever I wanted, just the two of us. I idolized him when I was younger, but I was starting to see that I idolized the idea of him more. The father I wanted him to be, the one he was on occasion, but not the one he was most of the time. That was the person I remembered most—my father, the iron fist.

I wanted more for my own potential family, and look how well that had turned out for me. I'm in bed with the Mafia for life—literally.

Nick's not my father, though, and he's already gone above and beyond to show me how different things can be. It's reassuring to some extent, but it doesn't make the decision I have to make any easier. Every logical part of me knows Nick is the better choice, but my heart is still undecided. Even after all the terrible things my father's done, I don't want to believe he's capable of what Nick says. I want to overlook the bad and hold on to the few precious good memories I have with him. I want to believe he can change. That he didn't really mean it. That if he knew how badly he was hurting me, he might turn it around.

If I choose to trust Nick and go through with this wedding, I have to be prepared to walk away from my entire family. From everything I've ever known. From any hope of ever reconciling with my dad. My dad will hate me, and for someone who has spent her whole life chasing his approval, that's a tough pill to swallow.

I'd never in a million years expected my wedding to cause such a rift, and as much as it kills me, part of me wonders if it's worth it. What if Nick can't protect me like he thinks he can? What if all this does is provoke people even more? What if Nick's wrong?

My stomach turns at the thought, not because I think he might be wrong, but because, deep in my soul, I know that he's right. If his word isn't enough, the glaring proof he has should be. No matter how badly I want them to, things aren't going to change. If anything, they're only going to get worse until someone I love gets hurt. Or killed.

My mind flashes to Andrew, and that's all the nudge I need. My dad's shown his true colors time and time again, and as tough as it might be, it's time I realize that.

I curl up next to Nick as a tear falls onto my pillow, and I stifle it, not wanting him to recognize that I'm crying. Right as the sun comes up, I fall asleep, my body finally giving in to exhaustion.

When I wake up a few hours later, Nick's gone, and my immediate reaction is frustration. It was only a few hours ago he was apologizing for being absent and distracted, and now I'm alone again.

I throw the covers off and make my way to the room phone, planning to make a very large, very expensive room service order, but something on the table catches my eye. There's a full tray of breakfast already waiting next to an overflowing bouquet of roses and a note.

When I read the note, a smile pulls at my lips as every bit of frustration I was feeling dissolves.

Good morning, my love!

You looked so peaceful sleeping that I didn't want to wake you. As I promised last night, today is all about you! I have big plans, so I hope you got some rest. Your first stop is the spa. Rose will have your next adventure waiting there. I'll be seeing you soon :)

Nick

In true Nick fashion, he's going above and beyond to prove himself. I'm curious to see what he has planned, and excitement washes over me. Somehow, whenever I doubt him, he finds a way to prove me wrong.

I eat a bit of the breakfast he had delivered and then slip some clothes on to head to the spa. It's a short walk from our villa, and I practically skip there. As soon as I open the door, scents of lavender and eucalyptus fill the air and a sense of peace consumes me. Soft instrumental music plays in the background and the woman behind the front desk gives me a warm smile.

"Hello. How can I help you?"

"I'm looking for Rose, my name is—"

"You must be Ava." She grins sweetly. "Please follow me, right this way."

She opens a set of double doors that lead to the interior of the spa and gives me a tour. There are several large hydrotherapy pools and she details the benefits of each to me. A hot tub, cold plunge pool, and rain shower are a few of the other amenities she points out. Before my services, I'll have an hour to be in here and try everything out.

At the end of the tour, she leads me into the locker room and hands me a key.

"In there, you will find a robe and slippers. Change into them and then you can go right through that door for your treatments. I will be back at the end to give you something." She smiles and then disappears quickly, leaving me to myself.

This place is so extravagant that it almost feels like a dream. She mentioned services, but I have no idea what Nick set up, and I'm anxious to find out. After soaking in some of the pools, I change into the robe and make my way to the lounge, where my therapist is already waiting for me.

"Good afternoon, Ms. Ava. My name is Jackie and I will be your therapist today. Are you ready?"

"I think so, but can you tell me what we will be doing?"

"Of course! First, you will have a ninety-minute hot stone massage, followed by a mud and seaweed wrap. Once you are done with that, we will do a hibiscus sugar scrub and you will soak in our hydrotherapy tubs. Rose will meet us after that to take you to the rest of your day."

Wow. I can get used to Nick's idea of relaxing.

Following the woman into the treatment room, I spend the next four hours in a state of bliss I didn't even know could exist. The only thing that could have made it better was having Nick with me, but I have a feeling I'll see him soon.

I sit in the lounge waiting for Rose and soon, she arrives.

"How was your morning, Ms. Ava?" She hands me a flute of champagne.

"Absolutely amazing." I smile. "Are you taking me to see Nick now?"

"Not yet. We still have a few things to do first." Apparently, she's in on whatever Nick has planned. "You can leave your stuff here and one of our workers will bring it over."

I follow her through another set of doors, and suddenly, we're in a salon.

"This is Angel. She is going to be your stylist." She introduces me to a woman behind the desk who has pastel hair and tiny, fairylike features.

"My stylist?"

"Yes, it was specified that the next place you're headed is very elegant, and that no expense should be spared in helping you get ready."

"Of course." I swallow a laugh. Nick wouldn't know how to spare an expense if his life depended on it. He's always over-the-top and extravagant, but this seems excessive even for him.

Angel leads me over to a chair and puts a cape over me. "Your husband must really love you."

"Oh, he's not my husband." I blush. *Not yet, anyway.*

She clicks her tongue, running her fingers through my hair. "Well, you better make it official soon, sweetie. I've seen a lot in my time here, but this guy must be crazy about you for what he's planning."

"You know where I'm meeting him?"

"Don't think you're getting anything out of me." She winks. "Now, let's see what we want to do here . . ."

She gets to work doing my hair while another attendant comes in and does my makeup. Another gives me a manicure and a pedicure, and I feel like an absolute queen. Nick has to be spending a fortune on all of this, and I feel a little guilty.

"Wow!" I exclaim when they finally turn me around and let me face the mirror. I walked in here looking like I'd just rolled out of bed, with my hair tied back and no makeup on, expecting a simple massage or something like that. Now I look like I walked off the red carpet at Cannes.

"You look stunning, sweetheart. You'll absolutely knock him off his feet." She squeezes my shoulders excitedly. "And now for the grand finale!"

"There's more?"

"You didn't think we were going to send you out of here in your swimsuit, did you?" Angel winks again and leads me into a room that's lined with clothing racks and floor-to-ceiling mirrors. There have to be at least a thousand dresses in here, and the selection of shoes and jewelry puts any Bergdorf Goodman store to shame. I run my fingers along one of the racks of dresses, each material softer than the one before.

"Pick whatever you like!" Angel grins, fanning her arms out around the room.

Is she serious? There isn't enough time in the world for me to consider all the options in here. As if reading my mind, Angel grabs a short white dress off a hanger and thrusts it at me. "Why don't you try this one? It will look beautiful with your complexion."

By the time I come out of the dressing room, she has a pair of shoes picked out that are exactly my size. Whatever Nick has planned, this isn't going to be a normal date. Everything is too perfect, working out too well. Something about today is special.

Angel dresses me up like her own personal Barbie doll, and when she's finally given her seal of approval, Rose leads me outside. We walk down the pathway and she makes small talk, but all I can think about is the pounding in my chest. My heart knows something is coming. Surprises aren't my favorite thing in the world, and with all this buildup, I'm a little anxious.

"If you go right down those stairs, I think you'll find what you're looking for. It was a pleasure to meet you, sweet Ava. Enjoy your evening."

Before I go down, I take a deep breath and step forward.

Nick stands with his back to me, talking to another man on the beach. My heart skips, watching as the sun sets behind him, white sand all around us. It's like the most beautiful painting I've ever seen. I'm overcome with emotion as I realize what's coming.

The day of pampering, the exotic location, the white dress. Our conversation last night. His pressed tuxedo is the final clue I need. It all makes sense now.

Nick doesn't hear me coming until I'm almost down the staircase, and when he turns to me, his face lights up. I love a bit of facial hair on him, but the way his jawline looks with a fresh shave and deep tan makes my stomach flutter. The smile he gives me nearly melts me right to my core, and there's an excitement behind it that reminds me of the very first night we met. God, he's so handsome.

"Wow, Ava, you look incredible."

"So do you." I smile. "What are we doing here?"

"Ava." He takes my hand without the slightest bit of hesitation. "I've loved you since the second I met you. Nothing about our relationship has been conventional, and I know how hard it's been for you." He pulls my ring out of his pocket and slides it gently on my finger. "When I gave this to you, I told you someday I would ask you for real, and that I hoped your answer would be the same. I'm not asking you to do this because there's a treaty or because our fathers say we should. I'm asking you because I love you, and I want to spend the rest of my life with you."

Hot tears pool in my eyes as he speaks.

Nick gets down on one knee, still holding my hand in his, and I can't stop shaking. "Marry me, Ava. Marry me, right here, right now, on this beach, just the two of us."

Even though I knew the moment was coming, it still takes me by surprise to see him kneeling on a beautiful beach, looking up at me with a smile so certain and sincere. I want to speak. To answer him. To tell him how head over heels in love I am with him and with the life we've started to build, but nothing feels adequate.

"Nothing else matters to me. Nothing but you and me. I don't want to let other people dictate our relationship anymore. I want us to do what we want to do. I want us to do this the right way. Say you'll marry me."

THIRTY-TWO

Nick

By the time I'm done with my speech, Ava is at a loss for words, but the look in her eyes tells me everything I need to know.

"Of course, I'll marry you," she whispers, soft tears trickling down her flawless skin. "This is perfect."

Hearing her say it out loud hits in a way that I never expected, and I get emotional myself. Marrying Ava on our own terms is more than I ever imagined could happen. After all the manipulation. After all the interference. After all that's been stacked against us from day one.

It's almost funny to look back now and think about how we met, and how that one passionate night together was enough to convince me that she was the girl for me. I wasn't exaggerating when I told Ava I loved her from the second I met her—from that very first night, she's been ingrained in me and I'd never be content with anyone else. Thank god she feels the same way.

My palm slides around the back of her neck, and I pull her in for an eager kiss. My lips find hers in a fervor of elation and instinct, her taste as sweet and sensual as it'd been in that hotel room. I've never wanted anything more in my entire life. It's one thing to see the excitement on her face, but it's a whole different thing to hear the words come off her painted lips. Ava is everything I never even knew I wanted, and way more.

If she doesn't want me to take her right on this very beach, we're going to need to get this show on the road.

The officiant, Oscar, joins us, handing us each one of the rings I bought earlier today. Hers is a simple band of diamonds and mine is titanium, both engraved with today's date. I want to remember this moment for the rest of my life.

Ava lets out a small gasp when she sees her ring, and my heart races. Pleasing her will never get old.

Oscar reads the vows about loving and honoring each other, and I'm sure it's all very nice, but all I can focus on is her.

"Ava, do you take Nick to be your lawfully wedded husband, to have and to hold, in sickness and in health, as long as you both shall live?"

She smiles, eyes locked on mine. "I do."

"Nick, do you take Ava to be your lawfully wedded wife, to have and to hold, in sickness and in health, as long as you both shall live?"

Fuck, yes.

"I do." I grin as we slip the bands onto each other's hands.

"I now pronounce you man and wife. You may now kiss your bride."

I snake my arm around Ava and pull her in tight. As she drapes her arms over my shoulders, I lean in and my lips find hers in a passionate kiss that puts every one before it to shame. I feel it through every part of my body, so compelling that it changes the very makeup of my soul. She's part of it, woven so deeply into my soul that I almost don't recognize the man I was before her. Nothing's really changed but there's an intimacy in the kiss that feels like the first time, and I guess it is. The first time as my wife.

When we finally break apart, we're both breathless and smiling uncontrollably. Oscar has us fill out the license and signs it as our witness before leaving us to ourselves on the sandy shore.

"I can't believe we did that." She lets out a giddy laugh, covering her mouth.

"Believe it, baby. We're married!"

"We're *married*," she repeats, a smile tugging at the corner of her lips.

"Let's go celebrate." I scoop her into my arms and carry her bridal-style back to our villa. She pretends to fight me the entire way, but it's the first time I've ever really seen her smile without holding something back.

The last days of our trip fly by in a blaze, mostly because we hardly leave the room. Ava and I try to soak in every last second of alone time we can. Once we touch down in New York, shit is going to blow up, but I expect that. By now, Alessandro must have heard that his plan was foiled, and I doubt he'll give up easily.

Now, though, there's no way he can break us apart. Ava's legally my wife, and there isn't a damn thing Alessandro can do about it. I quadruple-checked that everything about this marriage was legal and binding, and there are no loopholes he could conjure up.

When I reach for Ava's hand, I can tell she's a million miles away, the weight of the trip getting to her. The truth about her father, our marriage, getting a bit of herself back after the shooting . . . any of those things on its own would be a lot, and she took it all in one fell swoop.

"What are you thinking about, Avs?"

She bites her lip, not answering at first. "About our kids," she finally says.

Kids? What . . . Did she . . . She must read the expression on my face because she immediately backtracks.

"I'm not pregnant." She shakes her head wildly. "God, no, that's not what I meant. I was just wondering what their lives will be like. I always imagined I'd raise my children away from all of this."

This is a conversation I need to ease into. "I promise I will do whatever I can to give you and our kids a completely normal life."

"It's funny, I always thought my childhood *was* normal. I figured everybody's family was like that."

"The way your dad treated you, and continues to, is definitely not normal. Neither you nor our children will live like that—we'll have as normal a life as possible."

"Is it even possible to be part of the world and have a normal life?"

"If we try hard enough," I assure her. "My brothers and I played sports, went to public school, everything. And we always had a choice of whether or not we wanted to join. Our sons will too. I don't want to force this on them."

"You've already decided we're having sons?"

"Absolutely. At least that's one thing your dad and I agree on. Girls are tough." I'm mostly kidding. *Mostly.* The thought of having a tiny Ava running around is more than I could handle. I had my hands full with her already, and if I had a daddy's little girl to worry about, I'd be a wreck.

Her expression clouds when I mentioned her father again. "What if my dad is upset that we did this?"

Now that a confrontation is imminent, the initial high of the wedding is wearing off and the consequences are weighing on her heavily. I don't blame her, because I've been thinking about it too.

"He's going to be," I say definitively. There's no doubt in my mind Alessandro is going to raise hell when he finds out what we've done. "But, baby, none of this is about him. This is about us. You and me. Do you regret getting married?"

"Of course not." She shakes her head. "I'm happier with you than I think I've ever been."

"Then nothing else matters. Whatever happens next, we will face it together."

"Is your family going to be upset about it?"

I chuckle a little. "My mom will probably be pissed that she wasn't there, but I think overall they'll be excited. They love you. And a big ceremony would have only attracted attention—maybe even another shooting. That's something everyone will understand."

"You're right." She settles, nestling into my shoulder. "I wish we could have stayed there forever."

"Me too." I kiss her forehead. "But responsibility calls. At least you still have another week off from class. That will be nice to ease back into the swing of things."

"Yeah, I'm going to try to find an internship in that time, though."

"I'm sure that will be easy. There are a lot of defense attorneys in the city."

"Actually, I had another idea. The only reason I was going to be a defense attorney was for my father, and that seems kind of pointless now. I was thinking about maybe working with victims of abuse. Becoming a prosecutor and helping them confront their abusers and move on."

I stare back at her in awe. "That sounds incredible, Avs. It's a great idea."

"Thanks!" She lets out a sigh of relief. "It'll delay my graduation, but only by a semester while I take the extra classes. And Columbia has a really cool program where you get to work directly with victims and help them through the legal process so that they can hold their abusers accountable. It's kind of perfect for me."

"Ava, that's amazing. It *does* sound perfect for you. And I'm so proud of you for choosing to do something for yourself."

"Well, it's all thanks to you and your faith in me." She smiles. "I love you."

"I love you, too, Ava. More than anything."

She puts her head on shoulder and sleeps for the rest of the flight, her worries eased for now. It's one thing to be okay with all of this when we're thirty thousand feet in the air, but it'll be a lot harder when we are facing her family head on.

I have a few choice words I want to have with Alessandro after the stunt he pulled, but I won't put Ava in a situation where she has to listen to them. As far as I'm concerned, I don't want her within a hundred yards of the man, let alone without me. He's a snake, and now that I have her away from him, I'll stop at nothing to destroy him.

THIRTY-THREE

Nick

I've always loved New York in the fall. The leaves on the trees start to turn and the weather gets chillier. The streets thin out of tourists, who've all gone home after their summer adventures, and things quiet down, if only briefly. It's also the perfect time of year for fishing, and when we were younger, my dad used to take us all the time. We haven't been in years, though. Maybe my emotions are a little wrought after secretly getting married and then talking to Ava about our future family, but fall makes me a little nostalgic. Once everything settles down, maybe my dad and brothers and I can plan a trip.

The weather is nice, but after spending the last several days in the tropics, it's a harsh walk from my car to my dad's office. The warehouse is busy today, and I wave at a few people as I make my way up the back stairs.

I haven't seen him since the day of the shooting, and a lot's changed since then. He'll be pissed that he wasn't in on the plan for setting Alessandro up at the hotel, or our elopement in Saint Lucia, but this was something I needed to handle on my own. In a few weeks it all falls on me, anyway. He'll come around once he understands the full situation.

When I open the door, he glances up from his computer briefly and smirks. "Welcome home. Nice of you to come into work for a change."

"I worked a majority of the time I was down there, actually. Ava was pissed about it."

"As she should be." He shuts his laptop loudly and slides it to the corner of his desk. "You should have taken advantage of vacation while you had the chance. Once you're Don, vacations come few and far between."

"I'll keep that in mind." I let out a sharp laugh. He's right. I can count on one hand the number of times my dad has taken a real vacation since he took over for my grandfather. We traveled plenty, but it was always wrapped around the business in some way. "How have things been here?"

"Chaotic." He shakes his head with a sigh. "You'll be happy to hear the Morettis put a hit out on the Russian who shot up the dress shop."

"Vince told me."

For the most part, though, Alessandro's lying low, which I figure results from his botched plan to frame me for cheating on his daughter. For all of his faults, the man isn't stupid, and probably has figured out that something is up.

"I'm not so sure." My dad frowns. "I've known the Asnikovs for a long time, and a move like this will only fuel their fire. Everyone's upset, but I'm worried the hit is going to put everyone in even more danger."

"Yeah, I wanted to talk to you about that." I shift my weight, crossing an ankle over my knee. This isn't exactly how I planned on telling my father that I was married, but nothing about mine and Ava's relationship has gone according to plan. "I want full security on Ava at all times."

"Nick, we've been over this. Ava is part of Alessandro's family and that means she is his responsibility until—"

"Until we are married. I'm aware of the rules."

I pull a copy of our marriage certificate out of my pocket and hand it to him. As of this morning, our license is filed with the City of New York, which was the last step in making things legitimate. My father's brow furrows as he carefully unfolds the paper. His eyes scan the document, eyes widening as he realizes what I'm getting at.

"Nick, please tell me you didn't marry her in Saint Lucia." He's seething. Not exactly the reaction I was hoping for.

"I married her in Saint Lucia," I say with a smirk.

"Jesus Christ." He throws his head back dramatically. His voice is loud enough that the men downstairs probably hear his frustration. "Do you have any idea what this is going to do? Does Alessandro know?"

"No, he doesn't." I stiffen, a little put off that he thinks I did this without weighing all the options. "I'm well aware of what this is going to do. It's going to keep Ava safe, and as far away from Alessandro as possible."

"This is outrageous. Don't expect me to believe you thought about this any further than how it would benefit you," he hisses, standing up. "You're going to put us in the middle of a war with both the Morettis and the Asnikovs. You think we're equipped for something like that?"

"This isn't about business, Dad." I grit my teeth. "I love Ava, and I don't give two shits what Alessandro thinks of it. He is a bastard who has abused Ava her entire life, and he's been playing us from the very beginning. Leo said you wanted us to move the wedding up anyway—I don't know why you're so angry about this."

He rubs his jaw. "I'm angry because I'm still in fucking charge around here, Nick. You should have talked to me about this before you went ahead and did it."

"What, so you could tell me not to?"

"No," he barks. "So we could figure out the best course of action to get the wedding moved up. We, at least, needed it to look like we were working with Alessandro instead of you running off and getting married in a foreign country!"

"You really did it?" Leo appears, a goofy grin plastered on his face, holding a bag of bagels. He's got no idea what he walked into.

"You knew about this?" my dad bellows.

"Sure, we've been working with Vince and—" Leo stutters, looking back and forth between me and our dad.

"The two of you have been working with Vince Moretti behind my back?" My father's voice hinges with suspicion.

"Yeah. He's been feeding us information about Alessandro. That's why we knew that Nick needed to get Ava out of the country." Leo sets the bag of food down and takes the empty chair next to me

"Somebody better start explaining what the fuck is going on and why I wasn't made aware of it."

"Look, Dad, Alessandro was never going to let the wedding happen. Vince said he's gotten himself into some deep shit with the Asnikovs and he can't deliver. His only hope was getting Ava into our family and using her to feed the Russians information. When he saw that Ava and I truly loved each other and he wasn't going to control her anymore, he changed his tactics."

My dad taps his fingers on the desk, processing what I've told him.

"The treaty has always been a cover. He wanted to hand us to the Russians on a silver platter."

"He's been trying to drive a wedge between Nick and Ava from the beginning so that they would end things and he could be kept out of it," Leo adds.

"You married Ava before he could stop you?"

"Yeah. Vince tipped us off a few weeks ago and we've been careful about it since. We had to be sure Alessandro was spying on me before we could do anything, so when Ava and I left, we sent a guy to sit in a hotel room in Chicago booked under my name. Alessandro sent a bunch of hookers there to make it look like I was cheating on Ava."

My dad's never been one for performative action; that's Alessandro's specialty. "Why the fuck wouldn't he just say the deal is off? Why go to all this trouble?"

"Because he's trying to save face," Leo says. "He needs the Russians to believe he is doing everything he can to help them infiltrate us, and if he calls off the deal, he goes down as the bad guy. The Asnikovs will eat him alive."

"That's what the shooting was about," my dad says flatly.

I nod. "Mrs. Moretti took his car that day. Vince thinks that the Russians thought it was him in there, not even realizing it was a bridal boutique, and were trying to send him a message."

"Did you explain all of this to your *new wife*?" My dad turns his attention to me.

"More or less. I left out some of the details, but I told her that he was trying to set us all up."

"She must be devastated." He sighs, rubbing his chin.

"She's having a tough time with it, but she understands. She knows Alessandro is using her as a pawn and doesn't really care what happens to her." It sounds even more harsh as I say it out loud, reigniting my anger toward him.

"I'm still pissed you two decided not to tell me about this." My dad glares at us. "But I understand why you did it. We'll just need to be prepared for whatever is to come. Alessandro won't take this lying down."

"But I'm not taking any chances where Ava's safety is concerned. That's why I want to get men on her immediately. He's going to try to see her now that we're home."

"And she hasn't told her family that you're married?"

I shake my head.

"Let's keep it that way for now. I'd like to feel all this out with Alessandro."

I don't want to wait, but I'm not really in a bargaining position. I've already lied to my dad about most of this, so I expect that he'll keep me under his thumb for a while.

"What about Bella's wedding? Both families will be together, plus the Savinos, and this affects them as well."

"That could work," I say. It's only a few weeks away, but that feels like a lifetime when I want to shout the news of our marriage from the rooftops.

"In the meantime, you better make sure that this document is legit." He hands it back to me. "When Alessandro finds out about this, you want to be sure there are no loopholes and everything was done legally."

"I looked into everything, but I'll get it to the lawyers." I fold the certificate up carefully and put it back into my jacket pocket.

"I'll get some men for security for Ava. Make sure she knows, though. I want her aware of everything that is going on, so Alessandro can't argue that we've forced her into anything. It has to be on her terms."

"Good idea." Leo nods.

It's hard to admit defeat, but my dad's reaction only proves we should have brought him in sooner. As confident as I feel, I still have a hell of a lot to learn from him, and he thought of things that hadn't even crossed my mind, so I'm thankful for his support. We'll certainly need it if Ava and I are going to war with Alessandro.

Ava

There's nothing that ruins the vacation high quite like having a doctor's appointment the very next day. It's even worse because the appointment is to follow up on my wounds from the shooting that I've been trying to forget ever happened.

Thankfully, I don't have to go to the hospital to be seen, and my appointment is with my primary doctor.

The follow-up is to check on my mental state as much as my physical wounds, but I can't think of anything that will depress me more than having to rehash the details of the shooting and how I feel about it all with her. Dr. Chapman has been my doctor most of my life, and she knows the ins and outs of what I've been through. I can already tell this will set some alarm bells off in her mind.

But honestly, who is in a good mental state after a gruesome forty-five-minute wait just to be seen? Finally, a nurse takes me back to pull my blood and vitals, and then I wait for Dr. Chapman.

"Good morning, Ava." She smiles, washing her hands and then taking a seat in the chair.

"Hi, Dr. Chapman."

"How are you feeling? Wounds healing okay?"

"I think so. I don't have much pain anymore and they seem to be closed."

Dr. Chapman kneels next to me. "Let's have a quick look, then."

Her hands are cold as she runs her fingers along the outline of my wounds, and I try not to watch. After spending the last several days in a swimsuit, I've started to get used to the scars, but they're still awful looking, and a very tangible reminder of the danger I'm in.

"Everything looks really great, Ava," she says, standing up and snapping her gloves off. "They're healing up nicely and I don't see any signs of infection. I'll send you home with an ointment you can put on them that might help minimize the scarring."

"Great." I give her a tight-lipped smile. "Is that all for today, then?"

Before she responds, I hop off the table, ready to get out of here. But the look on her face stops me.

"Actually, there's something else I wanted to talk to you about."

"Okay." I sigh. Here we go with antidepressant speech. It's not the first time she's suggested them to me, but I have no interest in going on medication for my own reasons.

"When we ran your bloodwork to be sure there was no infection in your system, it flagged something else," she explains. "Ava, your HCG levels came back pretty elevated. They're consistent with someone who is about twelve weeks pregnant."

"What?"

My head starts to spin and I feel so dizzy that I can hardly breathe. Pregnant? There has to be some kind of mistake. "Are you sure you didn't get my test mixed up with someone else's?"

"We are very careful about that sort of thing, Ava. We'll confirm with an ultrasound in a week or so, but you're definitely pregnant."

"But I was on . . ." I lose my voice in the middle of the sentence.

"Birth control is effective, but it's not always a hundred percent. And it's also probably why you didn't notice your late period."

Dr. Chapman talks more about the statistics, but I drown her words out. All except for the one that really matters.

Pregnant.

I take a deep breath, trying to calm myself down. I should be happy about this, but a pit forms in my stomach and dread starts to creep in.

A baby. A tiny little life growing inside of me.

As much as I try to bite my tears back, I feel them start to fall. I have no idea how Nick's going to take the news. Of course, he wants kids, and so do I, but the timing couldn't be worse. Having a family with Nick was a wonderful thought when it was in the future, but now that it is an imminent reality, right in front of me, literally right inside of me, it paralyzes me.

THIRTY-FOUR

Ava

By the time I get dressed and leave Dr. Chapman's office, I'm an absolute wreck. I'm in a tailspin, every terrible possibility and outcome plaguing my mind. The thought of going home right now makes my stomach turn, so instead of heading to the parking lot where my car is, I decide to take a walk.

I should call Nick, but I don't know how to tell him yet. Besides my doctor, I'm the only one who knows, and something about having it out in the open makes it all too real. I'm not sure I'm ready for that.

Between his usual work and navigating an impending war between two rival families, the last thing he needs is another thing to worry about. Not to mention we haven't even announced our marriage yet, and I can already hear my father's assumptions and protests about the convenience of us rushing to the altar the same week we find out I'm knocked up.

God, this can't be happening.

A tinge of resentment passes through me. Even though the timing is off, Nick is getting the job, the family—everything he wants—while I'm having to adjust my own dreams to fit that. It's an incredibly selfish thought when he's been nothing but supportive of me and has probably saved my life in more ways than one. Whether it's the shock of the news or my hormones, I'm already feeling emotional.

Distracted by the news, I don't pay much attention as I walk, so I don't even notice someone calling my name until I feel a hand on my shoulder.

I whirl around, sucking in a sharp breath when I see my dad standing in front of me. Him? Really, universe? On top of everything else I have to worry about today?

"Sorry, Ava." He grins. "I didn't mean to scare you. I was calling your name for a while. Didn't you hear me?"

"I didn't." I shake my head. "Sorry, I guess I wasn't paying attention."

He comes in for an awkward hug and I try not to flinch. "It's good to see you. I was down here for a meeting and was about to leave when I saw you walking. What a coincidence!"

We haven't so much as spoken since the shooting, and after everything Nick told me, I'm uneasy around him. Maybe I'm paranoid, but this doesn't feel random in the slightest. Is he following me?

"Do you have time for lunch?" he asks.

"I'm kind of in a hurry. I have a few interviews for internships coming up that I need to get ready for, and I promised Bella I'd go with her to pick out some flowers for the wedding this afternoon."

"Coffee, then. There's a stand right over there and we can sit somewhere and catch up. I've hardly seen you since you moved in with Nick."

I don't want to spend another minute alone with him, but he doesn't leave much room for argument.

"As long as it's quick."

We walk over to the cart and get our drinks before finding a bench.

"How was your trip?" he asks, making himself comfortable. "I didn't realize you guys were going."

"It was last-minute. We wanted to get away for a bit after the shooting."

"Well, I'm sure you'll both be happy to know that I identified the shooter and we've completely eliminated any threat." I almost have to laugh at the way he wants to be a hero for solving a problem that he caused. Not to mention that Nick told me his men were the ones who identified the guy and gave my dad the information.

"That's great, Dad."

"I'm surprised Nick could sneak away. I'm sure he's busy prepping to take over for Gio." He pauses, studying my face for some type of reaction.

"He's been busy, but the break was good for us both."

"When is the big announcement coming?"

"Announcement?" All the air leaves my lungs. Does he know we're married? That I'm pregnant?

"That Nick is officially head of the family."

"It won't be until after our wedding." I press my lips together. "But that's all I really know."

I've always been a bad liar when it comes to him, so I keep my mouth shut instead of digging myself into a hole. He knows I know more than I'm saying, but he doesn't press.

"Why don't you come over for dinner this week? Your mom and I would love to see you. It seems like it's been a while since you've come around. You don't even have to bring Nick if he's busy."

"That would be nice." I smile, placating him. "I'm a little busy this week, though—Bella has me doing all kinds of last-minute things for the wedding and I'm on call to babysit Gigi in case Soph's mom can't make it when she goes into labor. And these internship interviews are really taking up my time. Maybe once things settle—"

"Don't forget who your real family is, Ava. You may be his fiancé by name, but you're still my daughter first and foremost." His words are venomous.

"Wasn't this what you wanted? For Nick and I to fall in love and . . ."

He chuckles, looking at me as if I'm a naïve child again. "Ava, this has never been about love. It's purely political. If Nick has you conned into thinking it's something more than that, you're sadly mistaken. This is business for him."

I don't respond, because he's trying to bait me, but that doesn't matter to him.

"Nick is too young and inexperienced to run his family. Once you're married, he'll need an advisor he can trust to make those big decisions, and I'm confident he'll turn to me with your influence."

For a moment I'm too stunned to respond. If I had any doubts about what Nick told me, they're all struck down by my dad's own admission. Any amount of hurt I feel is overshadowed by my intense anger that he thinks he can manipulate me this way. That he thinks so little of me. That he *cares* so little for me. "Nick's perfectly capable of running things."

"I wasn't asking for your assessment, Ava. You know nothing about this business. I've made up my mind, and you'll help me."

A surge of confidence winds through me like I've never felt before. Maybe it's out of loyalty to Nick, or maybe I feel a need to protect our unborn child, but for the first time ever I don't back down. "You can't control me, Dad. I'm not a child anymore."

"No." He flashes a sadistic grin at me. "You're certainly not, so you should know by now that it's in your best interest to follow my orders."

His brazen threat paralyzes me. I know better than anyone what he's capable of, and if I wasn't so confident in Nick, my dad would be right.

"With all due respect, Dad, you can't have it both ways. I'm as much a part of the Caponellis as I am a Moretti now, and I'm fully capable of making my own choices. I intend to stay out of whatever business dealings you have with Nick—after all, that's how you prefer it. If you have something to say, take it up with him. Now, if you'll excuse me, I need to be going. Tell Mom I said hi."

With every bit of gumption I've got, I stand up and walk away from him.

"Come out of your glass house sometime and tell her yourself," he calls after me, drawing the attention of several people passing on the street.

Adrenaline pulses through my veins, as if I've just won a gold medal. I don't know what came over me, but standing up to him feels good. Really good.

And I'm never going back to the way things were.

THIRTY-FIVE

Nick

The first couple of days that Ava and I are home, we're like two ships passing in the night with everything we've got going on. Between our battling schedules, we're barely able to talk, let alone see each other. When I get home late at night, she's usually already asleep, and then gone by the time I'm up in the morning.

The long hours are necessary right now, and even though it's temporary, it kills me not to be with her more often.

Somehow, we both ended up with a few free hours this evening, and I'm taking her out for a long overdue date night. I snagged reservations at a sushi restaurant that she'll love, and I get there early.

When I spot Ava walking in, my heart skips. She's so fucking beautiful, but something feels different tonight. A little confidence in her step. A glow in her cheeks. She looks happy. Really, really happy.

She smiles when she sees me, waving as she winds her way to our table. I stand up, pressing a thirsty kiss to her lips and helping her with her chair. "Hey, baby."

"Hi." She sits down. "This place looks nice."

"I thought you might like it. Leo was raving about how good the sushi is."

Ava bites her lip as if there's something she wants to say but decides against it. "How was your day?"

"It was long. And boring. How was yours?"

"About the same. I feel like I'm drowning in internship applications, and Bella has me running around the entire city on the most impossible wedding tasks." She rolls her eyes. "Today she asked me to track down a newspaper from the day she was born."

I let out a sharp laugh. "For what?"

"Exactly my question."

"Did you find it?" I ask, handing her a menu.

"Of course, I did." Ava smirks. "The library keeps archives for thirty years. You're not underestimating my abilities, are you?"

"Ava." I chuckle. "The very last thing I would ever do is underestimate you. You always find a way to come through."

The server comes over to the table, pen and paper in hand. "Are you guys ready to order?"

"Whiskey for me, and a cabernet for you?"

"Water is fine for me," Ava says, quickly waving me off.

I give her a strange look. "They have a huge wine list. We can take more time if you want to look."

"That's okay. I'm good with water for now."

"Okay. And what would you guys like to eat this evening?" the server asks.

"I'll take the salmon salad." Ava hands her the menu.

Salad? At a world-class sushi restaurant? Something seems off, but I finish the order before pressing her.

"Are you feeling okay?"

"I'm fine, Nick. Honestly," she insists. "I have to fit into my bridesmaid dress next weekend so I'm watching what I eat and drink."

Her answer sounds very unlike her, but she's been under a lot of pressure with her family, so I don't make a big deal of it.

"Do you think Bella's excited?"

Ava smiles. "I think it's going to be the greatest day of her life."

"Thanks to you. You've gone way above and beyond your maid of honor duties." Bella's wedding has been like a full-time job for Ava lately, and it'll take a lot of stress off her plate once it's done.

"I just want it to be special for her."

"I've been meaning to talk to you about the wedding," I start. I haven't had a chance to tell Ava that we'll be announcing our own marriage at the wedding yet, and it's better if she finds out sooner rather than later.

"About what?"

"You and I are going to announce our marriage at the reception. It's the perfect time with our families, plus the Savinos being there."

She lets out a sharp laugh. "You're kidding, right? You can't seriously think that's a good idea."

It's not exactly the reaction I was hoping for. I thought she'd be ecstatic to finally have it out in the open, but she's angry. She crosses her arms, leaning forward onto the table as her dark eyes narrow.

"It's the best we've got. We decided that—"

"Who is *we*?"

"My dad and me."

Her eyes widen. "You told your dad that we're married?"

"Yeah." I grimace. Without much time together the last few days, I haven't had a chance to fill her in. "I had to tell him so I could get protection on you."

"Who else knows?"

"Leo and Zane and Vince. Probably my mom."

Ava gives me a vicious glare. "So pretty much you get to tell whoever you want and I'm not allowed to tell anyone, right?"

"Ava, don't be ridiculous. I had to tell them so that we could be sure your dad didn't find out until the right time."

"And now the right time is on the biggest day of my sister's life?" She lets out a sharp laugh. "No, I won't do that. I've gone along with your plan this entire time. I've moved on your timeline, I've kept it to myself, but I'm not going to steal the spotlight from her like that."

"It's not about stealing the spotlight, Ava. It's business."

"Business," she repeats, a poisonous look in her eye.

Fuck. I regret my word choice the second it's out of my mouth.

"You know I didn't mean it like that."

"Do I? You push me for weeks to make this marriage happen, and then when it does, I'm not allowed to tell anybody or talk about it. And despite how much you tell me you don't want to control me and that things are different with you, your double standard and the way you're treating me says otherwise."

"Would you keep your voice down? This isn't the place to have this conversation." Our argument is drawing attention, and other tables are anxiously watching now.

"How about I try to catch you during business hours next week, since that's what this is, right? That's why we did it? For business."

I drop my head, rubbing my temples. *Jesus Christ.* "Can we just get home and have this discussion?"

"Great idea. I've completely lost my appetite."

Neither one of us seems to cool off on the ride home. Especially not Ava. She's out of her car and rushing inside before I've even parked the truck. She makes a beeline for our bedroom and slams the door sharply. I follow close behind, ready for whatever fight is about to ensue.

I can understand where she was originally coming from, but what I don't understand is how things spiraled so quickly. She's right—there are probably better ways to announce our marriage that won't interfere with Paul and Bella's celebration. As a man, the meaning behind it all slipped my mind, and if she had slowed down for one second, we could have talked about it.

I turn the handle to the bedroom door but it won't budge.

"Ava, open the door. We need to talk."

"Nick, please, leave me alone." Her voice cracks on the other side.

"Open the damn door, Ava. We need to talk even if you're upset."

She doesn't answer, but I hear whimpering on the other side.

"Ava, if you don't open the fucking door, I'm going to break it down." I try to level my voice as best I can.

"Don't be ridiculous, Nick."

Lowering my shoulder, I barrel into the door. It doesn't open, but it shakes with fury, and I'll easily get it open with another hit or two. The handle jiggles on the other side and then it flies open. "Jesus, Nick. Have you completely lost your mind?"

"I told you to open the door or I'd break it down. I'm a man of my word."

"A man of your word," she scoffs. "Right. I'm going to my sister's for a while."

Ava grabs her jacket and slips it on quickly.

"You're not going anywhere. We need to talk about this."

THIRTY-SIX

Ava

Things happen in slow motion. Nick catches my arm. I jerk away. My jacket slips off my shoulder. A small packet falls out of it and onto the floor, bouncing once before settling.

Nick bends down to pick it up, rolling the clear baggie filled with white powder over in his hand. We both know exactly what it is.

"Well, I guess we both have some explaining to do, don't we?"

My stomach lurches. I completely forgot about the pouch Jimmy gave me until right this second. I didn't even know I still had it, or that it happened to be in the jacket I chose tonight.

"Nick, I—"

"Ava, do you remember what I said would happen if you started using again?" He narrows his eyes at me harshly. Oh, I remember all right; he said he would make me go to rehab and that I would have no choice in the matter.

"I'm not using again," I blurt. "I can explain this."

Nick lets out a sharp laugh. "Oh, you mean you want me to give you a chance to explain yourself before I fly off the handle and rush to judgment? Funny, because you didn't give me the same courtesy back at the restaurant."

"Because you said our marriage was business." My voice is shaky as I try to justify what happened.

"I know exactly what I said, and you know that it isn't what I meant," he hisses, his anger only growing. He'd never hurt me, but it's got me on edge. "I'd be happy to explain it all to you, but right now, I'm more interested in this." He holds the bag up to me.

"Jimmy gave it to me a long time ago. I swear I'm not using. I haven't had anything since that night at the club. I'll take whatever test you want me to take," I defend myself, sitting down on the bed.

"See?" I reach into the pocket of my jacket and pull out a business card. "He gave it to me the same day he told me about his dad's job offer."

"So what? You just keep it in your jacket for safekeeping? Fun memories?" Nick's livid, and I can tell he doesn't believe me.

"Honestly, I forgot it was even there. I haven't worn this jacket since the night we had dinner at my parents'. I should have flushed it the first chance I got, but I shoved it in my pocket and forgot all about it until now."

"Sorry, but I'm having a tough time believing that."

"I'm your wife, Nick. Shouldn't that come with a little trust?"

"Ava, I do trust you, but that trust has to go both ways." He softens, reaching for my hand. "If you tell me you aren't using, I believe you. But you have to admit, hoarding cocaine in your jacket—the same jacket you were about to storm out of our house angry in—is a little hard to take."

"It looks bad, but I honestly had no intention of using it. I was angry with you and leaving, you're right, but using never even crossed my mind. It hasn't since that night, and it's because for the first time I feel like I'm in control of my own life. That's because of you, and what you've given me. I never want to risk the life we've got. I'm sorry, I've been a little emotional lately. I love you and I can't stand the thought of disappointing you." I wipe at the tears trickling down my cheek.

"I never want to disappoint you either," he says, fidgeting with my wedding rings. "I'm sorry that I didn't tell you my dad and the guys know. I didn't tell them for the hell of it or to hold you to a different standard, though. They needed to know for our safety, and I'm sorry I wasn't clearer about that. And about the wedding, you're right. It's not fair of us to overshadow Bella and Paul on such an important day, and we'll find a different time. Will that make you feel better?"

"It would. Thank you." I sniffle, wiping the tears off my cheek. There really is no perfect time to tell my family that we got married, but Bella's wedding seems like one of the worst, even if it might be convenient.

"Then I'll tell my dad that's the plan and we'll figure out another time." His lips curl. "And just so you know, I understand what a struggle you go through each day to stay clean, and I'm really proud of you for doing this for yourself."

I press my lips together. I'd planned to tell Nick about the baby at dinner, and with that completely ruined, now is as good a time as any.

"It's more than that, though, Nick." I take his hand, gently setting it on my stomach. "I wouldn't use because I'd never want to jeopardize the life of our baby."

Nick swallows, eyes widening as he realizes what I said. "Our . . . you're—"

"I'm pregnant, Nick."

"Ava, that's . . . I'm going to be a father?" He scratches his forehead.

"The timing kind of sucks. We're barely getting used to this husband-and-wife thing, and with you taking over for your dad—"

"Ava, that's the most incredible news I've ever heard. We're going to have a baby!" Nick sweeps me into his arms, spinning me around at the foot of our bed. When he finally sets me down he's got a grin on his face that absolutely melts me. "When did you find out?"

"When I went to my follow-up the other day. Dr. Chapman did

some bloodwork and my levels were high. We'll have to go back in for an ultrasound to make it official, but she says I'm about twelve weeks."

"That's why the sushi and the wine . . ."

"Yeah, that was about the worst possible place to have dinner." I laugh. "No raw fish or alcohol for the next several months."

"Wow. That's . . . this is . . ." Nick stutters, eyes wide as he stares back at me in wonder. It isn't often he's speechless.

"You're sure you're okay with this? We've already got so much going on, it's not a great time."

Nick lets out a sharp laugh. "Okay with it? Ava, I'm fucking ecstatic. Who cares about the timing? It'll never be perfect. The only thing that matters to me is you." His hand slips to my stomach, fingertips slipping underneath my shirt to my bare skin. "And our family. How do you feel about it?"

Terrified. Overwhelmed. Underqualified.

Now that I've seen Nick's reaction, though, there's no way to be anything but happy myself. His excitement is all the reassurance I need.

"Uh." I let out a heavy breath. "A little nervous. But excited. I've felt weird all week but I don't know if I'm reading into every little ache or pain now that I know."

"You're hurting now? Can I get you anything?"

"Easy, Nick. I'm fine." I laugh. This is already going exactly how I pictured. Nick doesn't know how to do anything halfway, so I anticipate him trying to wait on me hand and foot throughout this entire pregnancy.

"God, I love you so much." Nick presses a possessive kiss to my lips, his hand sliding to the back of my neck. When he pulls away, his forehead rests against mine. "You're going to be the most incredible mother."

I hope he's right.

THIRTY-SEVEN

Ava

"You're sure it's not too tight?" I grimace, running my hands over my velvet dress as I twist in front of the mirror. This dress is usually one of my favorites, with its off-the-shoulder sleeves and formfitting shape. It's the third outfit option I've had on, and it still feels off.

Nick sits on the edge of our bed, checking his watch because we're already running late. Tonight is Bella and Paul's rehearsal dinner, and I'm uneasy about more than just my dress. I haven't seen or spoken to my dad since he found me outside of the doctor's office last week, and the whole altercation has left a bad taste in my mouth. Thinking about being in the same room as him again has my nerves a wreck.

"Babe." He chuckles, sauntering over to me. He stands behind me and reaches around, resting his palm on the barely detectable swell of my stomach as he kisses my bare shoulder. At thirteen weeks, I have next to nothing to show in terms of a baby bump, but I'm still anxious that someone will notice. I was the one who wanted to wait to tell everyone, but we're not going to be able to hide it much longer. "It's not too tight. You look incredible. Now can we please go?"

After one more once-over in the mirror, I'm not thrilled, but it's as good as it's going to get, and I follow Nick out to the garage.

Instead of the truck parked in our spot, I see Leo's black SUV. "Where's the truck?"

"Leo needed it to move some stuff this weekend, so we made a switch," Nick says, opening the door for me.

My parents rented out a restaurant to host the dinner, and Nick pulls the car into the valet. He helps me out and I straighten my dress out for what has to be the thousandth time, already uncomfortable in it.

"You seem stressed. Is everything okay?" He slips his hand into mine as we walk inside.

"Nervous about seeing my dad."

Nick stiffens at the mention of him. "Baby, you have nothing to be worried about. He's not going to pull anything tonight. He'll be too distracted with sweet-talking the Savinos to even give us the time of day."

"You're right," I say, biting back the thousand scenarios that play through my mind. We're still at a bit of an impasse when it comes to my feelings about my dad, and I try to avoid the topic altogether.

He sweeps a kiss across my cheek, his palm finding my stomach. "Will you promise me that you'll try to relax? I don't like it when you're stressed. It's not good for the baby."

I bat his hand away before anyone can notice. "You can't touch me like that, or people are going to ask questions."

"It's almost like that's the point."

"Nick."

His lips find mine in a silencing kiss. "I'm kidding. I'll do my best to keep my hands to myself, I promise."

Nick

Ava is tense, and I hate it. I hate that Alessandro is still ruining things for her. This should be a fun and happy occasion, and instead she's nervous about seeing him. It isn't fair to her, and it makes me hate him even more, if that's possible.

Once he knows we're married we won't have to play so nice with him, and we can move on to more important things—like the child she's carrying. Everything has kind of taken a back seat to the pregnancy news over the last couple of days, especially after we got to hear the tiny heartbeat on the ultrasound. Nothing prepares a man for the first time he's sitting next to the woman he loves, holding her hand as they see their child for the first time, and seeing the joyful tears in her eyes wrecked me in the best of ways.

Ava's quickly gone from avoiding the topic of children to thinking about it all the time. She'll send me random texts throughout the day with potential names, and when I get home at night she wants to go over nursery plans. She's already thinking about logistics, like whether or not our balcony is safe or how we need to rearrange the bedroom to make room for a bassinet. And supposedly I'm the overbearing one.

I have my hand on her back as we wind through the sea of people at the party. It's crowded and I keep a protective hold on her. Something about knowing that she's pregnant makes me even more tender with her. She's already glowing, and I can't wait until there's no denying she's carrying my child anymore.

"Good evening, Mr. Caponelli, Ms. Moretti," one of the attendants greets us and takes our coats.

I nod politely to him, and we make our way into the reception area. Once we're inside, I follow Ava's lead and we make our way over to Bella and Paul, who stand at one of the cocktail tables, greeting their guests.

"Hi, guys!" Bella greets us, wrapping her arms around Ava and kissing her cheek. "Can you believe it's finally happening?"

"You look absolutely gorgeous, Bella," Ava gushes, and the two of them start running through a list of last-minute details before the big day tomorrow.

Paul reaches out to shake my hand. "Thanks for coming, man."

"We wouldn't miss it for the world."

"You're next." Bella grins, turning her attention back to us. "I'm sure your day will be every bit as beautiful."

Ava stiffens in my arms at the mention of our wedding and changes the subject. "Are Mom and Dad here yet?"

"They should be. Mom was coming straight from the hospital, though. Can you believe that Sophia went into labor on the same day as our rehearsal dinner? The timing couldn't be worse."

I stifle my laughter. Bella is about as self-absorbed as it gets.

"At least Vince and Gigi will still be able to come tomorrow. I'm not counting on Sophia and the baby, though."

I zone out for a few minutes, glancing around the room while Ava and Bella talk. I spot Alessandro exactly where I expected to find him. He's with Paul's father, no doubt trying to get on his good side. Mark Savino is a smart man, though, and he'll see right through Alessandro's bullshit.

Somehow, we make it through the entire happy hour without having to speak with him, but when it's time to take our seats for dinner, there's no avoiding him. Bella has her entire family seated at the same table, right at the front of the room. With Vince busy with his own family tonight, we've got no buffer, and I'm anxious to see how this goes.

"Nick, Ava!" Alessandro grins, extending his arms as he gives her a hug. "It's so good to see the two of you."

He's obviously aware of the crowd, and on his best behavior.

"Hi, Dad." Ava gives him a tight smile. "It's nice to see you too."

We make small talk for most of the meal, and everything goes uncharacteristically smoothly. I know never to get too comfortable with Alessandro, though. After the dessert course is served, he gets up to go greet some of the other guests.

"Doing okay?" I ask, checking in with Ava.

She nods. "Tired. Maybe we can make an early getaway."

"That sounds good to me, Avs. Tomorrow is going to be a long day. Want to start saying your goodbyes?"

I offer her my hand and she stands up.

"You're not leaving before I can make my speech, are you?" Something sinister is in Alessandro's smile when he returns.

"I didn't realize you were making one," she says.

"Of course, I am! It's my daughter's wedding tomorrow. Stay for a few minutes longer," he insists.

If it were up to me, we'd be out of here, but I recognize the hesitation in Ava's eyes.

"Sure. We can stay a little while longer."

Damn it, Ava.

She gives me an apologetic look and then sits back down. "Just a few minutes."

"Whatever you need, Avs." She's been stuck between the two of us for too long, and I'm not going to make it any harder on her.

Alessandro makes his way to the front of the room, unfastening the microphone from its stand. This is bound to be entertaining if nothing else.

"Good evening, everyone," he begins. "My name is Alessandro Moretti and I am Bella's father. On behalf of my entire family, I'd like to thank you all for joining us tonight to celebrate her marriage to Paul Savino. Sonya and I could not be more thrilled to be welcoming Paul into the family."

"Do you think he's going to say the same thing when he gives a speech for us?" I lean over, whispering into Ava's ear.

"Nick, stop." She laughs, rolling her eyes.

"Paul and Bella's marriage means the merger of our two families, and with it, we'll be combining our forces. In fact, earlier tonight, Mark and I agreed to an even larger expansion that will set both families up for decades to come. It's an exclusive partnership, and that means all other treaties will become null and void, effective immediately."

Alessandro has a vicious look on his face as his eyes meet mine all the way across the room. What the fuck is going on?

"My youngest daughter, Ava, was supposed to marry into the Caponelli family, but thanks to the generosity of Mark and the entire Savino family, that won't be necessary anymore."

"What is he talking about?" Ava looks to me for answers, but I'm as confused as she is.

"I don't know, babe. Let's just get out of here."

Ava and I go to get our coats while Alessandro finishes whatever he's got to say. Part of me wants to stay here and knock his fucking lights out, but I can't. I need to get Ava away, and I need to talk to my dad and Leo and find out what's going on.

While we're waiting, two men in security uniforms approach us. "Mr. Caponelli, we're going to have escort you out now. This is a closed party for the Savinos and the Morettis only."

One of the men grabs me, and I shrug him off. "Get your hands off me."

"What are you talking about?" Ava hisses, coming immediately to my defense. "Nick is my fiancé and this is my sister's wedding."

"*Was* your fiancé," Alessandro gloats, joining us at the back of the room. "With the new deal with Mark, your wedding isn't happening, which means the Caponellis are no longer welcome at this event."

"You stupid son of a bitch." I can't help but laugh. He's got no idea what he's done. Pulling out of a treaty is no simple thing, and this deep in, it's basically a declaration of war.

"Dad, this is ridiculous." Ava steps forward. "If the Caponellis aren't welcome here, then neither am I, because—" She looks at me with apprehension in her eyes, but I nod at her, bursting with pride at the way she stands up to him. "Because Nick and I already got married."

"You what?" The look on his face is worth the wait. Alessandro is so angry it looks like his head might pop right off. For a second I think

I actually see steam coming out of his ears, and I enjoy it more than I should.

"We got married a few weeks ago in Saint Lucia," she says, holding her ground.

Her father chuckles, and pretty soon, he's bellowing with laughter. "I should have known you'd find a way to screw this up for us. And for what? Some silly idea of love?"

"Alessandro—"

Ava steps forward before I can say anything. "Dad, I have tried my entire life to make you happy, and that's what I thought I was doing by agreeing to this in the first place. But you know what? If it takes me being a bartering chip that you give and take away on a whim, then I don't want it. I'm done letting you manipulate me. I love Nick, and you can either be happy for us or leave us alone, but you're not going to interfere in our relationship anymore."

I stand back, watching Ava in complete awe as she stands up to him. A few weeks ago this wouldn't have even been a possibility. Something entirely different has come over her tonight, and whatever it is, I'm so fucking proud of her. Alessandro doesn't know what to make of the shift in their dynamic, either, and he's stunned into silence.

"Come on, Nick." She reaches for my hand and pulls me to the entrance.

"Ava, don't you dare walk out that door," Alessandro calls after us, but she continues on as if she doesn't even hear him.

Once we're outside, she lets out a heavy breath and turns to me, her face flush with emotion. "Well, that could have gone better."

"No, I don't think it could have." I let out a sharp laugh. "You were absolutely incredible in there, Ava. I'm so proud of you."

"Thanks." Her halfhearted smile isn't convincing. "I just hope it doesn't cause even more issues for us."

I wrap my arm around her to shield her from the wind as we wait for the car to be pulled around, and kiss her. "You let me worry about that, okay?"

It will, but I don't tell her that. This is far from over with Alessandro, especially after the stunt he pulled tonight. I don't know what he's promised the Savinos, but this isn't going to go away as easily as he thinks. Getting Ava away from him was only half of the battle. Now I've got my sights on destroying him, and nothing's going to stand in my way.

The drive from the restaurant to our penthouse is about an hour, and Ava falls asleep almost immediately. She was exhausted to begin with, and the confrontation with Alessandro must have taken a lot out of her. I have no idea what's going to come of the wedding tomorrow, but she needs her rest, so I don't disturb her.

Sliding my jacket under her head for a little extra comfort, I look over at her. Suddenly, I'm blinded by blistering headlights.

Horns honking. Tires screeching. Glass shattering. Ava screaming.

I fly forward over the steering wheel, driving it so hard into my chest that it takes my breath away.

When the car finally skids to a stop, I look at Ava. She's hunched forward in the seat, blood dripping down the side of her face, and she's not moving or saying anything at all.

Fuck. Oh god, no.

"Ava, are you okay? Baby, can you hear me?"

No answer.

I unbuckle my seat belt and scoot toward her, tilting her head with my hand. "Ava, answer me, baby." The blood is coming from a deep gash on the side of her head above her ear, but it's mostly covered by her hair, and I can't see how bad it is.

"Ava!" I yell, shaking her a little, trying desperately to wake her up. This can't be happening. "Please, baby."

Still no response. I need to get out of the car.

I open my door and stumble out as smoke billows from the front of Leo's car. Whoever hit us is long gone by now, and wailing sirens fill the air. I head for Ava's door, but a wave of dizziness hits me and my legs seem to give out underneath me. My knees hit the pavement, and I call out for Ava one more time before everything goes black.

"Ava!"

She doesn't answer.

THIRTY-EIGHT

Nick

We've been here for over an hour, and the emergency room doctors still haven't let me back to see Ava. No amount of pacing in front of the doorway changes their minds, and I'm losing my shit.

By the time I woke up at the scene we were being loaded into separate ambulances. Paramedics assured me that Ava was being taken care of, but their words were less than comforting. I wanted to see her. I wanted to hear her voice. I wanted some confirmation that she was okay.

Between the mild head injury I had and the rush of everything, I'm still trying to piece together what happened. One minute we were headed home and Ava was sleeping peacefully next to me, and the next I was climbing out of splintered and folded metal and she was unconscious.

This was intentional. There's no doubt in my mind about that. It's too convenient, too coincidental to find us on back roads in the middle of the night when there's no one else around. Someone set out to hurt us, and when I find out who, I'll make sure they pay with every last breath they've got. Especially if anything happens to Ava or the baby.

Shit. The baby. In the heat of the commotion, I was so worried about Ava that I forgot to even mention that she's pregnant.

"Ma'am," I say, rushing toward the nurse's station. The charge nurse spots me and sighs heavily. She's fielded my attempts to get back to see Ava for the last hour, and even though she's understanding, her patience is wearing thin. "My wife, she's pregnant. I need to tell the doctor."

She gives me a sympathetic smile. "I'm sure they're aware of that, Mr. Caponelli. Why don't you have a seat and try to relax? As soon as they know anything, someone will come out to talk to you. Is there anyone I can call for you?"

I shrink back in defeat. If they'd only let me see her, I could relax. Until then, it's useless to even try.

"Out of my way!" A gruff voice comes from behind me and I turn to see Leo and my father bursting through hospital security.

"Dad!" My voice breaks with emotion as if I'm twelve all over again, but I don't care. Right now, I'm just happy to see him.

"Are you okay? Were you hurt?" His face is hard as he scans me for any sign of injury and then pulls me into a tight hug with a breath of relief, more flustered than I've ever seen him.

"I'm fine." I grimace. Apart from a few bruises and a mild concussion, I really am. The impact was mostly on Ava's side, and I made it out relatively unscathed. That only added insult to injury, though. Why am I okay when she's hurt so badly?

"What the hell happened? Where's Ava?"

"She's back there." I point at the large swinging metal doors that lead to the operating room. As the one thing between me and my wife, I've been battling them all night. "I don't know what happened. The car came out of nowhere. By the time I got out, whoever it was was gone."

"And you didn't get a good look at the guy?"

I shake my head, gutted that I let myself get so rattled that all my training went straight out the window. I should have paid better attention, or followed the guy, or done *something* so we weren't starting at square fucking one.

"It's Asnikov." Leo clenches his fist, fuming. "It has to be."

My dad quiets him. "We don't know that yet. Let's be cautious about this."

"Bullshit!" Leo growls, causing several people in the hallway to look at us, including my new nurse friend. "Fuck being cautious. If we would've taken care of the shit after the shooting, this never would've happened."

I hear them arguing back and forth, but none of it really registers. I can't even think about Asnikov or anything else until I know what's going on with Ava. Don't they know something by now? Why is this taking so damn long?

"Get a hold of yourself. I understand tensions are high right now, but we have to keep a level head. This could be any number of things." My dad gives Leo a silencing glare, his voice low to diffuse all the attention. "Let's not forget that they were in your car. It's possible you were the target, not Nick or Ava."

It's a possibility, but two cases of wrong place wrong time are a little too coincidental for my liking. Honestly, I'm beginning to think that both this and the dress shop shooting were intentional hits on Ava. No case of mistaken identity involved. And that means this person is close to us.

"You think they were after me?"

"I don't think anything at this point. The accident was barely ninety minutes ago and I'm trying to get you two to realize we can't move without the right information."

"Nick Caponelli?" Finally, a doctor emerges from the double doors, clipboard in hand.

I shoot up, nearly bounding toward him. "Is she okay?"

"Your wife is going to be fine. She is in recovery now, and you can go see her as soon as we're done here."

I nearly crumble with relief. My chest hurts as if I've been holding my breath the entire time that we've been here.

"And the baby?"

My dad and Leo both look at me in shock. At this point, ruining the surprise doesn't matter. I just want to be sure that my family is safe.

"Mr. Caponelli, Ava had quite a bit of internal damage from the force of the impact. We had to rush her into surgery to control the bleeding. In cases like these, the mother's life is our priority and . . ."

A sinking feeling creeps into my stomach. Why isn't he telling me the baby is okay? Why this long explanation?

"We were unable to save the baby. I'm so sorry."

His words are like a blade twisting in my throat. It's hard to breathe, hard to see, and I start to feel a little dizzy again. No. Please no.

This has to be some kind of sick joke. Maybe they have Ava mixed up with someone else. Maybe he's confused. It would be much too cruel to take something away from us like this that we only barely found out about. There has to be a mistake.

"You're sure?"

The doctor nods. "I'm so sorry. When you're ready to go see your wife, one of the nurses will take you down. And if you have any other questions, my name is Dr. Baker. Feel free to have them page me. Again, I'm sorry about the baby."

Rage avalanches through me as I try to restrain myself. I want to break everything in this damn hospital, but I can't, and without an outlet, I'm reeling. How dare he? How dare he say he's sorry as if we're talking about a small mistake or inconvenience? As if he has any idea what he's just taken from us?

My chest is so heavy that it feels like someone is sitting on top of me, and I brace myself on the wall to keep from collapsing. The doctor isn't responsible, but it doesn't make it any easier to hear those words. The last few days, knowing Ava was pregnant, that we were starting a family together, was utter heaven. It was the happiest I'd ever been in my entire life. And in one single second, that's all changed.

We were unable to save the baby.

Emotions have never been my strong suit, so I cling to what I know, already plotting and dialing in on revenge. Somewhere out there is the bastard who took a wrecking ball to our life, and I won't rest until I've got him. Until I've torn him to shreds and bled him dry. Until I've twisted a blade into his cold, calculated heart. Until I watched his eyes fill with a tiny sliver of the pain I feel right now. It might not make me feel any better, but it's the best I've got.

"Nick, you should go see Ava." My dad approaches carefully, setting his hand on my back. He handles me like I'm a stick of dynamite he's worried might explode at any second. And he might be right. The longer I stand here, the more rage and fury consume me.

Jerking away from him, I slam my fist into the hospital wall as hard as I can. I imagine it's the face of the person who's responsible, and I punch the wall over and over until the drywall crumbles under my fist.

"Look at me." My dad slips his hand underneath my shoulder and pulls me away. "You've got to pull it together. There will be plenty of time for this, but right now, Ava needs you. She needs you to be the strong one so that she can feel this however she needs to. And I promise you, Nick, there will be plenty of time for the rest. I can't imagine how badly you're hurting and I'm so fucking sorry, but now isn't the time. Ava first, then the rest. Got it?"

Suddenly I'm aware of all the eyes on me, and I pull myself together as best I can. I can't fall apart here. Not like this. Not when my wife needs me. I suck in a harsh breath, shoving my own pain as far out of my mind as I can so I can somehow make this okay for her.

"You find him, and you bring him to me." I don't even recognize my own voice, dripping as it is with rage and hatred as I speak to Leo.

Leo nods silently, and then he and my dad leave.

I follow a nurse down the hallway to Ava's room. It's late, and the hospital is quiet except for the hum of various machines. I stand in front of her door for a few minutes, trying to decide how I'm going to tell her that our baby is gone. Nothing seems right, though. Nothing carries enough sorrow.

Slowly, I nudge the door open, and in the darkness, I see Ava lying motionless on the bed with her back to me, her long dark hair spilling down her back. My heart skips a beat seeing her again for the first time. Both thankful that she's okay and in agony over what I have to do now.

As I get closer, I see her body heave and hear her soft, whimpering sobs.

She already knows.

Her cries shatter what's left of me. It's worse than any pain I've ever felt in my entire life, like my beating heart being ripped out of my chest and stomped on.

I make my way to her bed, sliding in next to her and draping my entire body around her protectively. I'm careful not to jostle her or her injuries too much, but she hardly moves or recognizes that I'm here.

"I'm right here, baby," I whisper hoarsely, leaning down and kissing her tearstained cheek. "It's going to be okay."

She melts into me a bit, and I bury my face into her soft curls, her faded perfume stinging my lungs. It's a sharp reminder that tonight was supposed to be a celebration. A happy event. And instead, it's ended in devastation.

Having her in my arms brings only a moment of peace. A false sense of relief. She's okay, but what comes next? She pulls away only long enough to turn over and bury her bruised face in my chest as she cries. I stroke her hair, my own tears falling onto the flimsy hospital pillow.

"Oh god, Nick. Why? Why did this happen?"

I don't have answers for her. I have no idea why this happened to us, and I'm every bit as lost as she is.

"I don't know, baby. But I promise you"—I kiss her forehead gently—"I'm going to fix this. I swear to god, I am going to make this right."

THIRTY-NINE

Nick

Seventy-three hours.

Four thousand three hundred and eighty minutes.

Two hundred sixty-two thousand and eight hundred seconds of agony like I've never felt before. Of a mental pain sharper than anything I've experienced physically. Or failure flashing in mind as I still haven't found the bastard who did this.

I have no doubt that Asnikov is responsible, but I can't attack without solid proof, and the wait is making me antsy.

Ava spent one night in the hospital, and then I was able to bring her home. I thought it would help to be here, but it's been the opposite. She walks around as if she's in a trance, hardly speaking or eating. She's lost a lot of weight in the last two days, and most of the time it's a struggle to even get her out of bed. This has crushed her in ways I can't even imagine, and as hard as I try to help, mostly she just wants to be left alone.

I busy myself doing anything I can to make it easier on Ava. I got rid of all her prenatal vitamins and supplements, donated the few baby items we'd accumulated, and even hid the ultrasound picture—anything that would remind her of the baby. Yesterday Dr. Chapman called to confirm our upcoming ultrasound appointment and Ava picked up before I knew what was happening. I had to pry the phone away from her and explain things to Dr. Chapman as Ava crumpled into a sobbing heap. This was absolutely killing both of us, and I didn't know if it would ever stop.

There was only so much I could do to keep busy, and when things quiet down at night, I'm left to my own thoughts. The silence is excruciating. All I want is for Ava to talk to me, but she's shutting down. Her sobs echo off the walls, and every time I hear her cry, I fight the urge to go to her. She doesn't want me right now, and I have to respect that.

The gym has become my sanctuary. I can crank the music up loud enough to drown out my thoughts and Ava's cries, and exercise is at least a healthy way to get my anger out. Besides, when I finally have my moment with Asnikov, I want to be in the best shape of my life.

Earlier, I tried to get Ava up and out of the house for a walk, but she wanted nothing to do with it. The pain I'm feeling is probably half of what she is, so, conceding to her once again, I found my way down to the warehouse office. Even if my dad and Leo aren't going to let me help with the investigation, I need some kind of human interaction.

I sit at my desk, staring at the frame in the corner. The picture behind the glass is of Ava and me in Saint Lucia only a few weeks ago, happy as could be. Tucked inside the corner is my copy of the ultrasound. I take it out, running my fingers over the glossy paper.

It hardly resembles a baby, more of a dust storm. *It.* We don't know if the baby we lost was a boy or girl, but I suspect that only would make all of this harder, the finer details stinging worse than the rest.

My thoughts are interrupted by someone pounding up the stairs.

"Sir, you can't go . . ." I hear my assistant's voice right as the door is thrown open and Alessandro and my father walk in.

I stand up, ready for whatever fight this will become. I didn't tell

Alessandro about the accident at Ava's request, and I'm pretty positive that's the reason for his visit. But I have more than enough anger to go around, so I welcome his visit more than most days.

"What kind of bullshit are you trying to pull here, Caponelli? My daughter was hospitalized and you don't have the decency to call me or my wife?"

My dad stands back, recognizing that this is something I need to handle myself.

"She's my wife, Alessandro. I will always respect her wishes, and she didn't want you there."

Alessandro's face turns into a harrowing glare. "Don't pretend you give a damn about her. You did this for your place in the business, and my daughter turned into a casualty."

"Right." I all but laugh. "Like you weren't using her for your own purposes from the very beginning. You're getting old and your memory may not be what it used to be, so let me remind you that *you're* the one who came up with this deal to begin with."

"A deal for your marriage, not for you to brainwash my daughter and whisk her off to a foreign country to get married. It's probably not even legal. I have my lawyer checking out the validity of it right now."

"Knock yourself out. Ava chose to marry me. She wasn't forced into anything like she would have been under your watch. Everything was done completely legally." He picked the wrong day to storm into my office; he's just the scapegoat I need. "You're lucky I don't put out a hit on you for trying to back out of the deal."

"The deal doesn't matter to either side anymore, Alessandro," my father interjects. "Nick and Ava made their own choice, and so did you when you started working behind our backs with both Asnikov and Savino. As far as I'm concerned, any arrangement you and I made is done. Nick will take over for me in a few weeks, and that will be the end of it."

"If you think you're getting your hands on my business, you have another thing coming," Alessandro snarls.

"I don't want anything to do with you, Alessandro. It's pretty telling that instead of asking me how your daughter is, you're still here arguing specifics of an agreement you already blew up."

"She wouldn't even be in this position if you guys had taken care of Asnikov after the shooting," Alessandro says. "After we took out the shooter, you basically had Asnikov on a silver platter and you didn't do anything. This is your fault."

"I'd appreciate it if you would get the fuck out of my office now."

"Not until you tell me when I can see my daughter." He stands his ground.

"I'm going to leave that up to her. She's going through a lot right now and—"

"She's going through a lot because you're keeping her from her family. You may think you're getting back at me, but you're only hurting Ava in the long run. You think Bella and Ava will ever fix their relationship after you didn't let her come to the wedding? Not to mention you're obliterated any future partnership you could have with the Savinos."

"You have no idea what the fuck you're talking about," I snap. "Ava was pregnant, Alessandro. She lost the baby in the accident and that's why we didn't come to the wedding. Bella and Paul will both understand that."

The color drains from his face. The baby is as much of a loss for their family as it is for us. Our child would've been an heir to both the Moretti and Caponelli crime families.

"And, yeah, she's hurting right now, so I'm going to do everything in my power to protect her. God knows you never did. And if that means keeping her from you and anybody else, I'll fucking do it."

"She shouldn't have even been in that damn car." For the first time ever, I see tears well up in his eyes. "This is your fault, Nick."

With that, he stalks out of my office and leaves the warehouse. My dad's gaze falls on me.

"Don't look at me like that," I growl. "He needed to know."

My dad sighs. "Go home, Nick. Be with your wife. She needs you right now more than we do, and you need her too."

He leaves, shutting the door softly behind him.

I fling my hand across my desk, knocking everything off it and onto the floor. I'm not usually one to let words get to me, but the truth behind what Alessandro said is haunting.

This is all my fault. If I had just taken my own car. If I had just killed Asnikov after the shooting. If I just quit this entire fucking thing and ran away with Ava.

If. If. If.

FORTY

Ava

I should have known.

I should have known that things were too good to be true. That it couldn't last much longer. That I was too comfortable.

I've never been happier than I was the last few months with Nick; everything seemed so perfect and starting our family together was the icing on the cake. I let my guard down, though, and now I'm reeling more than I ever thought possible.

The physical pain I feel is bearable. It took surgery to stop the internal bleeding, and I've got a pretty nasty concussion and cut on my forehead, but for the most part it's manageable. It's the mental pain that's the worst. Consuming. Suffocating. Like my body is eating away at itself from the inside out.

I spent a lot of time in therapy learning how to identify and name what I'm feeling, but this, this is a completely different thing.

I can't bear being around Nick. Every time I hear his voice or see his face all I can think about is how badly I've failed him. He's given me everything, saved my life in more ways than I can count, and I can't even give him the one thing he's asked for.

Maybe I should have done something different. Maybe taken better vitamins so the baby was stronger. Maybe eaten healthier or walked more, or anything at all that might have improved our chances.

I don't deserve Nick and the wonderful life he tried to give me. The last few days he's been so attentive and caring, and all I've done is rebuff his efforts.

In the beginning he'd come in every few hours to ask if I wanted something to eat or to go for a walk. Eventually he got tired of being shot down and would peek his head in to be sure I was still breathing. When he comes in at night, he drapes his arm over me and whispers how much he loves me, but I pretend to be asleep each time.

A small part of me feels like I'm being punished because of how I felt about the baby right off the bat. I was upset to be pregnant, but that was because it was a shock. After I came to terms with it, my whole mindset shifted and I was so excited. Why couldn't I have felt like that from the beginning?

All I want is a little space to process everything. I appreciate Nick more than I can ever say, but right now his attention feels suffocating. Every second he's trying to fix something he can't. He can't make this better, he can't make this go away, and every time I see him, all I can think about is our baby. He's a painful reminder of how much I lost.

As much as I'm ashamed to admit this, a small part of me blames him. Nick swore up and down that he wouldn't let anything like this happen, that he would take care of everything. I trusted that, but he didn't, and now our child is dead, my family hates me, and I'm completely isolated. Sometimes I feel like I'm avoiding Nick because I don't trust myself not to say that out loud. It isn't fair, and I hate myself for even thinking about it. It's only another reason why I don't deserve Nick.

I know it's irrational. The accident was just that—an accident. There's no way Nick could have stopped it or that I could have saved the baby. The doctor stressed that continuously. Neither one of us is to blame. Even the police who investigated the crash said the guy was driving drunk and it wasn't a targeted attack. I know all that, but it doesn't stop me from feeling that way.

Eventually, I'm going to have to face all of this. I can't keep myself locked away forever. I need to tell my family. I need to go back to work. I need to move on. But every time I even think about it, I am reduced to sobs again. Everything took a back seat to the baby the last few weeks, and now everything seems pale in comparison.

I heard Nick come home from the office about an hour ago, and I've been trying to get up the courage to go talk to him since. When I go out there, he'll jump back into protector mode again. The only thing he's doing, though, is making me feel inferior. I failed already by losing our baby, and I can't even pull myself back together on my own—I need him for that. It's pathetic.

I can hardly take care of myself; I would have been a terrible mother. Maybe that's why our baby was taken from us.

As I try to get up the courage to go out there, there's a soft knock on the door.

"Ava? Can I come in?" Nick's voice is broken and pained.

I don't answer, but he persists, nudging the door open slowly.

"Ava?" he asks again, hesitating at the door as if he's worried to come too far into the room. I don't blame him; every time he's been in here lately, I've bitten his head off.

The bed sinks in next to me and his fingers gently graze my shoulder. I can feel the desperation in his touch.

Finally, I roll over, realizing he isn't going to give up so easily today. He gazes down at me, waiting for me to make the first move. Giving up on all other methods he's tried before, he leaves the ball in my court and waits.

"Hi," I whisper, my voice scratchy. I've hardly said a word the last few days, and my throat is dry from dehydration.

"How are you feeling?" He rests his hand on the palm of my cheek, gently sweeping his thumb back and forth.

"I'm fine." I sigh. Truthfully, he doesn't want to know how I'm feeling, and by the look of pain he's already carrying, I don't think he can handle it.

There's obviously more to that answer, but Nick doesn't pry. "Can I get you something to eat? I brought Thai food home. I thought that might sound good."

If nothing else, he's relentless. He's been trying to get me to crack for days, and bringing home my favorite takeout even though he can't stand it is his latest attempt.

"Thank you, but I'm not very hungry."

"Baby, you need to eat something. We've got to keep your strength up." He tucks a piece of hair behind my ear, eyes pleading with me.

"I said I'm not hungry, Nick."

Taking my cue, he backs off a bit. "How about a movie, then?"

"I'm not sure if I feel up to it," I snap. My fuse is even shorter than normal, and though I hate myself for how I'm treating Nick, I can't seem to stop. I don't deserve him. I don't deserve his kindness, and the more he showers me with it, the worse I feel.

"We could watch it here if you want. I could bring a tray of dinner and we could get something on demand and just lie in bed."

I move away from him. "I don't want dinner, I don't want to watch a movie, I want to be alone."

He isn't going to do that, though. Instead, he wraps his body around mine. His usual gentle and loving touch feels like sandpaper on my skin, and it brings hot tears to my eyes as I realize how badly I've screwed all of this up.

"Ava, I know you're hurting right now. I can't imagine what you're going through, but please don't push me away. Let me help you. We can get through this together."

"Together?" I shriek, throwing the covers off and bolting up. Nick looks at me wide-eyed, as if he can't believe I'm capable of moving so fast. "Nick, you don't get it. This happened to me. I need to deal with it on my own, and if I want to stay in bed and cry for a few days, I'm going to do that. I lost my baby three days ago. I think that should give me a little leeway."

Nick's face falls. "*Our* baby."

"What?"

"*We* lost *our* baby." He moves to the edge of the bed and sits there as still as can be. "I'm hurting, too, Ava. This didn't only happen to you. I may not have been carrying our child, but trust me, I feel the loss all the same. But we don't have to go through this alone. We can figure it out together, but you've got to let me help you."

"I don't need your help," I cry, not even recognizing my own voice. It feels like the anger and grief overcome my body and I'm being possessed by something. "I just need some space, Nick."

"What do you mean?"

"You're smothering me!" I cry. "Every time I turn around, you're trying to be the hero and make all of this go away, but you can't. All I see when I look at you right now is our baby, and it feels like I'm losing it all over again. You swore you'd keep us safe and nothing like this would happen!" I freeze, the words come out of my mouth like I'm spewing venom. I don't mean it, and I regret them the second they come out.

Nick surprises me and lets out a sharp laugh. "Is that how you truly feel?"

I bite my lip, tears streaming down my cheeks. I want to tell him it isn't. That I don't blame him. That I'm just upset. I want to run to him and let him fix this for me, like he so desperately wants to. Instead, my feet stay cemented on our bedroom floor, my mouth clamped shut.

"Don't you think I have thought that a million times in the last few days? I screwed up. I shouldn't have taken Leo's car. I shouldn't have let Asnikov live after what happened at the dress shop. I should have kept you and the baby locked away somewhere until things were safe. There are a million things I wish I could have done differently, and I've been over them all because I have had nothing else to do. You've kept yourself holed up in this room like it's the end of the world, and I know it hurts. Trust me, I fucking know it hurts because my heart is breaking at the thought of never holding our child, never finding out if we were having a boy or girl, what we would name it. But it happened, Ava, and we can't go back and change anything. All we can do now is try to pick up the pieces of our life and piece it back together. That is, if that's what you still want."

Each of Nick's words hit me a bullet. He's hurting every bit as badly as I am, but all I can focus on is my own pain and loss. I'm in a vicious, depressive cycle and my thoughts are twisted.

"Is it what you want, Ava?" Nick asks, standing up and walking toward me.

"Ava!" Nick raises his voice at me and I flinch.

"I don't know, okay?" I cry, burying my face in my hands. "I don't know anything right now. I just need . . . I need some time, okay? Can you give me that?"

Nick bites his lip as if he's holding back his own tears. "I'll give you all the time you need, Ava. Until then, I'll be in the guest room."

Nick turns and walks to the door. He pauses for a moment before going out, giving me a chance to stop him. When I don't, he slams the door and I hear the sound of crashing and destruction out in the rest of the apartment. He is furious.

Disgust creeps up my body and I feel like I'm going to throw up. Why am I such an idiot? Why did I need to make this more difficult on him than it already is? Why couldn't I just go to him and make this right?

In my heart, I don't deserve him. Nick needs someone who is his equal—who is strong and confident and would never blame him for something out of his control like this. All I do is hurt Nick. Since we'd started dating, all I've done is make things harder on him and cause him stress. I hate myself, and Nick will be so much better off without me.

Staying here isn't an option. I desperately need some fresh air to clear my mind, and the thought of another confrontation with Nick is debilitating. This is his home, after all; he should be able to sleep in his own room in his own bed.

Grabbing my bag from the closet, I stuff a few of my things in it.

I don't know where I'm going to go, but I need to get out of here. I need to clear my head before I talk to Nick again; I need to stop putting him through all of this.

I want to talk to Bella, but she's on her honeymoon. I could go to my parents' house, but the thought of seeing them and facing more disappointment is too much. Angie would take me in, but she lives too far away. Vince seems like my only viable option right now.

I love Nick more than anything, but if I have any hope of salvaging our relationship, I need to put a little distance between us before I do something else that I'll regret. It will be better for him too. A few days to heal ourselves and then figure out what comes next. I hope he will see it that way too.

Nick

I wait a little while before going back into the bedroom, hoping Ava will be asleep by the time I go in. I have to get my toothbrush, but I want to avoid another confrontation at all costs.

Her words stung, but they didn't really surprise me. I could see the pain and regret on her face as soon as she said them. Deep down, she doesn't mean it. We're both hurting, and sometimes people say things they don't mean when they're backed into a corner.

It's my own fault. It was too soon. The accident was only three days ago, and this is all still very new and raw for her. I thought the tough-love approach might work, shake her out of her trance, make her realize that we can get through this and that it isn't the end of the world. She's right, though, if she wants to stay in bed and cry for a few days, who am I to stop her?

What hurt me most was the way she spoke like she's going through this on her own. Like it's her problem to deal with. Like she's the only one who lost something. She's in a really deep and dark place, and I have absolutely no idea how to pull her out of it. If anything, I'd only pushed her farther into it.

As much as I hate to admit it, maybe Alessandro's right. Maybe Ava needs to spend more time with her family. Her depression is something totally new to me, but they've dealt with it before.

I push our bedroom door open as quietly as I can, not wanting to wake her if she's asleep.

She isn't asleep, though. She's standing at the bed with an overnight bag, stuffing things inside of it.

"What the hell are you doing?"

Ava looks up at me like a deer in headlights. She probably hoped to make her escape before I noticed.

"Nick, I—" She scrambles for words. "I think we need a little time apart. We're not good for each other right now."

I let out an exasperated breath. "You're leaving me? Ava, don't do this."

"I need some space, okay? I need to figure this out and it's not fair of me to be here until I do. Those things I said . . . I'm sorry, Nick. You don't deserve that. Please don't be upset with me."

Watching her put her phone charger and a few clothes into her bag is a gut punch that knocks the air out of me. I can't even form words as I watch my entire life preparing to walk out the door.

"Ava, I could never be upset with you about how you're feeling.

Don't do this, please. I'll give you all the time and space you need. I'll do whatever—"

"No." She shakes her head definitively. "This is your house, Nick. It's not fair of me to ask you to do that. Look." She sighs. "It's just a few days. I'm going to go to Angie's or something. I'll be fine, I promise. And then in a few days when I'm thinking straight, we can talk."

She's clearly made up her mind. There's no way I can talk her out of it. All I can do is pretend it isn't slowly ripping my heart out.

I take her hand in mine, and she flinches. "Ava, I'm fine with you going to see your sister, but I want you to tell me you'll come home once these next few days are over. You said you weren't going to run anymore. Promise me you'll be back."

Ava turns away, heavy tears streaming down her face. "I'll text you when I get there."

FORTY-ONE

Ava

"Ava," Vince says flatly as he opens the door. "I wasn't expecting you to come by. Come inside, it's freezing out there." He ushers me inside and shuts the door tightly behind us.

"Is everything okay? It's really late."

"I—I wanted to come by and see the baby," I say quietly. I'm nervous to even be in his house, almost like an outsider.

"Of course you can." Vince's brow furrows. "Are you feeling okay? I thought you'd be at home resting. Where is Nick?"

"I came by myself. He's . . . busy tonight."

"Soph," Vince calls, leading me into the living room. "Ava came by to say hello."

Sophia is sitting on the couch, holding a little blue bundle in her arms. "Hey!" She smiles, standing to give me a hug. "It's so good to see you. You didn't have to come all this way when you're still recovering from the accident."

"I'm feeling much better," I say, gazing down into the blankets. My new nephew yawns, stretching a tiny arm up over his head and curling back up. "Wow, he's absolutely precious."

"Meet Rocco Moretti." Vince grins, doting on the little boy.

"Do you want to hold him?" Sophia offers.

"I'd love to." I swallow, carefully taking him out of her arms. Sophia excuses herself for a minute and I sit down next to Vince on the couch.

Holding a baby so soon after losing our own is as torturous as it is therapeutic. I'm so happy for my brother and sister-in-law, but my heart aches for what I'm missing out on. Tears bubble in my eyes as I stare at his perfect face and wonder what our baby would have looked like.

"Is everything okay, Ava?" Vince asks. "You said Nick's busy, but I can't imagine he'd want you to come all this way on your own. And your car's not here. Did you walk?"

I suck in a sharp breath. "I took a cab. Honestly, I don't know what Nick's doing tonight because we had a fight and I left."

"You did?"

I nod. "I said some pretty awful things to him."

"Ava, I'm sure Nick doesn't blame you. You guys have been through a lot the last few days."

We've certainly come a long way if Vince is defending Nick, and I almost can't bring myself to admit the entirety of our argument.

"I feel like I resent Nick for the accident. He swore he'd protect us and then he let—"

"Ava, I'm going to stop you right there. Looking at things like that isn't going to do anybody any good. Nick didn't let anything happen. If it was meant to happen, it would've happened either way. Nick isn't any more responsible for what happened than you are."

I swallow the growing lump in my throat. "I blame myself too."

"How do you figure that?" he asks. "You didn't cause the accident."

"It's not just the accident, though."

"I'm not following you, Ava. What do you mean?"

My lip quivers and knots twist in my stomach. All I can do is stare at the sweet, precious baby in my arms and cry. "I was pregnant. We lost the baby in the accident."

Vince's face turns white. "Ava . . . I'm so sorry." He puts his arm around me and pulls me into his shoulder. "I can't imagine how much you're hurting, but you can't blame yourself for that. Nick won't either."

"He should. It almost makes me angrier that he doesn't. When I first found out, I wasn't happy about it. I think this is my punishment for feeling that way."

"It doesn't work that way, Avs." He gives me a soft smile. "Did I ever tell you that before Sophia and I had Gigi and little Rocco here, we had a miscarriage?"

I shake my head. I had no idea.

"It happened so early that most people didn't even know she was pregnant. It was a long time ago, and I'm only telling you now because I want you to know that I understand what you're feeling. I understand what Nick's feeling. You're hurt and you're blaming yourselves and each other because you're grasping for some kind of explanation."

My tears flow freely now, and I can't stop them.

"It almost killed Sophia and me. We almost got divorced because of it. She was shutting me out, and I wanted to be strong for her, and neither one of us realized how much we could really help each other. You are never going to get an explanation for this, Ava. Sometimes bad things happen for no reason at all."

"What if this is some kind of sign that Nick and I aren't supposed to be together?"

"Ava." Vince smirks. "You and Nick are made for each other, and trust me, I was the last person who wanted to admit that. He loves you more than anything. Think about what he has already done for you. After Andrew died, you became a completely different person, and he brought you back. You're incredibly lucky to have found each other, but that doesn't mean it's always going to be easy. Things like this, things that hurt you and rock you to your core, are going to happen.

But that's when you should be leaning on each other and not pulling apart."

Hearing Vince talk like this has me convinced that something has possessed my brother. He's never sentimental or emotional like this, but I've never needed it more than I do at this moment.

"You're right." I nod. "I should go talk to him."

"You should." Vince agrees. "You're always welcome here, but you need to go fix things with your husband."

"Thank you. You have no idea how much I needed to hear that." I wipe my tears, ready to go back and face Nick.

"That's what I'm here for." He smiles, taking baby Rocco out of my arms. "Why don't you let me give you a ride? You're not exactly dressed for the weather."

"I left in a hurry."

Vince takes the baby back to Sophia, and I say goodbye to her as he puts his arm around my shoulder. "Let's get you home."

Vince drops me off in the front of our apartment building. I wave goodbye, thanking him again for the talk, and go inside. There's a crowd of people waiting to take the elevator and I don't feel like seeing any of our neighbors with my blotchy, tear-stained face.

I duck into the stairwell, deciding I can use the exercise, anyway. At about the fifth floor, I start to slow down a bit. A door opens and someone steps into the stairwell. Seconds later, I'm slammed against the hard concrete wall. One arm is pressed against the back of my neck so I can't move, while another holds the cool tip of a knife to my neck.

"If you scream, I'll slit your throat," a gritty, male voice whispers in my ear. "Nod if you understand."

I nod, frozen with fear.

"Good girl. Now, we are going to walk back downstairs and to my car. If you do anything to tip anyone off, I'll kill you, and then I'll go upstairs and kill Nick. Nod if you understand."

I nod again and the man pulls me back from the wall, twisting my arm behind my back so that I can't move away from him, the knife still pressed firmly against my neck.

"Walk."

Nick

Ava left.

No hug or kiss. No *I love you*. No indication of when I might see her again. She's just gone and that's it.

There's no way I can stay in the house by myself with only the reminders of her to keep me company, and I've already put so many holes in the wall and broken so much glass that it's starting to get expensive, so I call Leo to meet me at the bar.

An hour later I finish my seventh whiskey, and I've gone over every detail of what happened with my brother. He only listened, nodding occasionally and making supportive comments when needed.

"And you never got a text?"

I shake my head. "I called Angie, and she didn't show up there. She must have gone somewhere else." I'm the last person she wants to see, but that doesn't mean I'm willing to let her walk around while someone is trying to kill her. Zane's working on trying to find her right now.

"Do you want to look for her?"

"I want to, but I don't think that will do any good. Clearly, she doesn't want to talk to me." I throw back the rest of the drink and motion to the bartender.

Leo winces, swallowing his opinion about me having another drink. "This probably isn't what you want to hear, but maybe she just needs a little space. This has been a lot for her and she has to deal with it in whatever way she can. She'll come around."

Most of what Leo says goes over my head because I'm focused on what is in the corner of the bar. *Jimmy.* He sits at a dark booth with some blond girl hanging on his arm, half asleep and high as a kite.

Leo hasn't seen him yet, and if I play my cards right, I can go bash his skull in before Leo has time to stop me. I hate that guy, and he'd shown up at the same place as me on the wrong night. The only thing keeping me in my seat is the fact that Ava isn't with him. Wherever the fuck she is, at least she didn't run to Jimmy, and that's a small silver lining.

He catches me staring at him, and a darkness I don't recognize comes over his face. I stiffen when I see him stand up and approach me, readying myself for a fight.

"Hey, Nick. I, uh, I heard about the accident," Jimmy says, not meeting my eyes. There's a civility in his tone that I'm not used to with him.

"Yeah."

"Is Ava . . . I mean, how are you guys doing?" The sound of her name in his mouth makes my skin crawl.

"Fucking fantastic, Jimmy," I scoff, watching as the barkeep pours a hefty amount of whiskey into my nearly empty cup. I don't even have to ask anymore. He just knows.

Jimmy sighs uncomfortably. "Look, I know we got off on the wrong foot, and that was entirely my fault. I want to—"

Without thinking, I stand up abruptly, knocking my chair over. "The wrong foot?" I seethe. "Is that what you call shoving drugs down my wife's throat and trying to move in on her in her moment of weakness?"

"Nick, he's trying to apologize. Give the guy a break." Leo looks at me sympathetically.

"Stay the fuck out of this."

"It may not seem like it, but I care about Ava, and what happened with Alessandro . . . it wasn't right," Jimmy says.

"You care about her?" I shoot him a wicked smile. Before I know what's happening, my hands are at his throat, slamming him against the bar. "I'm sure you do care about her. Did she come running to you tonight when she left me? Is that what this fake apology is all about? You finally got your way and Ava is at home waiting for you while you're here rubbing it in my face?"

"Nick, get a grip, man." Leo pulls me off Jimmy, who quickly gets up and straightens his jacket.

"I'm sorry for whatever shit you two are going through right now, but I swear to god I haven't even spoken to Ava in weeks. She made her choice." His face falls. "I'll leave you guys alone now."

Jimmy walks away with his head down and ducks into the booth once again.

"You need to go home," Leo growls. "You are losing your shit and you're going to do something you regret."

"Funny, I don't regret one second of what just happened." I throw the rest of my drink back.

"I thought I might find you guys here." My father stands in front of me, judging my current state fervently.

"Oh, of course, you called Dad." I glare at Leo. "Perfect. The gang's all here."

My dad's icy stare shuts me up. Even drunk, I can take a hint. "Are you done? Because if you're through with all this self-pity, I have some news you might like to hear."

"Sorry, Dad, it's been a bit of a tough week. You know, losing my child and my wife and everything I've ever wanted in one fell swoop." My words slur together.

"This is pathetic, Nick." My dad frowns, shoving the row of empty glasses away from me. "I thought you cared more about Ava than this."

"She's the one who left me."

His eyes burn into me. "If you're willing to give up on her this easily, then you didn't deserve her in the first place. And you certainly don't deserve to lead this family."

"Fuck you." If there's one thing he's not going to do, it's doubt my love for that woman. She's absolutely everything to me, and being without her is fucking killing me.

"Are you going to sit here and act like a child all night, or do you want to know who was responsible for the accident?" He crosses his arms over his chest in annoyance.

"You know who it was and you haven't told me?"

"I came here to tell you, you haven't exactly been cooperative."

"Who is it?" I ignore his taunting. I need something to focus my anger on, and if I've got a name, I can take it out on them.

"The car that hit you belongs to Jeffrey Pratt. He's an associate of Alessandro's. Alessandro ordered the hit."

My blood runs cold. Alessandro? Alessandro did this? I've been wasting all this time thinking it was Asnikov, and it was my own fucking father-in-law?

Ava wasn't even supposed to be in that damn car.

What Alessandro did, it wasn't right.

It's all starting to make sense.

All I see is red hot rage. This is Alessandro's fault, and this time he's gone too far.

"I want him dead."

"You do what you have to do," my dad says stoically, giving me the green light.

I may not be able to win Ava back, but I can make sure Alessandro pays with his last breath.

FORTY-TWO

Nick

My fist collides with Alessandro's face again, and a fountain of red blood splatters in all directions. I've hit him so many times that I've lost track, and he doesn't even react anymore. I thought this would make me feel better, but the more I hit him, the angrier I become. I've waited months for this moment, and now that it's here, it's much less gratifying than I anticipated.

He's completely broken, disheveled, and looks like he hasn't slept in days. It's the first time I've ever seen him show any semblance of emotion.

It serves the bastard right. I hope this is eating him alive and keeping him up at night, like it is me and like it is Ava. If it isn't, I'll make sure he hurts all the same.

"I'm not the enemy here, Nick."

I don't even bother answering, landing my fist on his jaw. His head snaps back and then falls forward. He's motionless, but still conscious. "Shut the fuck up. I don't want to hear your excuses for one more second. I know everything, Alessandro. That you only wanted me to marry Ava so you could weasel your way into our organization. That you tried to use her to control everything and feed information to the Russians, and sold yourself out to them when you couldn't. That you caused the accident."

"Sounds like you've got it all figured out, then." He gives me a smug smirk, mustering all the strength he could. "What do you need me for? If you're going to kill me, why don't you do it already?"

"I want to know why," I hiss. "I want to hear it straight out of your fucking mouth—why my wife is gone and my child is dead."

Alessandro chuckles and shakes his head. "Contrary to what you think of me, Nick, I never meant to hurt my daughter. I set out with the best of intentions. I wanted her with you because I knew you would protect her and give her what she needed. God knows I never could."

I fight the urge to roll my eyes. He really has this caring father act down to a science. If I didn't know him better, I might fall for it.

"Ava has always been strong willed. I should have known from the start she would never agree with my plan. I overpromised the Russians. They were breathing down my neck trying to get answers that I didn't have, and the entire time this was going on, Ava was falling more and more in love with you. That's when I approached Savino about an exclusive deal, but that was ruined when I found out you were already married, so I needed a new plan. I knew if anything happened to you and Leo, Ava would assume responsibility, since she's your wife."

"That's what the accident was about."

Alessandro nods. "You have to understand Nick, I never expected her to be in the car and I certainly never expected that she was . . ."

Pregnant. He can't even say the fucking word.

Alessandro pauses, overcome with emotion. I'm not buying it. He doesn't care what he's done. Ava's gone, our baby is gone, and there is nothing else I care about. I can do this all day. Alessandro isn't walking out of here alive, and I want to be sure I get every last answer out of him.

"I screwed up, Nick. I admit that. I hurt Ava in more ways than I would ever like to admit, but you have to believe me—I never meant for any of this to happen. Not the accident, not the baby, certainly not Asnikov getting his hands on her."

It takes me a minute to process his words. Did he just say . . .

"Asnikov?" My jaw clenches.

"A call came in before you arrived. Alek picked her up last night. He sent me a picture; you can check my phone. I thought that was why you grabbed me, because Alek is going to kill Ava. You didn't know?"

"Where the fuck is your phone?" I hiss, throwing him out of the chair. This could be just another ploy to stall, so I'm not just taking his word for it.

"My back pocket." Alessandro groans in pain.

I rip the phone out of his pocket and search desperately. Just as he said, there's a picture of Ava from an unknown number. She's passed out on the floor of some cell, motionless and unconscious. Bruised, bloody, and fresh drag marks all over her legs. *Consider us even.* That's all the text says.

All the air is sucked out of my lungs. Alek sent this last night; he must have taken her when she left. I wasted all this time on this prick while Ava's in the hands of one of the most ruthless men in the world, who has a vendetta against both me and her father.

I drop Alessandro's phone and whip the gun off my hip. "You're a fucking bastard."

"Tell her I'm sorry, Nick. Go find her and tell her I'm sorry. And that I love her." His voice is shallow, and it's a struggle for him to get the words out. Before I can even pull the trigger, Alessandro slumps over, life completely drained out of him.

I'm shocked that it happened so suddenly. That he's truly gone. Dead from his injuries and blood loss. I should sort this out here, but the only thing on my mind is getting to Ava. I have to find her, and on the way there, I have to pray to god I'm not too late.

Ava

When I wake up I'm lying on a paper-thin mattress in a dark room, completely disoriented. The last thing I remember is the face of Alek Asnikov as he shoved me into the trunk of a car and a sharp stab and burning sensation in my arm. Alek must have drugged me so I wouldn't know where he'd taken me.

I'm not tied up, but there is still no way for me to get out of this room. The door doesn't even have a handle on the inside. The walls are cement and crumbly, and the only light comes from a dim bulb in the corner. It's musty, and the air feels heavy in my lungs. For a second I consider breaking the light bulb and using a shard of glass to defend myself, but my plan is interrupted by the jingling of keys in the door, and I scramble back against the wall.

Alek jerks the door open, and his face twists into an evil grin when he sees me cower away. "Oh good, you're awake. I was worried I had given you too much. You'll have to forgive me. I don't normally handle the dirty work."

Words are lost on my lips as Alek chats away as if this is completely normal. He reaches for my hand but I pull it away, trying to crawl farther away from him. It was no use, though. I'm literally backed into a corner.

Alek gives me a condescending smile. "Aw, don't be like that, Ava. You and I are friends, and I'd hate to have to tie my friend up."

He keeps his eyes locked on mine as he reached for my hand again. This time I freeze, letting him grab it. "That's a good girl."

He turns my arm over, inspecting it closely. There's a needle mark on the inside of my elbow that I assume is from when he drugged me. It's tender and bruised, and as he inspects it, Alek notices too.

"I'll get some cream for that."

"Why are you doing this?" I whisper, confused by his kindness. I've never been kidnapped before, but I've seen enough crime shows to know this isn't generally how it goes.

"Your father and I had a deal. He didn't follow through, so I decided to take matters into my own hands."

"Nick won't let you get away with this. He's probably looking for me right now."

"Now, you and I both know that's not true, Ava. He thinks you left him, remember?" Alek chuckles. "He's drowning his sorrows in a bar and whining about it right now. By the time he even realizes you're gone, you'll be dead. Get some rest. You'll need it later."

He knocks once on the door and someone opens it from the outside, and he disappears. Once he's gone, I burst into tears. He's right. Nick thinks I hate him. He thinks I left. And with the way I treated him, I'm not even sure he would come if he knew.

FORTY-THREE

Nick

In and out.

In and out.

In and out.

I focus on my breathing because if I don't, my head is going to fucking explode. Ava is with Alek and we're already ten steps behind him.

There's somewhat of an unspoken rule in the Mafia that women and children are off-limits, and a majority of groups abide by that, but not Alek. He's ruthless, absolutely evil, and he's had Ava for at least twenty-four hours. I can't even bring myself to think about what she's gone through in that amount of time, on top of the injuries she already had.

The thought that I might be too late guts me. That I might not see her again. That we might not have the chance to make up. That the last moments we shared could be full of agony and anger. It takes every bit of self-control I have to shove that to the back of my mind and focus on what I've got to do. One way or another, I'm going to bring Ava home.

Leo traced an abandoned warehouse in the Meatpacking District to Asnikov. It wasn't hard, because like with the shooting, he wanted us to know it was him and where he's hiding. Or rather, he wanted Alessandro to know.

It makes sense. It's practically on its own little island out here, far away from any functioning warehouses, and the place is nearly falling down. I feel like I have tetanus just from looking at the rusted sheet metal sides flapping in the wind. He can work out here and not be bothered by anyone at all.

Once we knew a location, Zane sent over blueprints, and I've been pouring over them for the last fifteen minutes. Ava is inside of that warehouse and every single minute counts, but going in there on my own would be a death trap for both Ava and me. My dad sent backup; they should have been here by now, and I'm getting restless.

When I finally can't take it any longer, I creep up to the side of the building and peer into a window. It's time I end this.

Just as I'm about to go in, my dad and Leo pull up with several other men, ready for a battle.

"I sure as hell hope you weren't about to go in there yourself, Nick," my dad hisses, slapping a bulletproof vest on and throwing one to me.

"Nope, just scoping things out," I lie, buckling the vest on. "What's the plan?"

"Bust through the door, charge our way through until we find Ava. Shoot anyone who gets in the way." Leo smirks, making it sound as easy as pie.

My dad shakes his head at Leo, less than amused. "Infrared is showing three men at the back entrance. For the last fifteen minutes of each hour, one of them goes on break. That's our window of opportunity. They're most likely holding Ava in one of the front cells, which is in the opposite corner of the entrance. We'll send Vince and Joey around this side. You and Leo will go the other way," my dad says, pointing and directing the group as we move through the shadows.

"Once we're inside, we'll have about ninety seconds before their backup gets here. We need to move fast. If they have Ava in the front, you're not going to be able to get to her and then get her out in that amount of time." He slaps a grenade into my hand. "You get her and you blow the side out of the building, and you get her out. Once we get the confirmation that everyone is out, we'll blow everything. We have to move. We've got eight minutes tops for all of this to go down."

Eight minutes to find Ava and get her out safely.

Eight minutes to end Asnikov and whatever threat he represents.

Eight minutes feels like both a flash and an eternity.

"And what if we need more time?" I ask, my confidence shaken.

My dad's face hardens. "Nick, you don't have more time. If their reserves show up and you don't have Ava, you throw that shit and you get the fuck out of there. Am I clear?"

I swallow the lump in my throat. He knows what he's asking me to do, but he also knows that he wouldn't follow that order if he was in my shoes. If my mom was inside, if one of us was inside, he'd fight until the bitter end, and that's exactly what I intend to do as well. I'm either coming out of there with my wife or not at all.

There's a knowing look in his eye. "Just do your job, and it won't come to that."

"All right. Listen up," he barks at the other men. "This is a rescue mission. Our top priority is getting Ava out of there alive. You take out anyone who gets in your way."

The men nod and we hang tight behind the cars until it's time to move.

I lead the group forward at my dad's signal, approaching Alek's soldiers from the side. They don't even see us coming before Leo and Zane drop them, snapping both of their necks silently.

Zane blows the door out and we charge inside. The noise draws the attention of a couple of Alek's men, who were sitting around a table playing cards. They scramble up, searching for weapons when they see us, but we're too quick.

"We'll hold them off. You go find her," my dad orders.

I nod, breaking off from the rest of the group and heading for the hallway. The main room fills up fast, the commotion attracting men from all over the warehouse. Zane is at my heels, shadowing every move I make as he covers me down the hall.

Sweeping every room, we search for any sign of Ava. She has to be here somewhere. When we get to the last doorway, it's shut. I make eye contact with Zane, and he nods in agreement, so I count to three and kick it in.

When I see her, both sickness and relief wash over me. Ava's in the center of the room, bound to a wooden chair. She's unconscious, her body limp and bruised, but she's breathing.

"Fuck." My voice cracks as I drop my gun and rush to her side. "Ava, baby, please, can you hear me?" I lightly tap her cheek, trying to wake her up. Blood streaks her face and is caked in her hair. The restraints cut into her wrists and ankles, and there's a large pool of fresh blood underneath the chair. Aside from a few shallow cuts, I don't see where she's injured, and I can't figure out where it's all coming from.

She moans, stirring slightly.

"That's it, Ava. I'm right here. We're going to get you out of here, okay?"

Behind me, one of Alek's guys steps out of the shadows, and Zane sprays him with bullets as I work to free Ava. The air is thick with gun smoke. "We need to get out, Nick." Zane glances over his shoulder.

More people are coming, which means their extra troops have shown up faster than we expected. The most heinous part of me wants to find Alek and hurt him in every way he's done to Ava. A bomb seems like too easy of a way to go for such a spineless bastard, but I have to get her out of here fast. I grab my knife, using it to loosen the restraints on her arms, and then scoop her up.

Zane clears the hallway and takes the grenade from me. "I'll hold them off and you get Ava out the back door."

I'm so focused on Ava that I can't think straight, and I appreciate Zane taking charge. I have her, but that's only half the battle. My dad and Leo and the rest of our guys are keeping things at bay in the main room, but a few other troops have found their way down the hallway, and we can hear them going through the empty rooms. Our timing has to be perfect.

Zane peeks into the hallway, then nods at me.

He goes first, fanning his gun in all directions. I follow him out and right as we get into the hallway, a few of Alek's men show up.

"Go!" Zane barks, pulling the pin out of the grenade. I run out as fast as I can, and right when the fresh night air hits my face, three bullets pierce my back. I fall to the ground on top of Ava.

"Nick!" Zane shrieks, rushing to my side.

My mouth fills with the metallic taste of blood and I can't answer, pain pulsing through my body. I fall limp into the dirt next to Ava, and with the last bit of strength I can muster, I reach for her hand.

"Nick," she whispers, just as everything goes black.

FORTY-FOUR

Ava

I can't breathe as I sit in the hospital chair next to Nick. I can't sit still, can't think straight, can't focus on anything besides the sharp peaked lines of the heart monitor, because it's the only thing telling me that he's still alive.

The heart monitor is just one of many machines he's hooked up to. There's one for fluids, one for antibiotics, one for his pulse, and about a dozen more. When the nurse comes in, she explains each of the levels to me, because by now she knows I'm going to ask anyway. That's been our routine for the last few days as I've sat here, waiting for some kind of sign, anything at all, that he's going to wake up.

The longer he doesn't, the less faith I have.

He looks so different from the man I'm used to. His tanned, olive skin is pale and sunken in, and his body is bruised from all the pokes and procedures. The surgeon was able to remove two of the bullets, but the third one, the one closest to his heart, was too splintered to remove.

I've only left his side long enough for the doctor to clear me, so for the last few days, this is where I've been. I can't stand the thought of him waking up without me, and so I've sat here, waiting on pins and needles for the moment he opens those gorgeous green eyes.

My family—the family Nick and I are building—is in shambles, and I have no idea how we'll ever recover. If I ever had any doubts about the true man my father is, all it took was twenty-four hours being beaten and tortured for his sins to make me see the light.

My dad dragged us into this mess. He's the reason I was kidnapped, and the reason Nick is lying in this hospital bed. It makes me sick to my stomach, and the thought of seeing him or even speaking to him right now is beyond anything that I can imagine.

At some point I'll have to talk to him and my entire family, but I want to put it off as long as I can. Right now I can't separate anyone else in my family from my dad and his mistakes. Battle lines have been drawn, and it feels like my family are all on the opposite side. I don't want to let myself think about my dad right now, though. Nick needs me, and this time I'm going to put him and our relationship first. Now, and for the rest of my life.

A few fresh tears trickle down my cheek and fall onto my hand as I clutch Nick's. His charcoal-colored wedding band is on his finger, and I spin it gently. I need him to know I'm here, and right now, this is the only way I can communicate with him.

The nurse said he can hear me talking, and even though I'm not convinced, I spent the last hour apologizing for everything. Maybe if I rehearse the words now it will make it easier when I say them to him while he's conscious. *If I get the opportunity.*

There is a sound at the door, and I look up right as Gio slips in.

"Hi, Ava." He smiles gently. "How are you feeling?"

I sniffle, wiping the remaining tears off my cheek. "I'm doing okay. I can leave so you can—"

"Nonsense." He gives me a sympathetic smile. "I actually came to see if you wanted to take a walk with me to the cafeteria. The coffee here is pretty shitty, but it gets the job done, and you've barely left his side since they brought him back."

"I want to be here when he wakes up." I'm not sure how Gio can even stand me right now.

"You need to take care of yourself, too, Ava. And besides, it's a short walk." He puts his hand on my shoulder gently. "Care to join me?"

I hesitate but eventually give in. Maybe a little fresh air will do me some good. I can go for one cup of coffee and then be back in just a few minutes.

Instead of drinking our coffee in the cafeteria, Gio and I decide to walk through the halls. He matches me step for step as we walk, comfortable in the silence for a few minutes before he finally speaks. "A lot has happened in the last few days. How are you doing with everything?"

"I'm fine." I muster up as much of a smile as I can. I don't really want to talk, but I don't want to be rude either.

"It's okay if you're not."

"I just feel kind of numb, I guess. I don't know what to feel."

"Ava, when you and Nick got married, you became one of my children. I am always here if you need to talk." Gio's support of me is almost more than I can bear. I don't deserve it, especially when I'm the reason his son is lying in a hospital bed fighting for his life.

I can feel tears pooling in my eyes again. We walk a little longer before I can bring myself to speak. "Nick and I had a fight."

Gio doesn't respond, just gives me a knowing nod and lets me continue.

"I should never have left his apartment that night. *Our* apartment. I should have stayed there and fixed things with him instead of—" I shake my head, biting my lip. We stop at the end of the hallway in front of a large window that looks out over the Hudson River. It's raining, and every once in a while a strike of lightning lights up the dark sky.

"Ava, this is not your fault, and please don't think it is for another second. Your father made some terrible mistakes, and that is the only reason this happened. You had a fight with your husband. You're allowed to blow off some steam. I know as well as anyone Nick can be stubborn. You fighting and leaving the house had nothing to do with Nick getting shot."

"Even if that's true, my dad orchestrated all of this. I should have seen it coming, and tried to stop it. I practically led him right to you guys."

"I fell for your father's act too," Gio says. "I genuinely thought he wanted to mend fences after all the years we've been at odds, and I started this whole thing with Nick. Does that make me responsible for this too?"

I don't say anything, watching raindrops streak down the glass.

"Let yourself off the hook for this. You're not responsible for the choices he made, and you certainly aren't responsible for believing in him. We like to believe that people are good, especially when it's our own family, and sometimes that's just not the case."

Gio puts his arm around my shoulder to comfort me, but it only makes me cry harder. Why couldn't my own father have been like this? Gio has become more of a father figure to me in the few months I've known him than my dad was my entire life.

"What's going to happen to him now?" I ask, sucking in a sharp breath. There's no way anyone is going to let my dad get away with this, and if I'm being honest, that makes me happy. The thought that he'll have to pay, and maybe even die, for all the hell he's put me through brings me an overwhelming sense of relief.

"Your father will get exactly what's coming to him, Ava. I can promise you that. Not only did he violate all our code, but he hurt you, and to me, that's something I can't let go. You're part of my family now, and Nick will say the same thing. What your father did is inexcusable, and once Nick wakes up, we'll come up with a plan and we'll go after him."

"I'm not upset at all. He's my father, and you're telling me that you're going to kill him. What kind of person does that make me?" I let out a sharp laugh, completely ashamed of myself. There has to be something wrong with me for feeling like I do.

"Ava, there is nothing wrong with how you're feeling. He hurt you in unimaginable ways, and it's perfectly normal to feel a sense of relief that he won't ever be able to do that again. I've known your father for a long time, and never agreed with the way he treated your mother and his children. I don't ever want you to feel like what he did was normal. That's not what a father is supposed to do, and I am so sorry that you had to go through that."

"Thank you, Gio. I'll try to remember that." A few errant tears trickle down my cheek. "Nick is so lucky to have you."

"You have me, too, Ava." He smiles, pulling me into a tight hug. "That's what family is for. Nick is very lucky to have *you* too. He adores you and would do anything under the sun to see you smile. It's okay to let yourself be loved that way."

Gio and I head back to Nick's room. Gio has the same calming and reassuring personality as Nick, and after talking with him, I feel a little better.

By now, Leo is back from the apartment with our stuff, and he follows us into the room.

I push the door open, expecting to find Nick just as I left him, but instead, I nearly faint when I see him sitting up in the bed, talking with the doctor.

"Nick!" I rush toward him, throwing my arms around his neck and holding on as if my life depends on it. Happy tears stream down my cheeks. Is this real? Is he really awake?

"Whoa, easy there." He chuckles sleepily. "I was shot, you know."

He takes me in his arms, pulling me into his chest and kissing the top of my head. I'm so overcome with emotion that I can't speak. For hours I sat here planning out everything I wanted to say to him, but now in the moment, words completely fail me and I'm a blubbering mess.

"It's so good to see you," Nick whispers, his lips grazing my ear. "I didn't know if I ever would again."

"How are you feeling, buddy?" Gio walks over to Nick, relief on his face.

"Like I could run a marathon." Nick smirks at the doctor.

"I'm glad to hear that, but I would advise against it. At least for six to eight weeks." The doctor smiles. "I want to keep you through the night for observation, but if all goes well, you'll be able to go home tomorrow."

"Thanks, Doc." Nick shakes the man's hand, and his doctor heads out of the room.

"You look like hell." Leo chuckles, giving Nick a big hug.

"Thanks, asshole." Nick shakes his head, laughing. "I feel like a million bucks!"

Gio groans. "Don't even start. I'm still in charge around here, and you're on mandatory leave for at least twelve weeks. It's not even remotely open for discussion."

"Twelve weeks?" Nick looks at his dad like he just handed down a death sentence.

"Nick, you just had major, life-saving surgery," I remind him.

"And still have one bullet inside of you," Gio echoes me. "We can talk about modified duty once we see how your recovery goes."

"You guys act like I almost died or something." Nick smirks. It's so good to see him strong enough to joke with his dad and brother.

"I don't generally agree with Dad on this kind of thing, but he's right. Everything else can wait. And since we obliterated Asnikov and Alessandro is in the wind, you need to take it easy," Leo chides him, arching his eyebrow at Nick.

A darkness comes over Nick's face. "Alessandro isn't exactly in the wind." He scratches his head. "Can you guys give Ava and me a minute? We need to talk."

Gio and Leo share a concerned glance, but oblige. "We'll be back later."

My mind starts to wander with possibilities. Obviously, Nick and I have a lot to discuss, but it doesn't feel like the appropriate time when he's just gotten out of surgery and is still pretty groggy. What he needs is rest and recovery.

I sit down next to Nick on the bed. "Are you really feeling okay?"

He puts his hand on my knee, gently rubbing with his thumb. "I'm fine, Ava, I promise. This isn't even the first time I've been shot."

I'm sure the sentiment is meant to be much more reassuring than it is.

"I'd much rather talk about you. How are you feeling?"

"Much better now that I'm with you."

Nick wastes no time getting to his point. "Ava, when you left that night—"

"We don't have to talk about any of this right now, Nick. I'm not going anywhere, I swear. I'm going to be right here next to you forever. Let's just focus on getting you healthy and then we can sort through all of this."

"I promise, I am feeling fantastic," he insists, brushing a piece of hair off my cheek. "And what I have to tell you can't wait, Avs."

"Okay."

"When you left that night, I was in a bad place. I was enraged about not being able to fix this, and the thought of losing you, and so Leo and I went to the bar."

I don't say anything, and he continues.

"My dad met us there. He had gotten the logistics back about the accident and found the car that hit us. It belonged to one of the men who works for your father, and it turned out your father had put a hit out on Leo, and you and I were caught in the cross fire. He was the one who caused the accident, the accident that made you lose our baby."

I lower my eyes. It really shouldn't surprise me anymore to learn the lengths my dad is willing to go to in order to get what he wants. He's nothing like the man I thought he was, and all I feel for him is disgust.

"Hearing that pushed me over the edge, and I went to find him." Nick props himself up a bit and squeezes my hand. "Ava, I couldn't stop myself once I got my hands on him. I'm sorry. He's . . ."

I swallow the lump growing in my throat, considering everything he's saying.

After a minute, it dawns on me that Nick is trying to tell me that my dad is dead. That Nick killed him. I should feel upset or sad that he's gone, but all I feel is numb. I almost don't feel anything at all for my dad anymore.

Nick stares back at me, waiting for my reaction. I reach out and gently rub his cheek. "I'm so sorry you had to do that."

Nick gives me a strange look and lets out a sharp laugh. "Did you get checked out by a doctor? Are you concussed?"

I can't help but laugh. "I'm not concussed. I just . . . I've come to terms with the kind of man my father was. I wanted him to be so much more, but he couldn't be. I got to talk to your dad for a little while this afternoon and he made me realize that there was nothing I could do to change that. I love you, and I accepted a long time ago that choosing you probably meant having to go against my family."

"You're incredibly brave, you know that?" Nick smiles and gives me a soft kiss.

"That's because you taught me how to be." I wipe away a tear. "Can you ever forgive me for the way I've been acting?"

"Ava, I don't ever want you to apologize for feeling the way you do. All I want is for us to be able to talk about it and work through it together," Nick says. "No matter what it is."

"I don't blame you for what happened. Not at all. I was just . . . I had no idea what I was feeling, and I was so worried that you were going to think I failed you." More tears pool in my eyes. After the last several days, I'm an emotional mess.

"There is nothing you're ever feeling that's too much for me. That will ever make me run, or leave you, or be mad at you as long as you're honest with me. Even if those feelings are anger and resentment toward me." He strokes my leg gently. "You're my entire world. I would do anything for you. Of course, I'd love to have kids, but if all I have is you for the rest of my life, that's everything I'll ever need."

I sigh heavily, laying my head on his shoulder. "You are everything to me too. And I promise to never forget how fortunate I am to have found you."

"How fortunate *we* are to have found *each other*," Nick corrects me. "But let's stop all this mushy stuff. I just want to hold you in my arms."

Nick leans back until we're both resting against the bed, and I nestle into his body as if I can't get close enough. There is still so much left to settle between us, but right now I can't imagine anything better than this. Nick's okay, we're going to be okay, and whatever comes tomorrow, we'll deal with it then.

EPILOGUE

Ava

"Babe, did you grab the—"

"Already in the car." Nick flashes me his million-dollar smile as he slides into the driver's seat.

I return it, reaching over and grabbing his hand. He brings my hand to his lips, pressing a soft kiss to it and setting it down on his thigh. "Are you ready for this?"

"Absolutely." Ready? Is he serious? I've never been more ready for something in my entire life.

As happy as I am that the day is finally here, it's Nick's excitement that makes me giddy. It takes a lot to get him worked up, thanks to his calm and cool nature, but today he's the bucket of nerves and I'm the steady hand.

Sometimes I like to remember the first night we met, in his restaurant, and think about how far we've come. I have to laugh at the way I snuck out of the hotel room that morning; if only I'd known what the next year would bring.

I glance into the back seat of Nick's newly bought SUV, at the empty car seat, realizing this is the last time I'll see it like this—empty. Today is the first day of the rest of our lives, in the best way possible, and it's as exhilarating as it is terrifying.

If I could sum up the last year with Nick in any way, that's how I would describe it: exhilarating and terrifying.

So much has changed, and I barely recognize the person I was in the beginning, but I'm happier than I've ever been, and that's all to Nick's credit.

That isn't to say these last few months haven't been trying. Today is nearly six months to the day that I was taken. That Nick killed my father. That he took three bullets trying to save my life. That we were given a second chance.

Things were off between us at first because we both still had a lot to work through. Everything about our relationship was in fast-forward from the very beginning, so we took a few steps back. We wanted to date and get to know each other, and experience all that came with that, like a normal couple, not one who was forced to go from strangers to husband and wife virtually overnight.

I moved out temporarily to give us that opportunity, but it took us all of two days to realize we couldn't be apart. We agreed we needed to get out of the penthouse. It always felt more like a museum than a home to me, and was definitely not a good place to raise a family. We found a place we both loved pretty quickly and moved in within three weeks. It was right between his family and mine, with plenty of space for us to grow.

I struggled a lot at first with my dad's death. I felt guilty because I wasn't more upset and knowing that I was with the person responsible for it. It was different than with Andrew.

Nick had killed my father out of vengeance, and as punishment for all the pain he'd caused us. I would like to say that if I had been in Nick's shoes I wouldn't have done the same thing, but deep down, I feel like I would have. I loved my father, but I was just a pawn in his game for more power.

When Nick told me what happened, all I felt was numb. Some

days, it's still hard for me to grasp all the horrible things my dad did. I think it is for everyone.

At first it was hard with my mom, but things are getting easier. She didn't want to accept what he had done or the person he had become. In her eyes he was still the man she married. Once the truth of everything that he did came out, she understood. Money and power ruined him. He wasn't the person any of us remembered.

Tomorrow, Nick and I are hosting both families at our house for a big announcement. We're all adjusting to a new normal, but so far, the future looks pretty great.

Tears pool in my eyes as Nick pulls up to the agency. I think I'm conditioned to things not working out in our favor, so I haven't really let myself get excited or emotional until this moment.

Nick reaches over, a big goofy grin on his face, and wipes the tears off my cheek. He immediately morphs into protector mode when I'm upset. This is different, though—this is a culmination of so many things over the last year, and me finally feeling like I'm exactly where I'm supposed to be. These are happy tears.

"Have I ever told you how beautiful you are?" Nick smiles at me.

"You tell me every day."

"That's because you get more beautiful as time goes on. I think I find something new I love about you every day."

I can't help but laugh. "Oh yeah? What did you find today?"

"Watching you cry with happiness as we're about to go meet our child. Now, that's a picture that will be burned in my mind forever."

I love hearing him say those words.

Our child.

When I first started thinking about this, I wasn't sure how Nick was going to react. I had been out shopping with Bella one day when this agency caught my eye. I'd never really considered adoption before, but this family walked out seconds after we passed.

The couple was sobbing, overcome with happiness, cradling this perfect little baby, who looked nothing like them, in their arms. My heart ached at the thought of someone not wanting their child. When I lost our baby, it nearly killed me. I couldn't fathom how someone could willingly give their baby up.

It was on my mind for days after, and it took a talk with Nick's mother to make me realize how beautiful it was. She was adopted. Her mother gave her up, realizing that she couldn't provide the kind of life that a baby deserved. She didn't do it because she wanted to, but because she loved that child enough to recognize that she couldn't take care of her. It changed my whole viewpoint, and suddenly I had an overwhelming urge to adopt a child.

I think Nick thought I was insane at first, going through some kind of crazy grief phase. But when the feeling persisted for a while, Nick opened up to the idea, and one day he came home ready to make it happen.

Having our own kids is important to both of us, and one day we will, but right now, we are about to pick up a one-year-old who's been through a lot. We don't know much more than that, but nothing else really matters.

He needs us, and we need him. What Nick doesn't know, though, is that I have another surprise up my sleeve.

Nick and I walk hand in hand into the agency.

"Mr. and Mrs. Caponelli," the receptionist greets us warmly. "We're so glad you could come so quickly. Mason was brought to us this morning. I have his file. You can look it over quickly before Brenda brings him out."

Mason.

Nick squeezes my hand and takes the stack of papers from the receptionist. We've been here a dozen times, filling out paperwork, looking through potential parents; we'd even gone through their parenting class.

The only thing left to do is to take him home. Nothing in his file will change our minds. We knew it was a done deal from the moment they called us, even though he was a little older than we'd expected.

Soon, Brenda emerges from the back, holding a perfect, healthy one-year-old. My heart nearly stops as I look at him. Everything about him is perfect, and I am in love immediately. With his dark hair and green eyes, he even looks like he's biologically ours.

"Nick, Ava, I'd like for you to meet Mason." Brenda smiles.

Mason beams, immediately reaching for Nick.

"Hi, buddy." I've never seen Nick smile so wide as he takes Mason out of her arms. "I'm going to be your dad."

Mason claps his hands, babbling loudly.

Nick looks at me with pure joy, causing Mason to turn his head too. "And this is your beautiful momma."

"Ma-ma!" Mason coos, lurching out of Nick's arms and reaching for me.

My heart immediately melts as I hold him in my arms for the first time. It seems so surreal. Nick and I have wanted this for a long time, and we are finally in a place to make it happen. Mason is actually ours.

"It looks like things are working out just fine," Brenda says. "Do you want to take him home in these clothes, or did you bring an outfit for him?"

Nick chuckles. "Ava's been waiting for this for a long time. She had an outfit picked out months ago."

"Wonderful."

"Why don't you go change him, babe, and I'll get the car pulled around?" Nick says, his hand firmly on the small of my back.

"Sounds great." Nick's right. I've had an outfit picked out for a long time. This is all part of my plan.

Brenda leaves us and I take Mason into the bathroom to change him. I pull out an adorable "Big Brother" onesie from my bag that fits him perfectly. Mason smiles and babbles the entire time. He seems like such a happy, easygoing baby, and I can't wait to get him home.

I also can't wait for Nick to see Mason's outfit. I found out a few weeks ago that I'm pregnant but haven't told Nick yet. We weren't trying, and now that we have Mason, the timing isn't ideal, but I know Nick will be through-the-roof ecstatic. We'll find a way to make it work; we always do.

Once we're done, I say goodbye to Brenda and walk outside to meet Nick.

"There's my two favorite people!" Nick grins. "Ready to get our baby home, baby?" He chuckles, clearly amused with himself. I guess the dad jokes come naturally.

"Yes, definitely. Will you put him in on your side?"

"Of course." He takes Mason out of my arms and walks around to the other side of the car.

I can't contain my smile as I wait for him to notice.

"Ava?" Nick's voice is concerned as he comes around the car wide-eyed, still holding Mason.

"Yes?"

"Did you dress him in this?"

I nod, biting my lip.

"Does that mean . . ." His eyes travel to my stomach.

"I'm pregnant, Nick."

"You're . . . but we just . . . holy shit." He's absolutely speechless, and I can see the wheels turning in his mind. I give him a minute to let it sink in, and then he breaks into a huge smile.

"We're going to have two babies." He looks at me, clarifying.

I can't help but laugh. "Technically, Mason will be a toddler when this baby comes. And you should probably start watching your language around him."

Nick rushes to me, enveloping me in a giant hug, with Mason still in his arms. The three of us stand there for a few minutes, hugging and laughing and crying.

"I love you so much," Nick finally says, cupping my chin in his hand, his lips finding mine in a passionate kiss that holds the promise of what's to come later.

"I love you too." I wipe away my tears. "This is going to be quite the adventure."

Nick presses his lips to mine. "The best one yet."

ACKNOWLEDGMENTS

Having a book published has been a dream of mine for as long as I can remember, and it would never have been possible without the help and support of so many people. First and foremost, to the W by Wattpad Books team—thank you for taking my dream and making it a reality, for your patience and guidance, and for believing in my stories. When I first wrote this book, I never could have imagined this day would come or what it would mean to me. The entire process has been surreal, and I am so thankful for all that I have learned from you along the way.

To my Wattpad readers—your encouragement and support pushed me to continue writing when I felt like I couldn't. Your feedback and words of encouragement have meant more to me than you could ever know. Thank you for loving this story and these characters as much as I do.

To my parents—for putting a book in my hand and for listening to my stories long before I started writing them down. To my husband—you believe in me and my work more than I ever could myself, and I never would have done this without you. And also, to my kids—I hope you always find the courage to follow your own dreams.

And lastly, thank YOU! By purchasing my book, you are supporting the dream of a little girl who grew from an avid reader to an author herself. Without someone to read them, stories are just words, and I am so thankful you decided to give mine a shot.

This was the first story I ever wrote and will forever hold a special place in my heart. To see my words and ideas transformed into this final product is more special than I could ever explain.

ABOUT THE AUTHOR

Nicole Knight is an award winning contemporary romance writer from Denver, Colorado. With over twenty million reads online, her books include feisty female leads and brooding bad-boy types that will have you loving and hating them all at once. If you like relatable characters, steamy connections, and a side of comedy with your dark romance, her books are for you! When she's not writing, she can be found traveling, listening to a true crime podcast, or spending time with her husband, kids, and giant furry friend, Finn.

Want more Caponelli family romance?

BREAKING TIES

Coming soon from W by Wattpad Books!

Turn the page for a sneak peek!

PROLOGUE

I see it happen in slow motion. The trigger pulls back. The bullet leaves the chamber and flies through the air. It pierces my shirt first, then my skin, and finally the muscle of my abdomen, where it lodges. The force sucks the wind right out of me, and I immediately reach for the wound, feeling the warmth of my blood as it seeps through the fabric.

Staggering backward, I use every ounce of strength I have to lift the gun and fire off two shots in return. The echoing booms fill the air, but I fall to the ground before I can see what my bullets hit, if anything at all.

Everything becomes still and quiet around me as I lie in a growing pool of my own blood. I fumble with the hem of my shirt, pulling it up and trying to look at the wound. It hurts too much to crunch my abs, so instead I feel for it with my fingers. I wince at the sting but press my hands firmly against it to try to stop the bleeding, or at the very least slow it down.

I'm losing too much blood, and it's happening too fast. No one knows where I am. No one knows how to find me, and by the time they figure it out, I'll be dead.